Favourite Sea Stories from

Seaside Al

SELECTED
AND
INTRODUCED
BY

ALAN MAITLAND

VIKING

VIKING
Published by the Penguin Group
Penguin Books Canada Ltd, 10 Alcorn Avenue, Toronto, Ontario M4V 3B2
Penguin Books Ltd, 27 Wrights Lane, London W8 5TZ, England
Viking Penguin, a division of Penguin Books USA Inc., 375 Hudson Street,
New York, New York 10014, U.S.A.
Penguin Books Australia Ltd, Ringwood, Victoria, Australia
Penguin Books (NZ) Ltd, 182–190 Wairau Road, Auckland 10, New Zealand

Penguin Books Ltd, Registered Offices: Harmondsworth, Middlesex, England

First published 1996
10 9 8 7 6 5 4 3 2 1

Introductions, Notes and Selection Copyright © Alan Maitland, 1996

Printed and bound in Canada on acid-free paper ∞

Canadian Cataloguing in Publication Data

Main entry under title:

Favourite sea stories from Seaside Al

ISBN: 0-670-86538-9

1. Sea stories. I. Maitland, Alan.

PN6120.95.S4F3 1996   808.8'032162   C95-932987-0

Copyright acknowledgments appear on page 324.

This book is dedicated to those who live
by the rise and fall of the tides,
who toil in the sea and seek its treasures,
who revel in its mysteries, who write about it,
who play in it, who fear its wrath and
are sometimes lost in it.

ACKNOWLEDGMENTS

I am indebted to CBC's Mark Starowicz for starting the stories on "As It Happens," and of course to those who continued them. To Barbara Frum who dubbed me Fireside Al. To Jackie Kaiser of Penguin for transferring them from tape to the written page. It's exciting to see them collected in print. To George Jamieson and Don Mason for doing much of the early work, and to Don for his help on historical matters. And to the many who have enjoyed the stories over the years on CBC radio. Now you can read them for yourselves. Enjoy!

Seaside Al

INTRODUCTION

Dark and strange and cold the sea-valleys opened
before him; blue sea-beasts ranged there, guarded
by strong-finned shepherds, and fishes like birds
darted to and fro...

Along the south coast of Nova Scotia, a short way from the village of Mahone Bay where I now live, a partially hidden pathway leads downward to the shore. Here, at path's end, the sea and sky are more blue than the bluest azure; the air, too, is threaded through with a glimmer of old salt; while silvered, spotted fishes gather like shadows to the shore, and seabirds cry of sands more distant than the sea. This is the place where stories come from.

Here are fabled shanties of the sea, and stories of the whispers that crowd the shoreline: stories of mermen and maids, the haunted tides, and the cliffs of Connemara; Squamish legends, and tales of old Provence; stories of the bottle imp, the isle of Inishmoor, and the waters about San Juan. Stories too of the fishermen of Nova Scotia, and of travellers returning to their native shore. Stories by Oscar Wilde, E. Annie Proulx, Malcolm Lowry. And then there's old widowed Doris, on a cargo ship to Bombay, and Emily Carr, on her way by boat to paint the Haida totems. Scattered throughout are a number of passages from Virginia Woolf's *The Waves*, moving from dawn to dusk, from tide to tide, forming a sort of lyrical framework for the stories that follow. Then, too, there's Turgenev's monkey, a small tale more keenly felt than a whole fishbowl of Moby Dicks.

This is a collection that has grown fondly from a small seed planted long ago. Sea-*side*, sea-*ward*, sea-*worthy*. Stories from port and starboard…from the place where stories *magically* are born.

TABLE OF CONTENTS

The Waves
(dawn)

The sun had not yet risen. The sea was indistinguishable from the sky, except that the sea was slightly creased as if a cloth had wrinkles in it. Gradually as the sky whitened a dark line lay on the horizon dividing the sea from the sky and the grey cloth became barred with thick strokes moving, one after another, beneath the surface, following each other, pursuing each other, perpetually.

As they neared the shore each bar rose, heaped itself, broke and swept a thin veil of white water across the sand. The wave paused, and then drew out again, sighing like a sleeper *whose breath comes and goes unconsciously. Gradually the dark bar on the horizon became clear as if the sediment in an old wine-bottle had sunk and left the glass green. Behind it, too, the sky cleared as if the white sediment there had sunk, or as if the arm of a woman couched beneath the horizon had raised a lamp and flat bars of white, green and yellow spread across the sky like the blades of a fan. Then she raised her lamp higher and the air seemed to become fibrous and to tear away from the green surface flickering and flaming in red and yellow fibres like the smoky fire that roars from a bonfire. Gradually the fibres of the burning bonfire were fused into one haze, one incandescence which lifted the weight of the woollen grey sky on top of it and turned it to a million atoms of soft blue. The surface of the sea slowly became transparent and lay rippling and sparkling until the dark stripes were almost rubbed out. Slowly the arm that held the lamp raised it higher and then higher until a broad flame became visible; an arc of fire burnt on the rim of the horizon, and all round it the sea blazed gold.*

VIRGINIA WOOLF
(1882–1941)

Three Villages

by
EMILY CARR
(1871–1945)

At odd angles always, and with a curious, playful solemnity, Emily Carr writes very much like she paints. "Three Villages" is Carr's written record of her first journey to the Queen Charlotte Islands, there to sketch and to paint the Haida poles and buildings along the shore. The year is 1912. For Carr, sketchbook in hand, it's "as if everything were waiting and holding its breath…"

Tanoo

J immie had a good boat. He and his wife, Louisa, agreed to take me to the old villages of Tanoo, Skedans and Cumshewa, on the southern island of the Queen Charlotte group. We were to start off at the Indian's usual "eight o'clock," and got off at the usual "near noon." The missionary had asked me to take his pretty daughter along.

We chugged and bobbed over all sorts of water and came to Tanoo in the evening. It looked very solemn as we came nearer. Quite far out from land Jimmie shut off the engine and plopped the anchor into the sea. Then he shoved the canoe overboard, and, putting my sheep dog and me into it, nosed it gently through the kelp. The grating of our canoe on the pebbles warned the silence that we were come to break it.

The dog and I jumped out and Jimmie and the canoe went back for the others.

It was so still and solemn on the beach, it would have seemed irreverent to speak aloud; it was as if everything were waiting and holding its breath. The dog felt it too; he stood with cocked ears, trembling. When the others came and moved about and spoke this feeling went away.

At one side of the Tanoo beach rose a big bluff, black now that the sun was behind it. It is said that the bluff is haunted. At its foot was the skeleton of a house; all that was left of it was the great beams and the corner posts and two carved poles one at each end of it. Inside, where the people used to live, was stuffed with elderberry bushes, scrub trees and fireweed. In that part of the village no other houses were left, but there were lots of totem poles sticking up. A tall slender one belonged to Louisa's grandmother. It had a story carved on it; Louisa told it to us in a loose sort of way as if she had half forgotten it. Perhaps she had forgotten some, but perhaps it was the missionary's daughter being there that made her want to forget the rest. The missionaries laughed at the poles and said they were heathenish. On the base of this pole was the figure of a man; he had on a tall, tall hat, which was made up of sections, and was a hat of great honour. On top of the hat perched a raven. Little figures of men were clinging to every ring of honour all the way up the hat. The story told that the man had adopted a raven as his son. The raven turned out to be a wicked trickster and brought a flood upon his foster parents. When the waters rose the man's nephews and relations climbed up the rings of his hat of honour and were thus saved from being drowned. It was a fine pole, bleached of all colour and then bloomed over again with greeny-yellow mould.

The feelings Jimmie and Louisa had in this old village of their own people must have been quite different from ours. They must have made my curiosity and the missionary girl's sneer seem small. Often Jimmie and Louisa went off hand in hand by themselves for a little, talking in Indian as they went.

A nose of land ran out into the sea from Tanoo and split the village into two parts; the parts diverged at a slight angle, so that the village of Tanoo had a wall-eyed stare out over the sea.

Beyond the little point there were three fine house fronts. A tall totem pole stood up against each house, in the centre of its front. When Jimmie cut away the growth around the foot of them, the paint on the poles was quite bright. The lowest figure of the centre pole was a great eagle; the other two were beavers with immense teeth—they held sticks in their hands.

All three base figures had a hole through the pole so that people could enter and leave the house through the totem.

Our first night in solemn Tanoo was very strange indeed.

When we saw the Indians carrying the little canoe down to the water we said:

"What are you going out to the boat for?"

"We are going to sleep out there."

"You are going to leave us alone in Tanoo?"

"You can call if anything is wrong," they said. But we knew the boat was too far out beyond the kelp beds for them to hear us.

The canoe glided out and then there was nothing but wide black space. We two girls shivered. I wanted the tent flaps open; it did not seem quite so bad to me if I could feel the trees close. But Miss Missionary wanted them tied tight shut to keep everything out.

Very early in the morning I got to work and two hours later Miss Missionary came out of the tent. The boat lay far out with no sign of life on her. The Indians did not come ashore; it got late and we wanted breakfast—we called and called but there was no answer.

"Do you remember what they said about those Indians being asphyxiated by the fumes from their engine while they slept?"

"I was thinking of that too."

We ran out on the point as far as we could so as to get nearer to the boat and we called and called both together. There was a horrible feeling down inside us that neither of us cared to speak about. After a long while a black head popped up in the boat.

"You must not leave us again like that," we told Jimmie and Louisa.

The Indians would not do a thing for Miss Missionary. They let her collect rushes for her own bed and carry things. The Mission house in their home village stood on the hill and looked down on the Indians. But here all of us were on the dead level, all of us had the same mosquito-tormented skins and everything in common, and were wholly dependent on the Indians' knowledge and skill.

I often wondered what Louisa and the white girl talked about while I was away from them working. Because of the mosquitoes, they tied their heads up in towels and were frightfully hot. I offered Miss Missionary some of the mosquito stuff a miner had told me of—bacon fat (it must be rancid) and turpentine. She refused—she said I looked so horrible dripping with it. She was bumped all over with bites. If you drew your hand down your face it was red with the blood the brutes had stolen from you.

I met them coming over the sand, Louisa hurrying ahead to get supper, Miss Missionary limping behind, draggled and weary. Away back I saw Jimmie carrying something dreadful with long arms trailing behind in the sand, its great round body speared by the stick on Jimmie's shoulder.

"We've took the Missionary's daughter hunting devilfish," chuckled Louisa, as she passed me.

We ate some of the devilfish for supper, fried in pieces like sausage. It was sweet like chicken, but very tough. Miss Missionary ate bread and jam.

"Father would not like me to eat devil," she said.

She told me the hunt was a disgusting performance. The devilfish were in the puddles around the rocks at low tide. When they saw people come, they threw their tenacles around the rocks and stuck their heads into the rocky creases; the only way to make them let go was to beat their heads in when you got the chance.

It was long past dinnertime. Louisa could not cook because there was no water in camp. That was Jimmie's job. The spring was back in the woods, nobody but Jimmie knew where, and he was far out at sea tinkering on his boat. Louisa called and called; Jimmie heard, because his head popped up, but he would not come. Every time she called the same two Indian words.

"Make it hotter, Louisa; I want to get back to work." She

called the same two words again.

"Are those swear words?"

"No, if I swore I would have to use English words."

"Why?"

"There are no swears in Haida."

"What do you say if you are angry or want to insult anybody?"

"You would say, 'Your father or your mother was a slave,' but I could not say that to Jimmie."

"Well, say something hot. I want dinner!"

She called the same two words again but her voice was different this time. Jimmie came.

Pictures of all the poles were in my sketch sack. I strapped it up and said, "That's that." The missionary's daughter revived. "Horrid place!" she said, scratching viciously at her ankle.

Then we went away from Tanoo and left the silence to heal itself—left the totem poles staring, staring out over the sea.

When we boarded the boat the missionary girl put her clumsy foot through my light cedar drawing-board. Nothing about her balanced—her silly little voice and her big foot; her pink and white face and big red hands. I was so mad about my board that I looked across the water for fear I'd hit her. Louisa's voice in my ear said,

"Isn't she clumsy and isn't she stupid!"

Almost immediately we were in rough water. Jimmie spread a sail in the bottom of the boat, and we women all lay flat. Nobody spoke—only groans. When the boat pitched all our bodies rolled one way and then rolled back. Under the sail where I was lying something seemed very slithery.

"Jimmie, what is under me?"

"Only the devilfish we are taking home to Mother—she likes them very much."

"Ugh!" I said. Sea-sickness on top of devilfish seemed too much.

Jimmie said, "They're dead; it won't hurt them when you roll over."

Skedans

Jimmie, the Indian, knew the jagged reefs of Skedans Bay by heart. He knew where the bobbing kelp nobs grew and that their long, hose-like tubes were waiting to strangle his propeller. Today the face of the bay was buttered over with calm and there was a wide blue sky overhead. Everything looked safe, but Jimmie knew how treacherous the bottom of Skedans Bay was; that's why he lay across the bow of his boat, anxiously peering into the water and motioning to Louisa his wife, who was at the wheel.

The engine stopped far out. There was the plop and gurgle of the anchor striking and settling and then the sigh of the little canoe being pushed over the edge of the boat, the slap as she struck the water. Jimmie got the sheep dog and me over to the beach first, so that I could get to work right away; then he went back for Louisa and the missionary's daughter.

Skedans was more open than Tanoo. The trees stood farther back from it. Behind the bay another point bit deeply into the land, so that light came in across the water from behind the village too.

There was no soil to be seen. Above the beach it was all luxuriant growth; the earth was so full of vitality that every seed which blew across her surface germinated and burst. The growing things jumbled themselves together into a dense thicket; so tensely earnest were things about growing in Skedans that everything linked with everything else, hurrying to grow to the limit of its own capacity; weeds and weaklings alike throve in the rich moistness.

Memories came out of this place to meet the Indians; you saw remembering in their brightening eyes and heard it in the quick hushed words they said to each other in Haida. The chatter of the missionary's daughter in solemn Skedans sounded like a sheep-bell tinkling outside a church.

Skedans Beach was wide. Sea-drift was scattered over it. Behind the logs the ground sloped up a little to the old village site. It was smothered now under a green tangle, just one grey roof still squatted there among the bushes, and a battered row of totem poles circled the bay; many of them were mortuary poles, high with square fronts on top. The fronts were carved with totem designs of birds and beasts. The tops of the poles behind these carved fronts were hollowed out and the coffins stood, each in its hole on its end, the square front hiding it. Some of the old mortuary poles were broken and you saw skulls peeping out through the cracks.

To the right of Skedans were twin cones of earth and rock. They were covered to the top with trees and scrub. The land ran out beyond these mounds and met the jagged reefs of the bay.

We broke through the growth above our heads to reach the house. It was of the old type, but had been repaired a little by halibut fishers who still used it occasionally. The walls were full of cracks and knot-holes. There were stones, blackened by fire, lying on the earth floor. Above them was a great smoke-hole in the roof; it had a flap that could be adjusted to the wind. Sleeping-benches ran along the wall and there was a rude table made of driftwood by the halibut fishers: Indians use the floor for their tables and seats.

When the fire roared, our blankets were spread on the plat-forms, and Louisa's stew-pot simmered. The place was grand—we had got close down to real things. In Skedans there were no shams.

When night came we cuddled into our blankets. The night was still. Just the waves splashed slow and even along the beach. If your face was towards the wall, the sea tang seeped in at the cracks and poured over it; if you turned round and faced in, there was the lovely smoky smell of our wood fire on the clay floor.

Early in the morning Jimmie stirred the embers; then he went out and brought us icy water from the spring to wash our faces in. He cut a little path like a green tunnel from the house to the beach, so that we could come and go easily. I went out to sketch the poles.

They were in a long straggling row the entire length of the bay and pointed this way and that; but no matter how drunk-en their tilt, the Haida poles never lost their dignity. They looked sadder, perhaps, when they bowed forward and more stern when they tipped back. They were bleached to a pinkish silver colour and cracked by the sun, but nothing could make them mean or poor, because the Indians had put strong thought into them and had believed sincerely in what they were trying to express.

The twisted trees and high tossed drift-wood hinted that Skedans could be as thoroughly fierce as she was calm. She was downright about everything.

Cumshewa

Tanoo, Skedans and Cumshewa lie fairly close to each other on the map, yet each is quite unlike the others when you come to it. All have the West Coast wetness but Cumshewa seems always to drip, always to be blurred with mist, its foliage always to hang wet-heavy. Cumshewa rain soaked my paper, Cumshewa rain trickled among my paints.

Only one house was left in the village of Cumshewa, a large, low and desolately forsaken house that had a carefully padlocked door and gaping hole in the wall.

We spent a miserable night in this old house. Louisa's cat and the missionary's daughter always looked and acted alike when it rained. All our bones were pierced with chill. The rain spat great drops through the smoke-hole into our fire. In comfortless, damp blankets we got through the night.

In the morning Jimmie made so hot a fire that the rain splatters hissed when they dropped into it. I went out to work on the leaky beach and Jimmie rigged up a sort of shelter over my work so that the trickles ran down my neck instead of down my picture, but if I had possessed the arms and legs of a centipede they would not have been enough to hold my things together, to defy the elements' meanness towards my canopy, materials and temper.

Through the hole in the side of the house I could hear the fretful mewings of the missionary's daughter and the cat. Indian people and the elements give and take like brothers, accommodating themselves to each other's ways without complaint. My Indians never said to me, "Hurry and get this over so that we may go home and be more comfortable." Indians are comfortable everywhere.

Not far from the house sat a great wooden raven mounted on a rather low pole; his wings were flattened to his sides. A few feet from him stuck up an empty pole. His mate had sat there but she had rotted away long ago, leaving him moss-grown, dilapidated and alone to watch dead Indian bones, for these two great birds had been set, one on either side of the doorway of a big house that had been full of dead Indians who had died during a small-pox epidemic.

Bursting growth had hidden house and bones long ago. Rain turned their dust into mud; these strong young trees were richer perhaps for that Indian dust. They grew up round the dilapidated old raven, sheltering him from the tearing winds now that he was old and rotting because the rain seeped through the moss that grew upon his back and in the hollows of his eye-sockets. The Cumshewa totem poles were dark and colourless, the wood toneless from pouring rain.

When Jimmie, Louisa, the cat and the missionary's daughter saw me squeeze back into the house through the hole and heard me say, "Done," they all jumped up. Curling the cat into her hat, Louisa set about packing; Jimmie went to prepare his boat. The cat was peeved. She preferred Louisa's hat near the fire to the outside rain. Even the missionary's daughter showed animation as she rolled up blankets.

The memory of Cumshewa is of great lonesomeness smoth-ered in a blur of rain. Our boat headed for the sea. As we rounded the point Cumshewa was suddenly like something that had not quite happened.

Coqueville on the *Spree*

by
EMILE ZOLA
(1840–1902)

A seaside tale of family rivalries and festivities, "Coqueville on the Spree" has about it that rare glimmer of a story that simply bubbles over in the telling. It's so delightfully well-salted that the very air about Coqueville is scented still (even down to this very day) with the sweetness of kirsch and kümmel and caraway seeded schnapps. A story so vigorously imagined that the Coquevillian sea is even now afloat with little barrels of delicious liqueurs bobbing about on the incoming tide.

oqueville is a little village snuggling down in a rocky inlet five miles from Grandport. A fine broad sandy beach stretches out at the foot of the ramshackle old cottages stuck halfway up the cliff-face like shells left high and dry by the tide. When you climb to the left, up on to the heights of Grandport, you can see the yellow expanse of beach very plainly to the west, looking like a tide of gold dust flowing out of the gaping slit in the rock; and if you have good eyes, you can even make out the tumbledown cottages standing out, rust-coloured against the stone, with the bluish smoke from their chimneys drifting upwards to the crest of the enormous ridge blocking the horizon.

It's an out-of-the-way hole. Coqueville has never succeeded in bringing its population up to the two hundred mark. The gorge running down to the sea, on the edge of which the village is situated, is so steep and winding that it is almost impassable for horses and carts. This prevents communication and isolates the village so that it seems miles away from any of the neighbouring hamlets. As a result, the inhabitants' only communication with Grandport was by water. They were almost all fishermen living from the sea and had to transport their catch there by boat every day. They had a contract with a large firm of wholesalers, Dufeu's, which bought their fish in bulk. Old Dufeu had been dead for some years but the business had been carried on by his widow; she had merely taken on an assistant, a tall fair-haired young fellow called Mouchel, whose job was to visit the villages along the coast and strike bargains with the villagers. This Monsieur Mouchel was the only link between Coqueville and the civilized world.

Coqueville deserves to have an historian. It seems certain that in the Dark Ages the village was founded by the Mahés, a family which found its way there, settled down and proliferated at the foot of the cliff. At first, the Mahés must have flourished by intermarriage, since for centuries you find nothing but Mahés. Then, under Louis XIII, there appeared a Floche. No one really knows where he came from. He married a Mahé and from that moment onwards a strange phenomenon occurred: the Floches prospered and were so prolific that they ended up by engulfing the Mahés, whose numbers decreased while their wealth passed into the newcomers' hands. Doubtless the Floches had brought new blood, a sturdier constitution and a temperament more suited to face the strong winds and rough seas of their profession. However that might be, the Floches were by now the bosses of Coqueville.

You will have realized that this shift in numbers and wealth had not taken place without terrible strife. The Mahés and the Floches hated each other like poison; centuries of loathing seethed between them. Despite their decline, the Mahés were proud, as befitted a former conqueror. After all, they were founders and ancestors. They would speak with scorn of the first of the Floches, a beggar and a tramp whom they had taken into their bosoms out of pity, and they expressed eternal regret at having given him one of their daughters. If you were to believe them, this Floche had produced nothing but a breed of lewd rogues who spent their nights in copulation and their days in pursuit of heiresses. There was no insult too foul to heap on the powerful tribe of Floches, with the bitter fury of ruined and decimated aristocrats against the arrogant and prolific middle classes who had dispossessed them of their mansions and their wealth that were theirs by right of inheritance. Needless to say, success had turned the Floches, on their part, into an arrogant lot. They were sitting pretty and could afford to sneer. They made fun of the ancient race of Mahé and swore to turn them out of the village if they didn't knuckle under. For them, the Mahés were down-and-outs who, instead of wrapping themselves proudly in their tattered finery, would be better employed mending it. Thus Coqueville found itself the prey of two warring clans; about one hundred and thirty of its inhabitants determined to take over the other fifty, for no other reason than that they were stronger. Struggles between mighty empires tell the same story.

Amongst the recent squabbles which had been tearing Coqueville apart, we may mention the famous feud between Fouasse and Tupain and the spectacular brawls between the Rouget couple. It must be explained that in the old days everyone was given a nickname, which later on became a sur-name, because it was difficult to disentangle all the cross-breedings of Mahé and Floche. Rouget had certainly once had an ancestor who had flaming red hair; as for Fouasse and Tupain, no one knew the reason for their names, since in the course of the years many nicknames had lost any rational explanation. Well, old Françoise, a sprightly old girl of eighty, still alive, had married a Mahé and produced Fouasse; then, after being widowed, had remarried a Floche and given birth to Tupain. Hence the mutual antagonism of the two brothers, a hatred kept alive by the fact that questions of inheritance were involved. As for the Rougets, they fought like cat and dog because Rouget accused his wife Marie of carrying on with a dark-haired Floche, the tall and sturdy Brisemotte. Rouget had already flung himself a couple of times on the latter, knife in hand, screaming that he would have his guts for garters. He was an excitable little man, always flying into rages.

But Coqueville's major concern at the moment was neither Rouget's rages nor Tupain's and Fouasse's squabbles. There was a wild rumour going round that a Mahé, Delphin, a whipper-snapper of twenty, had the audacity to be in love with Margot, the beautiful daughter of La Queue, the wealthiest of the

Floches and mayor of the village. This La Queue was a very considerable person indeed. He was called La Queue because under Louis-Philippe, his father, obstinately clinging to fashions prevalent in his youth, had been the last man in the village to tie his hair in a pigtail. Now La Queue owned *Zephyr*, one of Coqueville's two large fishing boats and by far the best, a fine seaworthy vessel, newly built. The other cutter was the *Whale*, a rotten old tub owned by Rouget and manned by Delphin and Fouasse, while La Queue sailed with a crew consisting of Tupain and Brisemotte. The latter were always making sarcastic comments about the *Whale*, describing it as an old tub which, one fine day, would disintegrate like a handful of mud. So when La Queue heard that this good-for-nothing young Delphin, the *Whale*'s cabin-boy, was daring to make sheep's eyes at his daughter, he gave her a couple of well-directed slaps in the face as a warning that she would never become a Mahé. Margot was furious and responded by loudly proclaiming that she would pass on the same treatment to Delphin if he ever had the nerve to start prowling around her. It was maddening to have your ears boxed because of a young man whom you'd never really bothered to look at properly. Although only sixteen, Margot was as strong as a man and already as lovely as any lady; she had the reputation of being high and mighty, a young madam who had no time for sweethearts. So you can well understand how those two slaps, Delphin's audacity and Margot's anger had kept every tongue wagging in Coqueville.

However, there were people who said that Margot was not as angry as all that at seeing Delphin hanging around her. This Delphin was a small young fellow with a face tanned by the sea and a mop of blond curls that hung down over his eyes and neck. And, despite his slender build, he was very strong and quite capable of tackling someone three times his size. Rumour had it that he would sometimes go off and spend the night in Grandport. This gave him a reputation with the girls of being something of a wolf, and when talking together they would accuse him of "living it up," a vague phrase which suggested all kinds of secret pleasures. Whenever she mentioned his name, Margot seemed to become rather too excited, while when he looked at her through his tiny bright eyes, he would give a sly grin and show not the slightest concern whether she was angry or scornful. He would walk past her front door, slip into the bushes and stay watching her for hours, as lithe and patient as a cat stalking a tom-tit; and when she suddenly discovered him right behind her, so close at times that she would detect his presence by the warmth of his breath, he did not take himself off but would put on such a gentle, wistful look that she was left speechless with surprise and remembered to be annoyed only after he had gone. There is no doubt that, had her father seen her, she would have collected another box on the ears. Things could certainly not go on like this for ever; but although she kept swearing that one day she would give Delphin the promised box on the ears, she never in fact took advantage of any opportunity of doing so when he was there. This made people say that she'd do better not to keep on talking so much about it, since the truth was that she still had given no sign of keeping her word.

All the same, nobody ever imagined that she would ever marry Delphin. It seemed merely a case of a passing fancy by a flirtatious young girl. As for marriage between the most poverty-stricken of the Mahés, who would find it hard to contribute even half a dozen shirts to the matrimonial estate, and the mayor's daughter, the richest heiress among the Floches, the whole idea would be monstrous. Unkind people hinted that she might none the less quite possibly get together with him but that she would certainly never marry him. A rich girl can enjoy herself as she pleases but when she has her head screwed on straight, she doesn't do anything silly. Anyway, the whole of Coqueville was taking a passionate interest in the matter and was curious to see the outcome. Would Delphin end up getting his ears boxed? Or would Margot get a kiss on her cheek in some remote corner of the cliffs? They'd have to wait and see. Some people supported the box on the ears, others the kiss on the cheek. Coqueville was all agog.

In the whole village there were only two people who did not belong either to the Mahé or the Floche camps: the priest and the gamekeeper. The latter, a tall lean man whose real name no one knew but whom everyone called the Emperor, doubtless because he had served under Charles X, in fact exercised no serious supervision whatsoever over the game of the district, which consisted of nothing but bare rock and deserted heathland. He had got the job because a *sous-préfet* had taken him under his wing and had created on his behalf this sinecure where he was free to squander his very modest salary undisturbed. As for Father Radiguet, he was one of those simple-minded priests whose bishops are anxious to get rid of by tucking them away in some God-forsaken hole where they can stay out of mischief. Radiguet was a decent sort of man who had reverted to his peasant origins and spent his time working in his exiguous little garden hewn out of the rock-face, and smoking his pipe as he watched his lettuces grow. His only weakness was a love of food, although he was hardly in a position to show a discriminating palate, since he was forced to make do with a diet of mackerel and cider, of which he sometimes drank more than he could hold. All the same, he was a good shepherd to his flock and they would come along, at infrequent intervals, to hear him say Mass, purely to oblige him.

However, after managing to remain neutral for a long time, the priest and the gamekeeper had been forced to take sides. Conservative at heart, the Emperor had opted for the Mahés while the priest had become a Flochite. This had given rise to complications. As the Emperor had absolutely nothing to do all day long and was tired of counting the boats leaving Grandport harbour, he had taken it into his head to act as the village policeman. As a Mahé supporter, he favoured Fouasse against Tupain, tried to catch Brisemotte and Rouget's wife red-handed and, above all, turned a blind eye when he saw Delphin slipping into Margot's back-yard. The trouble was that these goings-on led to violent disagreement between him and his direct superior, the mayor La Queue. While being sufficiently respectful of discipline to listen to the mayor's rebukes, the gamekeeper would then go away and do as he thought fit, thereby causing complete chaos in Coqueville's public administration. You could never go near the glorified shed that served as Coqueville's town hall without being deafened by the sound of some flaming row or other between the two. Father Radiguet, on the other hand, having joined the triumphant clan of the Floches, who showered him with gifts of superb mackerel, secretly encouraged Rouget's wife to stand up to her husband and threatened Margot with all the torments of hell if she ever let Delphin lay as much as a finger on her. In a word, anarchy reigned supreme, with the army in revolt against the civil authority and religion conniving at the frolics of the wealthier members of his flock, so that, in this dead-and-alive little hole looking out upon the infinite expanse of the sky and the vast sweep of the ocean, you had a whole community of fully one hundred and eighty souls at daggers drawn with each other.

In the midst of all this turmoil, Delphin alone never lost his good spirits; young and in love as he was, he did not give a damn for anything or anybody, as long as Margot would one day be his. He may well have been planning to snare her like a rabbit, but being a sensible lad despite his wild ways, he was going to see to it that the priest should tie the knot that would ensure that they would live happily ever after.

One evening as he was lying in wait for her in a lane, Margot finally took a swing at him and then blushed purple in confusion when, instead of waiting for the blow to land, Delphin caught hold of her hand and feverishly covered it in kisses.

She was trembling as he whispered to her:

"I love you. Will you love me?"

"Never!" she cried in a shocked voice.

He gave a shrug of his shoulders and said quietly, with a tender look in his eyes:

"Please don't say that... We'll get on very well together, the pair of us. You'll see just how nice it is."

2

That Sunday, the weather was dreadful, one of those sudden September storms which blow up with terrible force on the rocky coast round Grandport. As dusk was falling, Coqueville caught a glimpse of a vessel in distress being driven before the wind. But the light was failing and there was no question of going to her rescue. Since the previous day, *Zephyr* and the *Whale* had been tied up in the tiny natural harbour to the left of the beach, between the two granite sea-walls. Neither La Queue nor Rouget were going to risk venturing out. Unfortunately, Madame Dufeu's representative, Monsieur Mouchel, had taken the trouble to come over personally on Saturday to offer a bonus if they made a real effort: catches were poor and the Central Market was complaining. So when they went to bed on Sunday with the rain still pelting down, the fishermen of Coqueville were bad-tempered and full of grumbles. It was always the same old story: when the demand was good, the fish just weren't there. And they all discussed the ship that had been seen passing during the gale and which by now was no doubt lying at the bottom of the ocean.

Next day the sky was still black and the sea running high, booming and thundering and reluctant to calm down, even though the wind was blowing less strongly. It then dropped completely and though the waves were still rearing and tossing furiously, both boats went out that afternoon. *Zephyr* returned at about four o'clock, having caught nothing. While Tupain and Brisemotte were tying up in the little harbour, La Queue stood on the beach, shaking his fist angrily at the sea. And Monsieur Mouchel was expecting something from them! Margot was there with half Coqueville, watching the heavy swell of the dying storm and sharing her father's resentment against the sea and the sky.

"Where's the *Whale*?" someone asked.

"Over there, behind the point," replied La Queue. "If that old tub gets back safe and sound today, it'll be lucky."

His voice was full of scorn. He went on to suggest that it was quite understandable for the Mahés to risk their lives like that; when you haven't got two pennies to rub together, you don't have much choice. As for him, he'd sooner let Monsieur Mouchel go begging.

Meanwhile Margot was scrutinizing the rocky point behind which the *Whale* was hidden. Finally she asked her father:

"Did they catch anything?"

"Them!" he exclaimed. "Not a thing!"

Noticing that the Emperor was grinning, he calmed down and added more quietly:

"I don't know if they've caught anything but as they never do…"

"Perhaps they have caught something today after all," said the Emperor teasingly. "It has been known to happen."

La Queue was about to make a heated retort when Father Radiguet arrived and succeeded in soothing him. From the flat top of the church, Radiguet had just caught a glimpse of the *Whale* which seemed to be in pursuit of some large fish. This news created great excitement among the villagers gathered on the beach, with the Mahé supporters hoping for a miraculous catch and the Floches very keen for the boat to come back empty-handed. Margot was craning her neck and looking out to sea.

"There they are!" she exclaimed briefly.

And in fact a black speck could be seen beyond the point.

Everyone looked. It looked like a cork bobbing up and down on the sea. The Emperor could not even see the black speck: you had to be from Coqueville to recognize the *Whale* and its crew at that distance.

"Yes," Margot went on, for she had the best eyes of anyone in the village, "Fouasse and Rouget are rowing and the boy's standing in the bow."

She called Delphin "the boy" to avoid mentioning him by name. Now they were able to follow the course of the boat and try to understand its strange manoeuvres. As the priest had said, it seemed to be pursuing a fish which kept swimming away to escape. It was an extraordinary sight. The Emperor thought that their net had probably been carried away but La Queue exclaimed that they were just being lazy and fooling about. They wouldn't be catching seals, that was for sure! The Floches all found this an hilarious remark while the Mahés felt annoyed and pointed out that anyway Rouget had guts and was risking his life while certain other people stuck to dry land at the slightest puff of wind. Once again, Father Radiguet had to intervene because fists were being clenched.

"What on earth are they up to!" exclaimed Margot suddenly.

"They've gone again!"

They all stopped glowering at each other and everyone
scanned the horizon. Once more the *Whale* was hidden
behind the point. This time, even La Queue was becoming
uneasy. Since he was unable to explain to himself what they
were doing, and fearing that Rouget might really be making a
good catch, he was beside himself with rage. No one left the
beach even though there was nothing particular to see. They
stayed there for two hours, still waiting for the boat which
kept appearing and then vanishing. In the end it disappeared
altogether. La Queue declared it must have gone to the bottom
and in his anger he even found himself wishing in his heart of
hearts that this might be true; and as Rouget's wife happened
to be present with Brisemotte, he looked at them with a con-
spiratorial grin and gave Tupain a friendly tap on the shoulder
to console him for the loss of his half-brother Fouasse. But he
stopped laughing when he saw his daughter Margot on tiptoe
peering silently into the distance.

"What do you think you're doing here?" he said gruffly. "Off
you go back home... And have a care, Margot!"

She made no move but suddenly called out:

"Look, there they are!"

There was a cry of surprise. With her sharp eyes, Margot
swore that she couldn't see a soul on board. No Rouget, no
Fouasse, nobody! The *Whale* was running before the wind as
though abandoned, changing tack every minute as it bobbed
lazily up and down. Fortunately a breeze had sprung up from
the west which was driving the boat landwards, in an oddly
capricious way, so that it yawed first to port and then to starboard. The whole of Coqueville was by now assembled on the
beach. Everybody was calling out to everyone else and there
was not a woman or a girl left at home to prepare the supper.
It could only be some sort of disaster, something inexplicable
and so mysterious that they all felt quite at a loss. Rouget's wife
thought quickly and decided that she ought to burst into tears.
The most Tupain could do was to look miserable. All the
Mahés were looking distressed while the Floches were trying
hard to show some decorum. Margot had sat down on the

beach as if her legs had suddenly collapsed.

"What on earth are you doing there?" exclaimed La Queue, seeing her at his feet.

"I'm tired," she said simply.

And she turned her head to look out to sea, holding her face in her hands and peering through the tips of her fingers at the *Whale* bobbing up and down even more lazily, like a cheerful boat that has had too much to drink.

Theories were now flying thick and fast. Perhaps the three men had fallen into the sea? But for all three to do that at once seemed very odd. La Queue was trying to persuade people that the *Whale* had split open like a rotten egg. But as she was still afloat, the others merely shrugged their shoulders. Then he remembered that he was mayor and began to talk about various formalities, as if the men were really drowned.

"What's the point of talking like that!" exclaimed the Emperor. "How could people die as stupidly as that? If they'd fallen in, Delphin would have been here by now!"

They all had to agree; Delphin could swim like a fish. But in that case, where on earth could the three men be? Everyone was shouting. "I'm telling you it is!" "And I'm telling you it isn't!" "Stupid!" "Stupid yourself!" And they were getting to the stage of exchanging blows, so that Father Radiguet was forced to make an appeal for the cessation of hostilities while the Emperor hurriedly tried to restore order. Meanwhile the boat continued to bob lazily up and down under everyone's eyes. It was as though she was dancing and laughing at them all and as she drifted in on the tide, she seemed to be greeting the approaching land with a series of slow, rhythmical curtsies. She was a crazy boat, that was for sure!

Margot was still hiding her face and peering through her hands. A rowing-boat had just put out from the harbour to go to meet the *Whale*: losing patience, Brisemotte seemed anxious to put an end to Marie Rouget's uncertainty. Now Coqueville's whole attention was focused on the rowing-boat. They started shouting: Could he see anything? The *Whale* kept coming on, still looking mysterious and saucy. At last they saw him catch hold of one of the mooring ropes and stand up to look into the boat. Then suddenly he burst into fits of laughter. They were all mystified. What could he see that was so funny?

"Hi there! What's up?" they shouted excitedly. His only reply was to go on laughing even more loudly, making signs that they were soon going to find out. Then he tied the *Whale* to his own boat and towed her in. And the inhabitants of Coqueville were stunned at the extraordinary sight that met their eyes. The three men, Rouget, Fouasse and Delphin, were lying flat on their backs, fast asleep, blissfully snoring and dead drunk. In the middle, there lay a small cask that had been stoved in, a cask that had been full when they had picked it up. They had been drinking from it and it must have been good stuff, because they had drunk it all except for a litre or so that had spilled out into the boat and become mixed with seawater.

"Oh, what a pig!" cried Rouget's wife and stopped snivelling.

"Well, that's a fine catch, I must say," said La Queue, putting on a dignified air.

"Hang on!" said the Emperor. "People catch what they can and after all, they did catch a barrel at least, which is more than those who didn't catch anything."

Piqued by this remark, the mayor said no more. But Coqueville's other inhabitants were commenting excitedly. Now they could understand! When boats get drunk, they prance about, just like human beings, and that boat had certainly had a bellyful! The tipsy old so-and-so! She'd been zigzagging about just like a drunk who couldn't find his way home. And some were laughing at it and some were annoyed, for the Mahés found it funny and the Floches found it disgusting. They all gathered round the *Whale*, peering open-eyed at the three happy fellows snoring away with smiles all over their faces, completely oblivious to the crowd bending over them. Neither the insults nor the laughter could greatly disturb them. Rouget was unable to hear his wife accusing him of drinking the lot. Fouasse did not feel the sly kicks in his ribs being given him by his brother Tupain. As for Delphin, he looked charming, with his fair hair, pink cheeks and air of rapturous delight. Margot had stood up and was silently contemplating the young man with a hard look in her eyes.

"Better get them to bed!" a voice cried.

But at that very moment, Delphin started to open his eyes and, still with his blissful happy expression, began to look around at the crowd of people watching him. At once, everybody started questioning him, so excitedly that he felt quite bewildered, especially as he was still as drunk as a lord.

"Well, what's all the fuss?" he stammered. "It's a little cask. There wasn't any fish, so we caught a barrel."

That was all he could say. Each time he said it, he added simply:

"It was jolly good."

"But what was in it?" they asked him crossly.

"Oh, I don't know. It was jolly good."

By now the whole of Coqueville was bursting with curiosity. They all stuck their noses into the boat and sniffed hard. There was unanimous agreement that it was a liqueur of some sort but nobody could guess what liqueur. The Emperor, who flattered himself that he had drunk everything that a man can drink, said that he was going to see. Solemnly he took in the hollow of his hand a little of the liquid floating in the bottom of the boat. The crowd fell suddenly silent and waited expectantly. However, after taking a sip, the Emperor shook his head uncertainly, as if still in doubt. He tasted it twice again, with a surprised and worried look on his face, more and more embarrassed. Eventually he was forced to admit:

"I don't know... It's queer. I expect I'd be able to say if it wasn't for the seawater. But my word, it really is very queer."

People looked at each other in amazement that even the Emperor didn't dare to pass a definite judgement on what it was. Coqueville eyed the little cask with respect.

"It was jolly good," said Delphin once again. He seemed to be laughing up his sleeve.

Then, with a broad grin and a wave of his hand, he added:

"If you want some, there's still some left... I saw lots of little barrels...little...little barrels..."

He kept on humming the words like a refrain from some lullaby, looking fondly at Margot, whom he had only just caught sight of. She lifted her hand angrily but he did not blink an eyelid and waited for the slap with a tender look in his eyes.

Intrigued by the thought of this mysterious, delicious drink, Father Radiguet also dipped his finger into the bottom of the boat and sucked it. Like the Emperor, he too shook his head uncertainly: no, he couldn't place it, it was most surprising. One thing only they all agreed on: the cask must have come from the vessel in distress which they had noticed on Sunday and which must have been wrecked. English ships often carried cargoes of liqueurs and fine wines of that sort to Grandport.

The light was slowly fading and the villagers at last started to make their way home in the dark. Only La Queue stayed behind, sunk in thought, turning over in his mind an idea that he wanted to keep to himself. He stopped and listened for the last time to Delphin who was being carried away, still gently singing:

"Little barrels...little barrels...if you want some, there are still some left!"

3

That night the weather changed completely. When Coqueville woke up next day, the sun was shining brightly, the sea was as calm as a mill-pond, spread out like a piece of green silk. And it was warm, a golden autumnal warmth.

La Queue was first out of bed in the village, his mind still in confusion from last night's dreams. He stood for a long time looking out to sea, to left and right. Finally, he said irritably that he supposed that they'd better keep Monsieur Mouchel satisfied and immediately set out with Tupain and Brisemotte, threatening Margot that he would tickle her ribs if she didn't watch her step. As *Zephyr* was leaving harbour and he saw the *Whale* riding heavily up and down at her moorings, he cheered up somewhat and shouted:

"Well, anyway there'll be nothing doing from them today... Blow out the candle, lads, that drowsy lot are all in bed!"

As soon as he was out at sea, La Queue set his nets, after which he went to look at his pots, that is his long wicker lobster pots, in which you can occasionally catch red mullet as well. But despite the calm sea, his search went unrewarded; all

the pots were empty except the last one in which, as if to rub
salt into the wound, they found one tiny mackerel which he
angrily flung back into the sea. That was the way it went: sometimes weeks would pass and the fish would give Coqueville a
miss; and it always happened when Monsieur Mouchel was
keen to buy. When La Queue pulled his nets up an hour later,
the only thing he had caught was a bunch of seaweed. He
clenched his fist and swore; it was all the more irritating
because the Atlantic was unbelievably calm and was lying lazily
stretched out, drowsing under a blue sky like a sheet of burnished silver, on which *Zephyr* slid slowly and gently along on
an even keel. La Queue decided that he would make for harbour after he had dropped his nets once more. He would
return and have another look in the afternoon; and he threatened God and all his saints in outrageously blasphemous terms.

Meanwhile Rouget, Fouasse and Delphin were still sound
asleep and did not rouse themselves until lunch-time. They
could not remember anything except that they were vaguely
aware of having enjoyed an amazing treat such as they had
never known before. That afternoon, when they were down at
the harbour, the Emperor tried to question the three of them,
now that they had regained full use of their faculties. Perhaps
it was something like a sort of brandy mixed with liquorice
juice? Or could it be better described as a kind of sweet rum,
with a burnt flavour? First they said yes, then they said no.
The Emperor half suspected it might be ratafia but he couldn't
swear to it. Rouget and his crew were too exhausted to go fishing, especially as they knew that La Queue had gone out
unsuccessfully that morning; so they were thinking of waiting
until the following day before going to look at their pots. They
sat with parched throats slumped on blocks of stone, gazing at
the incoming tide and barely able to keep awake. Then suddenly Delphin sat up, sprang on to the block of stone and,
looking far out to sea, shouted:

"Look over there, guv'nor!"

"What is it?" asked Rouget, stretching himself.

"A barrel."

Their eyes lit up as the other two sprang to their feet and

scanned the horizon.

"Where is it, lad? Where is the barrel?" asked Rouget excitedly.

"See that black dot over there, on the left?"

The others could not see anything. Then Rouget uttered an oath:

"Christ Almighty!"

He had just caught sight of the barrel, no bigger than a lentil, against the pale sea, caught in the slanting rays of the setting sun. He ran down to the *Whale* with Delphin and Fouasse sprinting after him like startled rabbits, scattering showers of pebbles as they ran.

As the *Whale* was clearing the harbour mouth, the news of the sighting of the barrel spread like wildfire and the women and children rushed down to the beach. People were shouting:

"A barrel, a barrel!"

"Can you see it? The current's carrying it towards Grandport!"

"Hurry up! That's it, on the left. A barrel!"

And Coqueville streamed down on to the beach, with the children turning cartwheels and the women holding up their skirts with both hands so as to scramble down more quickly. Very soon the whole village was assembled on the beach, just as the evening before.

Margot appeared briefly and then ran back home as fast as she could to warn her father, who was discussing a summons with the Emperor. In the end La Queue came out livid with rage and said to the gamekeeper:

"Stop bothering me! Rouget must've sent you along to waste my time. Well, he's not going to get that one, you'll see!"

When he saw the crew of the *Whale* already three hundred yards off shore rowing madly towards the black dot bobbing up and down in the distance, he became even more enraged.

"No, they're not going to get it! Over my dead body!"

And now Coqueville saw a splendid sight, a wild race between *Zephyr* and the *Whale*. When the crew of the latter saw the other boat leaving harbour, realizing the danger they redoubled their efforts. Although they had a start of some four hundred yards, it was still an even contest, because *Zephyr* was far lighter and faster. Excitement on the beach was rising to fever pitch. The Mahés and the Floches had instinctively formed into two groups and were following the changing fortunes of the race with passionate interest, each cheering its own boat on. At first the *Whale* held on to its lead but once *Zephyr* was properly under way, she could be seen to be steadily overhauling the other boat. The *Whale* put in a final spurt and for a few minutes managed to hold her advantage, only to be again overhauled as *Zephyr* came up on her at tremendous speed. From that moment onwards, it became apparent that the two boats would reach the barrel roughly together. Victory would depend on circumstances and the slightest error of judgement would determine the issue.

"The *Whale*, the *Whale!*" the Mahés were yelling.

The words froze on their lips. Just as the *Whale* was almost touching the barrel, *Zephyr* boldly slipped in between and pushed the barrel away to the portside, where La Queue harpooned it with a boathook.

"*Zephyr*! *Zephyr*!" howled the Floches.

And as the Emperor muttered something about "foul play" under his breath, a few rough words were exchanged. Margot was clapping her hands. Father Radiguet, who had come down to the beach holding his breviary, uttered a profound remark which suddenly dowsed everyone's excitement and filled them all with alarm.

"Perhaps they're going to drink the lot, too," he muttered sadly.

Out at sea a violent squabble had arisen between the *Whale* and *Zephyr*. Rouget was accusing La Queue of being a thief while the latter replied by calling Rouget a ne'er-do-well. The two men even picked up their oars to knock each other on the head and the race showed signs of turning into a naval battle. As it was, shaking their fists at each other, they promised to settle the matter ashore, threatening to slit each other's throats as soon as they were on land.

"What a shyster," grunted Rouget. "You know, that cask was bigger than the one yesterday... It's yellow, too. It must be something special."

Then, in a resigned voice:

"Let's go and look at the pots. Perhaps there'll be some lob-sters."

And the *Whale* moved ponderously away to the point on the left.

On board *Zephyr*, La Queue had been obliged to speak sharply to Tupain and Brisemotte on the subject of the barrel, for the boathook had loosened one of the hoops and a red liq-uid was oozing out; the two young men took some of it on the tip of their finger and licked: it was delicious. Surely there wouldn't be any harm in trying just a glass of it? But La Queue put his foot down; he stowed the barrel away and said that the first person to try and have another lick would hear from him. Once ashore, they'd see.

"Shall we go and have a look at the pots, then?" asked Tupain sulkily.

"Yes, in a minute," replied La Queue. "There's no hurry."

He too had been casting fond glances at the cask and in a sudden fit of listlessness, he felt tempted to return to harbour straightaway to see what its contents tasted like. He was bored with fish.

All right," he said after a pause. "Let's get back, it's getting late. We'll look at the pots tomorrow."

But just as he was giving up any idea of fishing, he caught sight of another barrel to starboard, a very tiny cask which was floating upright and spinning like a top. That was the end of any thoughts of fishing nets or lobster pots; they weren't men-tioned again. *Zephyr* set off in pursuit of the cask which he picked up quite easily this time.

Meanwhile the *Whale* was engaged in a similar venture. When Rouget had already pulled up five completely empty lob-ster pots, Delphin, still on the lookout, shouted that he could see something. But it didn't look like a barrel, it was too long.

"It's a piece of wood," said Fouasse.

Rouget let his sixth lobster pot slide back into the sea with-out bothering to pull it completely out of the water.

"Let's go and have a look all the same," he said.

As they approached, it seemed to them like a plank, a crate

or a tree-trunk. Then they gave a cry of joy. It was a real barrel but a very queer one, a sort they had never seen before. It looked like a tube bulging in the middle with both ends closed by a layer of plaster.

"Isn't it strange!" exclaimed Rouget delightedly. "I want the Emperor to taste this one... Come on, you two, let's get back!"

They agreed not to broach the barrel straightaway and the *Whale* returned to harbour just as *Zephyr* was tying up. The villagers were all still waiting expectantly on the beach. Cheers greeted this unhoped-for catch of three barrels. The young boys flung their caps into the air while the women scurried off to fetch some glasses. They immediately decided to sample the drinks on the spot. Any flotsam and jetsam belonged to the whole community, there was no disputing that! However, they gathered in two groups, the Mahés with Rouget, while the Floches formed a circle round La Queue.

"The first glass is for the Emperor!" cried Rouget. "Tell us what it is!"

The liqueur was a lovely golden yellow. The gamekeeper raised his glass, looked at it, sniffed it and decided to take a sip.

"It's from Holland," he announced after a long pause.

He offered no further information, and the Mahés all drank with due deference. It was slightly viscous and they were surprised by the flowery taste. The women thought it was very good; the men would have preferred a little less sugar. However, in the end, after a third or fourth glass, it did seem quite strong. The more they drank, the better they liked it. The men were becoming merry and the women felt a bit funny.

Meanwhile, despite his recent exchange of words with the mayor, the Emperor was now hanging round the Floche group. The larger barrel contained a dark red liqueur, while the tiny cask held a liquid as clear as a mountain stream; and it was this last that was the deadliest of them, really peppery and strong enough to take the skin off the roof of your mouth. None of the Floches was able to place either the red or the clear one. Yet some of them were fairly expert and were annoyed not to know the name of the liqueurs that they were drinking with such enjoyment.

"Here you are, Emperor, see what you think of this," La Queue called out at last, making the first move.

The Emperor, who had been hoping for such an invitation, once again assumed his role as taster-in-chief. Having tried the red one, he said:

"There's some orange in it."

For the clear one, he merely said:

"That's a real beauty!"

That was all they could get out of him, because all he did was to keep nodding his head with a knowing look and a pleased expression on his face, like a man who has just done a good job.

Father Radiguet alone seemed unconvinced. He wanted to put a name to them and since, according to him, he had the names on the tip of his tongue, in order to complete his information he kept emptying one glass after another, repeating as he did so:

"Now, wait a second, I know what it is… I'll be able to tell you in a minute."

Meanwhile, everyone was becoming merry, the Mahés as well as the Floches. The latter were laughing particularly loudly because they were mixing their drinks and this made them all the merrier. Both groups were, however, keeping strictly to themselves and not offering any drinks to the other, although they were casting friendly glances at one another; but they were ashamed to admit openly that they would like to try the other group's drink, which was surely better than their own. Despite their rivalry, the two brothers Tupain and Fouasse spent the whole evening in close proximity to one another without once showing signs of wanting to square up to each other. It was noticed, too, that Rouget and his wife were drinking out of the same glass. As for Margot, she was serving drinks to the Floches and as she kept filling the glasses too full, the surplus spilt on to her fingers which she was continually licking, so that, although obeying her father's orders not to drink, she had become tipsy, like the girls during the grape-harvest. It was not unbecoming; on the contrary, she was looking all pink and her eyes were sparkling like candles.

The sun was setting; the evening was soft and springlike. Coqueville had demolished the contents of all three barrels and no one was thinking of going home to supper; they were too comfortable on the beach. When it was quite dark, Margot, sitting some distance away from the others, felt someone breathing down the back of her neck: it was Delphin, very merry, crawling on all fours and prowling round her like a wolf. She stifled a cry in order not to draw her father's attention, for he would certainly have booted his behind.

"Do go away, stupid!" she muttered, half laughing and half annoyed. "You'll get caught!"

4

Next day, when Coqueville awoke, the sun was already high in the heavens. It was an even warmer day and the sea lay stretched out sleepily under a cloudless sky. It was one of those lazy sorts of day when it's wonderful not to have to do anything. It was Wednesday and until lunch-time Coqueville recovered from its indulgence of the previous evening. Then everyone went down to the beach to take a look.

Fish, Madame Dufeu, Monsieur Mouchel and everything connected with them were forgotten. La Queue didn't even mention going to look at their lobster pots. At about three o'clock they sighted some barrels, four of them, bobbing up and down in front of the village. *Zephyr* and the *Whale* set off in pursuit but as there was enough for all, they didn't squabble and each boat took its share.

At six o'clock, after exploring the bay, Rouget and La Queue came back with three barrels each. And once more, they went on the spree. The women had brought tables down to the beach to make things more comfortable. They even fetched benches and set up two open-air cafés, just like those in Grandport. The Mahés sat on the left, the Floches on the right, separated from each other by a mound of sand. However, that evening the Emperor kept going from one group to the other, carrying round glassfuls of each liqueur, so that everybody could taste the contents of each of the six barrels. By about nine o'clock, everyone was much merrier than on the previous evening. And next morning, no one in Coqueville could even remember how they had managed to get to bed.

On Thursday, *Zephyr* and the *Whale* picked up only two barrels; that is, two barrels each: but they were enormous. On Friday, the catch was superb, and beyond their wildest dreams: seven barrels, three for Rouget and four for La Queue. And now for Coqueville there began the Golden Age. Nobody did a stroke of work. The fishermen slept off the effects of the night before and did not wake till noon. Then they would go down for a stroll along the beach and look longingly out to sea. Their only concern was which liqueur would come in on the tide. They would sit there for hours, gazing out to sea, and a cry of joy would go up as soon as a barrel hove into view. From the top of the rock, the women and children would wave their arms about wildly at the sight of the tiniest clump of seaweed bobbing up and down in the waves. *Zephyr* and the *Whale* held themselves in readiness to leave at a moment's notice. They sailed out and scoured the bay, fishing for barrels in the same way that people fish for tunny, spurning the carefree mackerel which disported themselves in the sun and the soles floating idly at the surface. Coqueville followed their expeditions from the beach, chuckling with delight. Then, when evening came, they drank their catch.

What really attracted Coqueville's fancy was that the barrels were never-ending. Whenever there seemed to be none left, still they came. The lost ship must have had a wonderful cargo on board and Coqueville, which had become cheerfully selfish, joked about the wrecked vessel: it must have been a proper liquor cellar, large enough to make every fish in the Atlantic tipsy! What is more, they never caught two identical barrels, for they were of every size, shape and colour, and in every barrel there was a different liqueur, so that the Emperor was in a permanent haze. He had drunk everything that was going and now he was all at sea! La Queue declared that he had never seen such a cargo in his whole life. Father Radiguet expressed the view that it must have been ordered by some native king wanting to set up a cellar. As a matter of fact, Coqueville was so drowsy and fuddled by drinking so many unknown liqueurs that it had given up any attempt to understand.

The ladies preferred the cordials: moka, cacao, peppermint and vanilla. One evening, Marie Rouget drank so much anisette that she was ill. Margot and the other girls went for curaçao, bénédictine, trappistine and chartreuse. The blackcurrant syrup was reserved for the children. The men, of course, enjoyed it most when they picked up brandies, rums and Holland gins, the sort of stuff that stings the palate. And then there were the surprise items. A cask of resinated raki from Chios threw Coqueville into a state of complete bewilderment; they thought that they'd come across a barrel of turpentine; all the same, they drank it up, because it's a shame to waste anything; but they talked about it long afterwards. Arak from Batavia, caraway seed schnapps from Sweden, tuica calugaresca from Romania and Serbian slivovitz also threw Coqueville's ideas on what you can pour down your throat into utter confusion. Basically, they betrayed a weakness for kümmel and kirsch, the sort of spirits that are as clear as crystal and powerful enough to fell an ox. How was it possible for such wonderful drinks to have been invented? Up till now, Coqueville had had experience of only the rawest of spirits; and not everyone had known them. And so their imagination began to run riot and they felt like going down on their knees to worship such an inexhaustible variety of intoxicating liquor. Fancy being able to get drunk every day on something new that you didn't even know the name of! It was like a fairy story, a shower of nectar, a fountain spurting with every sort of extraordinary liquid, distillations scented with the fruits and flowers of the whole of creation!

And so on Friday evening, there were seven barrels set up on the beach and the whole of Coqueville was there as well; indeed, the villagers were there all the time for, thanks to the mild weather, they were all living on the beach. Never had they known such a gorgeous week in September. They had been on the spree since Monday and there was no reason for it not to last for ever if divine Providence continued its supply of barrels. Father Radiguet saw the hand of God in all this. All business was suspended; why toil and sweat when pleasure was handed to you, in a bottle, while you slept? They had all become members of the leisured classes, people who were in a position to drink expensive liqueurs without having to worry who was footing the bill. With their hands in their pockets, the inhabitants of Coqueville lounged about in the sun awaiting their evening treat. As a matter of fact, they were never sober; kümmel, kirsch and ratafia were the links in an unbroken chain of jollification; in the space of seven days, Coqueville was being inflamed by gin, made sentimental by curaçao and hilarious by brandy. And they were as innocent and as ignorant as babes in arms, drinking everything the good Lord provided with the simple faith of true believers.

It was on Friday that the Mahés and the Floches started fraternizing. Everyone was very merry that evening. The barriers between them had already begun to crumble the previous day, when some of the tipsiest among them had kicked away the mound of sand separating the two groups. There was only one further step needed. The Floches were busily emptying their four barrels while the Mahés were similarly engaged in finishing off their three small casks, which happened to contain liqueurs of the same colours as the French flag, red, white, and blue. The Floches were very envious of the blue one because a blue liqueur seemed to them something quite out of the ordinary. Now that he was never sober, La Queue had become extremely genial and he suddenly went across unsteadily, with a glass in his hand, realizing that as mayor, it was up to him to make the first move.

"Look, Rouget," he said, stumbling somewhat over his words, "would you care to have a drink with me?"

"I don't mind if I do," replied Rouget, swaying with emotion.

And they fell on each other's necks. At this touching sight, everyone burst into tears and the Mahés and the Floches embraced each other after being at daggers drawn for three centuries. Father Radiguet, greatly stirred, again spoke of the hand of God. They drank each other's health in the three liqueurs, red, white and blue.

"*Vive la France!*" the Emperor cried.

The blue one was no good at all, the white one was just

passable; but the red one was terrific. After that, they set about the Floches' barrels. Then they started dancing. As there was no band, some of the young men obliged by whistling and clapping their hands. This set the girls going. It was a proper binge. The seven barrels were all placed in one long line and everyone could choose the one he liked best. Those who had had enough lay down on the sand and had a nap; when they woke up, they started again. The dancers gradually spread out until there was dancing all over the beach. This open-air hop went on till midnight. The sea lapped gently and the stars shone brightly in the calm of the fathomless depths of the heavens. It was like some primitive tribe, in the infancy of the world, peacefully cradled in the joyous intoxication of their first barrel of brandy.

However, Coqueville still went home when it was time to go to bed. When there was nothing left to drink, the Mahés and the Floches, supporting and carrying each other as best they could, eventually made their way back to their houses. On Saturday, the celebration went on until nearly two o'clock in the morning. During the day, they had caught six barrels, two of which were enormous. Fouasse and Tupain nearly came to blows and Tupain, who became aggressive when drunk, threatened to do his brother in. But everyone was disgusted at such an exhibition, the Floches as well as the Mahés. Was it sensible to go on squabbling like that when the whole village was overflowing with brotherly love? So they forced the two brothers to drink each other's health, which they reluctantly did. The Emperor promised himself to keep an eye on them. The Rouget couple were not very happy either. When Marie had been drinking anisette, she allowed Brisemotte to take liberties that were not to her husband's liking, all the more so as drink had made him also amorously inclined. Father Radiguet had tried to pour oil on troubled waters by preaching the forgiveness of sins, but everyone was apprehensive at the possibility of an outburst.

"Ah well," said La Queue, "things will sort themselves out. If there's a good catch tomorrow, you'll see… Your very good health!"

However, La Queue himself was not entirely guiltless. He

was still keeping a sharp eye on Delphin and trying to kick his backside every time he saw him sidling up to Margot. The Emperor indignantly pointed out that there was no sense in trying to prevent two young folk from having fun but La Queue still swore that he'd see his daughter dead rather than let Delphin have her. Anyway, Margot didn't want him.

"That's right, isn't it?" he shouted. "You're too proud ever to marry a tramp, aren't you?"

"No, I never would, papa!" Margot invariably replied.

On Saturday, Margot drank a good deal of a very sweet liqueur. You can't imagine how sweet it was. As Margot was quite unsuspecting, she soon found herself sitting on the ground beside the barrel. She was laughing happily to herself: it was heavenly, she could see stars and hear dance tunes singing in her ears. Then it was that Delphin slid up to her under the cover of the barrel and took her hand.

"Will you, Margot?" he asked her.

"It's papa who doesn't want me to," she replied, still smiling.

"Oh, that doesn't matter," retorted the boy. "Old people never do, you know... As long as you want to..."

And he boldly planted a kiss on her neck. She squirmed with pleasure and little shivers ran down her back.

"Stop it, you're tickling..."

But she made no mention of giving him a slap. For one thing, she couldn't have done it, because her hands had gone all weak, while for another, she was finding those little kisses on her neck rather nice. It was like the liqueur which was filling her with a delicious feeling of languor. After a while, she twisted her head and stretched out her chin, like a cat.

"Look," she said in a voice that trembled, "I'm itching just there, under my ear... Oh, that's wonderful..."

They had both forgotten La Queue. Fortunately the Emperor was on the alert. He drew Father Radiguet's attention to them.

"Look over there, Father. They'd better get married."

"Morality would certainly suggest so," observed the priest sententiously.

And he promised to see what he could do about arranging it

next day: he would personally have a word with La Queue. Meanwhile La Queue himself had drunk so much that the Emperor and the priest had to carry him home. On the way, they tried to make him see reason with regard to Delphin and his daughter; but all they could get out of him was grunts. Delphin followed behind them, taking Margot home under the bright starry sky.

Next day, *Zephyr* and the *Whale* had already picked up seven barrels by four o'clock. At six o'clock they caught two more. That made nine in all. And so Coqueville celebrated the Sabbath day. It was the seventh day of inebriation and it was a celebration to end all celebrations, a beano such as no one had ever seen before nor would ever see again. Mention this to anyone from Lower Normandy and they'll chuckle and say:

"Ah yes, what a binge they had in Coqueville!"

5

Meanwhile, even as early as Tuesday, Monsieur Mouchel had expressed surprise at seeing neither Rouget nor La Queue. What the devil were they up to? The sea was calm, they should have made a splendid catch. Perhaps they were waiting in the hope of getting a big haul of lobsters and sole which they could bring over all together. So he decided to be patient and see what happened on Wednesday.

But on Wednesday, Monsieur Mouchel got cross. It must be remembered that Dufeu's widow was an awkward customer; it did not take long for her to become abusive. So although he was a fine, upstanding young fellow, well-built, with a mop of fair hair, she made him quake in his shoes, despite his secret dreams of one day making her his wife; he was thus always careful to show her every attention while reserving the right to bring her to heel with a good slap round the face if he ever became the boss. Well, that Wednesday morning, the widow raged and swore, complaining that no fish was being delivered and putting the blame on him for gadding about with the local girls instead of concentrating on whiting and mackerel, of which there should have been a plentiful supply. Thus provoked, Monsieur Mouchel declared that it was Coqueville's fault for not having kept their word. For a brief moment, Madame Dufeu's surprise at the news of such strange behaviour made her forget her anger. What on earth was Coqueville thinking of? They'd never done that sort of thing before. But she hastened to add that she didn't give a damn about Coqueville, that it was Monsieur Mouchel's responsibility and if he kept on being taken in by the fishermen, she'd have to decide what measures to take. This remark made the young man very uneasy and he consigned Rouget and La Queue to the bottomless pit. But perhaps they'd come next day.

Next day was Thursday and still neither of them put in an appearance. In the late afternoon, a despairing Monsieur Mouchel climbed up to the rock to the left of Grandport, where he had a view of Coqueville in the distance, together with its yellow strip of beach. He stayed looking for a long time. It seemed peaceful enough under the sun. Wisps of smoke were coming out of the chimneys: no doubt wives were getting the supper ready. Monsieur Mouchel saw that Coqueville was still there and that it hadn't been crushed by a fall of rock. He was more mystified than ever. Just as he was about to go down, he thought he could see two dark spots in the bay, the *Whale* and *Zephyr*. He went back and reassured the widow: Coqueville was out fishing.

Night came and went; it was Friday and still no trace of Coqueville. Monsieur Mouchel climbed a dozen times up to the rock. He was beginning to lose his nerve; Madame Dufeu was treating him abominably and he could think of no possible explanation to give her. Coqueville was still there, lazily basking in the sun like a lizard. But this time Monsieur Mouchel could not see any smoke. The village seemed dead. Had they all crawled into their holes and given up the ghost? Certainly, the beach seemed to be swarming with people but that could well be heaps of seaweed brought in by the tide.

On Saturday, still nobody appeared. The widow had stopped shouting and was sitting tight-lipped and with eyes set hard. Monsieur Mouchel spent two hours up on his rock. He was becoming curious and beginning to feel that he must discover for himself why the village seemed so deserted.

Finally, the sight of those tumbledown old cottages blissfully drowsing in the sun irritated him so much that he resolved
to leave very early on Monday, so as to be there by nine
o'clock in the morning.

Getting to Coqueville was no easy matter. Monsieur
Mouchel decided to go by land, so that he could descend on
the village unawares. He drove in a horse and cart as far as
Robigneux, where he left them in a barn, since it would have
been foolhardy to risk driving down the gullies. He set off at a
steady pace for Coqueville, a distance of more than four miles
over the roughest landscape, twisting and turning as it
descends between two enormous sloping walls of rock, so narrow in parts that three men could not walk abreast. Further
on, it ran along a sheer drop, until the gorge suddenly opened
out to give views over the immense blue horizon and the sea.
But Monsieur Mouchel was in no mood to admire the landscape and he swore as the boulders rolled away under his feet.
It was all Coqueville's fault and he promised to show them the
rough edge of his tongue when he arrived. He was now nearly
there and as he came round the last bend in the rock he
caught sight of the twenty or so houses which comprised the
village, huddled together against the cliff-face.

It was just striking nine. The sky was blue and it was so
warm that you could have thought it was June. The air was
clear and there was a golden glow and a cool salty smell of sea.
Monsieur Mouchel set off down the only street of the village,
which he had often visited, and as he had to pass Rouget's
house, he went in. The house was empty. Then, he had a brief
look into Tupain's, Fouasse's and Brisemotte's cottages. Not a
soul to be seen; the doors were all open but the rooms were
empty. What could it mean? A cold shiver began to run down
his spine. Then he thought of the local authorities: the
Emperor would certainly be able to give him information. But
the Emperor's house was as empty as all the rest; so even the
gamekeeper wasn't there! By now, the silence of the deserted
village filled him with terror. He hurried on to the mayor's
house where another surprise awaited him. The inside of the
house was in a frightful mess: beds left unmade for the last

three days, dirty crockery lying about all over the place, chairs tipped up as if there had been a fight. Now completely unnerved and with thoughts of some dreadful cataclysm running through his mind, Monsieur Mouchel made for the church, determined to leave no stone unturned; but the priest was no more visible than the mayor. Religion had vanished together with any civil authority.

Coqueville had been abandoned and left with not a breath of life, not even a dog or a cat. And not even poultry, for the hens had left as well. Absolutely nothing at all: empty and silent, Coqueville lay plunged in slumber beneath the vast blue sky.

Heavens above! It wasn't surprising if Coqueville wasn't supplying any fish! Coqueville had moved out, Coqueville was dead! The police must be informed. Monsieur Mouchel was deeply moved by this mysterious disaster; but then, thinking that he might as well go down as far as the beach, he uttered a sudden cry. There, flat out on the sand, lay the entire population. He thought at first that there must have been a general massacre, but the sound of heavy snoring quickly disabused him. On Sunday night, Coqueville had celebrated until such a late hour that its inhabitants had been quite incapable of going home to bed. So they had slept on the beach, in the place where they had toppled over around the nine barrels of liqueur, now completely empty.

Yes, the whole of Coqueville lay there plunged in sleep; and I mean by that the women and children and old men, as well as the working men. There was not one still on his feet. Some were lying face down, some on their backs; others lay curled up. As you make your bed, so you must lie on it. And so the whole lot were scattered all over the beach where their drunkenness had landed them, like a handful of leaves blown at random by the wind. Some of the men had tipped over with their heads hanging down while some of the women were showing their backsides. It was all free and easy, a dormitory in the open air, good honest folk and not a trace of embarrassment, because embarrassment is the enemy of enjoyment. There happened to be a new moon and so, thinking that they had blown out their candles, the inhabitants of Coqueville had let themselves go.

Day had come and the sun was shining brightly, straight into the sleepers' eyes; but not one eye blinked. They were all sleeping like logs and beaming all over their faces with that wonderful innocence of the drunk. The hens, too, must have come down early to peck at the barrels, because they too were lying on the sand, dead drunk. There were even five cats and three dogs, flat on their backs with their paws in the air, tipsy from licking the sugary dregs left in the glasses.

Monsieur Mouchel picked his way through the sleepers for a while, taking care not to disturb anyone. He realized what had happened because they had picked up some casks from the wrecked English vessel in Grandport. His anger had completely evaporated. What a touching sight it was! Coqueville was reconciled and the Mahés were lying down with the Floches... When the last glass had been drained, the worst enemies had fallen into each other's arms: Tupain and Fouasse were snoring away hand in hand, like brothers who henceforth would find it impossible to quarrel over legacies. As for the Rougets, they offered an even more charming picture: Marie lay sleeping between Rouget and Brisemotte, as though saying that from now on they would live happily like that, for ever afterwards...

But there was one group that provided a particularly touching family scene: Delphin and Margot were lying with their arms round each other's necks, cheek to cheek, with their lips still open in a kiss, while the Emperor was lying crosswise at their feet, keeping guard over them; La Queue was sound asleep and snoring away like any happy father who had found a husband for his daughter; and Father Radiguet, who had toppled over like all the rest, was holding his arms outspread as though blessing them. In sleep, Margot was still holding up her pretty little face like the muzzle of a lovesick cat who enjoys being tickled under its chin.

So the spree ended in a wedding. And later on, Monsieur Mouchel himself married the widow and tanned her hide as he had promised.

Mention all this to anyone from Lower Normandy and they'll chuckle and say:

"Ah yes, what a binge they had in Coqueville!"

Port After Port, The Same Baggage

by
JANETTE TURNER HOSPITAL
(1942–)

Portugal, Morocco, Bombay…and port after port, the same old baggage, as if the passengers were carrying their very lives about on their backs. "We all manage as best we can," remarks Doris softly, a wise old widower on this, her maiden voyage. An intriguing tale of discovery from a writer who, each time I read her, impresses me more.

One wouldn't have expected daughters in full free flight to be so reactionary, Doris Mortimer thought. Yet there it was. The world was riddled with a lack of probity, double standards thick as dandelions in even the best-weeded lives.

But Mother, her daughters said, you know nothing about the predatory habits of men. And travelling alone, well, it's like an advertisement. You'll be fair game.

Doris knew what they meant: You need a man to go with you, to protect you from other men; you can't manage alone. But of course they couldn't come right out and say this, since it flew in the face of all their principles. She had to smile at their malaise.

You've led such a sheltered life, they said. You're so innocent and trusting.

Which is why you should stand up and cheer, Doris countered. Better, surely, to bloom so unseasonably late than never at all.

But both of her daughters were against the scheme from the start. They thought of it as a sudden madness brought on by the recent death of their father. Via elaborate desk phones, they conferred on her over-reaction. The views of colleagues in Legal Aid office and university department alike were passed on to Doris. There was unanimous disapproval of her plan. All the ex-husbands, with whom the two daughters were on the most cordial of terms, were brought in to concur.

To no avail.

Doris was quite stubborn.

But a *cargo* boat! they said. It's perverse. At least, her daughters pleaded, she should go by—she had *earned*—a luxury liner. If only, they cajoled, she would take along her teenage grandchildren, who would—

"No," Doris said.

Doris was fond of her grandchildren. Nevertheless it was her observation that few segments of society were as morally rigid as adolescents. And the first of their engraved absolutes was this: The elderly shall be above reproach.

Doris was tired of being above reproach.

It was not that she had outrageous plans. Not specifically. She did not expect occasions for transgression to flourish in the path of an elderly widow. It was simply that nothing in her life had ever allowed for the errant and the indiscreet, and she had a hankering to put herself in the way of temptation. After all, she thought, would St. Augustine's life, or Thomas Merton's, have meant anything at all without a counterpoint of piquant profligacy?

She did not, however, want to cause needless distress. Gillian and Geraldine had sufficient to worry about, and she had always put the family first—something deplored often enough by her daughters. Gillian had even given a paper at a conference on this subject; it was subtitled: "Can our fathers be forgiven?" and had discussed the slow debilitation of years of exemplary wifely support of an otherworldly scholar.

Now that this gentlest and most self-absorbed of pedants had been buried from the university chapel with full academic honours, it was true that Doris felt in some sense free; that she woke each morning to an aura of strangeness, to a part-frightening part-delicious sense of new beginnings. But her freedom seemed to her something at once overwhelmingly sad, quavering with promise, and infinitely private.

She did not, certainly, want to discuss it. She found her daughters' litany to past waste oppressive. Such dicta, she saw, sharpened their sense of purpose and made their own quite different brands of unhappiness worthwhile. She felt almost guilty for tampering with sacrosanct traditions, but the more she tried to settle into the role for which they were convinced she was (alas) destined, the more she toyed with startling subversions and new energies.

So finally she said fretfully: "After a lifetime of kowtowing to your father's needs, do I have to be bullied by my children and grandchildren?"

She knew that this was hitting below the belt. Jabbing them in the soft underbelly of their principles.

Gillian, a psychology professor at a major university, said bravely, "Certainly no one has more of a right to…to be a little *eccentric* for once. To self-indulge. It's just that…."

"If anything happens to you," Geraldine said lugubriously, "we'll never forgive ourselves."

Geraldine saw terrible things every day in Legal Aid. This did not make for optimism. Doris, who felt contrite because she hadn't disliked her life nearly as much as she felt she should have for her daughters' sake, had tried to join Geraldine's office as a volunteer. She had hoped it would cure her of congenital tranquillity and optimism. But Geraldine wouldn't hear of it.

"Mama," she said. "You've paid your dues. I don't even want you to know about some of what goes on."

But Doris was sick and tired of knowing about everything second-hand from books and newspapers and daughters, and when she finally stood on the deck of the cargo boat and waved to them all on the wharf, she had a deep inner certainty that an insurance settlement had never been put to better use.

Everyone came to the wharf. Gillian and Geraldine, and the four grandchildren, and the five former sons-in-law. Actually, only two of them had been sons-in-law, strictly and legally speaking, but in their various seasons Doris had regarded them all as such. She blew kisses and tossed coloured streamers and generally behaved (as one teenage granddaughter remarked to another) in an embarrassing manner. As the boat pulled away and the first of the streamers dipped soggily into the water, she called down to them: "I'm tough as nails, you know."

And her daughters laughed nervously, with tears in their eyes.

Doris sat at the captain's table. One of the pleasures of travelling by cargo boat was the intimacy possible between crew and passengers, of whom there were only four when the *Lord Dalhousie* left the St. Lawrence estuary, its belly full of Saskatchewan grain. Doris waited expectantly for salty tales of philandering in foreign parts, but the officers were disappointingly discreet.

"My little boy," the captain said, "my second one, the twelve-year-old, he's doing computers at school already. Astonishing." He shook his head, not so much in pride, Doris thought, as in bewilderment. "While I was home this time, he showed me a note from his teacher. It said he was ready to be individualized if we'd sign the consent slip. I called the teacher. He said electronic communications is where it's at, and there's no question my son can lock into fast track if he's individualized now."

Everyone pondered this cryptic future in silence.

"At twelve years of age," the captain said wonderingly.

"I hope you had the sense to say no." Wendell, a passenger, was on assignment for a book, *The Organics of Life*, commissioned by a New York publisher. "There's a lot of evidence coming in on the dangers. Not just eye strain and migraines from the video screen. Radiation risks too, I'm serious. They did tests on the programmers for a major corporation. Punching keys eight hours a day, watching that flickering monitor, I'm telling you, people think the exposure is negligible but it's a lie. A cover-up. I should know, my father's in Digital. You think he wants to broadcast the dangers? Hah.

Those tests would make your hair curl. Eczema, dermatitis, hair loss, way above average infertility, all the early signs. Soon even mid-ocean won't be safe."

"Do you have children, Mrs. Mortimer?" the captain asked.

"Two daughters," Doris said.

"How did they—you know—turn out?"

"Well, one became a lawyer, and the other became a college professor."

"Amazing, isn't it?" The captain sighed. "I suppose it all works out." He nodded at her vaguely and smiled, as though she had offered cautious promises and consolation. "It's a bit like planting squash and getting—I don't know—getting melons, isn't it? Of course I'm away for such long stretches. Still"—he raked his fingers through his hair—"I'd planned to take him canoeing. Wilderness trekking, you know? Sort of things boys are supposed to...but he's enrolled in computer camp for the summer."

"I intend to show," Wendell announced, "that a simple but physically demanding life is the answer."

"The answer for what?" Doris asked.

"For happiness. For vigour and potency to the very end. For example, look at what you're all drinking. Madness! If you had any idea what coffee and alcohol, either one of them...how toxic for the system...." He shared his extensive knowledge of herbal teas which cleanse the body without harmful side effects, rose hip especially, of which he had brought along a six-month supply. They would all notice the benefits within days. "I mean, look at you," he said to Doris. "Just like my mother. All pallor and soft flesh."

"I think Mrs. Mortimer is a very attractive lady," the captain said gallantly.

Wendell huddled into himself, sulking. "I'm only trying to be helpful. People don't *care* what they do to their bodies."

Doris saw that, like her daughters, he was pricked constantly by the burden of a proselytizing truth. He was so young. All his muscles and nerves were knotted, the guy wires of crusading righteousness. She thought of massaging the back of his neck with her fingers, the way she used to do when her girls were in high school—if they'd just lost a game, say; or if they hadn't done as well as expected in an exam.

Instead she raised her coffee mug to the captain by way of thanks for his support. She also agreed to do yoga on deck with Wendell every morning. She found it difficult to shed the habit of instinctive peace-making.

"You should be more assertive," the twins asserted. Or rather, Pam said this, and Pat said: "Pam's right, you know, Doris. You shouldn't let Wendell push you around."

The twins were supposed to be spending the year apart. Their parents, their teachers, and sundry therapists all insisted it was necessary. So Pam had been sent to college in New York and Pat had been packed off to Vermont. But now, as they joked, they were eloping. They had sent a ship's cable to their parents as soon as North America dipped safely below the horizon.

"Just so they won't panic," Pam said.

"And partly," Pat admitted, "to make them sorry for what they did."

"You have to follow your own star, Doris," Pam said. "You shouldn't take up yoga just to please Wendell."

"But I'm quite happy," Doris said, "for the chance to experience something quite new and different."

By the time they reached the Azores, Doris had mastered two or three elementary yogic contortions and had decided that the lotus position was as inaccessible as her own youth. This Wendell hotly denied.

"It's all in your mindset," he told her. "You're rigid through and through, you're the essence of rigidity. If you *think* limits, there'll *be* limits."

"You know, Wendell," Doris said mildly, as they watched the on-loading of citrus fruits, "I have been your age, but you haven't been mine."

"Just like my mother," he fumed. "A closed mind. You know it all, don't you. Can't tell you anything."

At Lisbon a cable awaited the twins. *We love you*, it said. *Come home and we'll work something out.*

"Hah!" Pam sniffed. "I'll bet. I can just see that therapist leaning over their shoulders and dictating."

"I don't think they've suffered enough yet," Pat agreed.

They sent a reply: *Hitch-hiking across Europe. Will communicate from time to time. Don't worry, everything fine.*

"And stop letting Wendell bully you," they said to Doris in farewell. "He's such a wimp."

They set out for the Pyrenees with backpacks, while the *Lord Dalhousie* off-loaded the Azorean oranges and half of its Canadian grain, and took on a cargo of wine and iron ore.

Doris admired the sheen of sweat on bare muscles. She wondered which of the dock workers beat their wives and which ones took home flowers on occasional impulse. She amused herself by speculating on the ones who might have ended up in Geraldine's Legal Aid office, and the ones who might have passed through Gillian's classes—if she and her family had lived in Portugal. But then of course the girls would have had different names and a different sort of education and different expectations. They wouldn't have been able to get divorces and perhaps wouldn't have wanted to.

She watched some old women moving along the docks as they sold fish from wicker baskets, and thought: And I would have been wearing black for the remainder of my life.

In Morocco, declining Wendell's offer of himself as chaperon, she went ashore and wandered through the bazaar alone.

"You'll be sorry," Wendell warned. "But of course, you can't let go the reins for a moment, can you? Don't blame me if something happens."

Doris felt that she would rather like something to happen.

In the bazaar, she was the only woman who was not moving

inside a private and portable tent. It's like a loose shroud, she thought. Perhaps they are buried in it, a garment for all purposes. She could feel male eyes like a film of sweat on her skin. It was strange to be a sexual object at the age of sixty-five. Perhaps it was the way she was dressed—in white linen pants and a long-sleeved white cotton blouse. The outfit had not seemed at all provocative when she packed it.

Smells assaulted her. Camel dung, exotic flowers, rotting vegetables, incense. She felt a quirky elation, and smiled into the startled faces of men. They did not respond. She might have been from the moon, a thought that pleased her. With a sandalled toe, she doodled *yes* in the virgin soil of new experience.

She stopped at an orange-seller's booth. Five, please, she indicated with her fingers, and offered a handful of coins. The merchant took all of her money without comment or expression—by which she knew she had offered more than was necessary—and handed her the oranges. A dilemma. She had expected to receive them in some sort of bag, and the extent of her pampered middle-class Western ignorance embarrassed her. She felt obscurely guilty.

It was difficult to carry five oranges without a container. Only two would fit in her handbag. She made a gesture of wry self-deprecation and handed three oranges back to the merchant. She smiled, as one human being to another, acknowledging the foibles of the species.

He turned his head away and spat forcefully on the ground between two of his wicker baskets. Her eyes widened in surprise and for a few seconds she remained motionless, staring at him. He spat again, this time close to her feet, and raised his right arm to cover his eyes. Warding off an evil presence.

She turned and walked on, under the shade of tamarind trees.

Stares. It was like a brushing of cobwebs, a sensation of being touched, molested, by something physically insubstantial yet malevolent. The whole world was staring. Young men, slim-hipped, the age of her eldest grandson—and of Wendell—stood in groups and pointed. How odd to be watched so intently by such green and blooming youths. She tried to savour the experience, to roll its irony around in her mind, to inhale its bouquet. But it was not the kind of staring that made one feel desirable.

She stopped and looked defiantly at a whispering group. Directly into their eyes. She would shame them, she would appeal to basic decency. But they did not lower their eyes or give any sign of being disconcerted. Some of them laughed lewdly. Was it possible that an old woman could be deemed to have loose morals because her face was unveiled?

I suppose they would be scandalized, she thought, to know that I am a mother and a grandmother.

It was late in the afternoon—when her feet were aching, her eyes felt scratched with grit, and red dust clung to her like a fine shawl—that she saw Wendell in an alleyway between market stalls. He was engaged in some negotiation with a boy who might have been sixteen or seventeen. The boy's dark curls and face were so beautiful that in any other country Doris would have assumed he was a girl. Fascinated by the androgynous perfection, she stood watching and admiring, and it was several minutes before she realized the nature of the business transaction taking place. Too late. As she turned to go, Wendell sensed a presence and saw her.

She spread her hands in a gesture of helplessness, of innocence of intention. Just an unlucky accident, she telegraphed silently. And in any case, it makes no difference to me. Who am I to make judgements?

She understood, nevertheless, that he had legitimate grounds for hating her at that moment.

She could feel a blush of sorrow on her cheeks. Wendell gave her a look of pure savagery and stormed off between the ragged awnings. And the Arab boy, his deal in ruins, spat in her direction. If I had agreed to Wendell's company? she wondered. She walked slowly back to the wharf, her feet dragging.

"Well?" Wendell demanded bitterly, materializing behind her. "Satisfied? Not just a food crank, but a pervert too. Who can blame my mother for giving up on me?"

"These oranges are delicious," she said, offering one. "Better than anything we get at home. Just taste."

"Hah. The ostrich strategy. My mother uses it all the time. Hide your head in the sand and the problem will go away. Pretend I'm out with girls and I'll turn out straight in the end."

"Oh Wendell. We all manage as best we can. You, me, your mother. Why don't you sit down here and watch the fishermen with me?"

He scowled, but sat down on the dock and leaned against her crate. "I'm not telling you anything."

"Of course not. There's no need."

Without being aware of it, she began to knead the muscles in the back of his neck, thinking of Gillian and Geraldine. Whenever they came to her mind these days, they came first as fresh-faced little girls. She had to think them up through time to assemble their faces as they looked now, in the present.

"It started in high school," Wendell began.

Capetown, Daar es Salaam, the Mauritius. She had seen diamonds, gold, cotton, bananas, ferried into the hold and out again. And sailors, she had discovered, really did have a woman in every port. Several women, in fact. Although not, it seemed, the captain, who sent postcards and presents from each stop to his wife and children, and especially to the son he had lost in the maze of high technology. Until somewhere— was it Capetown?—when that red sports car drove onto the wharf as the anchors were raised. A young woman got out and waved madly. She had long blonde hair; she had a little boy in her arms. Both were neatly—even expensively—dressed; and such exotic accessories; smiles and tears and smudged mascara, and a fluttering sea-blue scarf as long as the wind.

Doris glanced along the deck. The sailors were tossing boisterously suggestive jokes to the usual ship followers, but no one was returning the wave of the blonde woman with the child.

Surreptitiously, Doris studied the captain. He gazed at the spires of the city beyond the wharf, preoccupied; except, she observed, that the index finger of his right hand, which lay innocently on the railing, was raising and lowering itself in a rhythm that might be construed as a coded message of farewell.

Doris looked at the young woman on the wharf and back at the captain. His gaze did not shift from the spires in the middle distance. The woman waved on, undaunted. The captain's finger rose and fell.

"I think," Doris said finally, "that you should wave back to her properly. Who's going to mind?"

The captain flinched. His eyes implied that she had committed a gross impropriety. Nevertheless, a few seconds later, sheepishly, he did wave to the girl on the dock. A laughing sobbing sound floated up to them, and the girl held her little boy high up in her arms as though to receive a benediction.

"I would like you to know," the captain said awkwardly, as the wharf drifted from sight, "that I provide for the child."

Much later, coming upon Doris alone in the lounge, he said suddenly: "She called him Sailor—isn't that crazy? He loves to watch the ships, she takes him down to the wharf every day."

He opened his wallet and showed her a photograph, the kind taken in booths narrow as telephone boxes, with one slot for coins and another for finished photographs. The three heads were close together—the captain's, the pretty young woman's, and the little boy's.

"He's afraid of me," said the captain sadly. "He cries when I hold him. Already."

Bombay. When they left, Wendell was missing, but a sailor handed Doris a letter.

Dear Doris,
They have the right attitude here. Diet, meditation, healing, the spiritual needs, they know it's all organically related. Ideal

for finishing my book. I'm leaving you my supply of rose hip tea. (It's in the closet over my bunk.) Keep working on the lotus position and don't think limits.

You can write to me care of the Bombay YMCA if you want to, but I'm warning you, don't expect answers.

Love, Wendell

And then Cochin. "Jewel of the Arabian Sea," as they were told by the boatman who guided them in between islands green as jade, past the Chinese fishing nets in their hundreds, dipping in and out of the water like the gossamer veils of sea courtesans. Snake boats, with long curled prows and bellies pregnant with copra, shuddered in the *Lord Dalhousie's* wake, the boatmen resting on their bamboo paddles as they waited for the turbulence to pass.

They glided past Mattancheri, past the fabulous mansions of maharajahs, past the fifteenth-century Jewish synagogue. Past Bolghatty Island where the old Dutch Palace grew mouldy in the monsoons, a dowager empress fallen into soft times. Frangipani trees and marauding jasmine, extravagantly perfumed, sprawled beyond the bounds of gardens long since run amok.

The *Lord Dalhousie* docked at the mainland to take on a cargo of cinnamon and sandalwood.

When the ship itself becomes fragrant, thought Doris, is it possible that life will be the same?

The streets of Cochin were daunting: wide as the tropics, and teeming with cars, buses, bicycles, rickshaws, buffalo carts, pedestrians, cows, pigs; the heat also a tyrannical swaggering presence. Doris realized she should not have come ashore without a hat. She bought a black umbrella—there were no other colours, only black—from a roadside stall. When she opened it for shade, she could see the arabesque of small holes across two membranes, a map of insect exploration.

Vendors beckoned her into their shops, offering cool drinks

and exotic English. *Mem sahib is finding unique beauty as nowhere else, isn't it? they asked. Certainly she is wanting, she is buying, isn't it?* They courted her. Brasses and sandalwood carvings were brought on cushions, as tribute to a visiting monarch. Swathes of silk were unfurled. The wet heat and the incense that rose thickly from little brass holders made her feel faint. Faces began to merge with their wares, floating upwards. Of course, she thought drowsily. The Indian rope trick! Now she herself seemed to be drifting away from her chair, away from her own feet.

Perhaps she was dreaming. Or sleepwalking.

She was listing leeward from the anarchy of the street of vendors, she was in a maze of back alleyways. A large bird, with draggled feathers that trailed in the gutter slime, was pecking at something rotten. The air was oppressive with the too sweet smell of organic matter decomposing. Doris slipped on something—cow dung—and stumbled against the bird. With a screech it turned and flared its muck-spattered tail into a whiplash of blues and greens. Peacock! Was this a benign dream or a nightmare? The bird's lapis breast heaved with outrage, it fixed Doris with its brilliant blue-black eyes.

She fled, running and stumbling back toward the safe chaos of traffic and vendors, her legs trembling. She needed to sit down. She found a tiny eating place, its two tables covered with dirty oilcloths. For atmosphere: a corona of flies. A waiter came and flicked a rag at the flies so that they dispersed momentarily. She ordered tea. She had learned the word in Bombay: *chai.*

The tea was hot and very sweet and comforting, served in a glass tumbler patterned with circles of cloudy residue. Without feeling in any way disturbed by this, Doris studied the filth with tranquil fascination.

She felt drugged with peace.

Perhaps I am approaching enlightenment, she thought.

"Well!" A voice floated between the flies and the steam of hot tea and curled into her ears. "You *are* a find!" Some sort of vision, Doris thought. A visitation. It sat down opposite her. Its edges, mirage-like, wavered, but it had the appearance of an Edwardian Englishwoman. Hair coiled above an elegant aging face, lace bodice high at the neck, long sleeves, long skirt, parasol. Doris blinked several times, striving to keep her heavy eyes open.

"My dear," the vision said with some concern, "you tourists never learn. You're succumbing to sleeping sickness." The vision wagged an admonishing finger. "Only mad dogs and Englishmen, you know. Come on, I'll take you to my home."

There seemed to be a journey in a rickshaw and then a comfortable wicker chair on a verandah rampant with ferns. An overhead fan was turning, pushing offerings of hot air at Doris.

"I'm Emma," the vision said. "And I must say, you are a find. There's always someone of course, never a dearth of guests. Sailors, tourists, hippies, anthropologists, linguists, all kinds. But I can't even remember how long it's been since I talked to someone…well, of my own age and station, so to speak. I've just sent Agit down to the Queen's Bakery for some little English jam tarts so we can celebrate."

"You *live* here?" Doris asked in drowsy amazement, expecting the dream to float off course before an answer reached her.

"For thirty-five years, my dear. Minus a little spell back in England right after Independence."

Doris leaned forward, trying to concentrate. "But *why*?" she asked. Or tried to ask. She laced her fingers together to keep the dream from trickling away too quickly.

Emma raised her eyes in amusement. "Why not?" She stirred her tea reflectively, looking into the gentle whirlpool of its surface, examining reasons not looked at for a very long time. "We did go back in '47. Perhaps I would have stayed if it hadn't been for Teddy. Yes, I suppose I would have, though it's hard to imagine…cooking for church fêtes, doing the altar flowers once a month, that sort of thing, I suppose." She threw back her head and laughed heartily. "What I've been saved from!"

There was a long silence as they both sipped tea. One's dreams grow stranger with age, Doris thought. More colourful. She watched bright birds peck at berries in the courtyard.

"Yes, it was because of Teddy really...." Emma's voice seemed no louder than the soft humming of the mosquitoes which waited like a restive audience just beyond the lattice work. Lighted coils kept them at bay, coils that glowed like a row of tiny sentry fires around the edges of the verandah. "Teddy's our boy. Our only child. I don't understand why things turned out as they did. Julian was strict, I suppose, but I don't think more than other military fathers...."

What visions will come, Doris thought, when the ship is breathing cinnamon, when sandalwood seeps from its pores.

"Teddy had been away from us, of course," Emma sighed. "In boarding schools. Well, we all did that in those days, sent them back to England. We believed it was for the best. But Teddy, well...after he was sent down from his school.... I suppose the scandal... I suppose he wanted to leave it behind. Anyway, he ran away to sea. At least, that's how I like to think of it. A rather romantic thing to do, wasn't it?"

Whisper of spoon against cup; the tea stirred endlessly.

"I came to understand it after Julian died. Being totally alone, I mean." Pause. "I expect that's how it seemed at school, you know.... Of course it wasn't the sort of thing Julian could live with." Another long pause. "I think, once one knows one is absolutely alone, it is so much better to be among strangers. Don't you agree? An alien knows what to expect." Stir, stir. "And one day, you know, down at the wharf"—the voice dropped to a murmur—"I'm bound to bump into Teddy."

Doris sipped peacefully, at rest in her wicker chair.

"Anyway," Emma said brightly, "a pension goes a lot further in India..." but Doris drifted into sleep.

When she woke it was dusk and the yellow flame from an oil lamp threw fantastic shadows across the verandah. What was the smell? Coconut. Coconut oil. She tried to remember where she was.

"The ship!" she cried in alarm, jumping up and overturning the wicker chair. "How long have I been here?"

"You slept for a couple of hours, that's all," Emma said calmly. "When does your ship leave?"

"Tomorrow, I think. Oh thank god, I was afraid I'd...." With a shaking hand, Doris picked up the overturned chair and sat down again. "I'd better get back for the night."

"You could stay here. Anyway, *tiffin* is ready." She called back into the house. "Agit! Bring *tiffin*!"

A young man bearing platters of rice and curry and sweets emerged.

"And now," Emma said. "We can talk."

They spoke of many things as the oil lamps flickered and the perfume of the night-jasmine drifted in and out like fog. From time to time there was the soft thud of a bat hitting the verandah eaves. And whenever Emma laughed—which she did often—a chorus of nearby frogs responded throatily. Antiphonally. Or perhaps in protest.

"Isn't this fun?" Emma demanded. "Just like old times. A regular dinner party. Of course I have guests at least twice a week, usually sailors." She paused. "I don't suppose there's a Teddy on your ship's crew? No. Well, one of these days." She walked over to a hanging basket of ferns and pulled at some straggling fronds. "You know, you could stay on with me for a few weeks. Or months. We could...." She stopped, and when Doris said nothing, added quickly, almost harshly: "Just a passing thought. In fact, where would I put you? There simply isn't room. Agit! Brandy!"

And after the brandy, Emma said briskly: "Now before you go back to your ship, my *pièce de résistance*. I share it with all my guests. Agit! An autorick!"

They lurched their way back through the tumult of the main thoroughfares to a wooden building on low stilts. THEOSOPHICAL HALL, proclaimed a billboard in uneven hand-painted letters.

"She was one of us, more or less," Emma said, pointing to the sign. "Annie Besant, I meant. Couldn't be worn down."

Doris said carefully: "I don't think...it's quite to my taste, theosophical...."

Emma laughed. "The Kathakali dancers use the hall every night. It's a family troupe. Three generations. Absolutely first rate."

In the gloom inside—the power had failed, and a row of oil

lamps had been placed along the front of the stage—the dancers were still applying their elaborate facial make-up. The small audience was watching with interest. Perhaps this was part of the performance? There were, it seemed to Doris, peering about in the golden-misted twilight, about fifteen people in the audience. Some Indian families with children. A young tourist couple, probably German. And three sailors. Somewhat to Doris's dismay, Emma immediately introduced herself to the Westerners, conversing with animation and much gesture, hazarding her imperfect French and terrible German, asking the sailors their names and whether there was a Teddy (or an Ed, Eddy, Edward, or Ted) on their crews.

Then the performance began. To the accompaniment of a tabla player and a singer, the dancers, gorgeously costumed and dramatically and fantastically made-up, acted out the great legends of the *Ramayana* and the *Mahabharata*. It was primitive and splendid. Perhaps it was the drum beat, or the incense, or the rhythmic stamping of the dancers' feet, that gave Doris a sharp memory of love-making, that made her grieve with a sudden painful intensity for the presence, the body, of her husband who had slipped through some crack into non-being.

The Indians in the audience began to smile and lean forward eagerly in their seats. Doris could feel Emma touching her, was aware of Emma seizing her hand and whispering urgently: "This is the exciting part. This is where Rama destroys the demon Ravana, and right order prevails again in all the worlds."

She forgot to release Doris's hand.

Ever so slightly, they leaned inwards toward the stage and felt the damp pressure of shoulder against shoulder. It was an accidental and fleeting thing—as a child momentarily reaches for its mother; as lovers make discreet contact in public.

Neither drew back.

They sat there hand in hand in the darkness, waiting for Rama—upholder of right order in the universe—to triumph.

The
Ocean Spray

by
MALCOLM LOWRY
(1909–1957)

In 1941, still toiling away on Under the Volcano, *Malcolm Lowry moved into a small cottage on the beach at Dollarton (the Eridanus of the story), just north of Vancouver. In a letter to a friend written about this time, he described his new home as "a shack on the sea in a deserted village... It is a fine wet ruin of a forest full of snakes and snails and terrific trees blasted with hail and fire. We dive from our front porch into a wild sea troughing with whales and seals. We have a boat, now diving at anchor. Everywhere there is a good smell of sea and timber and life and death and crabs."*

"The Ocean Spray" is an extract from his unfinished novel, October Ferry to Gabriola, *a remarkable book now rarely seen. It captures something of Lowry's incredible love of Canada's west coast scenery, littered through with an almost unbearable sense of foreboding...*

I nside the Ocean Spray Inn, on the almost empty Ladies and Escorts side, the view from those same big windows looking straight out over the harbor and the Gulf of Georgia toward the mountainous mainland must have been about the best in the world, Ethan thought. Nothing could have been fresher, swifter, more wholesome, more brilliant. There was a tremendous sense of sunlight, and even sitting here, inside, you could feel the fresh sea wind and smell its sea salt.

Not a cloud in sight, so the thunder must have come from the mountains of Vancouver Island itself, behind them.

The sea was blue and rough, striated with lighter polar blue, the horizon line jagged with deep indigo and white peaks of the mainland mountains.

And there, far beyond a lighthouse in the immediate foreground, whose tower rose waggishly from its substructure of red roofs and white walls, lay Gabriola Island itself, the bartender was saying, or its tip, maybe seven miles away, shimmering like a mirage under the noonday sun.

The Llewelyns sat looking at this happy view without

speaking. Anything like it these days was almost unique in Canadian "beer parlours," which tended to combine the more lugubrious elements of the funereal and the genteel.

"Yes, that's Gabriola, sir," agreed the waiter. "Just beyond Hangman's Point there, sir."

"Just beyond—"

"And there's a ferry that runs to Gabriola Island, of course?" Jacqueline put in hastily.

"Ferry? Oh, absolutely.—Four?"

They gave themselves over to the enjoyment of the view again, sea gulls and lighthouses, blue sea and mountains—how grand it was! It touched your heart, too, filling it suddenly with a wild pride in your own country, a giant, yet so youthful, a clod of springtime mould after all. You felt proud even to be looking at such a dramatic beauty, as if you participated in all that dignity and cleanliness and sense of space and freedom; were, in some manner, clothed in this wholesomeness yourself, were what you were looking at. Do you see those mountains? That is ourselves, part of us.

It was a sudden feeling of love for one's land that had little to do with patriotism, but seemed part of a true pride. Ethan felt a pang: they were both looking past Gabriola, from which their toy passenger steamer was keeping an offing, straight over in the direction of Eridanus. At the same time he became aware that this was perhaps the main source of his pride. Perhaps the view, even though not their old view, really was part of them, its beauty they somehow deserved, had earned (so it seemed in this mood, until one remembered again): those wild forested mountains and the sea were the meaning of their whole life in the little house in Eridanus. In a way he couldn't have explained, they weren't looking at the view, but at something in themselves. Or that had once been in themselves. It was what they meant when they turned to one another, crossing the Second Narrows Bridge some stormy winter afternoon to stare through the streaming windows of their bus down the inlet through the wild weather, with the clouds sweeping low over the evergreens and only the lower slopes of the mountains visible, so that no place on earth seemed more grim and desperate and tempestuous and impossible, and looking forward to the lamps of evening still half an hour distant in the house to say, half-humorously, with such longing: "We *live* there!" And now?

"Hangman's Point," Ethan said aloud.

"I never saw so many lighthouses in my life."

"Nor I."

They counted seven from where they sat, planted on rocks near and far, the white towers of vigil all rising from port-wine-colored roofs and white walls of their keeper's houses, all with much the same pretty architecture. A lighthouse was surely the last thing you associated with a home: yet these scattered beacons on the rocks, these *farolitos* testifying to the extreme danger of the coast (and the extreme danger of living in such isolation: in his experience Ethan could remember more than one tragic crime committed in a light-house) not only were homes, but quite obviously and obsti-nately loved as such—around the nearer ones they could even see where efforts at gardens had been made, and among the rocks of the nearest lighthouse, roses still blooming, in defiance of the spray. And on a near island they saw a lovely little white house, built on piles: they looked at it, shining there against the bronze, russet and burnt gold of its maples (Jacqueline loved to name the colors) faded sage-green of alders and dark bottle-green of pines.

Flying shadows of herring gulls, glaucous-winged gulls, vio-let-green cormorants swept across the big C.P.R. building at the foot of the ramp. Their passenger boat for the mainland was now no more than a smudge of smoke, but a sister ship was coming in, her three yellow funnels, white bridge, foxglove-flower-shaped ventilators moving straight against the blue sky.

To the right, a half-mashie shot below the window, in a small sequestered harbor at the foot of the staircase, three-score freshly painted fishing boats with spiky masts swayed meekly at anchor, or were lying against a wharf. An old freighter was anchored out in the roadstead, just before them, an empty ship with water being pumped out of her side, riding so high she looked gigantic, ΑΡΙΣΤΟΤΕΛΗΣ.

Two men were working aloft, on the cross trees of the main-mast, doing something to the topping lift of a derrick. Derrick, it was a derrick because of the first hangman. It certainly was a curious place to meet Aristotle. Far to the left, remotely, a sea-weary-looking steamer with a great list, not much more than her stern visible, was taking on cargo.

"Loading coal for Australia," said the waiter, arriving at this moment, a tray of beer balanced on his palm, "and the funny thing about that there coal is, don't come from Nanaimo at all, but from somewhere in Alberta, I heard."

"Oh?"

"If you ask me, Nanaimo's getting too big for its boots these days," the waiter said, "ashamed to be among common working people like anyone else."

"And you're quite sure about that ferry to Gabriola?" Jacqueline asked again, shyly, as the waiter was going.

"Sure, there must be one, ma'am," the bartender, a stout, fatherly man called over from the bar. He had been rinsing glasses, and was now drying them. "Only question is, is it running?"

"That's right," said the waiter, "they might have stopped the summer service by now."

The bartender, glancing from time to time out of the window at the scene outside, began to pile the glasses one within another in a stack on the counter, a dull-seeming operation, about which, Ethan now understood from the bartender's glances of satisfaction at the stack, the position of which he altered now and then, evidently to suit some aesthetic whim, there was, on the contrary, something almost godlike: it was a creative process, an act of magic: for within each glass lay trapped the reflection of the window, within each window the reflected scene outside, extended vertically by the glasses themselves, the reflected windows flowing upward in a single attenuated but unbroken line in which could be seen a multiplicity of lighthouses, seabirds, suns, fishing crafts, passenger boats, Australia-bound colliers, the minuscule coal rushing audibly down the minute chute, minute S.S. *Aristotle* with minute Greeks working on the derricks. Ethan touched glasses with Jacqueline and drank.

It was now the end of the luncheon hour. People stood in the wind up and down the ramp. A bearded man in a bright red and black plaid shirt riding a chestnut mare stopped at the top, right under the window, to readjust the horse's blanket and cinch. A dark sedan with some faded gilt lettering on the front door—DEPARTMENT OF MINES AND RESOURCES—also drew up, revealing within, next to the man driving, a stout dowager in a seal coat lighting a cigarette. Ethan touched glasses again with Jacqueline and took another draught of beer watching, with one's eyes, where, diagonally across the street, sat the bastion.

"...Last ship to pass through the Panama...down to New Orleans...country where you can have some standard of living, like the U.S.A....?"

Sailors. The voices came from next door, from the Men's side; Ethan, peeping, thought he could see the speakers through a crack in the partition dividing the two rooms.

"Cargo of lead ore from Patagonia, in Argentina, for Trail, B.C....Vancouver...lumber and general cargo..."

These partitions were usually movable, for at crowded hours the Men's side was much fuller than the Ladies and Escorts: the partition would thus often be found slowly moving in on the territory of the latter, producing, sometimes, if you were obliged to leave your lady for several minutes, on your return a certain eerie feeling of perichoresis. An isolation that was, at the same time, begotten by an interpenetration. But this arrangement seemed an exception, though Ethan could make no sense of it. Alterations were evidently in process on the other side, as the bars appeared not really contiguous, but divided by a corridor, on the farther side of which was yet another partition, or maybe a wall, Ethan couldn't make out. The sailors, either by choice—there seemed a full sea wind blowing through this corridor that may have made it seem a home from home—or because the Men's bar was full, were sitting thus at a table in a kind of no-man's-land between the two.

"I'm English and I hail from Manchester—and don't forget

it!—but I'm married to an American girl in Mobile, so when I'm outward bound I'm homeward bound too."

"*Outward bound...*" the voice came from their first meeting, in the little movie theatre, in thunder and snow... "*But are we going to heaven or hell? But they are the same place, you see...*"

Voyage, the homeward-outward-bound voyage; everybody was on such a voyage, the Ocean Spray, Gabriola, themselves, the barman, the sun, the reflections, the stacked glasses, even the light, the sea outside, now due to an accident of sun and dislimning cloud looking like a luminosity between two darknesses, a space between two immensities, where it would set out on its way again, had already set out, toward the infinitely small, itself already expanding before you had thought of it, to replenish the limitless light of Chaos—

Blue, blue, deep blue: a white fishing boat slid across the foreground, which telegraph wires just outside the window intersected; and holding up the glass to the light and drinking the beer, one might have felt, forgetting everything, as though drinking down the day itself, and having drunk that the day was still there (there was another beer, this time Jacqueline's) in its inexhaustible coolness, its prospect of happiness to be engulfed once more.

But Jacqueline had scarcely finished her first glass of beer and now—Ethan had just drawn her attention to the scarcely perceptible *kaoiling kaoiling* of another very distant freight train—an expression of supplication came over her face.

"I'm sure we'll find a place on Gabriola, sweetheart," Ethan said.

But even as he said it, hoping it was true, he was aware of a certain sinking sense of fear that had been with him all morning, as though part of him did not want to find it, to commit himself finally, something of the feeling one has at the moment of commencing a long journey (however much one has dreamed of and longed for it) or the feeling he had had when he finally resigned from the law firm in Toronto and started west with Jacqueline, and he knew she felt this too, though if Gabriola proved impossible he felt already their exhausted and bitter disappointment at the same time.

And yet, finally to leave Eridanus, even though they knew they must, they had been warned of the new park that would encompass that stretch of forest and waterfront, warned that they were to be evicted, and even though they had never intended to live there permanently, still, to leave—

"Ethan," Jacqueline said, taking his hand.

"Yes."

"Do you remember, 'when you see the light in the sky, you see—'"

Two years ago last spring, in May, the Llewelyns, having followed the path through the forest ("follow this trail through the bush until you see the light in the sky, then you'll see the cabin you folks are looking for, at the bottom of the steps," the old fisherman had instructed them), and there below them, beneath a wild cherry tree in full bloom, its chimney capped by a bucket, shingled roof needing repair, its strong cedar foundations standing right in the sea, for it was high tide, they saw, for the first time, their third house, their beloved cabin. It was shimmering, awash in light; the reflections of the sun on the water sent forever millwheel reflections sliding up and down its weathered silver cedar sides. They stood there, looking at one another, in the lightness, greenness, the heavenliness of the forest, and always this first glimpse of their house was to be associated too, perhaps from memories of the carillon-sounding Sunday mornings of Niagara-on-the-Lake, with the unearthly chiming of a church bell through the mist. Actually the sound in Eridanus came from a freight train walking along the embankment on the other side of the inlet, its warning bell…

Entering the house with the key they had received from the owner, they gazed round the two rooms, slightly dusty, damp-smelling from disuse, but essentially clean, and bare of all but necessary articles: the wood-burning cookstove, table by the window and two plain wooden benches, the cupboard for the dishes; the second room with a bed like a ship's bunk set into the walls, and chest of drawers in one corner. Could they possibly—could Jacqueline—live in such a place, without electricity, without plumbing, without even running water?—There were two pails to be filled at the well. Jacqueline gazed round her, pulling off her white gloves she looked totally out of place. Ethan walked out on the porch, leaving her still gazing, with mute abstracted nods and astonished eyes round the rooms. But a moment later she joined him on the porch, and looking across the water toward the mountains: yes, she had said yes!

And then—"I know how you feel," Sigbjørn Wilderness said to them, last summer.

"God knows we've thought about it enough, but if you bought it would you like it?"

"Why not?"

"Well, we couldn't keep our houses on the beach then, we'd have to build houses back from the water twenty feet, I think it is—"

"Oh God, I'd forgotten about the Harbour Board."

"And then we'd have to cut it up into lots and chop down all the trees over twenty feet high and put in water mains—in short, you might as well just go round the point and buy a lot in the subsection. But hold on, we've been here ten years…"

But Ethan couldn't hold on, not like that. For between knowing that you are going to die, and knowing that you are going to die sometime within the next year there is a difference.

And once more, that day, the warning bell sounded through the mist, more frantically, and it had been high tide, and afterward they had stood in the house in anguish—and oh, my God, how was the house now? Perhaps at high tide the logs were banging underneath with a chewing breaking ruinous sound (and they not there to protect it) so that the house shook, hearing this, the *house* hearing this, for it was as if the house knew, with no sentimentality about it, knew its every timber and crossbrace precious to them, as if the house had heard that bell too, coming over the water, till the sound had driven in its last weary nail, the sound which was also like the cathedral bell—

> Vous qui passez
> Ayez pitié

The Feeding
of the Emigrants

by
LAURENCE HOUSMAN
(1865–1959)

This is a very odd, very beautiful little story. You may read it twice, or three or four times, and never be quite sure of its meaning. Though stories of the mer-folk were common throughout the Victorian era, Laurence Housman always succeeded in making the familiar strangely unfamiliar, and "The Feeding of the Emigrants" is a story as rare as a piece of Spaniard's gold.

Over the sea went the birds, flying southward to their other home where the sun was. The rustle of their wings, high over head, could be heard down on the water; and their soft, shrill twitterings, and the thirsty nibbling of their beaks; for the seas were hushed, and the winds hung away in cloud-land.

Far away from any shore, and beginning to be weary, their eyes caught sight of a white form resting between sky and sea. Nearer they came, till it seemed to be a great white bird, brooding on the calmed water; and its wings were stretched high and wide, yet it stirred not. And the wings had in themselves no motion, but stood rigidly poised over their own reflection in the water.

Then the birds came curiously, dropping from their straight course, to wonder at the white wings that went not on. And they came and settled about this great, bird-like thing, so still and so grand.

Onto the deck crept a small child, for the noise of the birds had come down to him in the hold. "There is nobody at home but me," he said; for he thought the birds must have come to call, and he wished to be polite. "They are all gone but me," he went on, "all gone. I am left alone."

The birds, none of them understood him; but they put their heads on one side and looked down on him in a friendly way, seeming to consider.

He ran down below and fetched up a pannikin of water and some biscuit. He set the water down, and breaking the biscuit sprinkled it over the white deck. Then he clapped his hands to see them all flutter and crowd round him, dipping their bright heads to the food and drink he gave them.

They might not stay long, for the water-logged ship could not help them on the way they wished to go; and by sunset they must touch land again. Away they went, on a sudden, the whole crew of them, and the sound of their voices became faint in the bright sea-air.

"I am left alone!" said the child.

Many days ago, while he was asleep in a snug corner he had found for himself, the captain and crew had taken to the boats, leaving the great ship to its fate. And forgetting him because he was so small, or thinking that he was safe in some one of the other boats, the rough sailors had gone off without him, and he was left alone. So for a whole week he had stayed with the ship, like a whisper of its vanished life amid the blues of a deep calm. And the birds came to the ship only to desert it again quickly, because it stood so still upon the sea.

But that night the mermen came round the vessel's side, and sang; and the wind rose to their singing, and the sea grew rough. Yet the child slept with his head in dreams. The dreams came from the mermen's songs, and he held his breath, and his heart stayed burdened by the deep sweetness of what he saw.

Dark and strange and cold the sea-valleys opened before him; blue sea-beasts ranged there, guarded by strong-finned shepherds, and fishes like birds darted to and fro, but made no sound. And that was what burdened his heart,—that for all the beauty he saw, there was no sound, no song of a single bird to comfort him.

The mermen reached out their blue arms to him, and sang; on the top of the waves they sang, striving to make him forget

the silence of the land below. They offered him the sea-life:
why should he be drowned and die?

And now over him in the dark night the great wings
crashed, and beat abroad in the wind, and the ship made great
way. And the mermen swam fast to be with her, and ceased
from their own song, for the wind sang a coronach in the canvas and cordage. But the little child lifted his head in his sleep
and smiled, for his soul was eased of the mermen's song, and it
seemed to him that instead he heard birds singing in a far-off
land, singing of a child whose loving hand had fed them, faint
and weary, in their way over the wide ocean.

In that far southern land the dawn had begun, and the
birds, waking one by one, were singing their story of him to
the soft-breathing tamarisk boughs. And none of them knew
how they had been sent as a salvage crew to save the child's
spirit from the spell of the sea-dream, and to carry it safely
back to the land that loved him.

But with the child's body the white wings had flown down
into the wave-buried valleys, and to a cleft of the sea-hills to
rest.

The Waves
(early morning)

The sun rose. Bars of yellow and green fell on the shore, gilding the ribs of the eaten-out boat and making the sea-holly and its mailed leaves gleam blue as steel. Light almost pierced the thin swift waves as they raced fan-shaped over the beach. The girl who had shaken her head and made all the jewels, the topaz, the aquamarine, the water-coloured jewels with sparks of fire in them, dance, now bared her brows and with wide-opened eyes drove a straight pathway over the waves. Their quivering mackerel sparkling was darkened; they massed themselves; their green hollows deepened and

darkened and might be traversed by shoals of wandering fish. As they splashed and drew back they left a black rim of twigs and cork on the shore and straws and sticks of wood, as if some light shallop had foundered and burst its sides and the sailor had swum to land and bounded up the cliff and left his frail cargo to be washed ashore.

VW

The Lighthouse of Les Sanguinaires

by
ALPHONSE DAUDET
(1840–1897)

*This little gem is from a wonderful collection of stories called
Letters from My Windmill, in which each story is written in
the form of a letter from the author's beloved windmill. Here
the windmill's canvas sail, sounding in the wind like the rigging of a ship, transports him back in time and imagination to
a venerable old lighthouse on the Corsican coast…*

L ast night I could not sleep. The mistral was in a bad temper, and the roaring of its loud voice kept me awake till morning. The whole mill kept creaking and the tattered sails, swinging heavily, whistled in the wind like the rigging of a ship. Tiles flew off its crumbling roof. In the distance, the close-packed pines that clothe the hill tossed and swished noisily in the darkness. You could have believed yourself out on the open sea…

It brought back to me so clearly those splendid vigils I used to keep three years ago, when I was living in the lighthouse of *Les Sanguinaires*, over there on the coast of Corsica, at the entrance to the Gulf of Ajaccio.

There I had found another pleasant corner in which to dream and to be alone.

Picture to yourself a grim little island of reddish-coloured rocks, with the lighthouse at one end and at the other an ancient Genoese tower in which, when I was there, there lodged an eagle. In between, down by the edge of the sea there stood the ruins of an old naval quarantine station, all overgrown with grass and weeds; around it, ravines, maquis, rocks, wild goats, small Corsican horses galloping with their manes flying in the wind; and then, high up there, in a swirling, tossing mass of sea-birds, the lighthouse, with its platform of white stone where the keepers walk to and fro, its green, arched doorway, its cast-iron tower, and, on top, the huge, many-sided lantern that glitters flame-like in the sun and gives out light, even during the day... Such was the island of *Les Sanguinaires*, as I saw it again last night listening to the roaring of my pines. It was to this island I used to go, before I had my windmill, when I felt the need of fresh air and solitude.

What did I used to do there?

What I do here, more or less. When the mistral or the tramontane did not blow too strongly, I used to settle down between two rocks near the water's edge, among the seagulls, the water-ousels, and the swallows, and there I would remain for almost the whole day in that soporific stupor, that languid sense of delight which comes from just looking at the sea. You must experience it, surely, that wonderful rapture of the spirit? You cease to think, even to dream. Your innermost self escapes, flying, drifting. You become the seagull swooping, the frothing foam floating in the sun between two waves, the white smoke of the liner far-off on the horizon, that little red-sailed, coral-fishing boat, this pearly drop of water, this drifting wisp of mist, you become everything but yourself... Oh, these wonderful hours I spent on my island, drifting, drifting, half-asleep!...

On days of high wind, when the water's edge was out of the question, I would shut myself away in the courtyard of the old quarantine station, a gloomy little courtyard, full of the smell of rosemary and wild absinthe, and huddled there against a bit of old wall, I would let myself be gently overwhelmed by the vaguely scented emanations of desuetude and sadness that hovered in the sunshine over the little stone cells which gaped all around me like ancient tombs. Now and then a door banged, the grass quivered...and a goat would come to feed out of the wind. On seeing me, she would stop quite disconcerted and stay, rooted to the ground, all alert, horns raised, looking at me with child-like eyes...

Above five o'clock, the lighthouse keepers' megaphone would summon me to dinner. I would then take a little path through the maquis that rose steeply from the sea and I would return slowly to the lighthouse, turning at each step to gaze at that immense horizon of water and of light that seemed to grow wider and wider as I climbed.

Up there in the lighthouse it was delightful. I can see still its fine dining-room with its wide flag-stones, its oak panelling, the bouillabaisse steaming on the table, the door flung wide open on to the white terrace and all the glory of the setting sun... The lighthouse keepers would be there, waiting for me before taking their seats at the table. There were three of them: one from Marseilles and two from Corsica, all small, bearded, their faces lined and weather-beaten, wearing similar short jackets of goat-skin, but completely different in manner and temperament.

The difference between them could be seen at once from their mode of life. The man from Marseilles, active, hardworking, always busy, always on the move, hastening about the island from morn till night, gardening, fishing, gathering sea-birds' eggs, lying in wait in the maquis to catch a goat and milk her; and always with some mayonnaise with garlic or some bouillabaisse in the making.

But the Corsicans, beyond their official duties they did absolutely nothing; they considered themselves to be civil servants and spent their days in the kitchen playing interminable games of cards, stopping only to light their pipes with a serious air, or to cut big leaves of green tobacco with a pair of scissors into the palms of their hands...

Apart from all this, all three were kindly fellows, simple, guileless, and full of attentions for their guest, though he must have seemed to them a most extraordinary person...

To come and shut himself up in a lighthouse just for the pleasure of it! What must they have thought of him, they who found the days so long and who were so happy when their turn came to go back to the mainland? In the fine season of the year this great good fortune is theirs once a month. Ten days ashore to every thirty days on the lighthouse, that is the rule; but in winter and during bad weather, all rules go by the board. The wind blows and the sea rises, *Les Sanguinaires* is white with foam, and the keepers on duty are stuck there for two or three months on end, and sometimes under the most terrible conditions.

"This is what happened to me personally, monsieur," old Bartoli related to me one day, while we were having dinner. "This is what happened to me five years ago, at this very table where we are now, one winter's evening, just like this one. That evening there were only two of us in the ligthhouse, myself and a comrade everyone called 'Tchéco'... The others were ashore, sick, off duty, I don't remember... We were finishing dinner, just like every night... Suddenly, my comrade stops eating, looks at me a moment, his eyes all strange, and then down he drops on to the table with his arms all spread out. So I go over to him. I shake him. I call him:

"'Tché!... Tché!...'

"No answer! He was dead!... You can guess how I felt! I sat there, beside his body for an hour, stunned and trembling. Then suddenly the thought came to me: 'The light!' I just had time to climb up to the lantern and light it as night fell. And what a night, monsieur! I know the voices of the wind and the sea, but that night they didn't sound natural. I kept thinking I could hear someone calling to me from down the stairs. I became feverish. And thirsty! But nothing would have made me go down those stairs again... I was too frightened of that dead man. However, when dawn came, my courage returned a little. I went down and carried my comrade to his bed, put a sheet over him, said a little prayer, and then quickly sent out the alarm signal.

"Unfortunately, the seas were too high: I sent it out again and again; nobody came... There I was alone in the lighthouse with my poor Tchéco, heaven knew for how long... At first I kept hoping I would be able to keep him there until the boat came! But after three days that became impossible... What was I to do? Carry him outside? Bury him? The rock was so hard, and there were so many crows on the island. He was a

Christian and I couldn't think of abandoning his body to the
crows... Then I thought of putting him one of the cells in the
quarantine station. It took me a whole afternoon, that sad
task, and I can tell you it need some courage. Yes, monsieur,
even today when I go down to that side of the island, on an
afternoon when the wind's high, I feel as if I still had that dead
man on my shoulders..."

Poor old Bartoli! Just from thinking of it, the sweat was running down his forehead.

We used to talk for a long time over our meals about such
things: about the lighthouse, the sea, tales of shipwreck, stories of Corsican bandits... Then, dusk falling, the keeper who
had to take the first watch would light his little lamp, pick up
his pipe, his water-bottle, the thick red-bound volume of
Plutarch, the only book on *Les Sanguinaires*, and disappear up
the stairs. A few moments later, the whole lighthouse started
echoing with the rattling of chains and pulleys as the pendu-
lum weights of the lantern were set in motion.

While this was being done, I would go out and sit on the
terrace. The sun, already well down, would descend quicker
and quicker into the sea, drawing the whole horizon after it.
The wind used to freshen, the island become the colour of violet. Near me, in the sky, a huge bird would pass slowly, heavily: the eagle of the Genoese tower returning to its home...
Little by little the mist would rise over the sea. Soon nothing
was visible save the white fringe of foam surrounding the
island... Suddenly, above my head, there would pour out a
great flood of soft light. The lantern was lit. Leaving all the
island in darkness, that clear beam stretched far and wide out
to sea, and there, below its piercing bright rays, which barely
touched me, I would sit on, lost in the night... But at last the
wind would grow stronger and colder and I'd have to go in
again. Feeling with my hands, I would shut the great door and
replace the iron bars. Then still feeling my way, I would climb
a narrow iron staircase which shook and rang under my feet.
At last the darkness gave way to light, and what a light it was.

Imagine a gigantic Carcel lamp with six rows of wicks,

around which revolve slowly the lantern's walls, some fitted with enormous lenses, others with great fixed mirrors which shelter the flames from the wind... At first I would be dazzled. The shining tinfoil, the copper brasses, the white metal reflectors, the convex crystal walls turning in great bluish circles, all the flashing, clashing lights, would make me feel dizzy for a few moments.

Gradually, however, my eyes would get used to it, and I would go and sit right at the foot of the lamp beside the keeper, who would be reading his Plutarch aloud, for fear he fell asleep...

Outside, the night, the dark abyss. On the little balcony which encircles the glass casing of the lantern the wind screams and howls like a madman. The lighthouse creaks, the sea roars. At the tip of the island, on the half-submerged rocks, the waves make a noise like cannon fire... At intervals, an invisible finger taps on the panes: some night bird, attracted by the light, has dashed itself against the crystal glass... Inside the lantern of the lighthouse, all is warm and bright: only the sounds of the crackling flames, the oil dripping, the chain unwinding, and the monotonous voice intoning the life of Demetrius of Phalerum.

At midnight, the keeper used to rise, throw a last glance at the wicks, and he would descend. On the stairs we would meet the keeper on the second watch, rubbing his eyes as he came up; he would be given the water-bottle, the Plutarch... Then, before finding our beds, we used to go into the back room, and there, amidst the clutter of chains, weights, tin reflectors, ropes, and by the light of his little lamp, the keeper would write in the big lighthouse log book, which is kept always open:

"Midnight. High seas. Gale. Ship sighted well away from the coast."

The Boat

by
JANE URQUHART
(1949–)

A strangely deserted boat drifts shoreward to the beach, and spawns a series of disturbing dreams. As always, Urquhart's handling of her subject is quietly masterful, and the story of "The Boat" unravels like a richly patterned cloth atop a sea of possible meanings.

The children spotted it first and simply watched it in an attitude children will take—plastic pails hanging, forgotten, from their hands, muscles tensed, alert. It looked to them like a wounded sea monster, thrashing and lurching in the waves. But when it moved closer and they saw it was a boat, they ran to us in great excitement. For although impressive yachts and sleek fibreglass sail-boats floated through their days at the beach, this craft, coming as it so obviously did from somewhere else, and heading for their very own shore, seemed to them to be the essence of what a boat should be.

I sat in my deck-chair under a colourful umbrella, reading the paper and staring at the ocean. My wife knitted. We seldom spoke, except to the grandchildren. To call them back in concern, to tie hats firmly on small heads to prevent sunstroke, or to apply more sun-tan lotion. I was golden brown and quite fat. I looked vaguely tired in the manner of older people who are only halfway through the two-week visit with children of whom they are overly fond. My wife had brought a picnic lunch with her to the beach and she was thinking about that now—the small problems associated with eating there:

keeping the grandchildren from eating too fast, or from eating nothing but chips and cookies, or from eating too much sand. The appearance of the boat interrupted her midday thoughts as even she shaded her eyes to determine the nature of the distressed vessel.

Its mast, which I would later come to know was made from the trunk of a slender tree, slapped the surface of the water, and then, as if involved in a desperate struggle, hauled itself upward, totem-like, against the sky. Hanging down from this, attached by a series of disorganized ropes, was a sail of real canvas. Part of it lay crumpled in the interior of the boat, but the major portion was draped over the gunwales and bubbled in the water. Unbleached, the beige colour seemed so unfamiliar, so non-plastic, that in its altered, broken state it was like the ghost of an earlier time and it frightened me somewhat, though I didn't know why.

Having caught the attention of everyone on the beach directly before it, the boat made its limping progress towards the shore. Propelled forward by one six-foot wave, it would pause briefly, rock slightly, sometimes forward as it was meant to. By now the life-guard, who was posted at our rear, could see through his binoculars that the boat, at one time, had probably belonged to a fisherman and was meant to be managed by a series of large oars. The mast and sail, then, would have had to be a later addition, made for the purpose of moving the boat out of the calm of some harbour and into the thick of an inexplicable journey. He could also see that whoever had planned this journey was absent, as were any passengers, that they had either been rescued at sea, or more likely had been swept overboard by the huge waves that had existed on the ocean for the last few days. Laying down his binoculars on his tanned thighs he relaxed his shoulders feeling functionless in this particular drama.

Within a half an hour the boat had ended its marine performance and had, with one last determined shove, buried its prow in the wet sand at the shoreline. There it rested, listing somewhat to the starboard side, its sail moving back and forth in the water with the motion of the waves. The children ran to it to peer inside. I, too, left my deck-chair, my Styrofoam cooler, my newspaper, to look at what the sea had brought in.

The children, of course, were most interested in the boat as an object. They responded instantly to the brightly coloured boards and twisted ropes. And they especially loved the broken parts of the boat where the flat planks had separated from the frame and tiny waterfalls appeared with each new wave. Small lakes had gathered at the bottom of the hull and beneath the prow was a perfect, enclosed, damp space where several small people might huddle together and giggle. Their hands automatically reached up to the gunwales in their desire to climb inside, to claim the boat as their own.

But I held them back. Sensing the blacker side, I knew that the boat called to my mind something I had forgotten so completely that I could not remember it even now with the fact of it rolling there in front of me at the edge of the ocean. And when I saw the open suitcase, the clothing, the portable baby's bed, the toothbrush, the shoes, all of which littered the hull, I understood that whoever had set out to sea in such a craft had arrived in my world despite rescue or death.

The life-guard and I hauled the boat farther up onto the beach, beyond the tide line. Then, standing slightly back, we began to speculate about its origins. The astonishing lack of synthetic fibre suggested to us that the boat was most certainly foreign. I thought it might have come from one of the smaller, more obscure Caribbean islands. He suggested South America. Our conversation dwindled. It seemed futile to discuss the fate of the boat's passengers, or even their reason for attempting to cross the sea in such a dangerous fashion. So we stood back and looked, our arms folded, feeling cheated, a bit, of the sensationalism that so often accompanies accidental death in our own country.

That night, tucked snugly away in our climate-controlled condominium, I dreamt a hundred dreams of the boat. In one dream I was building the boat, or at least working on part of it. Sometimes I pushed large sharp needles through tough canvas. Sometimes I wove ropes. In some far corner of my brain, where I remembered my father's carpentry shop, I steamed and bent wood for the frame long into the night. Then I fitted the skeleton-like construction together in record time. My mother, whom I had all but forgotten, appeared in one of the dreams, saying over and over in a carping, critical fashion, "It looks like the ribcage of a dead elephant. It looks like the ribcage of a dead elephant," until I shouted at her, in a way I never would have done in real life, "Well, *you* are elephant flesh; grey, loose and wrinkling!" Then I dreamt I was planking the frame—setting the then bevelled boards higher and higher, fastening them with bright galvanized nails. I whispered to myself in an unfamiliar language. "Garboard, shutter, sheer-stake," I said quietly, but with amazing confidence. The work went well.

My wife, because she had been a mother, dreamt about mending the boat—caulking the seams with cotton dresses she had thrown away years before and patching the holes with oilcloth and horse-hoof glue. She claimed she spent half the night untying the knots in the ropes and winding them up into well-organized, tidy coils. Then she carefully stitched the torn sail, sometimes with brightly coloured embroidery thread, sometimes with the more functional white variety. Later she repainted the simple geometric design, which had, in some places, been rubbed off the stern. And finally, she dreamt that she hauled the sail away from the place where it lay in the damp sand, put it through the wash cycle in an enormous machine, and hung it out to dry on a clothes-line strung between two telephone poles. And all the Lincolns, Chryslers and Cadillacs on Ocean Boulevard ground to a halt, amazed to see this expanse of canvas, like a brown flag with grommets, flap up towards the sky.

The children dreamt of sailing the boat, or of driving it, or of flying it, depending on their personalities, just as it was— injured, wrecked—with sand and water spilling into its hull and its sail dragging behind it like long drowned hair. They were too young, too satisfied, to actively search for change in their dreams and so they dreamt of the fact of the boat and of access to that fact; of scaling the sides, leaping over the gunwales and sitting at the rudderless helm. In truth they dreamt of taking command of the boat as something the sea had arbitrarily given them.

When we arrived at the beach the following morning the boat looked more familiar, less foreign to us. I brought my little black camera with me and marched down the beach with it to capture the image of the boat from all sides, forever. My wife fussed and clucked, almost affectionately, about the untidiness of the boat. Some of the clothing, which had earlier spilled from the hull, had been brought in by the waves and had formed a colourful strip at the tide line. She moved slowly towards this and, gingerly picking up the pieces of fabric, dropped them in a neat pile, hoping that the machine that came at night to bury seaweed would dispose, as well, of this reminder of the human factor.

The children began to play with the portable baby's bed. Unnoticed behind the stern they constructed a sail from a large stick and a plaid cotton shirt. Borrowing the laces from an unmatched shoe that hung from the port gunwale, they were able to tie miniature ropes through the buttonholes and pull the fabric tight enough to catch the wind. They pounded the stick through the canvas bottom of the tiny bed and placed the youngest child inside as a navigator. Then, screaming with joy, they propelled their little craft out to sea where it turned slowly round a few times before being pushed under by the white froth of an incoming wave.

So all that day my stock market quotations and the children's plastic pails lay untouched in the sand beside the deckchairs as we all responded to the boat. Sometimes we just stood and stared at it. It was something that could not be interpreted but could not be turned away from either. Sometimes we commented to each other that it really was a strong boat and might, in fact, be made seaworthy once again. The children played around the edges of the boat, having been forbidden, since the incident of the baby's bed, to touch either the vessel or its contents.

On the second night the dreams revisited us but in slightly different form. I, for instance, dreamt that I had discovered a miniature model of the boat. Walking through the streets of an unfamiliar city I had seen it in a junk shop window and had decided to purchase it though the price was much too high. When I placed it on the mantelpiece in my living-room, my wife had demanded: "Who told you I wanted a family portrait over the fireplace?" and I had replied, "You'll never know till you light the fire." I awakened with my heart pounding to discover that my wife, in the twin bed opposite, had been dreaming of adopting a child from a small obscure Caribbean island.

But before this she dreamt of her childhood home, which had miraculously evolved into the boat. Upside down, the keel had become the peak of the roof, and, with little alteration, planks had turned to clapboard. Inside, the windows were gaping holes, providing a variety of ocean views and covered with curtains made of torn clothing and shoe laces. Her father crouched in the left-hand corner of the overturned stern, reading the Bible and writing stock market quotations in the damp sand of the floor. When we went back to sleep I dreamt I was a fisherman considering immigration to a new land.

One of the children dreamt that he could see the pattern of the boat clearly charted by stars in a navy-blue sky. It was situated right between the Big and Little Dippers. He pointed it out to a crowd that had assembled somewhere vaguely to his left but they had been unable to see even the Big or Little Dipper and spoke only of fireflies and satellites.

The next day we were all easy with the boat, as if our vision of the beach had expanded just enough to include it. And so, when late in the morning we watched the uniformed men tie the boat to their own authoritative coast guard vessel, we felt remotely sad and guilty too, as if the boat had committed some obscure crime, to which we were a party. We asked and were told that the boat would be filled with weights and sunk at sea. Our last glimpse of it was a spot of red on the horizon—its painted stern glowing in the sun.

The following week vacation ended and the children returned to their home in the north where winter gradually bleached their brown skins. When they spoke of the boat, they did so with such confusion that their mother assumed that they had been taken on a fishing excursion, and their father believed that they had been presented with an expensive toy by us, their over-indulgent grandparents. Even their drawings, which often included the boat, were quickly glanced at by their parents and then forgotten.

We quickly adjusted to our childless existence and finally forgot about the boat altogether except when it entered our unremembered dreams. Each day we went to the beach and sat beneath our colourful umbrellas. My wife knitted. We seldom spoke. I read stock market quotations. She unpacked the Styrofoam cooler. Sleek fibreglass sail-boats and impressive yachts sailed across our constant vision of the sea. And when, a month later, our attention focused on the horizon, we did not recognize the subject of our dreams, the object of our very own design, believing instead that it was merely a wounded sea monster, thrashing and lurching in the waves. But the children had gone. This time we had caused the image, created it. This time it was our unsubstantial pride, moving slowly, painfully back to shore.

The Fisherman and His Soul

by
OSCAR WILDE
(1854–1900)

Taking Hans Christian Andersen's "The Little Mermaid" as the basis for his story, the tale of "The Fisherman and His Soul" becomes for Wilde a sort of Arabian Night—a journey into the heart of the exotic, a litany of all that is rare and precious in this world. A story whose glittering surface, like the surface of the sea itself, conceals the shadows of its hidden depths.

Every evening the young Fisherman went out upon the sea, and threw his nets into the water.

When the wind blew from the land he caught nothing, or but little at best, for it was a bitter and black-winged wind, and rough waves rose up to meet it. But when the wind blew to the shore, the fish came in from the deep, and swam into the meshes of his nets, and he took them to the market-place and sold them.

Every evening he went out upon the sea, and one evening the net was so heavy that hardly could he draw it into the boat. And he laughed, and said to himself, "Surely I have caught all the fish that swim, or snared some dull monster that will be a marvel to men, or some thing of horror that the great Queen will desire," and putting forth all his strength, he tugged at the coarse ropes till like lines of blue enamel round a vase of bronze, the long veins rose up on his arms. He tugged at the thin ropes, and nearer and nearer came the circle of flat corks, and the net rose at last to the top of the water.

But no fish at all was in it, nor any monster or thing of horror, but only a little Mermaid lying fast asleep.

Her hair was as a wet fleece of gold, and each separate hair as a thread of fine gold in a cup of glass. Her body was as white ivory, and her tail was of silver and pearl. Silver and pearl was her tail, and the green weeds of the sea coiled round it; and like sea-shells were her ears, and her lips were like sea-coral. The cold waves dashed over her cold breasts, and the salt glistened upon her eyelids.

So beautiful was she that when the young Fisherman saw her he was filled with wonder, and he put out his hand and drew the net close to him, and leaning over the side he clasped her in his arms. And when he touched her, she gave a cry like a startled sea-gull, and woke, and looked at him in terror with her mauve-amethyst eyes, and struggled that she might escape. But he held her tightly to him, and would not suffer her to depart.

And when she saw that she could in no way escape from him, she began to weep, and said, "I pray thee let me go, for I am the only daughter of a King, and my father is aged and alone."

But the young Fisherman answered, "I will not let thee go save thou makest me a promise that whenever I call thee, thou wilt come and sing for me, for the fish delight to listen to the song of the Sea-folk, and so shall my nets be full."

"Wilt thou in very truth let me go, if I promise thee this?" cried the Mermaid.

"In very truth I will let thee go," said the young Fisherman.

So she made him the promise he desired, and sware it by the oath of the Sea-folk. And he loosened his arms from about her, and she sank down into the water, trembling with a strange fear.

Every evening the young Fisherman went out upon the sea, and called to the Mermaid, and she rose out of the water and sang to him. Round and round her swam the dolphins, and the wild gulls wheeled above her head.

And she sang a marvellous song. For she sang of the Sea-folk who drive their flocks from cave to cave, and carry the little calves on their shoulders; of the Tritons who have long green beards, and hairy breasts, and blow through twisted conchs when the King passes by; of the palace of the King which is all of amber, with a roof of clear emerald, and a pavement of bright pearl; and of the gardens of the sea where the great filigrane fans of coral wave all day long, and the fish dart about like silver birds, and the anemones cling to the rocks, and the pinks bourgeon in the ribbed yellow sand. She sang of the big whales that come down from the north seas and have sharp icicles hanging to their fins; of the Sirens who tell of such wonderful things that the merchants have to stop their ears with wax lest they should hear them, and leap into the water and be drowned; of the sunken galleys with their tall masts, and the frozen sailors clinging to the rigging, and the mackerel swimming in and out of the open portholes; of the little barnacles who are great travellers, and cling to the keels of the ships and go round and round the world; and of the cuttlefish who live in the sides of the cliffs and stretch out their long black arms, and can make night come when they will it. She sang of the nautilus who has a boat of her own that is carved out of an opal and steered with a silken sail; of the happy Mermen who play upon harps and can charm the great Kraken to sleep; of the little children who catch hold of the slippery porpoises and ride laughing upon their backs; of the Mermaids who lie in the white foam and hold out their arms to the mariners; and of the sea-lions with their curved tusks, and the sea horses with their floating manes.

And as she sang, all the tunny-fish came in from the deep to listen to her, and the young Fisherman threw his nets round them and caught them, and others he took with a spear. And when his boat was well-laden, the Mermaid would sink down into the sea, smiling at him.

Yet would she never come near him that he might touch her. Oftentimes he called to her and prayed of her, but she would not; and when he sought to seize her she dived into the water as a seal might dive, nor did he see her again that day. And each day the sound of her voice became sweeter to his ears. So sweet was her voice that he forgot his nets and his cunning, and had no care of his craft. Vermilion-finned and with eyes of bossy gold, the tunnies went by in shoals, but he heeded them not. His spear lay by his side unused, and his baskets of plaited osier were empty. With lips parted, and eyes dim with wonder, he sat idle in his boat and listened, listening till the sea-mists crept round him, and the wandering moon stained his brown limbs with silver.

And one evening he called to her, and said: "Little Mermaid, little Mermaid, I love thee. Take me for thy bridegroom, for I love thee."

But the Mermaid shook her head. "Thou hast a human soul," she answered. "If only thou wouldst send away thy soul, then could I love thee."

And the young Fisherman said to himself, "Of what use is my soul to me? I cannot see it. I may not touch it. I do not know it. Surely I will send it away from me, and much gladness shall be mine." And a cry of joy broke from his lips, and standing up in the painted boat, he held out his arms to the Mermaid. "I will send my soul away," he cried, "and you shall be my bride, and I will be thy bridegroom, and in the depth of the sea we will dwell together, and all that thou hast sung of thou shalt show me, and all that thou desirest I will do, nor shall our lives be divided."

And the little Mermaid laughed for pleasure and hid her face in her hands.

"But how shall I send my soul from me?" cried the young Fisherman. "Tell me how I may do it, and lo! it shall be done."

"Alas! I know not," said the little Mermaid: "the Sea-folk have no souls." And she sank down into the deep, looking wistfully at him.

Now early on the next morning, before the sun was the span of a man's hand above the hill, the young Fisherman went to the house of the Priest and knocked three times at the door.

The novice looked out through the wicket, and when he saw who it was, he drew back the latch and said to him, "Enter."

And the young Fisherman passed in, and knelt down on the sweet-smelling rushes of the floor, and cried to the Priest who was reading out of the Holy Book and said to him, "Father, I am in love with one of the Sea-folk, and my soul hindereth me from having my desire. Tell me how I can send my soul away from me, for in truth I have no need of it. Of what value is my soul to me? I cannot see it. I may not touch it. I do not know it."

And the Priest beat his breast, and answered, "Alack, alack, thou art mad, or hast eaten of some poisonous herb, for the soul is the noblest part of man, and was given to us by God that we should nobly use it. There is no thing more precious than a human soul, nor any earthly thing that can be weighed with it. It is worth all the gold that is in the world, and is more precious than the rubies of the kings. Therefore, my son, think not any more of this matter, for it is a sin that may not be forgiven. And as for the Sea-folk, they are lost, and they who would traffic with them are lost also. They are the beasts of the field that know not good from evil, and for them the Lord has not died."

The young Fisherman's eyes filled with tears when he heard the bitter words of the Priest, and he rose up from his knees and said to him, "Father, the Fauns live in the forest and are glad, and on the rocks sit the Mermen with their harps of red gold. Let me be as they are, I beseech thee, for their days are as the days of flowers. And as for my soul, what doth my soul profit me, if it stand between me and the thing that I love?"

"The love of the body is vile," cried the Priest, knitting his brows, "and vile and evil are the pagan things God suffers to wander through His world. Accursed be the Fauns of the woodland, and accursed be the singers of the sea! I have heard them at night-time, and they have sought to lure me from my beads. They tap at the window and laugh. They whisper into my ears the tale of their perilous joys. They tempt me with temptations, and when I would pray they make mouths at me. They are lost, I tell thee, they are lost. For them there is no heaven nor hell, and in neither shall they praise God's name."

"Father," cried the young Fisherman, "thou knowest not what thou sayest. Once in my net I snared the daughter of a King. She is fairer than the morning star, and whiter than the moon. For her body I would give my soul, and for her love I would surrender heaven. Tell me what I ask of thee, and let me go in peace."

"Away! Away!" cried the Priest: "thy leman is lost, and thou shalt be lost with her." And he gave him no blessing, but drove him from his door.

And the young Fisherman went down into the market-place, and he walked slowly, and with bowed head, as one who is in sorrow.

And when the merchants saw him coming, they began to whisper to each other, and one of them came forth to meet him, and called him by name, and said to him, "What hast thou to sell?"

"I will sell thee my soul," he answered: "I pray thee buy it of me, for I am weary of it. Of what use is my soul to me? I cannot see it. I may not touch it. I do not know it."

But the merchants mocked at him, and said, "Of what use is a man's soul to us? It is not worth a clipped piece of silver. Sell us thy body for a slave, and we will clothe thee in sea-purple, and put a ring upon thy finger, and make thee the minion of the great Queen. But talk not of the soul, for to us it is nought, nor has it any value for our service."

And the young Fisherman said to himself: "How strange a thing this is! The Priest telleth me that the soul is worth all the gold in the world, and the merchants say that it is not worth a clipped piece of silver." And he passed out of the market-place, and went down to the shore of the sea, and began to ponder on what he should do.

And at noon he remembered how one of his companions, who was a gatherer of samphire, had told him of a certain young Witch who dwelt in a cave at the head of the bay and was very cunning in her witcheries. And he set to and ran, so eager was he to get rid of his soul, and a cloud of dust followed him as he sped round the sand of the shore. By the itching of her palm the young Witch knew his coming, and she laughed and let down her red hair. With her red hair falling around her, she stood at the opening of the cave, and in her hand she had a spray of wild hemlock that was blossoming.

"What d'ye lack? What d'ye lack?" she cried, as he came panting up the steep, and bent down before her. "Fish for thy net, when the wind is foul? I have a little reed-pipe, and when I blow on it the mullet come sailing into the bay. But it has a price, pretty boy, it has a price. What d'ye lack? What d'ye lack? A storm to wreck the ships, and wash the chests of rich treasure ashore? I have more storms than the wind has, for I serve one who is stronger than the wind, and with a sieve and a pail of water I can send the great galleys to the bottom of the sea. But I have a price, pretty boy, I have a price. What d'ye lack? What d'ye lack? I know a flower that grows in the valley, none knows it but I. It has purple leaves, and a star in its heart, and its juice is as white as milk. Shouldst thou touch with this flower the hard lips of the Queen, she would follow thee all over the world. Out of the bed of the King she would rise, and over the whole world she would follow thee. And it has a price, pretty boy, it has a price. What d'ye lack? What d'ye lack? I can pound a toad in a mortar and make a broth of it, and stir the broth with a dead man's hand. Sprinkle it on thine enemy while he sleeps, and he will turn into a black viper, and his own mother will slay him. With a wheel I can draw the Moon from heaven, and in a crystal I can show thee Death. What d'ye lack? What d'ye lack? Tell me they desire, and I will give it thee, and thou shalt pay me a price, pretty boy, thou shalt pay me a price."

"My desire is but for a little thing," said the young Fisherman, "yet hath the Priest been wroth with me, and driven me forth. It is but for a little thing, and the merchants have mocked at me, and denied me. Therefore I am come to thee, though men call thee evil, and whatever be thy price I shall pay it."

"What wouldst thou?" asked the Witch, coming near to him.

"I would send my soul away from me," answered the young Fisherman.

The Witch grew pale, and shuddered, and hid her face in her blue mantle. "Pretty boy, pretty boy," she muttered, "that is a terrible thing to do."

He tossed his brown curls and laughed. "My soul is nought to me," he answered. "I cannot see it. I may not touch it. I do not know it."

"What wilt thou give me if I tell thee?" asked the Witch, looking down at him with her beautiful eyes.

"Five pieces of gold," he said, "and my nets, and the wattled house where I live, and the painted boat in which I sail. Only tell me how to get rid of my soul, and I will give thee all that I possess."

She laughed mockingly at him, and struck him with the spray of hemlock. "I can turn the autumn leaves into gold," she answered, "and I can weave the pale moonbeams into silver if I will it. He whom I serve is richer than all the kings of this world, and has their dominions."

"What then shall I give thee," he cried, "if thy price be neither gold nor silver?"

The Witch stroked his hair with her thin white hand. "Thou must dance with me, pretty boy," she murmured, and she smiled at him as she spoke.

"Nought but that?" cried the young Fisherman in wonder, and he rose to his feet.

"Nought but that," she answered, and she smiled at him again.

"Then at sunset in some secret place we shall dance together," he said, "and after that we have danced thou shalt tell me the thing which I desire to know."

She shook her head. "When the moon is full, when the moon is full," she muttered. Then she peered all round, and listened. A blue bird rose screaming from its nest and circled over the dunes, and three spotted birds rustled through the coarse grey grass and whistled to each other. There was no other sound save the sound of a wave fretting the smooth pebbles below. So she reached out her hand, and drew him near to her and put her dry lips close to his ear.

"Tonight thou must come to the top of that mountain," she whispered. "It is a Sabbath, and He will be there."

The young Fisherman started and looked at her, and she

showed her white teeth and laughed. "Who is He of whom thou speakest?" he asked.

"It matters not," she answered. "Go thou tonight, and stand under the branches of the hornbeam, and wait for my coming. If a black dog run towards thee, strike it with a rod of willow, and it will go away. If an owl speak to thee, make it no answer. When the moon is full I shall be with thee, and we will dance together on the grass."

"But wilt thou swear to me to tell me how I may send my soul from me?" he made question.

She moved out into the sunlight, and through her red hair rippled the wind. "By the hoofs of the goat I swear it," she made answer.

"Thou art the best of the witches," cried the young Fisherman, "and I will surely dance with thee tonight on the top of the mountain. I would indeed that thou hadst asked of me either gold or silver. But such as thy price is thou shalt have it, for it is but a little thing." And he doffed his cap to her, and bent his head low, and ran back to the town filled with a great joy.

And the Witch watched him as he went, and when he had passed from her sight she entered her cave, and having taken a mirror from a box of carved cedarwood, she set it up on a frame, and burned vervain on lighted charcoal before it, and peered through the coils of the smoke. And after a time she clenched her hands in anger. "He should have been mine," she muttered, "I am as fair as she is."

And that evening, when the moon had risen, the young Fisherman climbed up to the top of the mountain, and stood under the branches of the hornbeam. Like a targe of polished metal the round sea lay at his feet, and the shadows of the fishing-boats moved in the little bay. A great owl, with yellow sulphurous eyes, called to him by his name, but he made it no answer. A black dog ran towards him and snarled. He struck it with a rod of willow, and it went away whining.

At midnight the witches came flying through the air like bats. "Phew!" they cried, as they lit upon the ground, "there is some one here we know not!" and they sniffed about, and chattered to each other, and made signs. Last of all came the young Witch, with her red hair streaming in the wind. She wore a dress of gold tissue embroidered with peacocks' eyes, and a little cap of green velvet was on her head.

"Where is he, where is he?" shrieked the witches when they saw her, but she only laughed, and ran to the hornbeam, and taking the Fisherman by the hand she led him out into the moonlight and began to dance.

Round and round they whirled, and the young Witch jumped so high that he could see the scarlet heels of her shoes. Then right across the dancers came the sound of the galloping of a horse, but no horse was to be seen, and he felt afraid.

"Faster," cried the Witch, and she threw her arms about his neck, and her breath was hot upon his face. "Faster, faster!" she cried, and the earth seemed to spin beneath his feet, and his brain grew troubled, and a great terror fell on him, as of some evil thing that was watching him, and at last he became aware that under the shadow of a rock there was a figure that had not been there before.

It was a man dressed in a suit of black velvet, cut in the Spanish fashion. His face was strangely pale, but his lips were like a proud red flower. He seemed weary, and was leaning back toying in a listless manner with the pommel of his dagger. On the grass beside him lay a plumed hat, and a pair of riding-gloves gauntleted with gilt lace, and sewn with seed-pearls wrought into a curious device. A short cloak lined with sables hung from his shoulder, and his delicate white hands were gemmed with rings. Heavy eyelids drooped over his eyes.

The young Fisherman watched him, as one snared in a spell. At last their eyes met, and wherever he danced it seemed to him that the eyes of the man were upon him. He heard the Witch laugh, and caught her by the waist, and whirled her madly round and round.

Suddenly a dog bayed in the wood, and the dancers stopped, and going up two by two, knelt down, and kissed the man's hands. As they did so, a little smile touched his proud lips, as a bird's wing touches the water and makes it laugh.

But there was disdain in it. He kept looking at the young Fisherman.

"Come! let us worship," whispered the Witch, and she led him up, and a great desire to do as she besought him seized on him, and he followed her. But when he came close, and without knowing why he did it, he made on his breast the sign of the Cross, and called upon the holy name.

No sooner had he done so than the witches screamed like hawks and flew away, and the pallid face that had been watching him twitched with a spasm of pain. The man went over to a little wood, and whistled. A jennet with silver trappings came running to meet him. As he leapt upon the saddle he turned round, and looked at the young Fisherman sadly.

And the Witch with the red hair tried to fly away also, but the Fisherman caught her by her wrists, and held her fast.

"Loose me," she cried, "and let me go. For thou hast named what should not be named, and shown the sign that may not be looked at."

"Nay," he answered, "but I will not let thee go till thou hast told me the secret."

"What secret?" said the Witch, wrestling with him like a wild cat, and biting her foam-flecked lips.

"Thou knowest," he made answer.

Her grass-green eyes grew dim with tears, and she said to the Fisherman, "Ask me anything but that!"

He laughed, and held her all the more tightly.

And when she saw that she could not free herself, she whispered to him, "Surely I am as fair as the daughter of the sea, and as comely as those that dwell in the blue waters," and she fawned on him and put her face close to him.

But he thrust her back frowning, and said to her, "If thou keepest not the promise that thou madest to me I will slay thee for a false witch."

She grew grey as a blossom on the Judas tree, and shuddered. "Be it so," she muttered. "It is thy soul and not mine. Do with it as thou wilt." And she took from her girdle a little knife that had a handle of green viper's skin, and gave it to him.

"What shall this serve me?" he asked of her, wondering.

She was silent for a few moments, and a look of terror came over her face. Then she brushed her hair back from her forehead, and smiling strangely she said to him, "What men call the shadow of the body is not the shadow of the body, but is the body of the soul. Stand on the sea-shore with thy back to the moon, and cut away from around thy feet thy shadow, which is thy soul's body, and bid thy soul leave thee, and it will do so."

The young Fisherman trembled. "Is this true?" he murmured.

"It is true, and I would that I had not told thee of it," she cried, and she clung to his knees weeping.

He put her from him and left her in the rank grass, and going to the edge of the mountain he placed the knife in his belt and began to climb down.

And his Soul that was within him called out to him and said, "Lo! I have dwelt with thee for all these years, and have been they servant. Send me not away from thee now, for what evil have I done thee?"

And the young Fisherman laughed. "Thou hast done me no evil, but I have no need of thee," he answered. "The world is wide, and there is Heaven also, and Hell, and that dim twilight house that lies between. Go wherever thou wilt, but trouble me not, for my love is calling to me."

And his Soul besought him piteously, but he heeded it not, but leapt from crag to crag, being sure-footed as a wild goat, and at last he reached the level ground and the yellow shore of the sea.

Bronze-limbed and well-knit, like a statue wrought by a Grecian, he stood on the sand with his back to the moon, and out of the foam came white arms that beckoned to him, and out of the waters rose dim forms that did him homage. Before him lay his shadow, which was the body of his soul, and behind him hung the moon in the honey-coloured air.

And his Soul said to him, "If indeed thou must drive me from thee, send me not forth without a heart. The world is cruel, give me thy heart to take with me."

He tossed his head and smiled. "With what should I love my love if I gave thee my heart?" he cried.

"Nay but be merciful," said his Soul: "give me thy heart, for the world is very cruel, and I am afraid."

"My heart is my love's," he answered, "therefore tarry not, but get thee gone."

"Should I not love also?" asked his Soul.

"Get thee gone, for I have no need of thee," cried the young Fisherman, and he took the little knife with its handle of green viper's skin, and cut away his shadow from around his feet, and it rose up and stood before him, and looked at him, and it was even as himself.

He crept back, and thrust the knife into his belt, and a feeling of awe came over him. "Get thee gone," he murmured, "and let me see thy face no more."

"Nay, but we must meet again," said the Soul. Its voice was low and flute-like, and its lips hardly moved while it spake.

"How shall we meet?" cried the young Fisherman. "Thou wilt not follow me into the depths of the sea?"

"Once every year I will come to this place, and call to thee," said the Soul. "It may be that thou wilt have need of me."

"What need should I have of thee?" cried the young Fisherman, "but be it as thou wilt," and he plunged into the water, and the Tritons blew their horns, and the little Mermaid rose up to meet him, and put her arms around his neck and kissed him on the mouth.

And the Soul stood on the lonely beach and watched them. And when they had sunk down into the sea, it went weeping away over the marshes.

And after a year was over the Soul came down to the shore of the sea and called to the young Fisherman, and he rose out of the deep, and said, "Why dost thou call to me?"

And the Soul answered, "Come nearer, that I may speak with thee, for I have seen marvellous things."

So he came nearer, and couched in the shallow water, and leaned his head upon his hand and listened.

And the Soul said to him, "When I left thee I turned my face to the East and journeyed. From the East cometh everything that is wise. Six days I journeyed, and on the morning of the seventh day I came to a hill that is in the country of the Tartars. I sat down under the shade of a tamarisk tree to shelter myself from the sun. The land was dry and burnt up with the heat. The people went to and fro over the plain like flies crawling upon a disk of polished copper.

"When it was noon a cloud of red dust rose up from the flat rim of the land. When the Tartars saw it, they strung their painted bows, and having leapt upon their little horses they galloped to meet it. The women fled screaming to the waggons, and hid themselves behind the felt curtains.

"At twilight the Tartars returned, but five of them were missing, and of those that came back not a few had been wounded. They harnessed their horses to the waggons and drove hastily away. Three jackals came out of a cave and peered after them. Then they sniffed up the air with their nostrils, and trotted off in the opposite direction.

"When the moon rose I saw a camp-fire burning on the plain, and went towards it. A company of merchants were seated round it on carpets. Their camels were picketed behind them, and the negroes who were their servants were pitching tents of tanned skin upon the sand, and making a high wall of the prickly pear.

"As I came near them, the chief of the merchants rose up and drew his sword and asked me my business.

"I answered that I was a Prince in my own land, and that I had escaped from the Tartars, who had sought to make me their slave. The chief smiled, and showed me five heads fixed upon long reeds of bamboo.

"Then he asked me who was the prophet of God, and I answered him Mohammed.

"When he heard the name of the false prophet, he bowed and took me by the hand, and placed me by his side. A negro brought me some mare's milk in a wooden dish, and a piece of lamb's flesh roasted.

"At daybreak we started on our journey. I rode on a red-haired camel by the side of the chief, and a runner ran before us carrying a spear. The men of war were on either hand, and the mules followed with the merchandise. There were forty camels in a caravan, and the mules were twice forty in number.

"We went from the country of the Tartars into the country of those who curse the Moon. We saw the Gryphons guarding their gold on the white rocks, and the scaled Dragons sleeping in their caves. As we passed over the mountains we held our breath lest the snows might fall on us, and each man tied a veil of gauze before his eyes. As we passed through the valleys the Pygmies shot arrows at us from the hollows of the trees, and at night-time we heard the wild men beating on their drums. When we came to the Tower of Apes we set fruits before them, and they did not harm us. When we came to the Tower of Serpents we gave them warm milk in bowls of brass, and they let us go by. Three times in our journey we came to the banks of the Oxus. We crossed it on rafts of wood with great bladders of blown hide. The river-horses raged against us and sought to slay us. When the camels saw them they trembled.

"The kings of each city levied tolls on us, but would not suffer us to enter their gates. They threw us bread over the walls, little maize-cakes baked in honey and cakes of fine flour filled with dates. For every hundred baskets we gave them a bead of amber.

"When the dwellers in the villages saw us coming, they poisoned the wells and fled to the hill-summits. We fought with the Magadae who are born old, and grow younger and younger every year, and die when they are little children; and with the Laktroi who say that they are the sons of tigers, and paint themselves yellow and black; and with the Aurantes who bury their dead on the tops of trees, and themselves live in dark caverns lest the Sun, who is their god, should slay them; and with the Krimnians who worship a crocodile, and give it earrings of green grass, and feed it with butter and fresh fowls; and with the Agazonbae, who are dog-faced; and with the Sibans, who have horses' feet, and run more swiftly than horses. A third of our company died in battle, and a third died of want. The rest murmured against me, and said that I had brought them an evil fortune. I took a horned adder from beneath a stone and let it sting me. When they saw that I did not sicken they grew afraid.

"In the fourth month we reached the city of Illel. It was night-time when we came to the grove that is outside the walls, and the air was sultry, for the Moon was travelling in Scorpio. We took the ripe pomegranates from the trees, and brake them, and drank their sweet juices. Then we lay down on our carpets and waited for the dawn.

"And at dawn we rose and knocked at the gate of the city. It was wrought out of red bronze, and carved with sea-dragons and dragons that have wings. The guards looked down from the battlements and asked us our business. The interpreter of the caravan answered that we had come from the island of Syria with much merchandise. They took hostages, and told us that they would open the gate to us at noon, and bade us tarry till then.

"When it was noon they opened the gate, and as we entered in the people came crowding out of the houses to look at us, and a crier went round the city crying through a shell. We stood in the market-place, and the negroes uncorded the bales of figured cloths and opened the carved chests of sycamore. And when they had ended their task, the merchants set forth their strange wares, the waxed linen from Egypt, and the painted linen from the country of the Ethiops, the purple sponges from Tyre and the blue hangings from Sidon, the cups of cold amber and the fine vessels of glass and the curious vessels of burnt clay. From the roof of a house a company of women watched us. One of them wore a mask of gilded leather.

"And on the first day the priests came and bartered with us, and on the second day came the nobles, and on the third day came the craftsmen and the slaves. And this is their custom with all merchants as long as they tarry in the city.

"And we tarried for a moon, and when the moon was waning, I wearied and wandered away through the streets of the city and came to the garden of its god. The priests in their yellow robes moved silently through the green trees, and on a pavement of black marble stood the rose-red house in which the god had his dwelling. Its doors were of powdered lacquer, and bulls and peacocks were wrought on porcelain and the jutting eaves were festooned with little bells. When the white doves flew past, they struck the bells with their wings and made them twinkle.

"In front of the temple was a pool of clear water paved with veined onyx. I lay down beside it, and with my pale fingers I touched the broad leaves. One of the priests came towards me and stood behind me. He had sandals on his feet, one of soft serpent-skin and the other of birds' plumage. On his head was a mitre of black felt decorated with silver crescents. Seven yellows were woven into his robe, and his frizzed hair was stained with antimony.

"After a little while he spake to me, and asked me my desire.

"I told him that my desire was to see the god.

"'The god is hunting,' said the priest, looking strangely at me with his small slanting eyes.

"'Tell me in what forest, and I will ride with him,' I answered.

"He combed out the soft fringes of his tunic with his long pointed nails. 'The god is asleep,' he murmured.

"'Tell me on what couch, and I will watch him,' I answered.

"'The god is at the feast,' he cried.

"'If the wine be sweet I will drink it with him, and if it be bitter I will drink it with him also,' was my answer.

"He bowed his head in wonder, and, taking me by the hand, he raised me up and led me into the temple.

"And in the first chamber I saw an idol seated on a throne of jasper bordered with great orient pearls. It was carved out of ebony, and in stature was of the stature of a man. On its forehead was a ruby, and thick oil dripped from its hair on to its thighs. Its feet were red with the blood of a newly-slain kid, and its loins girt with a copper belt that was studded with seven beryls.

"And I said to the priest, 'Is this the god?' And he answered me, 'This is the god.'

"'Show me the god,' I cried, 'or I will surely slay thee.' And I touched his hand, and it became withered.

"And the priest besought me, saying, 'Let my lord heal his servant, and I will show him the god.'

"So I breathed with my breath upon his hand, and it became whole again, and he trembled and led me into the second chamber, and I saw an idol standing on a lotus of jade hung with great emeralds. It was carved out of ivory, and in stature was twice the stature of a man. On its forehead was a chrysolite, and its breasts were smeared with myrrh and cinnamon. In one hand it held a crooked sceptre of jade, and in the other a round crystal. It wore buskins of brass, and its thick neck was circled with a circle of selenites.

"And I said to the priest, 'Is this the god?' And he answered me, 'This is the god.'

"'Show me the god,' I cried, 'or I will surely slay thee.' And I touched his eyes, and they became blind.

"And the priest besought me, saying, 'Let my lord heal his servant, and I will show him the god.'

"So I breathed with my breath upon his eyes, and the sight came back to them, and he trembled again, and led me into the third chamber, and lo! there was no idol in it, nor image of any kind, but only a mirror of round metal set on an altar of stone.

"And I said to the priest, 'Where is the god?'

"And he answered me: 'There is no god but this mirror that thou seest, for this is the Mirror of Wisdom. And it reflecteth all things that are in heaven and on earth, save only the face of him who looketh into it. This it reflecteth not, so that he who looketh into it may be wise. Many other mirrors are there, but they are mirrors of Opinion. This only is the Mirror of Wisdom. And they who possess this mirror know everything, nor is there anything hidden from them. And they who possess it not have not Wisdom. Therefore is it the god, and we worship it.' And I looked into the mirror, and it was even as he had said to me.

"And I did a strange thing, but what I did matters not, for in a valley that is but a day's journey from this place have I hidden the Mirror of Wisdom. Do but suffer me to enter into thee again and be thy servant, and thou shalt be wiser than all the wise men, and Wisdom shall be thine. Suffer me to enter into thee, and none will be as wise as thou.

But the young Fisherman laughed. "Love is better than Wisdom," he cried, "and the little Mermaid loves me."

"Nay, but there is nothing better than Wisdom," said the Soul.

"Love is better," answered the young Fisherman, and he plunged into the deep, and the Soul went weeping away over the marshes.

And after the second year was over, the Soul came down to the shore of the sea, and called to the young Fisherman, and he rose out of the deep and said, "Why dost thou call to me?"

And the Soul answered, "Come nearer, that I may speak with thee, for I have seen marvellous things."

So he came nearer, and couched in the shallow water, and leaned his head upon his hand and listened.

And the Soul said to him, "When I left thee, I turned my face to the South and journeyed. From the South cometh everything that is precious. Six days I journeyed along the highways that lead to the city of Ashter, along the dusty red-dyed highways by which the pilgrims are wont to go did I journey, and on the morning of the seventh day I lifted up my eyes, and lo! the city lay at my feet, for it is in a valley.

"There are nine gates to this city, and in front of each gate stands a bronze horse that neighs when the Bedouins come down from the mountains. The walls are cased with copper, and the watch-towers on the wall are roofed with brass. In every tower stands an archer with a bow in his hand. At sunrise he strikes with an arrow on a gong, and at sunset he blows through a horn of horn.

"When I sought to enter, the guards stopped me and asked of me who I was. I made answer that I was a Dervish and on my way to the city of Mecca, where there was a green veil on which the Koran was embroidered in silver letters by the hands of the angels. They were filled with wonder, and entreated me to pass in.

"Inside it is even as a bazaar. Surely thou shouldst have been with me. Across the narrow streets the gay lanterns of paper flutter like large butterflies. When the wind blows over the roofs they rise and fall as painted bubbles do. In front of their booths sit the merchants on silken carpets. They have straight black beards, and their turbans are covered with golden sequins, and long strings of amber and carved peach-stones glide through their cool fingers. Some of them sell galbanum and nard, and curious perfumes from the islands of the Indian Sea, and the thick oil of red roses, and myrrh and little nail-shaped cloves. When one stops to speak to them, they throw pinches of frankincense upon a charcoal brazier and make the air sweet. I saw a Syrian who held in his hands a thin rod like a reed. Grey threads of smoke came from it, and its odour as it burned was as the odour of the pink almond in spring. Others sell silver bracelets embossed all over with creamy blue turquoise stones, and anklets of brass wire fringed with little pearls, and tigers' claws set in gold, and the claws of that gilt cat, the leopard, set in gold also, and earrings of pierced emerald, and finger-rings of hollowed jade. From the tea-houses comes the sound of the guitar, and the opium-smokers with their white smiling faces look out at the passers-by.

"Of a truth thou shouldest have been with me. The wine-sellers elbow their way through the crowd with great black skins on their shoulders. Most of them sell the wine of Schiraz, which is as sweet as honey. They serve it in little metal cups and strew rose leaves upon it. In the market-place stand the fruitsellers, who sell all kinds of fruit: ripe figs, with their bruised purple flesh, melons, smelling of musk and yellow as topazes, citrons and rose-apples and clusters of white grapes, round red-gold oranges, and oval lemons of green-gold. Once I saw an elephant go by. Its trunk was painted with vermilion and turmeric, and over its ears it had a net of crimson silk cord. It stopped opposite one of the booths and began eating the oranges, and the man only laughed. Thou canst not think how strange a people they are. When they are glad they go to the bird-sellers and buy of them a caged bird, and set it free that their joy may be greater, and when they are sad they scourge themselves with thorns that their sorrow may not grow less.

"One evening I met some negroes carrying a heavy palanquin through the bazaar. It was made of gilded bamboo, and the poles were of vermilion lacquer studded with brass peacocks. Across the windows hung thin curtains of muslin embroidered with beetles' wings and with tiny seed-pearls, and as it passed by a pale-faced Circassian looked out and smiled at me. I followed behind, and the negroes hurried their steps and scowled. But I did not care. I felt a great curiosity come over me.

"At last they stopped at a square white house. There were no windows to it, only a little door like the door of a tomb. They set down the palanquin and knocked three times with a copper hammer. An Armenian in a caftan of green leather peered through the wicket, and when he saw them he opened, and spread a carpet on the ground, and the woman stepped out. As she went in, she turned round and smiled at me again. I had never seen any one so pale.

"When the moon rose I returned to the same place and sought for the house, but it was no longer there. When I saw that, I knew who the woman was, and wherefore she had smiled at me.

"Certainly thou shouldst have been with me. On the feast of the New Moon the young Emperor came forth from his palace and went into the mosque to pray. His hair and beard were dyed with rose-leaves, and his cheeks were powdered with a fine gold dust. The palms of his feet and hands were yellow with saffron.

"At sunrise he went forth from his palace in a robe of silver, and at sunset he returned to it again in a robe of gold. The people flung themselves on the ground and hid their faces, but I would not do so. I stood by the stall of a seller of dates and waited. When the Emperor saw me, he raised his painted eyebrows and stopped. I stood quite still, and made him no obeisance. The people marvelled at my boldness, and counselled me to flee from the city. I paid no heed to them, but went and sat with the sellers of strange gods, who by reason of their craft are abominated. When I told them what I had done, each of them gave me a god and prayed me to leave them.

"That night, as I lay on a cushion in the tea-house that is in the Street of Pomegranates, the guard of the Emperor entered and led me to the palace. As I went in they closed each door behind me, and put a chain across it. Inside was a great court with an arcade running all round. The walls were of white alabaster, set here and there with blue and green tiles. The pillars were of green marble, and the pavement of a kind of peach-blossom marble. I had never seen anything like it before.

"As I passed across the court two veiled women looked down from a balcony and cursed me. The guards hastened on, and the butts of the lances rang upon the polished floor. They opened a gate of wrought ivory, and I found myself in a watered garden of seven terraces. It was planted with tulip-cups and moon-flowers, and silver-studded aloes. Like a slim reed of crystal a fountain hung in the dusky air. The cypress-trees were like burnt-out torches. From one of them a nightingale was singing.

"At the end of the garden stood a little pavilion. As we approached it two eunuchs came out to meet us. Their fat bodies swayed as they walked, and they glanced curiously at me with their yellow-lidded eyes. One of them drew aside the captain of the guard, and in a low voice whispered to him. The other kept munching scented pastilles, which he took with an affected gesture out of an oval box of lilac enamel.

"After a few moments the captain of the guard dismissed the soldiers. They went back to the palace, the eunuchs following slowly behind and plucking the sweet mulberries from the trees as they passed. Once the elder of the two turned round, and smiled at me with an evil smile.

"Then the captain of the guard motioned me towards the entrance of the pavilion. I walked on without trembling, and drawing the heavy curtain aside I entered in.

"The young Emperor was stretched on a couch of dyed lion skins, and a ger-falcon perched upon his wrist. Behind him stood a brass-turbaned Nubian, naked down to the waist, and with heavy earrings in his split ears. On a table by the side of the couch lay a mighty scimitar of steel.

"When the Emperor saw me he frowned, and said to me, 'What is thy name? Knowest thou not that I am Emperor of this city?' But I made him no answer.

"He pointed with his finger at the scimitar, and the Nubian seized it, and rushing forward struck at me with great violence. The blade whizzed through me, and did me no hurt. The man fell sprawling on the floor, and when he rose up his teeth chattered with terror and he hid himself behind the couch.

"The Emperor leapt to his feet, and taking a lance from a stand of arms, he threw it at me. I caught it in its flight, and brake the shaft in two pieces. He shot at me with an arrow, but I held up my hands and it stopped in mid-air. Then he drew a dagger from a belt of white leather, and stabbed the Nubian in the throat lest the slave should tell of his dishonour. The man writhed like a trampled snake, and a red foam bubbled from his lips.

"As soon as he was dead the Emperor turned to me, and when he had wiped away the bright sweat from his brow with a little napkin of purfled and purple silk, he said to me, 'Art thou a prophet, that I may not harm thee, or the son of a prophet, that I can do thee no hurt? I pray thee leave my city tonight, for while thou art in it I am no longer its lord.'

"And I answered him, 'I will go for half of thy treasure. Give me half of thy treasure, and I will go away.'

"He took me by the hand, and led me out into the garden. When the captain of the guard saw me, he wondered. When the eunuchs saw me, their knees shook and they fell upon the ground in fear.

"There is a chamber in the palace that has eight walls of red porphyry, and a brass-scaled ceiling hung with lamps. The Emperor touched one of the walls and it opened, and we passed down a corridor that was lit with many torches. In niches upon each side stood great wine-jars filled to the brim with silver pieces. When we reached the centre of the corridor the Emperor spake the word that may not be spoken, and a granite door swung back on a secret spring, and he put his hands before his face lest his eyes should be dazzled.

"Thou couldst not believe how marvellous a place it was. There were huge tortoise-shells full of pearls, and hollowed moonstones of great size piled up with red rubies. The gold was stored in coffers of elephant-hide, and the gold-dust in leather bottles. There were opals and sapphires, the former in cups of crystal, and the latter in cups of jade. Round green emeralds were ranged in order upon thin plates of ivory, and in one corner were silk bags filled, some with turquoise-stones, and others with beryls. The ivory horns were heaped with purple amethysts, and the horns of brass with chalcedonies and sards. The pillars, which were of cedar, were hung with strings of yellow lynx-stones. In the flat oval shields there were carbuncles, both wine-coloured and coloured like glass. And yet I have told thee but a tithe of what was there.

"And when the Emperor had taken away his hands from before his face he said to me: 'This is my house of treasure, and half that is in it is thine, even as I promised to thee. And I will give thee camels and camel drivers, and they shall do thy bidding and take thy share of the treasure to whatever part of the world thou desirest to go. And the thing shall be done tonight, for I would not that the Sun, who is my father, should see that there is in my city a man whom I cannot slay.'

"But I answered him, 'The gold that is here is thine, and the silver also is thine, and thine are the precious jewels and the things of price. As for me, I have no need of these. Nor shall I take aught from thee but that little ring that thou wearest on the finger of thy hand.'

"And the Emperor frowned, 'It is but a ring of lead,' he cried, 'nor has it any value. Therefore take thy half of the treasure and go from my city.'

"'Nay,' I answered, 'but I will take nought but that leaden ring, for I know what is written within it, and for what purpose.'

"And the Emperor trembled, and besought me and said, 'Take all the treasure and go from my city. The half that is mine shall be thine also.'

"And I did a strange thing, but what I did matters not, for in a cave that is but a day's journey from this place have I hidden the Ring of Riches. It is but a day's journey from this place, and it waits for thy coming. He who has this Ring is richer than all the kings of the world. Come therefore and take it, and the world's riches shall be thine."

But the young Fisherman laughed. "Love is better than Riches," he cried, "and the little Mermaid loves me."

"Nay, but there is nothing better than Riches," said the Soul.

"Love is better," answered the young Fisherman, and he plunged into the deep, and the Soul went weeping away over the marshes.

And after the third year was over, the Soul came down to the shore of the sea, and called to the young Fisherman, and he rose out of the deep and said, "Why dost thou call to me?"

And the Soul answered, "Come nearer, that I may speak with thee, for I have seen marvellous things."

So he came nearer, and couched in the shallow water, and leaned his head upon his hand and listened.

And the Soul said to him, "In a city that I know of there is an inn that standeth by a river. I sat there with sailors who drank of two different-coloured wines, and ate bread made of barley, and little salt fish served in bay leaves with vinegar. And as we sat and made merry, there entered to us an old man bearing a leathern carpet and a lute that had two horns of amber. And when he had laid out the carpet on the floor, he struck with a quill on the wire strings of his lute, and a girl whose face was veiled ran in and began to dance before us. Her face was veiled with a veil gauze, but her feet were naked. Naked were her feet, and they moved over the carpet like little white pigeons. Never have I seen anything so marvellous, and the city in which she dances is but a day's journey from this place."

Now when the young Fisherman heard the words of his Soul, he remembered that the little Mermaid had no feet and could not dance. And a great desire came over him, and he said to himself, "It is but a day's journey, and I can return to my love," and he laughed, and stood up in the shallow water, and strode towards the shore.

And when he reached the dry shore he laughed again, and held out his arms to his Soul. And his Soul gave a great cry of joy and ran to meet him, and entered into him, and the young Fisherman saw stretched before him upon the sand that shadow of the body that is the body of the Soul.

And his Soul said to him, "Let us not tarry, but get hence at once, for the Sea-gods are jealous, and have monsters that do their bidding."

So they made haste, and all that night they journeyed beneath the moon, and all the next day they journeyed beneath the sun, and on the evening of the day they came to a city.

And the young Fisherman said to his Soul, "Is this the city in which she dances of whom thou didst speak to me?"

And his Soul answered him, "It is not this city, but another. Nevertheless let us enter in."

So they entered in and passed through the streets, and as they passed through the Street of the Jewellers the young Fisherman saw a fair silver cup set forth in a booth. And his Soul said to him, "Take that silver cup and hide it."

So he took the cup and hid it in the fold of his tunic, and they went hurriedly out of the city.

And after that they had gone a league from the city, the young Fisherman frowned, and flung his cup away, and said to his Soul, "Why didst thou tell me to take this cup and hide it, for it was an evil thing to do?"

But his Soul answered him, "Be at peace, be at peace."

And on the evening of the second day they came to a city, and the young Fisherman said to his Soul, "Is this the city in which she dances of whom thou didst speak to me?"

And his Soul answered him, "It is not this city, but another. Nevertheless let us enter in."

So they entered in and passed through the streets, and as they passed through the Street of the Sellers of Sandals, the young Fisherman saw a child standing by a jar of water. And his Soul said to him, "Smite that child." So he smote the child till it wept, and when he had done this they went hurriedly out of the city.

And after that they had gone a league from the city the young Fisherman grew wroth, and said to his Soul, "Why didst thou tell me to smite the child, for it was an evil thing to do?"

But his Soul answered him, "Be at peace, be at peace."

And on the evening of the third day they came to a city, and the young Fisherman said to his Soul, "Is this the city in which she dances of whom thou didst speak to me?"

And his Soul answered him, "It may be that it is in this city, therefore let us enter in."

So they entered in and passed through the streets, but nowhere could the young Fisherman find the river or the inn that stood by its side. And the people of the city looked curiously at him, and he grew afraid and said to his Soul, "Let us go hence, for she who dances with white feet is not here."

But his Soul answered, "Nay, but let us tarry, for the night is dark and there will be robbers on the way."

So he sat him down in the market-place and rested, and after a time there went by a hooded merchant who had a cloak of cloth of Tartary, and bare a lantern of pierced horn at the end of a jointed reed. And the merchant said to him, "Why dost thou sit in the market-place, seeing that the booths are closed and the bales corded?"

And the young Fisherman answered him, "I can find no inn in this city, nor have I any kinsman who might give me shelter."

"Are we not all kinsmen?" said the merchant. "And did not one God make us? Therefore come with me, for I have a guest-chamber."

So the young Fisherman rose up and followed the merchant to his house. And when he had passed through a garden of pomegranates and entered into the house, the merchant brought him rose-water in a copper dish that he might wash his hands, and ripe melons that he might quench his thirst, and set a bowl of rice and a piece of roasted kid before him.

And after that he had finished, the merchant led him to the guest-chamber, and bade him sleep and be at rest. And the young Fisherman gave him thanks, and kissed the ring that was on his hand, and flung himself down on the carpets of dyed goat's-hair. And when he had covered himself with a covering of black lamb's-wool he fell asleep.

And three hours before dawn, and while it was still night, his Soul waked him and said to him, "Rise up and go to the room of the merchant, even to the room in which he sleepeth, and slay him, and take from him his gold; for we have need of it."

And the young Fisherman rose up and crept towards the room of the merchant, and over the feet of the merchant there was lying a curved sword, and the tray by the side of the merchant held nine purses of gold. And he reached out his hand and touched the sword, and when he touched it the merchant started and awoke, and leaping up seized the sword and cried to the young Fisherman, "Dost thou return evil for good, and pay with the shedding of blood for the kindness that I have shown thee?"

And his Soul said to the young Fisherman, "Strike him," and he struck him so that he swooned, and he seized then the nine purses of gold, and fled hastily through the garden of pomegranates, and set his face to the star that is the star of morning.

And when they had gone a league from the city, the young Fisherman beat his breast, and said to his Soul, "Why didst thou bid me slay the merchant and take his gold? Surely thou art evil?"

But his Soul answered him, "Be at peace, be at peace."

"Nay," cried the young Fisherman, "I may not be at peace, for all that thou hast made me to do I hate. Thee also I hate, and I bid thee tell me wherefore thou hast wrought with me in this wise."

And his Soul answered him, "When thou didst send me forth into the world thou gavest me no heart, so I learned to do all these things and love them."

"What sayest thou?" murmured the young Fisherman.

"Thou knowest," answered his Soul, "thou knowest it well. Hast thou forgotten that thou gavest me no heart? I trow not. And so trouble not thyself nor me, but be at peace, for there is no pain that thou shalt not give away nor any pleasure that thou shalt not receive."

And when the young Fisherman heard these words he trembled and said to his Soul, "Nay, but thou art evil, and has made me forget my love, and hast tempted me with temptations, and has set my feet in the ways of sin."

And his Soul answered him, "Thou hast not forgotten that when thou didst send me forth into the world thou gavest me no heart. Come, let us go to another city, and make merry, for we have nine purses of gold."

But the young Fisherman took the nine purses of gold, and flung them down, and trampled on them.

"Nay," he cried, "but I will have nought to do with thee, nor will I journey with thee anywhere, but even as I sent thee away before, so will I send thee away now, for thou has wrought me no good." And he turned his back to the moon, and with the little knife that had the handle of the green viper's skin he strove to cut from his feet that shadow of the body which is the body of the Soul.

Yet his Soul stirred not from him, nor paid heed to his command, but said to him, "The spell that the Witch told thee avails thee no more, for I may not leave thee, nor mayest thou drive me forth. Once in his life may a man send his Soul away, but he who receiveth back his Soul must keep it with him for ever, and this is his punishment and his reward."

And the young Fisherman grew pale and clenched his hands and cried, "She was a false Witch in that she told me not that."

"Nay," answered his Soul, "but she was true to Him she worships, and whose servant she will be ever."

And when the young Fisherman knew that he could no longer get rid of his Soul, and that it was an Evil Soul, and would abide with him always, he fell upon the ground weeping bitterly.

And when it was day, the young Fisherman rose up and said to his Soul, "I will bind my hands that I may not do thy bidding, and close my lips that I may not speak thy words, and I will return to the place where she whom I love has her dwelling. Even to the sea will I return, and to the little bay where she is wont to sing, and I will call to her and tell her the evil I have done and the evil thou hast wrought on me."

And his Soul tempted him and said, "Who is thy love, that thou shouldst return to her? The world has many fairer than she is. There are the dancing-girls of Samaris who dance in the manner of all kinds of birds and beasts. Their feet are painted with henna, and in their hands they have little copper bells. They laugh while they dance, and their laughter is as clear as the laughter of water. Come with me and I will show them to thee. For what is this trouble of thine about the things of sin? Is that which is pleasant to eat not made for the eater? Is there poison in that which is sweet to drink? Trouble not thyself, but come with me to another city. There is a little city hard by in which there is a garden of tulip-trees. And there dwell in this comely garden white peacocks and peacocks that have blue breasts. Their tails when they spread them to the sun are like disks of ivory and like gilt disks. And she who feeds them dances for pleasure, and sometimes she dances on her hands and at other times she dances with her feet. Her eyes are coloured with stibium, and her nostrils are shaped like the wings of a swallow. From a hook in one of her nostrils hangs a flower that is carved out of a pearl. She laughs while she dances, and the silver rings that are about her ankles tinkle like bells of silver. And so trouble not thyself any more, but come with me to this city."

But the young Fisherman answered not his Soul, but closed his lips with the seal of silence and with a tight cord bound his hands, and journeyed back to the place from which he had come, even to the little bay where his love had been wont to sing. And ever did his Soul tempt him by the way, but he made it no answer, nor would he do any of the wickedness that it sought to make him do, so great was the power of the love that was within him.

And when he had reached the shore of the sea, he loosed the cord from his hands, and took the seal of silence from his lips, and called to the little Mermaid. But she came not to his call, though he called to her all day long and besought her.

And his Soul mocked him and said, "Surely thou hast but little joy out of thy love. Thou art as one who in time of death pours water into a broken vessel. Thou givest away what thou hast, and nought is given to thee in return. It were better for thee to come with me, for I know where the Valley of Pleasure lies, and what things are wrought there."

But the young Fisherman answered not his Soul, but in a cleft of the rock he built himself a house of wattles, and abode there for the space of a year. And every morning he called to the Mermaid, and every noon he called to her again, and at night-time he spake her name. Yet never did she rise out of the sea to meet him, not in any place of the sea could he find her though he sought for her in the caves and in the green water, in the pools of the tide and in the wells that are at the bottom of the deep.

And ever did his Soul tempt him with evil, and whisper of terrible things. Yet did it not prevail against him, so great was the power of his love.

And after the year was over, the Soul thought within himself, "I have tempted my master with evil, and his love is stronger than I am. I will tempt him now with good, and it may be that he will come with me."

So he spake to the young Fisherman and said, "I have told thee of the joy of the world, and thou hast turned a deaf ear to me. Suffer me now to tell thee of the world's pain, and it may be that thou wilt hearken. For of a truth pain is the Lord of this world, nor is there any one who escapes from its net. There be some who lack raiment, and others who lack bread. There be widows who sit in purple, and widows who sit in rags. To and fro over the fens go the lepers, and they are cruel to each other. The beggars go up and down on the highways, and their wallets are empty. Through the streets of the cities walks Famine, and the Plague sits at their gates. Come, let us go forth and mend these things, and make them not to be.

Wherefore shouldst thou tarry here calling to thy love, seeing she comes not to thy call? And what is love, that thou shouldst set this high store upon it?"

But the young Fisherman answered it nought, so great was the power of his love. And every morning he called to the Mermaid, and every noon he called to her again, and at night-time he spake her name. Yet never did she rise out of the sea to meet him, nor in any place of the sea could he find her, though he sought for her in the rivers of the sea, and in the valleys that are under the waves, in the sea that the night makes purple, and in the sea that the dawn leaves grey.

And after the second year was over, the Soul said to the young Fisherman at night-time, and as he sat in the wattled house alone, "Lo! now I have tempted thee with evil, and I have tempted thee with good, and thy love is stronger than I am. Wherefore will I tempt thee no longer, but I pray thee to suffer me to enter thy heart, that I may be one with thee even as before."

"Surely thou mayest enter," said the young Fisherman, "for in the days when with no heart thou didst go through the world thou must have much suffered."

"Alas!" cried his Soul, "I can find no place of entrance, so compassed about with love is this heart of thine."

"Yet I would that I could help thee," said the young Fisherman.

And as he spake there came a great cry of mourning from the sea, even the cry that men hear when one of the Sea-folk is dead. And the young Fisherman leapt up, and left his wattled house, and ran down to the shore. And the black waves came hurrying to the shore, bearing with them a burden that was whiter than silver. White as the surf it was, and like a flower it tossed on the waves. And the surf took it from the waves, and the foam took it from the surf, and the shore received it, and lying at his feet the young Fisherman saw the body of the little Mermaid. Dead at his feet it was lying.

Weeping as one smitten with pain he flung himself down beside it, and he kissed the cold red of the mouth, and toyed with the wet amber of the hair. He flung himself down beside it on the sand, weeping as one trembling with joy, and in his brown arms he held it to his breast. Cold were the lips, yet he kissed them. Salt was the honey of the hair, yet he tasted it with bitter joy. He kissed the closed eyelids, and the wild spray that lay upon their cups was less than his tears.

And to the dead thing he made confession. Into the shells of its ears he poured the harsh wine of his tale. He put the little hands round his neck, and with his fingers he touched the thin reed of the throat. Bitter, bitter was his joy, and full of strange gladness was his pain.

The black sea came nearer, and the white foam moaned like a leper. With white claws of foam the sea grabbled at the shore. From the palace of the Sea-King came the cry of mourning again, and far out upon the sea the great Tritons blew hoarsely upon their horns.

"Flee away," said his Soul, "for ever doth the sea come nigher, and if thou tarriest it will slay thee. Flee away, for I am afraid, seeing that thy heart is closed against me by reason of the greatness of thy love. Flee away to a place of safety. Surely thou wilt not send me without a heart into another world?"

But the young Fisherman listened not to his Soul, but called on the little Mermaid and said, "Love is better than wisdom, and more precious than riches, and fairer than the feet of the daughters of men. The fires cannot destroy it, nor can the waters quench it. I called on thee at dawn, and thou didst come to my call. The moon heard thy name, yet hadst thou no heed of me. For evilly had I left thee, and to my own hurt had I wandered away. Yet ever did thy love abide with me, and ever was it strong, not did aught prevail against it, though I have looked upon evil and looked upon good. And now that thou art dead, surely I will die with thee also."

And his Soul besought him to depart, but he would not, so great was his love. And the sea came nearer, and sought to cover him with its waves, and when he knew that the end was at hand he kissed with mad lips the cold lips of the Mermaid, and the heart that was within him brake. And as through the fullness of his love his heart did break, the Soul found an entrance and entered in, and was one with him even as before.

And the sea covered the young Fisherman with its waves.

And in the morning the Priest went forth to bless the sea, for it had been troubled. And with him went the monks and the musicians, and the candle-bearers, and the swingers of censers, and a great company.

And when the Priest reached the shore he saw the young Fisherman lying drowned in the surf, and clasped in his arms was the body of the little Mermaid. And he drew back frowning, and having made the sign of the cross, he cried aloud and said, "I will not bless the sea nor anything that is in it. Accursed be the Sea-folk, and accursed be all they who traffic with them. And as for him who for love's sake forsook God, and so lieth here with his leman slain by God's judgement, take up his body and the body of his leman, and bury them in the corner of the Field of the Fullers, and set no mark above them, nor sign of any kind, that none may know the place of their resting. For accursed were they in their lives, and accursed shall they be in their death also."

And the people did as he commanded them, and in the corner of the Field of the Fullers, where no sweet herbs grew, they dug a deep pit, and laid the dead things within it.

And when the third year was over, and on a day that was a holy day, the Priest went up to the chapel, that he might show to the people the wounds of the Lord, and speak to them about the wrath of God.

And when he had robed himself with his robes, and entered in and bowed himself before the altar, he saw that the altar was covered with strange flowers that never had been seen before. Strange were they to look at, and of curious beauty, and their beauty troubled him, and their odour was sweet in his nostrils, and he felt glad, and understood not why he was glad.

And after that he had opened the tabernacle, and incensed the monstrance that was in it, and shown the fair wafer to the people, and hid it again behind the veil of veils, he began to speak to the people, desiring to speak to them of the wrath of God. But the beauty of the white flowers troubled him, and their odour was sweet in his nostrils, and there came another word into his lips, and he spake not of the wrath of God, but of the God whose name is Love. And why he so spake, he knew not.

And when he had finished his word the people wept, and the Priest went back to the sacristy, and his eyes were full of tears. And the deacons came in and began to unrobe him, and took from him the alb and the girdle, the maniple and the stole. And he stood as one in a dream.

And after that they had unrobed him, he looked at them and said, "What are the flowers that stand on the altar and whence do they come?"

And they answered him, "What flowers they are we cannot tell, but they come from the corner of the Fullers' Field." And the Priest trembled, and returned to his own house and prayed.

And in the morning, while it was still dawn, he went forth with the monks and the musicians, and the candle-bearers and the swingers of censers, and a great company, and came to the shore of the sea, and blessed the sea, and all the wild things that are in it. The Fauns also he blessed, and the little things that dance in the woodland, and the bright-eyed things that peer through the leaves. All the things in God's world he blessed, and the people were filled with joy and wonder. Yet never again in the corner of the Fullers' Field grew flowers of any kind, but the field remained barren even as before. Nor came the Sea-folk into the bay as they had been wont to do, for they went to another part of the sea.

Far Enough Island

by
LESLEY CHOYCE
(1951–   )

A sort of homespun tale, charmingly told, of coastal Nova Scotia, in which a family's hard-won hopes and dreams rekindle slowly in the face of hardship and trial (and a very real shortage of cod). The island itself, far enough away to lie just out of small Sarah's reach, but not so far away as to seem absolutely unreachable, embodies the unspoken answers and possibilities of a small child's small world...

Sarah MacNeil wished that her mother could be happier. But there was nothing she seemed to be able to do about it. Sarah was afraid that maybe her mother was the unhappiest mother in the whole world. When twelve-year-old Sarah woke up on a sunny summer morning in Nova Scotia, she found it hard to believe that anyone could be unhappy there.

Her bedroom looked out over a blue sparkling inlet. Sea gulls swooped up and down and a great blue heron walked gingerly through the shallows. Off toward the ocean, she could see the outline of Far Enough Island. Sarah thought that there was something magical about Far Enough Island because nobody lived there and she had never set foot on it. It was always there in her bedroom window, full of interesting possibilities.

Jeremiah was scratching at the door. Good old Jeremiah. He was her pure black Labrador retriever, and the best friend she ever had in the world.

"Sarah, get up and let your dog out!" her mother yelled from the kitchen.

Sarah jumped up from bed and let Jeremiah into her room.

Jeremiah dove at her and knocked her down on the floor, licking her nose and slobbering all over her face.

"What's going on up there?" her mother yelled again.

"Nothing," Sarah answered. Good old Jeremiah. "Dad didn't let you go on the boat again today, did he?" she said to her dog.

Jeremiah just rolled over on the floor and scratched his back by wiggling back and forth, upside down on the floor.

Sarah changed into her clothes in seconds and ran outside, with Jeremiah right on her heels. Without even saying good morning to her mother, she raced at top speed to the end of the wharf, stopping at the very last second before she would have toppled over into the icy water. Jeremiah galloped along behind her but forgot to stop at the end of the wharf. He just kept running straight out over the end, his feet kicking at the empty air. Then he splashed down hard into the water, surfaced and turned around to swim back to the shore.

Sarah laughed and laughed. It was one of her games she liked to play with Jeremiah in the summer. He probably could have stopped if he wanted to, but Sarah knew he was a good swimmer and Jeremiah always seemed so happy after she had tricked him into flying off the end of the wharf. Now he was on the shoreline, shaking himself, water flying in a million directions.

Out past Far Enough Island, Sarah could see her dad's boat coming back from sea. That seemed strange. It was way too early for that.

Sarah walked back to the house and went into the kitchen where her mother was worrying over a pile of papers at the kitchen table. Jeremiah bounded past her and shook himself in the middle of the kitchen floor.

"Get that mangy beast out of here!" Sarah's mother went off like a cannon.

"Sorry, I'll clean it up," Sarah said. The last thing she needed was to get her mother mad at her. Sarah grabbed a towel; and began to mop the water drops off everything, including her mother. She grabbed poor Jeremiah by the collar and skidded him across the floor and out the door. Jeremiah looked very hurt that he was being thrown out.

"Why is Daddy headed back in so soon?" she asked her mother. She was used to her father's boat arriving back from fishing at around eleven or twelve o'clock. She saw that it was only nine thirty.

"The fish are gone. There are hardly any left," Sarah's mother said, her voice like dry gravel.

"But there's millions of fish in the sea."

"Well, not around here, there's not. Get yourself some cereal for breakfast."

"Sure." Sarah filled a bowl to the very top.

"Sarah, that's too much. Don't waste it. Money doesn't grow on trees, you know."

Sarah poured half of it back into the box. Why didn't money grow on trees, she wondered. In fact, it should. Her parents were always worrying about money and Sarah couldn't see why. They weren't exactly poor.

Jeremiah had managed to stand up outside the door and turn the doorknob with his paw. He had it open a crack just big enough so that he could stick his nose through. He looked so funny that Sarah thought she was going to burst out laughing and spit her cereal all over the floor. Instead, she held it in. But she couldn't help having a big funny lopsided grin on her face as she tried to chew her cereal.

Her mother looked up at her. She was very annoyed about something. But it couldn't just be Sarah. Sarah was just being herself.

"Why are you smiling like that?" she asked.

Sarah shrugged her shoulders.

"Well, never smile without a good reason. You should know that. People will think there's something wrong with you. Never smile before Christmas. That's what my mother used to say." She let out a deep sigh. "And even then there's not always something to smile about."

Jeremiah had arrived in the middle of the night, six years before. It was during the worst hurricane Nova Scotia had seen in fifty years.

"What was that?" six-year-old Sarah asked. Sarah, her mother and her dad were sitting around the kitchen table. They had on a smelly kerosene lantern because the storm had knocked down a power line.

"That was just the wind," her mother said. Her mother looked frightened by the storm and her father was holding her hand.

"It will calm down by morning," Sarah's father said, trying to be reassuring.

"What if you lose the boat?"

"I have her tied up real good. She won't go anywhere. That ole boat wouldn't know where else to go."

"Be serious," Sarah's mother said. She was staring deep into the flame.

"Stop worrying," he said.

"That's easy for you to say," Sarah's mother snapped back.

"There, I heard it again," Sarah said. "It sounded like someone crying."

"It's just your imagination," her mother explained.

"No, it wasn't," Sarah insisted. She ran to the back door and threw it open. A torrent of wind and rain blew into the room. The wind blew out the lamp and they were thrown into total darkness.

"Now what?" Sarah's mother groaned, always expecting the worst.

"Just be calm," her father said. "I'll find the flashlight. Sarah, close the darned door!"

The door slammed shut hard and Sarah's father fell over a chair in the dark as he tried to find the flashlight. Outside the wind howled.

Her father found the flashlight and flicked it on. There was little Sarah sitting on the wet floor by the door. In her arms was a little black puppy.

"Well, I'll be darned," her father said. "Where'd he come from?"

"I don't know, but he's found us now," Sarah answered. "We're keeping him."

Her father was relighting the old kerosene lantern. "Well, I don't know. Your mother was never very fond of dogs. Besides, he probably belongs to someone. What do you think, dear?" he asked his wife.

Sarah was so busy hugging the little squirmy puppy that she didn't even look up to see her mother crying and shaking her head up and down. "Yes," she said. "We'll keep him until we find his real home."

Now the storm had picked up even more strength. The waves pounded at the wharf. The wind tore at the wooden shingles on the roof until it had set some of them free.

"It's going to be a long night," her father said.

"This is the best night of my life," Sarah said.

No one ever laid claim to the puppy so Sarah's mother said she could keep it.

"What do you want to name him, Sarah?" she asked.

Sarah thought long and hard. "I don't know. There are so many good names. You pick one."

"I always liked the name Jeremiah," her mother said. "I think maybe if you had a brother, I might have called him Jeremiah." Her mother looked at her with sad, gentle eyes.

"But maybe you should save that name in case I do have a brother."

"No, I don't think that will happen. I want you to use the name for the puppy."

Those were the years when the fishing was good. Sarah's dad went to sea during the good weather and nearly filled the boat with cod and hake and haddock and flounder. He sold it to the fish plant further up the inlet and came home with money in his pockets.

Her dad seemed to like getting up at five thirty in the morning when it was still dark and going off to sea in his boat alone. "It's good to get back up the inlet before the winds come up," he'd explain. But Sarah's mother worried about him out there all alone. She always expected the worst to happen. Even in good times.

"Stop your frettin'," he'd say. "I'm very careful." He had a big, wonderful smile on his face.

"Never smile before Christmas," his wife chided him. "You never know what can go wrong. You don't want to tempt fate with all that over-confidence."

But her dad kept smiling anyway.

Sarah didn't have many friends because she lived such a long way from town and from school. It took a half-hour drive in their old Chevy pick-up truck to drive down the muddy gravel road to get her to school. Sarah had tried to keep track of the number of potholes.

"Three thousand and seventy-five."

"What?" her mother asked.

"Three thousand and seventy-five potholes to school and back."

"And next year, there'll be four thousand and seventy-five," her mother answered.

Jeremiah would ride in the back of the pick-up and sniff at the air. He looked strong and proud riding back there. And when Sarah would come home from school, they would go hiking along the beaches where Sarah would imagine them having all sorts of adventures.

Even though Jeremiah never hurt another animal, he loved to chase any living thing he came across—spruce grouse, weasels, otters or ducks. Sarah would try to stop him, but Jeremiah just had too much wild energy that had to be released.

That was until one day when he got too close to a porcupine. Jeremiah howled with regret. He was only playing when he ran up close and nipped at the porcupine's fur which turned out not to be fur at all but hundreds of sharp needles.

Jeremiah howled in pain. Sarah ran to him and found his mouth filled with porcupine needles and blood. Sarah thought Jeremiah might die. She didn't know what to do. Jeremiah didn't seem to want to follow her. He was acting crazy from the pain. Sarah tried to pick him up but he was almost as big as she was.

She heard an engine from a boat coming from the inlet and ran to the stony beach. There was her father just rounding Far Enough Island and headed home. She stood on the shore and waved and yelled for almost twenty minutes until her dad was close enough to see her. He pulled his boat in close and jumped into the shallow water.

"What is it?"

"It's Jeremiah. He chased a porcupine. Now I think he's going to die."

Sarah's father ran into the woods with her and found Jeremiah lying in a pool of blood. He wasn't moving.

Sarah's father picked him up and ran him to the boat. "Come on, honey," he said to Sarah. "We have to get the boat up the inlet to town before the tide gets too low."

On the boat, Sarah's father roared the engine and they charged toward town.

Sarah knew that her father would never take the boat up the tricky inlets unless it was a dire emergency. It was too easy to hit a rock or get stuck on a sand bar. And the boat was his life. It was what her father needed to make enough money for them to live.

"Sit up front and look for logs or rocks or shallow water," he yelled. "Just hold on good."

Sarah had to lie down on the bow of the boat with both hands braced on the wood railing. She yelled to her father to go right or left whenever she saw something ahead. The tide was dropping and the water seemed to keep getting more shallow.

Jeremiah lay very still in the back on top of the fish. He was breathing but his eyes looked funny.

"Is he going to die, Daddy?" Sarah asked.

"No," he shouted. "Just keep a look out."

Sarah knew that if they got stuck, they'd never get Jeremiah to the vet in time. She watched the water ahead very carefully, shouting when she saw a grassy shallow or a rock ahead.

At the vet's, the woman gave Jeremiah a needle. "This way he won't feel any pain," she said.

Sarah thought she meant she was putting him to sleep for good. "No! You can't!" she screamed.

Her father pulled her back and the vet smiled. "No. It's not that. He's not going to die." When she pulled out the needle, she took a pair of pliers and began to gently remove the porcupine quills. Sarah counted twenty in all.

"He's a very lucky dog to have two friends like you," the vet said.

Sarah's dad had to phone her mother to come pick them up. The tide was too low to get the boat back down the inlet toward the sea, toward home.

"You could have wrecked the boat!" her mother said to them in the truck. Jeremiah was asleep across her dad's lap.

"I couldn't just let him die, could I?" her father said. He seemed really mad at her for saying it. Sarah just remained quiet.

"Well, it's just an old dog," her mother said. "If you wrecked the boat, then what would we do for money?"

"It's not just an old dog," Sarah said, angry now at what her mother said. She didn't understand at all.

Her mother stopped the truck and slapped her across the face. Sarah felt it like a hot burn across her cheek. Sarah raised her arm to hit her mother back but her father grabbed onto her wrist, firm but gently.

"You shouldn't have slapped her," he said.

Sarah's mother turned off the truck. She threw the keys at Sarah's father. Then she got out, slammed the door and began walking.

"I'm walking home. You drive home just the two of you. I'm the one who does all the worrying around here. Get on with you."

Sarah's father tried to stop her but it did no good. He lay Jeremiah on the seat and slid over to drive.

"Why is she like that?" Sarah asked.

"It's hard to explain," her father said. "Her mother was very cruel to her. And I think she always hoped I'd be something more than a fisherman."

"What's wrong with being a fisherman?"

"Well, sometimes you have good times and sometimes you have bad times. And you know her father drowned."

"Yeh, but you can swim."

"Sure, I can swim good," he said, even though it was a lie but it was one he had repeated over and over so many times that he half believed it.

Sarah's father couldn't get out to sea the next day to fish because his boat was tied up in town and he had missed the high tide in the middle of the night. So he lost a day's fishing, which cost the family needed money.

Just like Sarah's mother had predicted, things did get worse. It seemed that every year there were fewer and fewer fish. The weather was getting stormier and colder early in the fall. With less fish and fewer days in the season, the fish plant closed down and there was no place to sell what little catch there was. Her father lost his boat to the bank because he couldn't keep up payments. He took a job at a garage in town fixing cars but he hated it.

"At least it's money coming in," his mother would say. "But I know it's gonna get worse before it gets better. If it ever gets better."

Sarah didn't like school very much and now that her father was working in town, she had to hang around the gas station until five o'clock when he got off work so he could drive her home.

She missed her long walks along the beach with Jeremiah in the afternoons. She hated the garage, which always smelled of cigarettes and grease and gasoline. Men and boys stood around and talked tough. Her father was always telling them to use good language when Sarah was around but it didn't do any good.

And she really missed waking up in the morning and seeing her father's boat way off out to sea toward Far Enough Island. She missed how happy her father had been coming home to the wharf with a boat load of fish.

"Since you're not fishing any more, we might as well sell the place and move to town. It would be better for Sarah and it would be better for us," her mother said in a sour voice.

"Jeremiah would hate it in town," Sarah said.

"Then we'd just have to find Jeremiah a new home. He costs us an arm and a leg to feed anyway. And we need to save all the money we can. Hard times might be ahead."

Sarah's father looked down at the floor and didn't say a thing. But the next day when he took Sarah to town, he said he didn't want her to go to school, that he needed her help. First they went to the bank and he took out almost all their saved money. Then they drove over to Old Man Fogerty's little run-down wharf on a narrow channel of the inlet.

Old Man Fogerty was eighty-five years old. "She's a good boat," he said. "Old, but good. You treat her well, she'll last you a few years."

The boat certainly was old. But it didn't look so good.

"All it needs is a little paint," her father said. "With a little luck I'll be able to afford better in a couple of years."

Her father handed over the money.

"You bought it? What will Mother say?" Sarah asked.

"I don't know. I just know I'm fed up with the garage and I don't want to move to town. Now lie down up front here and help me steer out the channel to home before the tide slips."

So Sarah helped steer her dad and his new boat home.

The engine made loud coughing noises. It sputtered and stalled several times but eventually they made it. When they pulled up, there was Sarah's mother on the wharf with her arms folded and a dirty look on the face. When Jeremiah spotted them he came racing down the boards and launched himself out off the wharf before her mother could stop him. He jumped halfway to the boat before splashing down and swimming the rest of the way. Sarah's dad helped him up over the side and as Jeremiah shook the water off, he sprayed Sarah and her dad until they were soaked.

It should have been a funny scene. But Sarah's mother wasn't laughing at all.

Sarah's father worked night and day at fixing up the boat.

"It's too old," Sarah's mother said.

"Fogerty says there's life in her yet."

"I don't trust you out there alone in that old boat. Something could happen."

"Why don't you take Jeremiah along," Sarah said. "Just for company."

"He'd only get in the way," her father said. "A dog's not much good on a boat."

"But he likes the water."

Sarah's mother scowled. "Yes, why not take the dog with you. Get him out from being underfoot."

Sarah's father nodded okay. He didn't mind having a little dog company on board if it gave his wife one less thing to complain about.

It was getting late in the year for a good start but the fish had come back now and there was plenty to catch.

Sarah was in school when her father came back each day with the boat, but she knew things were going well.

She missed Jeremiah jumping up and licking her in the face every morning but she did get to play with him after school. And she liked the idea of good old Jeremiah being out there with her father every day, out beyond Far Enough Island. The only problem was that Jeremiah now always smelled like fish and he wasn't allowed into the house any more, except when Sarah sneaked him in when her mother wasn't home.

"I knew everything would work out," her father told the family one night at dinner. "I got the boat. The cod are back. I'm even getting a pretty good price from the new buyer. I'll have a newer boat soon."

"I think it's Jeremiah on the boat that brings good luck," Sarah said. Sarah and her father looked at each other and beamed.

Sarah's mother wasn't convinced. "It's always calmest just before the storm," she said. "Season's not over yet. Just wait. Never smile before Christmas, that's what I'd say."

But things were going well. And everyone should have been happy, only Sarah's mother couldn't convince herself things were going to be all right.

Then one morning that started out bright and cheery, the

wind switched and a heavy fog pulled up the inlet.

It was a Saturday and Sarah was not in school. Her mother stared out the window and began to wring her hands together. "I hope he gets back in here soon."

"He'll be okay. He knows the inlet out there. Don't worry," Sarah said.

But she worried.

Her father might have high-tailed it shoreward before the fog if he wasn't having trouble with the engine. But the old contraption was giving him problems. Water in the carburettor. He was stalled and drifting, still trying to fix it, when the fog pulled in sight so that he couldn't see a thing. Then the wind stopped and it was dead still.

Jeremiah was nervous, nosing around the boat, wondering why it was quiet and they weren't moving.

Sarah's father had the lid off the engine and was pouring gasoline down the carburettor. He tried the ignition. It backfired a couple of times. Then suddenly it coughed a long flame out the mouth of the carburetter, knocking her father off balance and back onto the slimy pile of the day's catch. Before he could turn off the ignition, gasoline was leaking out of the fuel line and the flame had caught it on fire.

Sarah's father grabbed a heavy tarp and threw it across the engine. But it too caught fire. Jeremiah was barking loud and fiercely as if the fire was a living thing and he was going to fend it off.

The fire began to creep out onto the floorboards. It was headed toward the gas tank. Sarah's father tried to sneak past it toward the small cabin to grab for a life vest but a new, more violent burst of flame roared up from below the deck, knocking him overboard. In the water, he flailed his arms. He kept telling himself that he did know how to swim. He had told that to his wife so often that he truly believed it. The water was cold. It was like sharp knives sticking into his arms and legs.

On the boat, Jeremiah continued to bark. What should he do, Sarah's father wondered. Should he get back in the boat or try to swim away from it? He tried to stay calm, kept himself floating, and tried to think it through.

"Here. Jeremiah. Jump!" He yelled.

Jeremiah launched into the water and swam towards him.

Now the entire boat was aflame. Within minutes it would be down. There was no explosion, just the crackle of wood.

All too soon, the water was up the gunwales and the flame diminished to nothing as the boat sank beneath. Still hanging onto Jeremiah to keep himself afloat, Sarah's father swam back toward where the boat had gone down, hoping to find a plank, some sort of wood to hold onto and keep him up. He found a section of the hull that had been left floating. It wasn't much but it was enough to keep his head above water. Around them was a sickly pool of oil and gas and black ash. The fog was now so dense he couldn't see more than ten feet in any direction. Jeremiah pulled himself up onto a section of deck that was afloat. At first he began to whine. But then he shook himself and began to bark loudly.

"I'm sorry old boy," Sarah's father said. "I don't know what good barking will do you. You might as well save your breath."

But Jeremiah went on barking louder and louder. It was like he had gone crazy and couldn't stop himself.

Sarah's father felt so cold and weak from being in the water that he grew discouraged. He could think of no plan of action. He felt helpless and doomed. The dog barked on and he wished he could make Jeremiah shut up.

After what seemed to be an hour, he thought he heard a boat engine. It was far off in the fog but coming closer.

"Keep barking!" he now shouted to Jeremiah, but Jeremiah was floating away from him.

The boat was coming closer. Sarah's father convinced himself he had to move. He let go of the wood and began to swim toward the engine noise. Then he heard Jeremiah splash into the water and swim up to him. "Over here!" he yelled to who-ever was coming to help. But as he did so, his mouth filled with water. He felt himself sink under. He reached out with his hands and there was Jeremiah. He grabbed the collar, pulled the dog under with him, but Jeremiah kicked his legs and kept swimming.

The boat was nearly on top of them.

"Cut the engine quick," someone shouted. Arms were reaching down. Sarah's father was fighting to stay above water. He knew he was pushing down on Jeremiah. It was the only thing keeping him from sinking altogether. He knew he was probably drowning the dog. But he couldn't help it.

Then the arms grabbed him. He was being hauled up into a boat. He was flat on the deck and his lungs were heaving. He was gasping for air.

"Anybody else out here?" a man's voice as frantically.

"A dog," Sarah's father said. "Jeremiah. Did you get the dog?"

"I didn't see no dog but that's why I came this way. I heard some fool dog barking his head off. But if he was out there he's not around now," the man said.

Sarah's father pulled himself up to the gunwale and looked over the side. There was nothing to see. No Jeremiah, nothing but a thick ugly fog.

They circled around for twenty minutes but saw and heard nothing.

"He saved my life," Sarah's father said and sunk back onto the floor.

"I told you things would get worse. I felt it in my bones. We're just a family of bad luck."

"That's not true," Sarah shouted back at her mother. "If it wasn't for Jeremiah, Dad would be dead by now."

Her dad hung his head down. "That's right. I have to go look for him. I'll get Hopper to loan me his boat."

"Not in this weather, you're not!" Sarah's mother insisted.

"I suppose you're right. One swim in the sink is one too many."

"But we need to look for him!" Sarah screamed. "He might be alive."

"He couldn't swim all the way back here," her father said.

"But he might have made it to the island. He could have, you know?"

Her father shook his head. "It's unlikely. I don't know how close to the island we were. Besides, how could he find it in all that fog?"

"He's just dead and that's all there is to it," her mother said. "Now let's just leave it at that."

But by morning the sun was out. "I'm going looking for him. Hopper said I could borrow his boat." Sarah's father had a life jacket on. Just then Sarah burst out of her room. She had on one as well. "I'm going too," she announced.

Her father put an arm around her and gave her a hug. "Sure. We'll both look for him."

Her mother looked furious. "Sure, get both of you drowned now! That's all I need."

Sarah's father walked up to her and took her by the shoulders, kissed her on the cheek and whispered something in her ear. "Please, we'll be careful," Sarah said. "We won't go past the island. We just have to look once."

They were gone most of the day. Sarah and her father walked all around the island and looked everywhere along the beaches. But there was no sign of Jeremiah.

"I'm sorry, honey," her father said.

Sarah tried not to cry but she couldn't help it. "He was my only real friend," she said, and the tears kept coming all the way home. But when she entered the kitchen and saw how happy her mother was to have the two of them home safe, she brightened a little.

They had a big dinner without any arguing at all and her father promised to try to get his job back at the garage.

After that the weather turned very cold for so early in the year. All the fishermen pulled up their boats weeks before they normally would. Raging northeast storms pummelled the coast. Then came snow in October. Sleet and ice and snow. Schools were closed. Sarah's father got fired from his garage job and went on unemployment.

Sarah's mother always wore a frown on her face. "We should have just packed up and moved long ago. Now's the time. Let's get away from here."

But Sarah didn't want to move. She kept remembering those happy sunny days walking the shoreline with Jeremiah and discovering all sorts of things. She still couldn't believe he was gone. Some mornings she'd wake up and expect him to come bounding into her room, smelling of fish and mud. But she kept reminding herself that if it wasn't for Jeremiah, she wouldn't have a father.

It was Christmas morning and things had been so rotten around Sarah's house for so long that she knew even today was going to be rotten.

The only thing that would make it better was a miracle. Her parents argued all the time about money and about moving. Sarah, herself, would get so tired of it all that she'd just scream, "Shut up!" and run out of the living room and lock herself in her bedroom.

It had been a strange December. The harbour froze up early and the ice grew thick across the shallows and even out into the channel.

"It's a sign of worse things to come," her mother said. "I've never seen anything like it."

They could no longer afford oil for the furnace so her father spent much of his time each day cutting spruce logs and hauling them home for firewood, splitting them and stoking the stoves.

The ice had crept all the way out the inlet almost to Far Enough Island. It was the first time that had happened this early, Old Man Fogerty said, since 1915. It was going to be a long, cold, sad winter.

"But today is Christmas," her mother said. "And I'm not going to worry about a thing. Today I want all of us to be happy!"

She wasn't very convincing but she tried. She had always said it was the one day that she refused to worry about any-thing. She woke Sarah early in the morning, even before the sun was up, with a peck on the cheek.

"Merry Christmas, Sarah."

But Sarah woke up thinking about Jeremiah and all the other Christmases he had been there. She remembered how he had torn up the wrapping paper to get at his presents—dog bones and leather chew toys. He had been so funny and so cute. And now she would never, ever see him again.

Her mother tried singing to Sarah to cheer her up but it didn't do any good.

The presents were opened and Sarah tried to act surprised and happy but nothing there interested her.

Her father tried to be cheerful but he was a lousy faker.

By the end of the day, her mother's good humour had worn off and they all sat around tired and depressed.

"This is the worst Christmas of my life," Sarah finally said out loud. "I never want to have another Christmas as long as I live." She sulked off to her room, slammed her door and went to bed.

The day after Christmas was something else. The ice storm had stopped. The sun was shining brightly and Sarah flipped open the shade on her window. All the trees were coated in ice and the inlet was like one sheet of pure, clear glass. The wharf was like some magical creation coated in crystal. And off in the distance, Far Enough Island, with all the trees glazed with ice, shone like a magical kingdom.

Sarah just wanted to keep looking out her window. She didn't want to go down to her family and face all the gloom and worry. If only she could just stare out her window like this forever and see the world as a gleaming magical place, everything would be all right.

And then, off in the far distance, she saw a small black speck that arrested her attention. Out towards Far Enough Island, something was moving on the ice. An otter, she decided. She should get her father's binoculars and watch him.

She quietly slipped out of her bed and into her parents' bedroom. They were still asleep. But by the window were the binoculars. She returned with them to her room.

At first she couldn't relocate the animal in the glare of ice. But then she found it. Maybe it wasn't an otter, after all. It was larger than an otter, for sure. And it had longer legs. It was running. Running towards her.

Her eyes began to tear up. She couldn't focus properly. She wiped her face. Yes, whatever it was, it was running. And it was black. It kept slipping and falling on the ice. But it was running towards her from the island. She closed her eyes and pinched herself to make sure she was awake. She had had dreams like this before. And always when she opened her eyes, she was alone, and the image was gone.

She re-opened her eyes. The pinch had hurt. She was awake. She put the binoculars to her eyes again.

It was him. The ice now stretched from Far Enough Island all the way to her shore. He was on his way home.

Sarah ran downstairs and on outside into the bright cold air. She yelled "Jeremiah!" out across the vast expanse of ice.

Then she heard the first bark. It was his unmistakable bark. She started to run toward him, out across the frozen yard, but she slipped and fell. Everything was covered with ice and it was almost impossible to take a step.

Her shout had awakened her father and mother. They were there beside her now, her father helping her up.

"He was there after all," her father said, his eyes fixed on the black animal still making his difficult way toward them across the ice. "He had made it to the island and he was too tired or injured for us to find him. And now that the inlet has froze up all the way to the island, he's coming back."

"Today is the day for all of us to smile," Sarah's mother said.

All three of them, still in their night clothes, began a slow slippery walk across the icy yard toward the inlet, toward Jeremiah. Sarah wanted to run, but her parents held her back. When they reached the wharf, there was Jeremiah, his feet going every which way as he scratched the ice to make his way home.

Sarah knelt down on the cold glassy surface and felt the hot, familiar breath of Jeremiah. She let him lick her face and bark loud as a cannon shot right in her ear.

With a lot of slipping and sliding, they all found their way back into the warm kitchen where Jeremiah was treated to all the leftover Christmas dinner he wanted.

And as soon as Sarah had calmed down enough to allow her brain half a chance to think, she realized by looking at her mother and her father and at Jeremiah that things were going to get better after this. It wouldn't matter if the fish never came back or if the money was tight or if the whole world froze solid. There would always be this moment that would make every one of them smile, any time of the year, long before Christmas.

On *the* Sea

by
IVAN TURGENEV
(1818–1883)

As Lewis Carroll's Alice would say, "Curiouser and curiouser!"
Turgenev's monkey seems to me the most likeable of crea-
tures. There is, by the way, a sort of tradition of literary mon-
keys (or, more gruesomely, monkey body-parts) that is strange-
ly connected to the sea. This seems to have originated with the
trade and transportation of these creatures by ship (often, pre-
sumably, for the purposes of vivisection and research). That is
(thankfully) not the case here; the monkey is travelling to its
new owner's home, and it's the poor creature's vulnerability,
and the sadness of her plight into the unknown, that makes this
small sketch such a curiously powerful piece of simple observa-
tion.

151

I was going from Hamburg to London in a small
steamer. We were two passengers; I and a little
female monkey, whom a Hamburg merchant was
sending as a present to his English partner.

She was fastened by a light chain to one of the seats on
deck, and was moving restlessly and whining in a little plaintive pipe like a bird's.

Every time I passed by her she stretched out her little,
black, cold hand, and peeped up at me out of her little
mournful, almost human eyes. I took her hand, and she
ceased whining and moving restlessly about.

There was a dead calm. The sea stretched on all sides like a
motionless sheet of leaden colour. It seemed narrowed and
small; and thick fog overhung it, hiding the very mast-tops in
cloud, and dazing and wearying the eyes with its soft obscurity. The sun hung, a dull red blur in this obscurity; but before
evening it glowed with strange, mysterious, lurid light.

Long, straight folds, like the folds in some heavy silken stuff,
passed one after another over the sea from the ship's prow, and
broadening as they passed, and wrinkling and widening, were
smoothed out again with a shake, and vanished. The foam

flew up, churned by the tediously thudding wheels; white as milk, with a faint hiss it broke up into serpentine eddies, and then melted together again and vanished too, swallowed up by the mist.

Persistent and plaintive as the monkey's whine rang the small bell at the stern.

From time to time a porpoise swam up, and with a sudden roll disappeared below the scarcely ruffled surface.

And the captain, a silent man with a gloomy, sunburnt face, smoked a short pipe and angrily spat into the dull, stagnant sea.

To all my inquiries he responded by a disconnected grumble. I was obliged to turn to my sole companion, the monkey.

I sat down beside her; she ceased whining, and again held out her hand to me.

The clinging fog oppressed us both with its drowsy dampness; and buried in the same unconscious dreaminess, we sat side by side like brother and sister.

I smile now...but then I had another feeling.

We are all children of one mother, and I was glad that the poor little beast was soothed and nestled so confidingly up to me, as to a brother.

The Waves
(early afternoon)

The waves broke and spread their waters swiftly over the shore. One after another they massed themselves and fell; the spray tossed itself back with the energy of their fall. The waves were steeped deep-blue save for a pattern of diamond-pointed light on their backs which rippled as the backs of great horses ripple with muscles as they move. The waves fell; withdrew and fell again, like the thud of a great beast stamping.

VW

Ebb Tide

by
L. ROSSITER
(1957–   )

I won't reveal by what circuitous route this story first made its way to my desk or, having found its way there, how it managed to rise to the top of its teetering pile. This accomplished, however, "Ebb Tide" drew me in as assuredly as Verna, the old crank at the centre of this story, is drawn to the coast. A fine story, gathering in power and momentum as it moves from Calgary to the shores of Vancouver Island.

It was a bitter November day and Verna dreaded the prospect of stepping back outside. Each day the cold seemed to find a new way into her bones. No matter how many layers she heaped onto her bulky body, it seeped into her marrow. The metal edges of Calgary sliced cleanly through her flesh.

She shifted heavily on the high stool and huddled deeper into her rumpled, greywash scarves. Her feet dangled like a child's, feeling for a rung on which to hook her toes. The current trend for cramped, over-priced coffee shops seemed to breed these cruelly designed stools. Once the pungent scent of the cafe had lured you in, the reality of the place did everything possible to hasten your exit.

Verna was aware of intrusive eyes, but she had half her coffee left and she wasn't leaving until it was done. She knew that her presence was unsettling. It was obvious when she picked her way down the aisle at the grocer's or sidled onto an occupied park bench. People would politely find an excuse to move away. It was as if she had become some kind of alien, the very hint of her existence vaguely disturbing. This seemed to happen all at once, but perhaps it had been a gradual evolution.

Today, two teenagers in great baggy jeans, whose sleeves dipped into their mugs, snickered when Verna had eased her way through the door. Who could blame them? She was certainly a sight. And, admittedly, she had been cleaner. When she slumped onto her stool, the smartly dressed couple next to her bristled. As if by accident, Verna leaned closer until they were compelled to move. Management asked if they could clear her cup. She said yes, but then, in a rash moment, she ordered another. This made her feel powerful.

As she sat facing the frosty window, her back warmed by the rich blanket of mountain grown, Verna grinned. Weeks ago, she had felt the first stirrings of it. She had felt foolish and light-headed and had dismissed the thought. Now, as she coddled her precious cup between trembling hands, Verna knew. It was time.

Back in her little room, Verna rifled through her depressingly small collection of belongings. She stuffed a bundle of old clothing, a shoebox of tattered letters and a large pill jar filled with shells and stones into her overnight bag. She had just enough money to get there. The rent on the tiny bedsit was minimal, and she'd only splurged now and then on a good cup of coffee. She glanced around. It was pitiful. This was the culmination of her life.

As she pulled herself up onto the bus, Adele, her one remaining friend, held out Verna's shabby bag. These past years, Adele felt that everything she thought she'd known about Verna had faded. Like a clear image on television slowly lost to a passing plane. Adele now believed that Verna was following a predetermined path, and that nothing she could say or do could alter that.

Verna grasped her bag and hefted herself onto the steps. When she reached the uniformed driver, she turned, smiled a strangely bright smile at Adele, then moved on down the aisle. Adele stared hard at the filthy windows, trying to get a final glimpse of Verna's face. A blast of diesel obliterated her last glance, and she walked away.

Once on the highway, the Greyhound lumbered toward the

mountains, settling into a steady, rocking rhythm. Tucked into a rumpled ball next to the window, Verna slipped in and out of memory. She drifted back to her mother's funeral where she had numbly served up sweet biscuits and old coffee. The ancient silver urn grumbled in the corner, churning out enough to appease the catty bats who had come to gawk and gossip. Her mother had not seen these wasps in years, yet here they swarmed to gulp and munch and finger the pristine china cups saved for just such an occasion. Verna gripped her stoneware mug and shambled though a haze of childhood mementos. Her biddy aunts clacked on, oblivious. She resolved never to provide for such an unnatural reunion.

After the wake, Verna had retreated briefly to the little cottage on the sea. Here her father once brought her exotic treasures, picked from the ragged shore that fronted the tiny summer house. He'd gather bits of coloured glass, rounded and dulled by the grinding sand, limpet shells or "Chinese hats," with which she could dress up the ends of her fingers, and minute pink crabs, preserved on the rocks when the tide pools receded. Rarely, he'd find the most precious treasure of all, a perfectly round glass float which had escaped the net of a Japanese fisherman. Tucked craftily into the folds of the sweeping bull kelp, even the shyest of them would be located. He'd hold out his huge cupped hand, then slowly reveal the surprise. Verna felt her throat constrict with unshed tears.

The bus bumped through the Rocky Mountains. Verna knew she should take one last look, but her neck, limp and overcooked by her scarves, bobbed back and forth on the headrest. Instead, she drifted. Her life, always kept so safely distant, now seemed to dog the churning wheels of the bus. She pressed her cheek against the cool window and closed her eyes.

The first time Stephen had asked her out, it was to a greasy spoon near the harbour. Verna's stomach, tightly wound around itself, could barely handle the aroma of her milky coffee. Stephen had urged her to eat something, anything, but Verna kept her eyes cast down into the fascinating swirls of her drink, rather than risk the fascinating swirls of his eyes.

Strangely, Verna summoned the nerve to return with Stephen to that cafe, this time graduating to a slice of lemon meringue pie. Stephen knew then that she would marry him.

Long after the "I do's," Verna would regularly lay awake into the small hours, staring in hunger at his face, pressed into the pillow beside her. No matter how badly she wanted to nestle there next to him, something would urge her away. Stephen, soft and gentle, was there so close, yet she was stranded on the other side of an invisible chasm. Each day Verna felt it grow wider.

Verna would slip out of bed and pad barefoot into the prickling night air. When she reached the water she would perch on her favourite rock, sipping from her father's little silver flask. The tide gently kissed its way around the hem of her nightdress. For hours at a time, she'd allow the sea to lap softly at her toes, and was always surprised by the warmth she felt at its touch.

The filtering dawn would prod her back to their home where she'd drift briefly into brandied sleep, her dreams carrying her over every minute detail of Stephen's body. Each morning when she awoke, her mouth dry and salty, she felt strangled by fear. But when Stephen's kind brown eyes would flutter open, she'd smile.

Through the years, Verna and Stephen dawdled over hundreds of morning coffees, their thoughts concealed behind two walls of newsprint. The world beyond their arborite breakfast table was abstracted into a single dimension of jarring headlines. The chasm taunted and beckoned to Verna between the gently rustling pages. Her throat chafed with captive screams and she feared her madness. Her compulsion to drift with the moonlit tide ceased to ease her. Verna's nightgown, always scented with seawater, now constricted around her like a huge, gloved fist. One day, after Stephen had left for work, Verna understood that she had to escape.

Bus travel made Verna nauseous and this journey was particularly arduous. Like a salmon returning, battered, to its spawning ground, driven solely by primordial instinct, she was equally compelled. Verna's limbs balked as she shifted over the lap of the man beside her and squeezed down the narrow aisle. The tiny washroom was not a good fit either. This bus was definitely a means to an end. Her head was clear and, despite the discomforts, she sighed. For the moment, she felt safe and relaxed.

She changed buses in Vancouver, trying not to panic in the stinking, crowded station. Once on the ferry she felt nearly home-free. The Strait of Georgia lay ahead, blue and serene. Verna made herself as small as possible against the brown vinyl seat. She tried to ignore the screaming children running up and down the aisles. A Chinese couple played cards next to her. The open water gave way to hummocks of evergreens and the ferry passed nearly close enough to scrape the stoney out-croppings of the gulf islands. Verna was shocked to find that these once untouched hideaways had fallen prey to develop-ers. The islands were now infiltrated by stylish homes and manicured lawns. People had to possess everything. Verna started sharply when the ship's horn blasted its way through Active Pass. She strained her eyes to get a glimpse of the cocky little harbour seals, but could see none. When Vancouver Island finally came into her view, Verna exhaled relief.

Initially, she was quite turned around. Nothing was as she'd remembered it. It was urban and fast and commercial. She was forced to ask for directions, and managed to catch a city bus to the outskirts of town. Eventually, Verna was able to get a ride up-island. Here the landscape became slightly more familiar, with its twisting, narrow road couched in fir trees and hobby farms. She found that the little community had expanded con-siderably, bustling with pottery studios and whole food cafes. It was a far cry from the rustic hamlet populated solely by hard-drinking loggers and their ragtag families.

The grey sky was close. Rain fell in a steady drizzle. The dri-ver worried when Verna requested he let her out in the middle of nowhere, but she convinced him to leave her. By some mira-cle, she located the start of the old path which had been ren-dered almost invisible. Ironically for Verna, this was the first time in years that she didn't feel lost. She stumbled her way down the trail which was nearly concealed by a dense net of salal and bracken. As she crashed toward the ocean, the undergrowth eased its grip on the path. After such a long, uncomfortable trip she was surprised at the comparative lightness with which she could now move. Her joints were almost lubricated by their pain. She paused, closing her eyes for a moment. Her body's memory could navigate without her. She could taste the breath of the ocean on her tongue. Although her skin sucked at her cold wet clothing, Verna stumbled onward.

When the trees finally cleared, she could just barely see it. It was nearly collapsed with rot. Like a barnacle on the hull of a rusting ship, the softening shell of her cottage had steadfastly defied years of punishing coastal storms. The wood was black and moist, the tarpaper roof buckled with moss and fallen branches. Bits of plastic patching had been added here and there, probably by wandering hikers stopping over for a night. Through the shaggy, grey-green curtain of old man's beard, Verna's eyes burned, her breath shallow.

She approached the cottage as if she was afraid it would startle and spring off into the woods. There was no doorknob on the tilting door, and she had to shoulder it open with a firm push. She stepped forward, inhaling the sudden rush of images that had, for decades, been locked tightly inside. She stood, frozen. The stinging salt-sea welled from her eyes. The interior room was a shambles of broken furniture and peeling walls. She stared intently, seeing the face of a lost friend, deeply aged yet still familiar. Verna caressed the decrepit walls and fingered the slivering windowsill. It was vaguely discoloured from the overwatered plants which once occupied it. After here, Verna had given up raising plants.

Engorged slugs clung to the filigreed windowpane. It was surprising, with the air so steeped in salt, that the fleshy, slime-slickered creatures could ever exist here. Verna gazed absently through their mucous trails and huddled deeper into her scarves and heavy plaid jacket. Her hands were mottled with stubborn circulation. Her cropped hair, clotted with sea air, was doused by a weighty woolen turban. *Klee Wyck*. A passing resemblance.

That one glorious summer, the only summer during her marriage that she'd allowed herself to return, she had brought Stephen. After surveying the little house in its creeping decrepitude, Stephen had insisted that he replace that old windowpane. The original glass was poor quality, rippled and warped—you couldn't get a proper view. He had set the new pane so carefully, laying in the putty just so, when with the one final tap of the hammer, a tiny crack exploded in the corner. Enraged, he pounded his fist on the sill. She laughed and told him that the glass would forever hold his signature. Now, as she strained to see the Pacific through the filthy window, Stephen's name remained etched in that glass. Her eyes traced it over and over again. Her heart still ached.

The late November wind urged the cedars surrounding the cabin into a reluctant, creaking rhythm. Verna believed that the elephant-skin bark of these ancient coastal trees etched the stories of their lifetime. Much as her own creased and sagging skin was imprinted by the pain and pleasures of her years.

Exhaustion seeped through her. She realised that she hadn't eaten since leaving Calgary, how many days ago? Verna shuffled toward the corner and lowered herself onto a tattered cot. After rummaging through her sodden bag, she produced a sweaty cheddar cheese sandwich wrapped snugly in plastic. Adele had insisted that she pack a thermos of coffee which Verna had resisted drinking on the bus. She had wanted to avoid that trip to the bathroom as much as possible. Now she unscrewed the lid and poured the black liquid into the cup. She rolled the dry sandwich around in her cheek and took a gulp of the cold coffee. It tasted fine. Verna shifted carefully to avoid the cot's protruding springs and gently lay down. She burrowed into the deepest sleep she'd had in years.

When she finally stirred, Verna had no idea for how many hours or days she had slept. Here, her past and present all melded together in the moment. The relentless thrum of the ocean had an hypnotic effect on her, and she drifted with its hush, drugged and drowsy. She now felt as stiff as she'd ever been. The fog clung heavily outside the walls, nosing at the window. She half-smiled to herself, remembering how

Calgarians would justify that their cold was somehow superior to the coastal chill. "Well it's a dry cold, eh?" To Verna, this damp that now permeated her every pore felt infinitely less bitter than the relentless prairie wind.

She felt around in her bag and withdrew another ghastly turban which she squashed onto her head. She had never cared about appearances. That was part of what turned her invisible. Verna's bunions throbbed through two pairs of damp, unwashed socks, crammed into cheap running shoes. She raised herself slowly, and made her way to the door of the shack. The floorboards exhaled wet rot under her gnarled feet.

With all the strength she could muster, Verna pried open the door and stepped out onto the mossy welcome mat. She pressed her toes down into it. Everything here was soft and wet as her flesh. Verna thought it must be evening as the greyfog sky had closed in around her. She scratched about and found a sturdy stick which was still young and firm enough to bear the burden of her weight. With painfully slow progress, Verna inched her way down the narrow, darkening trail to the sea.

She reached the clearing and carefully picked her way over the slippery black rocks and scattered logs. She crouched down, which hurt her knees, and slid partway to the gravelly beach. She shook her head as she remembered how easily she had navigated this terrain as a child. Now, it must have taken her an hour or more to come this short way from the cottage. Completely worn, Verna had to stop and get her breath. She groped through the damp folds of her pockets and found the pill jar. Verna unscrewed the lid and emptied the contents onto the beach. After years in captivity, the little stones and bits of glass gratefully blended with others of their kind until Verna was unable to tell them apart. She dropped the bottle and pressed her rounded spine against a hard pillow of granite. She tipped her head back, allowing dusk to settle wetly on her face.

Verna dizzily traced the action of the massive, sweeping seagulls tossing across the sky. A splash of vermilion lit the end of their yellow beaks, their pristine grey and white plumage glinting as they combed and plundered the seascape. Verna admired their impudence. Not scavengers, but opportunists. She closed her eyes so she could absorb their calls. Lusty and vigorous, she could feel them slicing the sky above her.

Drunk with the elixir of sky and sea and wind, Verna's breath came hoarse and rapid, her chest swelling. Her parched lungs thirstily drew the salt air deeper and deeper until they threatened to burst. Her eyes squeezed tightly shut. With a jolt, her mouth opened wide, cracking its corners. Verna screamed. She screamed and screamed as loud a scream as she had in her. It shook frighteningly from deep inside—a twisted, orgiastic, joyous noise that blended and swirled with the wildness around her. The wind lifted her ragged voice, rolling it over the slick grey rocks, above the surging current. The sound was carried aloft, borne past the startled eagles nesting at the top of the giant cedar, then gently, softly, Verna's plaintive lament was set down and released, like petals of sweetly whispered music.

A crevice of sunlight tickled the ragged little beach. A silent lover, the tide had come and gone in the night. It had swept tidepools clean, leaving fresh offerings, like St. Nicholas exchanging the milk and cookies of tiny believers for sparkling boxes festooned with tinsel and wonder. Driftwood, from the smallest splinter to the mammoth root of an upturned cedar, landscaped the rocks, snagging wreaths of unresisting seaweed. Miniscule sea creatures ensnared with the slick licorice ribbons of kelp waited, unseen, for the next turn of tide to release them back to the sea.

The shrieking laughter of herring gulls pierced the daylight. Swooping and diving, they plucked shimmering fish from the shallows. The seabreeze gently prodded at bits of bark and plantlife deposited on the beach by the exiting night tide.

Sheathed in a tumble of rope and weed and scarves and seawash, nestled for a brief moment on this beach, lay a perfect, luminescent globe of green glass, released from a fisherman's net half a world away.

Deadman

by

E. ANNIE PROULX

(1935–   )

It is a truth universally acknowledged that E. Annie Proulx accomplished something quite out of the ordinary with The Shipping News, *her novel of Newfoundland life. "Deadman" is an extract from it, and there are a few things you should know: 1) Quoyle is a journalist writing for the local rag:* The Gammy Bird. *He writes a regular column known as "The Shipping News." 2) Petal, Quoyle's errant wife, was earlier killed in a car crash: thus Quoyle's nightmares. 3) Finally as Quoyle learns, there is meaning in the making of knots. Enjoy.*

"Deadman—An 'Irish pennant,' a loose end hanging
about the sails or rigging."
THE MARINER'S DICTIONARY

T he end of September, tide going out, moon in its last quarter. The first time Quoyle had been alone at the green house. The aunt was in St. John's for the weekend buying buttons and muslin. Bunny and Sunshine had howled to stay with Dennis and Beety for Marty's birthday.

"She's my best friend, Dad. I wish she was my sister," Bunny said passionately. "Please please please let us stay." And in the Flying Squid Gift & Lunchstop she chose a ring made from pearly shell for Marty's present, a sheet of spotted tissue for wrapping.

Quoyle came across the bay in his scorned boat on Friday afternoon with a bag of groceries, two six-packs of beer. All of his notes and the typewriter. A stack of books on nineteenth-century shipping regulations and abuses. In the kitchen, stooped to put the beer in the ice cooler under the sink, then thought of ice. He'd meant to get some, but the empty cooler was still empty, still in the boat. It didn't matter. In the evening he drank the beer as it was, scribbled by the light of the gas lamp.

On Saturday Quoyle stumped around the underfurnished

rooms; dusty air seemed to wrinkle as he moved through it. He split wood until lunch; beer, two cans of sardines and a can of lima beans. In the afternoon he worked at the kitchen table, started on the first draft, banging the keys, swearing when his fingers jammed between them, writing about Samuel Plimsoll and his line.

"FOR GOD'S SAKE, HELP ME"

Everybody has seen the Plimsoll lines or loading marks on vessels. They mark the safe load each ship can carry.

These loading marks came about because of a single concerned individual, Samuel Plimsoll, elected MP from Derby in 1868. Plimsoll fought for the safety of seamen in a time when unscrupulous shipowners deliberately sent overloaded old ships to sea. Plimsoll's little book, *Our Seamen*, described bad vessels so heavily laden with coal or iron their decks were awash. They knew the crews would drown. They did it for the insurance.

Overloading was the major cause of thousands of wrecks each year. Plimsoll begged for a painted load line on all ships, begged that no ship be allowed, under any circumstances, to leave port unless the line was distinctly visible.

He wrote directly to his readers. "Do you doubt these statements? Then, for God's sake—oh, for God's sake, help me to get a Royal Commission to inquire into their truth!" Powerful shipping interests fought him every inch of the way.

When he stopped the evening was closing in again. Cooked two pounds of shrimp in olive oil and garlic, sucked the meat from the shells. Went down to the dock in the twilight with the last beer, enduring the mosquitoes, watching the lights of Killick-Claw come on. The lighthouses on the points stuttering.

The Old Hag came in the night, saddled and bridled Quoyle. He dreamed again he was on the nightmare highway.

A tiny figure under a trestle stretched imploring arms. Petal, torn and bloody. Yet so great was his speed he was carried past. The brakes did not work when he tramped them. He woke for a few minutes, straining his right foot on the dream brake, his neck wet with anxious sweat. The wind moaned through the house cables, a sound that invoked a sense of hopeless abandonment. But he pulled the sleeping bag corner over his upper ear and slept again. Getting used to nightmares.

By Sunday noon the Plimsoll piece was in shape and he needed a walk. Had never been out to the end of the point. As he pulled the door to behind him a length of knotted twine fell from the latch. He picked it up and put it in his pocket. Then down along the shore and toward the extremity of land.

Climbed over rocks as big as houses, dropping down their sides into damp rooms with seaweed floors. The stones clenched lost nets, beaten into hairy frazzles of mussel shells and seaweed. Gulls flew up from tidal pools. The rock was littered with empty crab shells still wet with rust-colored body fluids. The shoreline narrowed to cliff. He could go no further that way.

So, backtracked, climbed up to the heather that covered the slope like shriveled wigs. Deep-gullied stone. Followed caribou paths up onto the tongue of granite that thrust into the sea. To his right the blue circle of Omaloor Bay, on the left the rough shore that reeled miles away to Misky Bay. Ahead of him the open Atlantic.

His boots rang on the naked stone. Stumbled on juniper roots embedded in fissures, saw veins of quartz like congealed lightning. The slope was riddled with gullies and rises, ledges and plateaus. Far ahead he saw a stone cairn; wondered who had made it.

It took half an hour to reach this tower, and he walked around it. Thrice the height of a man, the stones encrusted with lichens. Built a long time ago. Perhaps by the ancient Beothuks, extinct now, slain for sport by bored whalers and cod killers. Perhaps a marker for Basque fishermen or wrecker Quoyles luring vessels onto the rocks with false lights. The booming thunge of sea drew him on.

At last the end of the world, a wild place that seemed poised on the lip of the abyss. No human sign, nothing, no ship, no plane, no animal, no bird, no bobbing trap marker nor buoy. As though he stood alone on the planet. The immensity of sky roared at him and instinctively he raised his hands to keep it off. Translucent thirty-foot combers the color of bottles crashed onto stone, coursed bubbles into a churning lake of milk shot with cream. Even hundreds of feet above the sea the salt mist stung his eyes and beaded his face and jacket with fine droplets. Waves struck with the hollowed basso peculiar to ovens and mouseholes.

He began to work down the slant of rock. Wet and slippery. He went cautiously, excited by the violence, wondering what it would be like in a storm. The tide still on the ebb in that complex swell and fall of water against land, as though a great heart in the center of the earth beat but twice a day.

These waters, thought Quoyle, haunted by lost ships, fishermen, explorers gurgled down into sea holes as black as a dog's throat. Bawling into salt broth. Vikings down the cracking winds, steering boats, breathing, breathing, rhythmic suck of frigid air, iced paddles spiraling down. Millennial bergs from the glaciers, morbid, silent except for waves breaking on their flanks, the deceiving sound of shoreline where there was no shore. Foghorns, smothered gun reports along the coast. Ice welding land to sea. Frost smoke. The glare of ice erasing dimension, distance, subjecting senses to mirage and illusion. A rare place.

As Quoyle descended, he slipped on the treacherous weed, clung to the rock. Reached a shelf where he could stand and crane, glimpse the maelstrom below. Could go no further.

He saw three things: a honeycomb of caves awash; a rock in the shape of a great dog; a human body in a yellow suit, head under the surface as though delighted in patterns of the sea bottom. Arms and legs spread out like a starfish, the body slid in and out of a small cave, a toy on a string tugged by the sea. Newspaper Reporter Seems Magnet for Dead Men.

There was no way down to the body unless he leaped into the foam. If he had brought a rope and grapnel... He began to

climb back up the cliff. It struck him the man might have fall-
en from where he now climbed. Yet more likely from a boat.
Tell someone.

Up on the headland again he ran. His side aching. Tell
someone about the dead man. When he reached the house it
would take still another hour to drive around the bay to the
RCMP station. Faster in the boat. The wind at his back swept
his hair forward so that the ends snapped at his eyes. At first
he felt the cold on his neck, but as he trotted over the rock he
flushed with heat and had to unzip his jacket. A long time to
get to the dock.

Caught in the urgency of it, that yellow corpse shuttling in
and out, he cast free and set straight across the bay for Killick-
Claw. As though there were still a chance to save the man. In
ten minutes, as he moved out of the shelter of the lee shore
and into the wind, he knew he'd made a mistake.

Had never had his boat in such rough water. The swells
came at him broadside from the mouth of the bay, crests like
cruel smiles. The boat rolled, rose up, dropped with sickening
speed into the troughs. Instinctively he changed course, taking
the waves at an angle on his bow. But now he was headed for a
point northeast of Killick-Claw. Somewhere he would have to
turn and make an east-southeast run for the harbor. In his
inexperience Quoyle did not understand how to tack a zigzag
across the bay, a long run with the wind and waves on his bow
and then a short leg with the wind on his quarter. Halfway
across he made a sudden turn toward Killick-Claw, presented
his low, wide stern to the swell.

The boat wallowed about and a short length of line slid out
from under the seat. It was knotted at one end, kinked and
crimped at the other as if old knots had finally been untied.
For the first time Quoyle got it—there was meaning in the
knotted strings.

The boat pitched and plunged headlong, the bow digging
into the loud water while the propellor raced. Quoyle was
frightened. Each time, he lost the rudder and the boat yawed.
In a few minutes his voyage ended. The bow struck like an
axe, throwing the stern high. At once a wave seized, threw the

boat broadside to the oncoming sea. It broached. Capsized. And Quoyle was flying under water.

In fifteen terrifying seconds he learned to swim well enough to reach the capsized boat and grasp the stilled propeller shaft. His weight pulled one side of the upturned stern down and lifted the bow a little, enough to catch an oncoming wave that twisted the boat, turned it over and filled it. Quoyle, tumbling through the transparent sea again, saw the pale boat below him, sinking, drifting casually down, the familiar details of its construction and paint becoming indistinct as it passed into the depths.

He came to the surface gasping, half blinded by some hot stuff in his eyes, and saw bloody water drip.

"Stupid," he thought, "stupid to drown with the children so small." No life jackets, no floating oars, no sense. Up he rose on a swell, buoyed by body fat and a lungful of air. He was floating. A mile and a half from either shore Quoyle was floating in the cold waves. The piece of knotted twine drifted in front of him and about twenty feet away a red box bobbed— the plastic cooler for the ice he'd forgotten. He thrashed to the cooler through a flotilla of wooden matches that must have fallen into the boat from the grocery bag. He remembered buying them. Guessed they would wash up on shore someday, tiny sticks with the heads washed away. Where would he be?

He gripped the handles of the cooler, rested his upper breast on the cover. Blood from his forehead or hairline but he didn't dare let go of the box to reach up and touch the wound. He could not remember being struck. The boat must have caught him as it went over.

The waves seemed mountainous but he rose and fell with them like a chip, watched for the green curlers that shoved him under, the lifting sly crests that drove saltwater into his nose.

The tide had been almost out when he saw the dead man, perhaps two hours ago. It must be on the turn now. His watch was gone. But wasn't there an hour or so of slack between low water and the turn of the tide? He knew little about the currents in the bay. The moon in its last quarter meant the smaller neap tide. There were, Billy said, complex waters along the west side, shoals and reefs and grazing sunkers. He feared the wind would force him five miles up to the narrows and then out to sea, heading for Ireland on a beer cooler. If only he were nearer to the west shore, the lee shore, where the water was smoother and he might kick his way toward the rock.

A long time passed, hours, he thought. He could not feel his legs. When he rose high on the waves he tried to gauge where he was. The west shore seemed nearer now, but despite the wind and incoming tide, he was moving toward the end of the point.

Later he was surprised to glimpse the cairn he had walked around that morning. Must be in some rip current that was carrying him along the shore toward land's end, toward the caves, toward the dead man. Ironic if he ended up sliding in and out of a booming water cave, companion to the man in yellow.

"Not while I have this hot box," he said aloud, for he had begun to think the red cooler was filled with glowing charcoal. He deduced it because when he raised his chin from the cover his jaw chattered uncontrollably, and when he rested it back against the box the chattering ceased. Only a wonderful heat could have that effect.

He was surprised to see it was almost dusk. In a way he was glad, because it meant he could go to bed soon and get some sleep. He was tremendously tired. The rising and falling billows would be deliciously soft to sink into. This was something he'd worked out. He didn't know why he hadn't thought of it before, but the yellow man was not dead. Sleeping. Resting. And in a minute Quoyle thought he would roll over too and get some sleep. As soon as they shut the lights out. But the hard light was shining directly into his swollen eyes and Jack Buggit was wrenching him from the hot box and onto a pile of cod fish.

"Jesus Cockadoodle Christ! I *knowed* somebody was out here. Felt it." He threw a tarpaulin over Quoyle.

"I told you that damn thing would drown you. How long you been in the water? Couldn't be too long, boy, can't live in this too long."

But Quoyle couldn't answer. He was shaking so hard his heels drummed on the fish. He tried to tell Jack to get the hot box so he could get warm again, but his jaw wouldn't work.

Jack half-dragged him, half-shoved him into Mrs. Buggit's perfect kitchen. "Here's Quoyle I fished out of the bloody drink," he said.

"If you knew how many Jack has saved," she said. "How many." All but one. She got Quoyle's clothes off, laid hot-water bottles on his thighs and wrapped a blanket around him. She made a mug of steaming tea and forced spoonsful of it between his teeth with the swift competence of practice. Jack mumbled a cup of rum would do more good.

In twenty minutes his jaw was loose enough and his mind firm enough to choke out the sinking of the boat, the illusion of the hot box, to take in details of the Buggit domicile. To have a second cup of tea loaded with sugar and evaporated milk.

"That's a nice oolong," said Mrs. Buggit. Rum couldn't come near it for saving grace.

Everything in the house tatted and doilied in the great art of the place, designs of lace waves and floe ice, whelk shells and sea wrack, the curve of lobster feelers, the round knot of cod-eye, the bristled commas of shrimp and fissured sea caves, white snow on black rock, pinwheeled gulls, the slant of silver rain. Hard, tortured knots encased picture frames of ancestors and anchors, the Bible was fitted with sheets of ebbing foam, the clock's face peered out like a bride's from a wreath of worked wildflowers. The knobs of the kitchen dresser sported tassels like a stripper in a bawd house, the kettle handle knitted over in snake-ribs, the easy chairs wore archipelagoes of thread and twine flung over the reefs of arms and backs. On a shelf a 1961 Ontario phone book.

Mrs. Buggit stood against the Nile green wall, moved forward to the stove to refill the kettle, her hands like welded scoops. Great knobby knuckles and scarred fingers. The boiling water gushing into the teapot. Mrs. Buggit was bare armed in a cotton dress. The house breathed tropical heat and the torpor of comfort.

She had a voice built up from calling into the wind and stating strong opinions. In this house Jack shrank to the size of a doll, his wife grew enormous in the waxy glitter and cascade of flowers. She searched Quoyle's face as though she had known him once. His teeth clattered less against the mug. The shudders that had racked him from neck to arch eased.

"You'll warm," she said, though she herself could not, coming at him with a hot brick for his feet. A mottled, half-grown dog stirred on the mat, cocked her ears briefly.

Jack, like many men who spend their days in hard physical labor, went slack when he sat in an easy chair, sprawled and spread as if luxury jellied his muscles.

"It was your build there, all that fat, y'know, that's what insulated you all them hours, kept you floating. A thin man would of died."

Then Quoyle remembered the yellow man and told his story again, beginning with the walk on the point and ending with the light in his eyes.

"At the ovens?" Jack went to the telephone in a wedge of space under the stairs to call the Coast Guard. Quoyle sat, his ears ringing. Mrs. Buggit was talking to him.

"People with glasses don't get on with dogs," she said. "A dog has to see your eyes clear to know your heart. A dog will wait for you to smile, he'll wait a month if need be."

"The Newfoundland dog," said shuddering Quoyle, still weak with the lassitude of drowning.

"The Newfoundland dog! The Newfoundland dog isn't in it. That's not the real dog of this place. The real dog, the best dog in the world that ever was, is the water dog. This one here, Batch, is part water dog, but the pure ones all died out. They were all killed generations ago. Ask Jack, he'll tell you about it. Though Jack's a cat man. It's me as likes the dogs. Batch is from Billy Pretty's Elvis. Jack's got his cat, you know, Old Tommy, goes out in the boat with him. Just as good a fisherman."

And at last, Billy Pretty and Tert Card told, the Coast Guard informed of the yellow man, Quoyle's tea mug emptied. Jack went down to the stage to clean and ice his fish. Had saved, now let the wife restore.

Quoyle followed Mrs. Buggit up to the guest room. She handed him the replenished hot-water bottles.

"You want to go to Alvin Yark for the next one," she said.

Before he fell asleep he noticed a curious pleated cylinder near the door. It was the last thing he saw.

In the morning, ravenous with hunger, euphoric with life, he saw the cylinder was a doorstop made from a mail-order catalog, a thousand pages folded down and glued, and imagined Mrs. Buggit working at it day after winter day while the wind shaved along the eaves and the snow fell, while the fast ice of the frozen bay groaned and far to the north the frost smoke writhed. And still she patiently folded and pasted, folded and pasted, the kettle steaming on the stove, obscuring the windows. As for Quoyle, the most telling memento of his six-hour swim were his dark blue toenails, dyed by his cheap socks.

And when her house was empty again, Quoyle gone and the teapot scalded and put away on the shelf, the floor mopped, she went outside to hang Quoyle's damp blanket, to take in yesterday's forgotten, drenty wash. Although it was still soft September, the bitter storm that took Jesson boiled around her. Eyes blinked from the glare; stiff fingers pulled at the legs of Jack's pants, scraped the fur of frost growing out of the blue blouse. Then inside again to fold and iron, but always in earshot the screech of raftering ice beyond the point, the great bergs toppling with the pressure, the pans rearing hundreds of feet high under the white moon and cracking, cracking asunder.

The Wreck

by
GUY DE MAUPASSANT
(1850–1893)

"The Wreck" begins with a simple premise: a shipwreck near to shore. The situation seems simple enough, then becomes slowly more peculiar, and more peculiar still. You settle in, thinking yourself secure…and then, suddenly—cruelly— comes the plunge and twist of the Maupassant knife…

esterday, December 31st, I had been dining with my old friend, Georges Garin, when the servant brought him a letter covered with seals and foreign stamps. Georges said: "Do you mind if I read it?"

"Of course not!"

He began to read, eight pages criss-crossed in a sprawling English hand. He read slowly and carefully with an attention that suggested some sentimental interest. At last he put the letter down on a corner of the chimney-piece and said: "This letter recalls a curious incident, that I've never told you, an incident that genuinely moved me—and it's quite true. I had an odd New Year's Day that year. It must be twenty years ago, for I was thirty at the time and I'm fifty now.

"In those days I was an inspector in the Maritime Insurance Company, of which I am Managing Director to-day. I was intending to spend the New Year holiday in Paris, for there is a general conspiracy to regard New Year's Day as a holiday, when I got a letter from the manager telling me to start at once for the Île de Ré, where a three-masted schooner from Saint-Nazaire, insured with us, had been wrecked. It was eight o'clock in the morning. I went to the office to get my instructions and that evening I caught the express which put me down at La Rochelle next morning, December 31st.

"I had two hours to wait for the *Jean-Guiton*, the boat to the island; so I strolled round the town. La Rochelle is an unusual town, full of character, with its labyrinth of narrow alleys. The pavements run under interminable galleries, arcaded galleries like those in the Rue de Rivoli. The galleries and their arches are low and stunted, breathing mystery; they look as if they had been originally built, and had remained ever since, as hiding places for conspirators. They are the striking setting of the wars of past ages, those wars of religion, so heroic and so pitiless. It is an old Huguenot town, unobtrusively solid, without any out-standing artistic gems like those wonderful monuments which are the glory of Rouen; but its whole appearance is stern with a suggestion too of cunning, a city of stubborn fighters, a home of fanatics, where the mystical faith of the Calvinists flourished and the conspiracy of the Three Sergeants* was hatched.

"After wandering round these interesting streets for some time I went on board the little steamer, broad in the beam and dirty, which was to take me to the Île de Ré. She puffed asth-matically as she steamed between the two ancient towers guarding the harbour, crossed the roadstead and made her way out past the mole built by Richelieu, the huge stones of which can be seen at water level and which encircles the town like a great necklace; then she turned to the right.

"It was one of those thick heavy days, which stifle the brain and chill the heart and sap all strength and energy, a grey day, bitterly cold, under a pall of dense mist, as drenching as rain, icy, and poisonous to breathe like the fumes from a sewer.

"Under a ceiling of low, threatening fog, the muddy sea, quite shallow here and thick with sand from the miles of beaches, was flat calm; no movement, not a sign of life in the oily, soupy, stagnant water. The *Jean-Guiton* steamed along, rolling slightly from habit, cutting through the glassy, opaque

---

* These men were members of the 4th Regiment of the Line, affiliated to the Carbonari of Italy; they sought to spread revolutionary doctrines and were executed in Paris in 1822, where their tomb can still be seen.

sheet of water, leaving in her wake a few waves, a few splashes, a few undulations which soon disappeared.

"I began to chat with the skipper, a short man with practically no legs, as round as his ship with a roll like hers. I was anxious to get a few facts about the accident that I was going to investigate.

"A great square-rigged three-master from Saint-Nazaire, the *Marie-Joseph*, had run aground on a stormy night on the sands of the Île de Ré. 'The hurricane had driven the ship so far up the sand,' wrote the owner, 'that it had been impossible to refloat her and they had had to clear everything movable out of her as quickly as possible.' My job was to investigate her condition before the stranding and decide whether adequate steps had been taken to refloat her. I was there as the company's agent in order to be able to correct from personal observation the owner's statements when the matter came into court. On receipt of my report the director would take such steps as he might consider necessary to safeguard our interests.

"The skipper of the *Jean-Guiton* knew all about the incident, having been called in, with his boat, to assist in the attempts at salvage.

"He told me what had happened. It was quite simple; the *Marie-Joseph* had been caught by a violent squall and had lost her bearings in the darkness in clouds of flying spray—'The sea had been like milk soup' was how the captain put it—and she had run aground on one of those huge sand-banks which at low tide make the coast hereabouts look like the Sahara desert.

"As we talked, I was looking round and ahead. Between the sea and the lowering sky there was a luminous streak visible on the horizon. I asked: 'Is that the Île de Ré?'

"'Yes, Sir.'"

"And suddenly the skipper, pointing straight ahead, showed me a speck only just distinguishable, surrounded by water, and said: 'Look! There's your boat!'

"'You mean the *Marie-Joseph*?'

"'Yes, of course!'

"I was amazed. This almost invisible black speck, which I should have taken for a reef, appeared to me to be at least two miles from the shore. I went on: 'But, Captain, there must be a hundred fathoms of water at the spot you indicate.'

"He began to laugh: 'A hundred fathoms, my dear Sir! Not two fathoms, I assure you.' He was a Bordeaux man and he continued: 'It's just high water, 9.40. You go out for a walk on the sands with your hands in your pockets after lunch at the Dauphin Hotel, and I promise you that at 2.50 or three o'clock at latest you'll reach the wreck without getting your feet wet, my dear Sir. You can stay there for an hour and three-quarters or two hours—don't stay any longer or you'll be caught. The further the tide goes out, the faster it comes back. This coast is as flat as a bug. Start back at 4.50—take my word for it. Then come aboard the *Jean-Guiton* at half past seven and you'll be on the quay at La Rochelle the same evening.'

"I thanked the captain and went and sat down in the fore-part of the ship to watch the little town of Saint-Martin, which we were rapidly approaching.

"It was just like the rest of the miniature harbours which serve as capitals to all the small islands scattered along the coasts of continents. It was a large fishing village, with one foot in the sea and one on land; it lived on fish and poultry, vegetables and shell-fish, radishes and mussels. The island is very low-lying with only a small area under cultivation but the population seems large; I did not, however, go any distance inland.

"After lunch I crossed a small headland and then, as the tide was going out fast, I set off across the sands towards a sort of black projection rising out of the water at some distance.

"I walked fast across the sandy flat, which was resilient like human flesh and seemed to exude moisture under foot. The sea had been there a moment earlier and now I saw it disappearing in the distance and I could no longer distinguish the line between sand and water. It was like being the spectator of some supernatural transformation scene on a gigantic scale. A moment before the Atlantic had been in front of me and now it had been swallowed up in the sand like scenery disappearing down a trap-door on the stage, and I was walking in the middle of a desert. All I could still detect was the tang of salt water in my nostrils. I could smell the sea-weed, the scent of the sea waves and the strong kindly tang of the land. I walked fast and no longer felt cold; I kept my eyes on the wreck, which grew larger as I approached and now resembled a huge stranded whale.

"She seemed to be rising out of the ground, towering to a surprising height above the boundless sandy flat all round. After an hour's walk I reached her. She was lying on her side, burst open and shattered; her broken ribs of tarred wood were visible with huge nails sticking in them. The sand had already got into her, infiltrating through the cracks; it had gripped and mastered her and would never let her go. She now seemed rooted in the sand. The fore-part had sunk deep into the soft treacherous bank, while the stern stuck up and seemed to be raising to heaven a desperate cry for help, shouting the two words of her name, *Marie-Joseph*, painted white on the black timbers.

"I climbed on to the corpse of the boat where the side was lowest and, reaching the deck, made my way inside her. The hatches had been stove in and let in light, which also penetrated through the holes in her sides, and I could dimly see long dark passages full of broken woodwork. There was nothing else in her except sand, which formed the floor of this tunnel of planking.

"I started to make notes on the condition of the boat. I had sat down on an empty broken cask and I was writing by the light from a big hole through which I could see the boundless expanse of beach. The cold and the loneliness sent a strange shiver through me from time to time and I stopped writing at intervals to listen to vague mysterious noises from the wreck; crabs were scratching the planking with their crooked claws and there were the sounds of the thousand tiny sea-creatures which had already found their way into this corpse, and also the low regular tap of the borer with its ceaseless gnawing, a grating sound like a gimlet boring into and devouring all the rotting woodwork.

"Suddenly I heard human voices quite close to me. I jumped up as if expecting to see a ghost. I genuinely believed for a moment that I was about to see the apparitions of two of the drowned men, who would tell me the story of their death. It certainly did not take me long to pull myself up on the deck. There I saw standing in front of the bows of the ship a tall gentleman with three girls, or rather a tall Englishman with three equally English daughters. They were certainly more frightened than I, when they saw a figure shoot up from below on the deserted ship. The youngest girl ran away; the two others clung tightly to their father, whose open mouth was his only sign of surprise. After a few seconds he said in atrocious French: 'Are you the owner of this boat, Sir?'

"'Yes, Sir!'

"'Can I go over it?'

"'Certainly, Sir!'

"Then he spoke a long sentence in English, in which the only word I could make out was 'gracious,' several times repeated.

"As he was looking for somewhere to climb on board, I showed him the best place and gave him a hand up; when he had clambered up, we helped the three girls, who had got over their fear, on to the deck. They were charming, especially the eldest, a fair girl of eighteen, with the dainty fresh loveliness of a flower.

"She spoke French a little better than her father and acted as interpreter. I had to give a detailed account of the shipwreck; I invented all the little details as if I had been there. After that the whole family made their way down into the bowels of the boat. As soon as they got down into the long dim passage, they uttered cries of astonishment and admiration; and in no time the father and the three girls had pulled out sketch-books from the pockets of their loose water-proofs and started to make pencil drawings of this strange grim place.

"They were sitting side by side on a projecting beam and the four sketch-books supported on eight knees were soon covered with little black lines meant to represent the gaping hold of the *Marie-Joseph*.

"As they worked, the eldest of the girls kept up a conversation with me, while I continued my inspection of the skeleton of the boat.

"I discovered that they were spending the winter at Biarritz and had come to the Île de Ré on purpose to see this schooner buried in the sand. They had none of the usual English stand-offishness, these folk, they were just plain simple souls, a bit mad, belonging to the class of travellers from England whom one meets all over the world. The father was tall and spare, with a florid face framed in white whiskers, an animated sand-wich in fact, just a slice of ham cut to the shape of a head between two pads of white hair. The lanky girls held them-selves well, like young wading birds, and were slim like their father, except the eldest; all three were attractive, particularly the eldest. She had such an amusing way of speaking, telling stories, laughing, understanding or failing to understand, rais-ing her eyes, which were as blue as the depths of the sea, to ask some question, pausing in her drawing to guess, going back to her work and saying 'yes' or 'no,' that I could have stayed indefinitely listening to her and watching her. Suddenly she whispered: 'I can hear something moving gently in the boat.'

"I listened and immediately heard a low, mysterious, contin-uous sound. What could it be? I got up and went to look out of one of the holes in the side and uttered a loud cry. The tide had come back and we should be cut off in no time.

"We rushed on deck but it was already too late; the sea was all round us and the tide was running towards the shore with increasing speed. It was not running, it was gliding, creeping, spreading out like some gigantic ink-blot. As yet there were only a few inches of water over the sand, but the front line of the tide had already passed far beyond us in its imperceptible onward march.

"The Englishman was anxious to start back at once, but I restrained him; escape was no longer possible owing to the deep pools, which we had had to go round on our way out and into which we should have fallen on our way back.

"We felt a sudden chill of fear in our hearts. But the little English girl began to smile and said: 'Now it's we who are shipwrecked!'

"I tried to smile but fear choked me, a cowardly overmaster-ing panic, as base and sneaking as the tide itself. I realized all at once the danger we were in and I wanted to shout for help;

but there was no one to hear.

"The two younger English girls were clinging to their father, whose terrified gaze was fixed on the expanse of the water all round. Night was falling as quickly as the water was rising, and the darkness was oppressive, damp and ice-cold. I said: 'We can do nothing but stay on the boat.'

"The Englishman replied: 'No, I suppose not.'

"We stayed where we were for a quarter of an hour, perhaps half an hour, I don't know how long it was, watching all round us the yellow water getting thicker, eddying, seething, as if it was disporting itself over the sands in its triumphant advance.

"One of the girls felt cold and it occurred to me we might go below again to shelter from the light but icy wind which was blowing upon us and pricking our faces.

"I peered down the hatchway. The boat was full of water; so we had to crouch against the stern timbers, which afforded some protection. It was now quite dark and we stayed there, pressed against each other, hemmed in by the darkness and the water. I felt the little English girl's shoulder shivering against mine, while her teeth chattered, but I was also conscious of the delicious warmth of her body through her clothes, a warmth as exciting to me as a kiss. We were not talking now, we stayed there, not moving, silent, crouching down like animals in a ditch during a storm. And yet in spite of everything, in spite of the darkness and the imminent danger, increasing every minute, I began to feel glad I was there; I welcomed the cold and the risk, I welcomed the long hours of darkness and anxiety on those shattered planks, because I was close to this lovely, fascinating girl.

"I wondered at the time at the strange sensation of happiness and content that I felt.

"Why was it? I can't explain. Was it because she was there? She, an unknown little English girl? I wasn't in love with her, I didn't even know her, and yet my emotions were deeply stirred—I was her slave; I would gladly have sacrificed my life to save hers, quite irrationally. It is extraordinary how the proximity of a woman will unbalance any man. Is it the power of beauty which acts as a charm, the attraction of grace and youth which intoxicates us like wine?

"Perhaps it is rather the magic touch of Love, that mysterious god, who is always seeking to unite all living creatures. He is eager to test his power as soon as he has brought a man and a woman face to face; he thrills the very depth of their being with emotion, an undefined, unconfessed emotion, as a gardener waters the earth to make the flowers grow.

"The silence of the night was becoming terrifying, the silence of the sky, for we heard all round a low murmur, undefined but unceasing, the dull swish of the rising tide and the monotonous splash of the waves against the sides of the boat.

"Suddenly I heard sobs; the youngest of the English girls was crying. Her father tried to comfort her and they began to speak in their own language, which I could not follow. I guessed that he was trying to reassure her but that she was still frightened.

"I asked the one next me: 'You're not too cold, I hope?'

"'Oh! yes, I'm frozen!'

"I offered her my coat and she refused it, but I had already taken it off and I put it round her in spite of her refusal.

"For some minutes the air had been getting colder and the splash of the waves against the side louder. I stood up and a strong gust buffeted me in the face. The wind was rising.

"The Englishman noticed it too and he said simply: 'This is a poor look-out for us.'

"It certainly was a poor look-out; it was certain death if waves, even small waves, broke upon the wreck and shook her; she was so shattered and weakened that the first waves of any size would pound her to match-wood.

"Our anxiety increased every minute as the squalls increased in violence. The waves were now curling over and in the darkness I saw white lines of foam appearing and disappearing, while each breaker buffeted the shell of the *Marie-Joseph* and made her shift with a shuddering shock which made our hearts stop beating.

"In the distance ahead to right and left the lighthouses were winking on the coast, white, yellow, and red, revolving like the huge eyes of some giant watching us and waiting eagerly for us to disappear. One of them in particular annoyed me; every thirty seconds it went out and immediately lighted up again; it was exactly like an eye, winking an eyelid over a fiery stare.

"At intervals the Englishman struck a match to look at the time and then put his watch back in his pocket. Suddenly he said to me with magnificent gravity over the heads of his daughters: 'A happy New Year to you, Sir!'

"It was midnight. I held out my hand and he shook it; presently he said something in English and he and his daughters immediately broke into 'God Save the Queen!' the notes soaring up into the dark silent air and fading away into space.

"My first reaction was a desire to laugh, but almost at once the singing evoked in me a strange but powerful emotion.

"There was something sinister and at the same time inspiring in this song of people condemned to death by shipwreck, a sort of prayer and something even finer like the sublime cry of the Roman gladiators: 'Hail, Caesar, those about to die salute thee!'

"When they had finished, I asked the girl next me to sing some ballad or folk-song, anything she liked, to make us forget our anxiety. She consented and immediately her fresh young voice soared aloft into the night. The song, no doubt, was something sad, for the notes were long drawn out; they came from her lips slowly and fluttered like wounded birds over the waves.

"The sea was rising and now the waves were beating against our wreck; but I could think of nothing but her voice. It reminded me of the Sirens. If a boat had passed near us, what would the sailors have imagined? My anxious thoughts wandered off into dreamland. A Siren? Surely she was really a Siren, this daughter of the sea, who was the cause of my staying on this mouldering wreck and who would soon be engulfed together with me in the waves.

"Suddenly all five of us were flung down the deck as the Marie-Joseph settled on her right side. The English girl had fallen on top of me and I had clasped her tight in my arms and, without realizing what I was doing, thinking my last hour had come, I was kissing her cheek, her forehead, her hair passionately. The boat ceased to roll and she and I stayed where we were.

"Her father shouted: 'Kate,' and from my arms she answered: 'Yes!' and made a movement to disengage herself. At that moment I wished the boat would split in two so that I might fall into the water with her.

"'It was certainly a bit of a roll,' went on the Englishman, 'but I've got all my daughters safe anyhow!' Not seeing the eldest, he had thought she had gone overboard.

"I got up slowly and all at once I saw a light quite close on the sea. I shouted and an answer came back. It was a boat looking for us, the hotel-keeper having anticipated our folly.

"We were saved. I was seriously disappointed! They took us off our wreck and brought us back to Saint-Martin. Back in the hotel, the Englishman murmured, rubbing his hands: 'Now for a good meal!'

"We did have supper, but I wasn't feeling a bit festive; I wished we were still on the *Marie-Joseph!*

"We had to part next morning after affectionate farewells and promises to write. They set off for Biarritz and I very nearly followed them.

"I was quite crazy and I was ready to ask the girl to marry me. If we had a week together, I'm sure I should have married her. Sometimes a man is unaccountably weak!

"It was two years before I heard of them. Then I got a letter from her from New York to tell me she was married. Since that time we have written to each other for every New Year's Day. She speaks of her life and her children but never says a word about her husband. I often wonder why. And I only talk about the *Marie-Joseph*. Perhaps she is the only woman I have ever loved...no, whom I might have loved... But I wonder...one gets carried away by things... Nothing lasts forever... And by now she must be an old woman... I shouldn't recognize her... But the girl on the wreck long ago... How adorable she was!... She tells me her hair is quite white...and that hurts, it was golden once... No, the girl of my dreams is no more... What a depressing thought!"

The Aran Islands: First Visit

by

J.M. SYNGE

(1871–1909)

J.M. Synge's visits to the Aran Islands, off the west coast of Ireland, would later form the basis for Riders to the Sea *and* The Playboy of the Western World, *two plays that shook Ireland. And though the stories and conversations recorded here relate to all manner of island and seafaring life, from style of dress to the price of kelp in neighbouring Connemara, the sea is never really very far away. But whether it be old Pat Dirane telling his stories—and what stories they are—by the side of a smoking fire, or the young women out washing their clothes in the tidepools by the bay, "The Aran Islands" is a compelling portrait of a people who live out their lives on the edge of the sea.*

I am in Aranmor, sitting over a turf fire, listening to a murmur of Gaelic that is rising from a little public-house under my room.

The steamer which comes to Aran sails according to the tide, and it was six o'clock this morning when we left the quay of Galway in a dense shroud of mist.

A low line of shore was visible at first on the right between the movement of the waves and fog, but when we came further it was lost sight of, and nothing could be seen but the mist curling in the rigging, and a small circle of foam.

There were few passengers; a couple of men going out with young pigs tied loosely in sacking, three or four young girls who sat in the cabin with their heads completely twisted in their shawls, and a builder, on his way to repair the pier at Kilronan, who walked up and down and talked with me.

In about three hours Aran came in sight. A dreary rock appeared at first sloping up from the sea into the fog; then, as we drew nearer, a coastguard station and the village.

A little later I was wandering out along the one good road-way of the island, looking over low walls on either side into small flat fields of naked rock. I have seen nothing so desolate.

Grey floods of water were sweeping everywhere upon the limestone, making at times a wild torrent of the road, which twined continually over low hills and cavities in the rock or passed between a few small fields of potatoes or grass hidden away in corners that had shelter. Whenever the cloud lifted I could see the edge of the sea below me on the right, and the naked ridge of the island above me on the other side. Occasionally I passed a lonely chapel or schoolhouse, or a line of stone pillars with crosses above them and inscriptions asking a prayer for the soul of the person they commemorated.

I met few people; but here and there a band of tall girls passed me on their way to Kilronan, and called out to me with humorous wonder, speaking English with a slight foreign intonation that differed a good deal from the brogue of Galway. The rain and cold seemed to have no influence on their vitality, and as they hurried past me with eager laughter and great talking in Gaelic, they left the wet masses of rock more desolate than before.

A little after midday when I was coming back one old half-blind man spoke to me in Gaelic, but, in general, I was surprised at the abundance and fluency of the foreign tongue.

In the afternoon the rain continued, so I sat here in the inn looking out through the mist at a few men who were unlading hookers that had come in with turf from Connemara, and at the long-legged pigs that were playing in the surf. As the fishermen came in and out of the public-house underneath my room, I could hear through the broken panes that a number of them still used the Gaelic, though it seems to be falling out of use among the younger people of this village.

The old woman of the house had promised to get me a teacher of the language, and after a while I heard a shuffling on the stairs, and the old dark man I had spoken to in the morning groped his way into the room.

I brought him over to the fire, and we talked for many hours. He told me that he had known Petrie and Sir William Wilde, and many living antiquarians, and had taught Irish to Dr. Finck and Dr. Pedersen, and given stories to Mr. Curtin of America. A little after middle age he had fallen over a cliff, and since then he had had little eyesight, and a trembling of his hands and head.

As we talked he sat huddled together over the fire, shaking and blind, yet his face was indescribably pliant, lighting up with an ecstasy of humour when he told me anything that had a point of wit or malice, and growing sombre and desolate again when he spoke of religion or the fairies.

He had great confidence in his own powers and talent, and in the superiority of his stories over all other stories in the world. When we were speaking of Mr. Curtin, he told me that this gentleman had brought out a volume of his Aran stories in America, and made five hundred pounds by the sale of them.

"And what do you think he did then?" he continued; "he wrote a book of his own stories after making that lot of money with mine. And he brought them out, and the divil a halfpenny did he get for them. Would you believe that?"

Afterwards he told me how one of his children had been taken by the fairies.

One day a neighbour was passing, and she said, when she saw it on the road, "That's a fine child."

Its mother tried to say, "God bless it," but something choked the words in her throat.

A while later they found a wound on its neck, and for three nights the house was filled with noises.

"I never wear a shirt at night," he said, "but I got up out of my bed, all naked as I was, when I heard the noises in the house, and lighted a light, but there was nothing in it."

Then a dummy came and made signs of hammering nails in a coffin.

The next day the seed potatoes were full of blood, and the child told his mother that he was going to America.

That night it died, and "Believe me," said the old man, "the fairies were in it."

When he went away, a little bare-footed girl was sent up with turf and the bellows to make a fire that would last for the evening.

She was shy, yet eager to talk, and told me that she had good spoken Irish, and was learning to read it in the school, and that she had been twice to Galway, though there are many grown women in the place who have never set a foot upon the mainland.

The rain has cleared off, and I have had my first real introduction to the island and its people.

I went out through Killeany—the poorest village in Aranmor—to a long neck of sandhill that runs out into the sea towards the south-west. As I lay there on the grass the clouds lifted from the Connemara mountains and, for a moment, the green undulating foreground, backed in the distance by a mass of hills, reminded me of the country near Rome. Then the dun top-sail of a hooker swept above the edge of the sandhill and revealed the presence of the sea.

As I moved on a boy and a man came down from the next village to talk to me, and I found that here, at least, English was imperfectly understood. When I asked them if there were any trees in the island they held a hurried consultation in Gaelic, and then the man asked if "tree" meant the same thing as "bush," for if so there were a few in sheltered hollows to the east.

They walked on with me to the sound which separates this island from Inishmaan—the middle island of the group—and showed me the roll from the Atlantic running up between two walls of cliff.

They told me that several men had stayed on Inishmaan to learn Irish, and the boy pointed out a line of hovels where they had lodged running like a belt of straw round the middle of the island. The place looked hardly fit for habitation. There was no green to be seen, and no sign of the people except these beehive-like roofs, and the outline of a Dun that stood out above them against the edge of the sky.

After a while my companions went away and two other boys came and walked at my heels, till I turned and made them talk to me. They spoke at first of their poverty, and then one of them said—

"I dare say you do have to pay ten shillings a week in the hotel?"

"More," I answered.

"Twelve?"

"More."

"Fifteen?"

"More still."

Then he drew back and did not question me any further, either thinking that I had lied to check his curiosity, or too awed by my riches to continue.

Repassing Killeany I was joined by a man who had spent twenty years in America, where he had lost his health and then returned, so long ago that he had forgotten English and could hardly make me understand him. He seemed hopeless, dirty, and asthmatic, and after going with me for a few hundred yards he stopped and asked for coppers. I had none left, so I gave him a fill of tobacco, and he went back to his hovel.

When he was gone, two little girls took their place behind me and I drew them in turn into conversation. They spoke to me with a delicate exotic intonation that was full of charm, and told me with a sort of chant how they guide "ladies and gintlemins" in the summer to all that is worth seeing in their neighbourhood, and sell them pampooties and maidenhair ferns, which are common among the rocks.

We were now in Kilronan, and as we parted they showed me holes in their own pampooties, or cowskin sandals, and asked me the price of new ones. I told them that my purse was empty, and then with a few quaint words of blessing they turned away from me and went down to the pier.

All this walk back had been extraordinarily fine. The intense insular clearness one sees only in Ireland, and after rain, was throwing out every ripple in the sea and sky, and every crevice in the hills beyond the bay.

This evening an old man came to see me, and said he had known a relative of mine who passed some time on this island forty-three years ago.

"I was standing under the pier-wall mending nets," he said, "when you came off the steamer, and I said to myself in that moment, if there is a man of the name of Synge left walking the world, it is that man yonder will be he."

He went on to complain in curiously simple yet dignified language of the changes that have taken place here since he left the island to go to sea before the end of his childhood.

"I have come back," he said, "to live in a bit of a house with my sister. The island is not the same at all to what it was. It is little good I can get from the people who are in it now, and anything I have to give them they don't care to have."

From what I hear this man seems to have shut himself up in a world of individual conceits and theories, and to live aloof at his trade of net-mending, regarded by the other islanders with respect and half-ironical sympathy.

A little later when I went down to the kitchen I found two men from Inishmaan who had been benighted on the island. They seemed a simpler and perhaps a more interesting type than the people here, and talked with careful English about the history of the Duns, and the Book of Ballymote, and the Book of Kells, and other ancient MSS., with the names of which they seemed familiar.

In spite of the charm of my teacher, the old blind man I met the day of my arrival, I have decided to move on to Inishmaan, where Gaelic is more generally used, and the life is perhaps the most primitive that is left in Europe.

I spent all this last day with my blind guide, looking at the antiquities that abound in the west or north-west of the island.

As we set out I noticed among the groups of girls who smiled at our friendship—old Mourteen says we are like the cuckoo with its pipit—a beautiful oval face with the singularly spiritual expression that is so marked in one type of the West Ireland women. Later in the day, as the old man talked continually of the fairies and the women they have taken, it seemed that there was a possible link between the wild mythology that is accepted on the islands and the strange beauty of the women.

At midday we rested near the ruins of a house, and two beautiful boys came up and sat near us. Old Mourteen asked them why the house was in ruins, and who had lived in it.

"A rich farmer built it a while since," they said, "but after two years he was driven away by the fairy host."

The boys came on with us some distance to the north to visit one of the ancient beehive dwellings that is still in perfect preservation. When we crawled in on our hands and knees, and stood up in the gloom of the interior, old Mourteen took a freak of earthly humour and began telling what he would have done if he could have come in there when he was a young man and a young girl along with him.

Then he sat down in the middle of the floor and began to recite old Irish poetry, with an exquisite purity of intonation that brought tears to my eyes though I understood but little of the meaning.

On our way home he gave me the Catholic theory of the fairies.

When Lucifer saw himself in the glass he thought himself equal with God. Then the Lord threw him out of Heaven, and all the angels that belonged to him. While He was "chucking them out," an archangel asked Him to spare some of them, and those that were falling are in the air still, and have power to wreck ships, and to work evil in the world.

From this he wandered off into tedious matters of theology, and he repeated many long prayers and sermons in Irish that he had heard from the priests.

A little further on we came to a slated house, and I asked him who was living in it.

"A kind of schoolmistress," he said; then his old face puckered with a gleam of pagan malice.

"Ah, master," he said, "wouldn't it be fine to be in there, and to be kissing her?"

A couple of miles from this village we turned aside to look at an old ruined church of the Ceathair Aluinn (The Four Beautiful Persons), and a holy well near it that is famous for cures of blindness and epilepsy.

As we sat near the well a very old man came up from a cottage near the road, and told me how it had become famous.

"A woman of Sligo had a son who was born blind, and one night she dreamed that she saw an island with a blessed well in it that could cure her son. She told her dream in the morning, and an old man said it was of Aran she was after dreaming.

"She brought her son down by the coast of Galway, and came out in a curagh, and landed below where you see a bit of a cove.

"She walked up then to the house of my father—God rest his soul—and she told them what she was looking for.

"My father said that there was a well like what she had dreamed of, and that he would send a boy along with her to show her the way.

"'There's no need, at all,' said she; 'haven't I seen it all in my dream?'

"Then she went out with the child and walked up to this well, and she kneeled down and began saying her prayers. Then she put her hand out for the water, and put it on his eyes, and the moment it touched he called out: 'O mother, look at the pretty flowers!'"

After that Mourteen described the feats of poteen drinking and fighting that he did in his youth, and went on to talk of Diarmid, who was the strongest man after Samson, and of one of the beds of Diarmid and Grainne, which is on the east of the island. He says that Diarmid was killed by the druids, who put a burning shirt on him,—a fragment of mythology that may connect Diarmid with the legend of Hercules, if it is not due to the "learning" in some hedge-school master's ballad.

Then we talked about Inishmaan.

"You'll have an old man to talk with you over there," he said, "and tell you stories of the fairies, but he's walking about with two sticks under him this ten year. Did ever you hear what it is goes on four legs when it is young, and on two legs after that, and on three legs when it does be old?"

I gave him the answer.

"Ah, master," he said, "you're a cute one, and the blessing of God be on you. Well, I'm on three legs this minute, but the old man beyond is back on four; I don't know if I'm better than the way he is; he's got his sight and I'm only an old dark man."

I am settled at last on Inishmaan in a small cottage with a continual drone of Gaelic coming from the kitchen that opens into my room.

Early this morning the man of the house came over for me with a four-oared curagh—that is, a curagh with four rowers and four oars on either side, as each man uses two—and we set off a little before noon.

It gave me a moment of exquisite satisfaction to find myself moving away from civilisation in this rude canvas canoe of a model that has served primitive races since men first went on the sea.

We had to stop for a moment at a hulk that is anchored in the bay, to make some arrangements for the fish-curing of the middle island, and my crew called out as soon as we were within earshot that they had a man with them who had been in France a month from this day.

When we started again, a small sail was run up in the bow, and we set off across the sound with a leaping oscillation that had no resemblance to the heavy movement of a boat.

The sail is only used as an aid, so the men continued to row after it had gone up, and as they occupied the four cross-seats I lay on the canvas at the stern and the frame of slender laths, which bent and quivered as the waves passed under them.

When we set off it was a brilliant morning of April, and the green, glittering waves seemed to toss the canoe among themselves, yet as we drew nearer this island a sudden thunderstorm broke out behind the rocks we were approaching, and lent a momentary tumult to this still vein of the Atlantic.

We landed at a small pier, from which a rude track leads up to the village between small fields and bare sheets of rock like those in Aranmor. The youngest son of my boatman, a boy of about seventeen, who is to be my teacher and guide, was waiting for me at the pier and guided me to his house, while the men settled the curagh and followed slowly with my baggage.

My room is at one end of the cottage, with a boarded floor and ceiling, and two windows opposite each other. Then there is the kitchen with earth floor and open rafters, and two doors opposite each other opening into the open air, but no windows. Beyond it there are two small rooms of half the width of the kitchen with one window apiece.

The kitchen itself, where I will spend most of my time, is full of beauty and distinction. The red dresses of the women who cluster round the fire on their stools give a glow of almost Eastern richness, and the walls have been toned by the turf-smoke to a soft brown that blends with the grey earth-colour of the floor. Many sorts of fishing tackle, and the nets and oil-skins of the men, are hung upon the walls or among the open rafters; and right overhead, under the thatch, there is a whole cowskin from which they make pampooties.

Every article on these islands has an almost personal charac-ter, which gives this simple life, where all art is unknown, something of the artistic beauty of mediaeval life. The curaghs and spinning-wheels, the tiny wooden barrels that are still much used in the place of earthenware, the home-made cra-dles, churns, and baskets, are all full of individuality, and being made from materials that are common here, yet to some extent peculiar to the island, they seem to exist as a natural link between the people and the world that is about them.

The simplicity and unity of the dress increases in another way the local air of beauty. The women wear red petticoats and jackets of the island wool stained with madder, to which they usually add a plaid shawl twisted round their chests and tied at the back. When it rains they throw another petticoat over their heads with the waistband round their faces, or, if they are young, they use a heavy shawl like those worn in Galway. Occasionally other wraps are worn, and during the thunderstorm I arrived in I saw several girls with men's waist-coats buttoned round their bodies. Their skirts do not come much below the knee, and show their powerful legs in the heavy indigo stockings with which they are all provided.

The men wear three colours: the natural wool, indigo, and a grey flannel that is woven of alternate threads of indigo and natural wool. In Aranmor many of the younger men have adopted the usual fisherman's jersey, but I have only seen one on this island.

As flannel is cheap—the women spin the yarn from the

wool of their own sheep, and it is then woven by a weaver in Kilronan for fourpence a yard—the men seem to wear an indefinite number of waistcoats and woollen drawers one over the other. They are usually surprised at the lightness of my own dress, and one old man I spoke to for a minute on the pier, when I came ashore, asked me if I was not cold with "my little clothes."

As I sat in the kitchen to dry the spray from my coat, several men who had seen me walking up came in to talk to me, usually murmuring on the threshold, "The blessing of God on this place," or some similar words.

The courtesy of the old woman of the house is singularly attractive, and though I could not understand much of what she said—she has no English—I could see with how much grace she motioned each visitor to a chair, or stool, according to his age, and said a few words to him till he drifted into our English conversation.

For the moment my own arrival is the chief subject of interest, and the men who come in are eager to talk to me.

Some of them express themselves more correctly than the ordinary peasant, others use the Gaelic idioms continually and substitute "he" or "she" for "it," as the neuter pronoun is not found in modern Irish.

A few of the men have a curiously full vocabulary, others know only the commonest words in English, and are driven to ingenious devices to express their meaning. Of all the subjects we can talk of war seems their favourite, and the conflict between America and Spain is causing a great deal of excitement. Nearly all the families have relations who have had to cross the Atlantic, and all eat of the flour and bacon that is brought from the United States, so they have a vague fear that "if anything happened to America," their own island would cease to be habitable.

Foreign languages are another favourite topic, and as these men are bilingual they have a fair notion of what it means to speak and think in many different idioms. Most of the strangers they see on the islands are philological students, and the people have been led to conclude that linguistic studies, particularly Gaelic studies, are the chief occupation of the outside world.

"I have seen Frenchmen, and Danes, and Germans," said one man, "and there does be a power a Irish books along with them, and they reading them better than ourselves. Believe me there are few rich men now in the world who are not studying the Gaelic."

They sometimes ask me the French for simple phrases, and when they have listened to the intonation for a moment, most of them are able to reproduce it with admirable precision.

When I was going out this morning to walk round the island with Michael, the boy who is teaching me Irish, I met an old man making his way down to the cottage. He was dressed in miserable black clothes which seemed to have come from the mainland, and was so bent with rheumatism that, at a little distance, he looked more like a spider than a human being.

Michael told me it was Pat Dirane, the storyteller old Mourteen had spoken of on the other island. I wished to turn back, as he appeared to be on his way to visit me, but Michael would not hear of it.

"He will be sitting by the fire when we come in," he said; "let you not be afraid, there will be time enough to be talking to him by and by."

He was right. As I came down into the kitchen some hours later old Pat was still in the chimney-corner, blinking with the turf smoke.

He spoke English with remarkable aptness and fluency, due, I believe, to the months he spent in the English provinces working at the harvest when he was a young man.

After a few formal compliments he told me how he had been crippled by an attack of "old hin" (i.e. the influenza), and had been complaining ever since in addition to his rheumatism.

While the old woman was cooking my dinner he asked me if I liked stories, and offered to tell one in English, though he added, it would be much better if I could follow the Gaelic. Then he began:—

There were two farmers in County Clare. One had a son, and the other, a fine rich man, had a daughter.

The young man was wishing to marry the girl, and his father told him to try and get her if he thought well, though a power of gold would be wanting to get the like of her.

"I will try," said the young man.

He put all his gold into a bag. Then he went over to the other farm, and threw in the gold in front of him.

"Is that all gold?" said the father of the girl.

"All gold," said O'Conor (the young man's name was O'Conor).

"It will not weigh down my daughter," said the father.

"We'll see that," said O'Conor.

Then they put them in the scales, the daughter in one side and the gold in the other. The girl went down against the ground, so O'Conor took his bag and went out on the road.

As he was going along he came to where there was a little man, and he standing with his back against the wall.

"Where are you going with the bag?" said the little man.

"Going home," said O'Conor.

"Is it gold you might be wanting?" said the man.

"It is, surely," said O'Conor.

"I'll give you what you are wanting," said the man, "and we can bargain in this way—you'll pay me back in a year the gold I give you, or you'll pay me with five pounds cut off your own flesh."

That bargain was made between them. The man gave a bag of gold to O'Conor, and he went back with it, and was married to the young woman.

They were rich people, and he built her a grand castle on the cliffs of Clare, with a window that looked out straightly over the wild ocean.

One day when he went up with his wife to look out over the wild ocean, he saw a ship coming in on the rocks, and no sails on her at all. She was wrecked on the rocks, and it was tea that was in her, and fine silk.

O'Conor and his wife went down to look at the wreck, and when the lady O'Conor saw the silk she said she wished for a dress of it.

They got the silk from the sailors, and when the Captain came up to get the money for it, O'Conor asked him to come again and take his dinner with them. They had a grand dinner, and they drank after it, and the Captain was tipsy. While they were still drinking, a letter came to O'Conor, and it was in the letter that a friend of his was dead, and that he would have to go away on a long journey. As he was getting ready the Captain came to him.

"Are you fond of your wife?" said the Captain.

"I am fond of her," said O'Conor.

"Will you make me a bet of twenty guineas no man comes near her while you'll be away on the journey?" said the Captain.

"I will bet it," said O'Conor; and he went away.

There was an old hag who sold small things on the road near the castle, and the lady O'Conor allowed her to sleep up in her room in a big box. The Captain went down on the road to the old hag.

"For how much will you let me sleep one night in your box?" said the Captain.

"For no money at all would I do such a thing," said the hag.

"For ten guineas?" said the Captain.

"Not for ten guineas," said the hag.

"For twelve guineas?" said the Captain.

"Not for twelve guineas," said the hag.

"For fifteen guineas?" said the Captain.

"For fifteen I will do it," said the hag.

Then she took him up and hid him in the box. When night came the lady O'Conor walked up into her room, and the Captain watched her through a hole that was in the box. He saw her take off her two rings and put them on a kind of a board that was over her head like a chimney-piece, and take off her clothes, except her shift, and go up into her bed.

As soon as she was asleep the Captain came out of his box, and he had some means of making a light, for he lit the candle. He went over to the bed where she was sleeping without disturbing her at all, or doing any bad thing, and he took the two rings off the board, and blew out the light, and went down again into the box.

He paused for a moment, and a deep sigh of relief rose from the men and women who had crowded in while the story was going on, till the kitchen was filled with people.

As the Captain was coming out of his box the girls, who had appeared to know no English, stopped their spinning and held their breath with expectation.

The old man went on—

When O'Conor came back the Captain met him, and told him that he had been a night in his wife's room, and gave him the two rings.

O'Conor gave him the twenty guineas of the bet. Then he went up into the castle, and he took his wife up to look out of the window over the wild ocean. While she was looking he pushed her from behind, and she fell down over the cliff into the sea.

An old woman was on the shore, and she saw her falling. She went down then to the surf and pulled her out all wet and in great disorder, and she took the wet clothes off of her, and put on some old rags belonging to herself.

When O'Conor had pushed his wife from the window he went away into the land.

After a while the lady O'Conor went out searching for him, and when she had gone here and there a long time in the country, she heard that he was reaping in a field with sixty men.

She came to the field and she wanted to go in, but the gate-man would not open the gate for her. Then the owner came by, and she told him her story. He brought her in, and her husband was there, reaping, but he never gave any sign of knowing her. She showed him to the owner, and he made the man come out and go with his wife.

Then the lady O'Conor took him out on the road where there were horses, and they rode away.

When they came to the place where O'Conor had met the little man, he was there on the road before them.

"Have you my gold on you?" said the man.

"I have not," said O'Conor.

"Then you'll pay me the flesh off your body," said the man.

They went into a house, and a knife was brought, and a clean white cloth was put on the table, and O'Conor was put upon the cloth.

Then the little man was going to strike the lancet into him, when says lady O'Conor—

"Have you bargained for five pounds of flesh?"

"For five pounds of flesh," said the man.

"Have you bargained for any drop of his blood?" said lady O'Conor.

"For no blood," said the man.

"Cut out the flesh," said lady O'Conor, "but if you spill one drop of his blood I'll put that through you." And she put a pistol to his head.

The little man went away and they saw no more of him.

When they got home to their castle they made a great supper, and they invited the Captain and the old hag, and the old woman that had pulled the lady O'Conor out of the sea.

After they had eaten well the lady O'Conor began, and she said they would all tell their stories. Then she told how she had been saved from the sea, and how she had found her husband.

Then the old woman told her story, the way she had found lady O'Conor wet, and in great disorder, and had brought her in and put on her some old rags of her own.

The lady O'Conor asked the Captain for his story, but he said they would get no story from him. Then she took her pistol out of her pocket, and she put it on the edge of the table, and she said that any one that would not tell his story would get a bullet into him.

Then the Captain told the way he had got into the box, and come over to her bed without touching her at all, and had taken away the rings.

Then the lady O'Conor took the pistol and shot the hag through the body, and they threw her over the cliff into the sea.

That is my story.

It gave me a strange feeling of wonder to hear this illiterate native of a wet rock in the Atlantic telling a story that is so full of European associations.

The incident of the faithful wife takes us beyond Cymbeline to the sunshine of the Arno, and the gay company who went out from Florence to tell narratives of love. It takes us again to the low vineyards of Würzburg on the Main, where the same tale was told in the middle ages, of the "Two Merchants and the Faithful Wife of Ruprecht von Würzburg."

The other portion, dealing with the pound of flesh, has a still wider distribution, reaching from Persia and Egypt to the *Gesta Romanorum*, and the *Pecorone* of Ser Giovanni, a Florentine notary.

The present union of the two tales has already been found among the Gaels, and there is a somewhat similar version in Campbell's *Popular Tales of the Western Highlands.*

Michael walks so fast when I am out with him that I cannot pick my steps, and the sharp-edged fossils which abound in the limestone have cut my shoes to pieces.

The family held a consultation on them last night, and in the end it was decided to make me a pair of pampooties, which I have been wearing to-day among the rocks.

They consist simply of a piece of raw cowskin, with the hair outside, laced over the toe and round the heel with two ends of fishing-line that work round and are tied above the instep.

In the evening, when they are taken off, they are placed in a basin of water, as the rough hide cuts the foot and stocking if it is allowed to harden. For the same reason the people often step into the surf during the day, so that their feet are continually moist.

At first I threw my weight upon my heels, as one does naturally in a boot, and was a good deal bruised, but after a few hours I learned the natural walk of man, and could follow my guide in any portion of the island.

In one district below the cliffs, towards the north, one goes for nearly a mile jumping from one rock to another without a single ordinary step; and here I realised that toes have a natural use, for I found myself jumping towards any tiny crevice in the rock before me, and clinging with an eager grip in which all the muscles of my feet ached from their exertion.

The absence of the heavy boot of Europe has preserved to these people the agile walk of the wild animal, while the general simplicity of their lives has given them many other points of physical perfection. Their way of life has never been acted on by anything much more artificial than the nests and burrows of the creatures that live round them, and they seem, in a certain sense, to approach more nearly to the finer types of our aristocracies—who are bred artificially to a natural ideal—than to the labourer or citizen, as the wild horse resembles the thoroughbred rather than the hack or cart-horse. Tribes of the same natural development are, perhaps, frequent in half-civilised countries, but here a touch of the refinement of old societies is blended, with singular effect, among the qualities of the wild animal.

While I am walking with Michael some one often comes to me to ask the time of day. Few of the people, however, are sufficiently used to modern time to understand in more than a vague way the convention of the hours, and when I tell them what o'clock it is by my watch they are not satisfied, and ask how long is left them before the twilight.

The general knowledge of time on the island depends, curiously enough, on the direction of the wind. Nearly all the cottages are built, like this one, with two doors opposite each other, the more sheltered of which lies open all day to give light to the interior. If the wind is northerly the south door is opened, and the shadow of the door-post moving across the kitchen floor indicates the hour; as soon, however, as the wind changes to the south the other door is opened, and the people, who never think of putting up a primitive dial, are at a loss.

The system of doorways has another curious result. It usually happens that all the doors on one side of the village pathway are lying open with women sitting about on the thresholds, while on the other side the doors are shut and there is no sign of life. The moment the wind changes everything is reversed, and sometimes when I come back to the village after an hour's walk there seems to have been a general flight from one side of the way to the other.

In my own cottage the change of the doors alters the whole tone of the kitchen, turning it from a brilliantly-lighted room looking out on a yard and laneway to a sombre cell with a superb view of the sea.

When the wind is from the north the old woman manages my meals with fair regularity, but on the other days she often makes my tea at three o'clock instead of six. If I refuse it she puts it down to simmer for three hours in the turf, and then brings it in at six o'clock full of anxiety to know if it is warm enough.

The old man is suggesting that I should send him a clock when I go away. He'd like to have something from me in the house, he says, that way they wouldn't forget me, and wouldn't a clock be as handy as another thing, and they'd be thinking of me whenever they'd look on its face.

The general ignorance of any precise hours in the day makes it impossible for the people to have regular meals.

They seem to eat together in the evening, and sometimes in the morning, a little after dawn, before they scatter for their work, but during the day they simply drink a cup of tea and eat a piece of bread, or some potatoes, whenever they are hungry.

For men who live in the open air they eat strangely little. Often when Michael has been out weeding potatoes for eight or nine hours without food, he comes in and eats a few slices of home-made bread, and then he is ready to go out with me and wander for hours about the island.

They use no animal food except a little bacon and salt fish. The old woman says she would be very ill if she ate fresh meat.

Some years ago, before tea, sugar, and flour had come into general use, salt fish was much more the staple article of diet than at present, and, I am told, skin diseases were very common, though they are now rare on the islands.

No one who has not lived for weeks among these grey clouds and seas can realise the joy with which the eye rests on the red dresses of the women, especially when a number of them are to be found together, as happened early this morning.

I heard that the young cattle were to be shipped for a fair on the mainland, which is to take place in a few days, and I went down on the pier, a little after dawn, to watch them.

The bay was shrouded in the greys of coming rain, yet the thinness of the cloud threw a silvery light on the sea, and an unusual depth of blue to the mountains of Connemara.

As I was going across the sandhills one dun-sailed hooker glided slowly out to begin her voyage, and another beat up to the pier. Troops of red cattle, driven mostly by the women, were coming up from several directions, forming, with the green of the long tract of grass that separates the sea from the rocks, a new unity of colour.

The pier itself was crowded with bullocks and a great number of the people. I noticed one extraordinary girl in the throng who seemed to exert an authority on all who came near her. Her curiously-formed nostrils and narrow chin gave her a witch-like expression, yet the beauty of her hair and skin made her singularly attractive.

When the empty hooker was made fast its deck was still many feet below the level of the pier, so the animals were slung down by a rope from the mast-head, with much struggling and confusion. Some of them made wild efforts to escape, nearly carrying their owners with them into the sea, but they were handled with wonderful dexterity, and there was no mishap.

When the open hold was filled with young cattle, packed as tightly as they could stand, the owners with their wives or sisters, who go with them to prevent extravagance in Galway, jumped down to the deck, and the voyage was begun. Immediately afterwards a rickety old hooker beat up with turf from Connemara, and while she was unlading all the men sat along the edge of the pier and made remarks upon the rottenness of her timber till the owners grew wild with rage.

The tide was now too low for more boats to come to the pier, so a move was made to a strip of sand towards the southeast, where the rest of the cattle were shipped through the

surf. Here the hooker was anchored about eighty yards from
the shore, and a curagh was rowed round to tow out the animals. Each bullock was caught in its turn and girded with a
sling of rope by which it could be hoisted on board. Another
rope was fastened to the horns and passed out to a man in the
stern of the curagh. Then the animal was forced down through
the surf and out of its depth before it had much time to struggle. Once fairly swimming, it was towed out to the hooker and
dragged on board in a half-drowned condition.

The freedom of the sand seemed to give a stronger spirit of
revolt, and some of the animals were only caught after a dangerous struggle. The first attempt was not always successful,
and I saw one three-year-old lift two men with his horns, and
drag another fifty yards along the sand by his tail before he
was subdued.

While this work was going on a crowd of girls and women
collected on the edge of the cliff and kept shouting down a
confused babble of satire and praise.

When I came back to the cottage I found that among the
women who had gone to the mainland was a daughter of the
old woman's, and that her baby of about nine months had
been left in the care of its grandmother.

As I came in she was busy getting ready my dinner, and old
Pat Dirane, who usually comes at this hour, was rocking the
cradle. It is made of clumsy wicker-work, with two pieces of
rough wood fastened underneath to serve as rockers, and all
the time I am in my room I can hear it bumping on the floor
with extraordinary violence. When the baby is awake it
sprawls on the floor, and the old woman sings it a variety of
inarticulate lullabies that have much musical charm.

Another daughter, who lives at home, has gone to the fair
also, so the old woman has both the baby and myself to take
care of as well as a crowd of chickens that live in a hole beside
the fire. Often when I want tea, or when the old woman goes
for water, I have to take my own turn at rocking the cradle.

One of the largest Duns, or pagan forts, on the islands, is
within a stone's-throw of my cottage, and I often stroll up

there after a dinner of eggs or salt pork, to smoke drowsily on the stones. The neighbours know my habit, and not infrequently some one wanders up to ask what news there is in the last paper I received, or to make inquiries about the American war. If no one comes I prop my book open with stones touched by the Fir-bolgs, and sleep for hours in the delicious warmth of the sun. The last few days I have almost lived on the round walls, for, by some miscalculation, our turf has come to an end, and the fires are kept up with dried cow-dung—a common fuel on the island—the smoke from which filters through into my room and lies in blue layers above my table and bed.

Fortunately the weather is fine, and I can spend my days in the sunshine. When I look round from the top of these walls I can see the sea on nearly every side, stretching away to distant ranges of mountains on the north and south. Underneath me to the east there is the one inhabited district of the island, where I can see red figures moving about the cottages, sending up an occasional fragment of conversation or of the old island melodies.

The baby is teething, and has been crying for several days. Since his mother went to the fair they have been feeding him with cow's milk, often slightly sour, and giving him, I think, more than he requires.

This morning, however, he seemed so unwell they sent out to look for a foster-mother in the village, and before long a young woman, who lives a little way to the east, came in and restored him his natural food.

A few hours later, when I came into the kitchen to talk to old Pat, another woman performed the same kindly office, this time a person with a curiously whimsical expression.

Pat told me a story of an unfaithful wife, which I will give further down, and then broke into a moral dispute with the visitor, which caused immense delight to some young men who had come down to listen to the story. Unfortunately it was carried on so rapidly in Gaelic that I lost most of the points.

This old man talks usually in a mournful tone about his ill-health, and his death, which he feels to be approaching, yet he has occasional touches of humour that remind me of old Mourteen on the north island. To-day a grotesque twopenny doll was lying on the floor near the old woman. He picked it up and examined it as if comparing it with her. Then he held it up: "Is it you is after bringing that thing into the world," he said, "woman of the house?"

Here is his story:—

One day I was travelling on foot from Galway to Dublin, and the darkness came on me and I ten miles from the town I was wanting to pass the night in. Then a hard rain began to fall and I was tired walking, so when I saw a sort of house with no roof on it up against the road, I got in the way the walls would give me shelter.

As I was looking round I saw a light in some trees two perches off, and thinking any sort of a house would be better than where I was, I got over a wall and went up to the house to look in at the window.

I saw a dead man laid on a table, and candles lighted, and a woman watching him. I was frightened when I saw him, but it was raining hard, and I said to myself, if he was dead he couldn't hurt me. Then I knocked on the door and the woman came and opened it.

"Good evening, ma'am," said I.

"Good evening kindly, stranger," says she. "Come in out of the rain."

Then she took me in and told me her husband was after dying on her, and she was watching him that night.

"But it's thirsty you'll be, stranger," says she. "Come into the parlour."

Then she took me into the parlour—and it was a fine clean house—and she put a cup, with a saucer under it, on the table before me with fine sugar and bread.

When I'd had a cup of tea I went back into the kitchen where the dead man was lying, and she gave me a fine new pipe off the table with a drop of spirits.

"Stranger," says she, "would you be afeard to be alone with himself?"

"Not a bit in the world, ma'am," says I; "he that's dead can do no hurt."

Then she said she wanted to go over and tell the neighbours the way her husband was after dying on her, and she went out and locked the door behind her.

I smoked one pipe, and I leaned out and took another off the table. I was smoking it with my hand on the back of my chair—the way you are yourself this minute, God bless you—and I looking on the dead man, when he opened his eyes as wide as myself and looked at me.

"Don't be afeard, stranger," said the dead man; "I'm not dead at all in the world. Come here and help me up and I'll tell you all about it."

Well, I went up and took the sheet off of him, and I saw that he had a fine clean shirt on his body, and fine flannel drawers.

He sat up then, and says he—

"I've got a bad wife, stranger, and I let on to be dead the way I'd catch her goings on."

Then he got two fine sticks he had to keep down his wife, and he put them at each side of his body, and he laid himself out again as if he was dead.

In half an hour his wife came back and a young man along with her. Well, she gave him his tea, and she told him he was tired, and he would do right to go and lie down in the bedroom.

The young man went in and the woman sat down to watch by the dead man. A while after she got up and "Stranger," says she, "I'm going in to get the candle out of the room; I'm thinking the young man will be asleep by this time." She went into the bedroom, but the divil a bit of her came back.

Then the dead man got up, and he took one stick, and he gave the other to myself. We went in and we saw them lying together with her head on his arm.

The dead man hit him a blow with the stick so that the blood out of him leapt up and hit the gallery.

That is my story.

In stories of this kind he always speaks in the first person, with minute details to show that he was actually present at the scenes that are described.

At the beginning of this story he gave me a long account of what had made him be on his way to Dublin on that occasion, and told me about all the rich people he was going to see in the finest streets of the city.

A week of sweeping fogs has passed over and given me a strange sense of exile and desolation. I walk round the island nearly every day, yet I can see nothing anywhere but a mass of wet rock, a strip of surf, and then a tumult of waves.

The slaty limestone has grown black with the water that is dripping on it, and wherever I turn there is the same grey obsession twining and wreathing itself among the narrow fields, and the same wail from the wind that shrieks and whistles in the loose rubble of the walls.

At first the people do not give much attention to the wilderness that is round them, but after a few days their voices sink in the kitchen, and their endless talk of pigs and cattle falls to the whisper of men who are telling stories in a haunted house.

The rain continues; but this evening a number of young men were in the kitchen mending nets, and the bottle of poteen was drawn from its hiding-place.

One cannot think of these people drinking wine on the summit of this crumbling precipice, but their grey poteen, which brings a shock of joy to the blood, seems predestined to keep sanity in men who live forgotten in these worlds of mist.

I sat in the kitchen part of the evening to feel the gaiety that was rising, and when I came into my own room after dark, one of the sons came in every time the bottle made its round, to pour me out my share.

It has cleared, and the sun is shining with a luminous warmth that makes the whole island glisten with the splendour of a gem, and fills the sea and sky with a radiance of blue light.

I have come out to lie on the rocks where I have the black edge of the north island in front of me, Galway Bay, too blue almost to look at, on my right, the Atlantic on my left, a perpendicular cliff under my ankles, and over me innumerable gulls that chase each other in a white cirrus of wings.

A nest of hooded crows is somewhere near me, and one of the old birds is trying to drive me away by letting itself fall like a stone every few moments, from about forty yards above me to within reach of my hand.

Gannets are passing up and down above the sound, swooping at times after a mackerel, and further off I can see the whole fleet of hookers coming out from Kilronan for a night's fishing in the deep water to the west.

As I lie here hour after hour, I seem to enter into the wild pastimes of the cliff, and to become a companion of the cormorants and crows.

Many of the birds display themselves before me with the vanity of barbarians, forming in strange evolutions as long as I am in sight, and returning to their ledge of rock when I am gone. Some are wonderfully expert, and cut graceful figures for an inconceivable time without a flap of their wings, growing so absorbed in their own dexterity that they often collide with one another in their flight, an incident always followed by a wild outburst of abuse. Their language is easier than Gaelic, and I seem to understand the greater part of their cries, though I am not able to answer. There is one plaintive note which they take up in the middle of their usual babble with extraordinary effect, and pass on from one to another along the cliff with a sort of an inarticulate wail, as if they remembered for an instant the horror of the mist.

On the low sheets of rock to the east I can see a number of red and grey figures hurrying about their work. The continual passing in this island between the misery of last night and the splendour of to-day, seems to create an affinity between the moods of these people and the moods of varying rapture and dismay that are frequent in artists, and in certain forms of alienation. Yet it is only in the intonation of a few sentences or some old fragment of melody that I catch the real spirit of the island, for in general the men sit together and talk with endless iteration of the tides and fish, and of the price of kelp in Connemara.

After Mass this morning an old woman was buried. She lived in the cottage next mine, and more than once before noon I heard a faint echo of the keen. I did not go to the wake for fear my presence might jar upon the mourners, but all last evening I could hear the strokes of a hammer in the yard, where, in the middle of a little crowd of idlers, the next of kin laboured slowly at the coffin. To-day, before the hour for the funeral, poteen was served to a number of men who stood about upon the road, and a portion was brought to me in my room. Then the coffin was carried out sewn loosely in sailcloth, and held near the ground by three cross-poles lashed upon the top. As we moved down to the low eastern portion of the island, nearly all the men, and all the oldest women, wearing petticoats over their heads, came out and joined in the procession.

While the grave was being opened the women sat down among the flat tombstones, bordered with a pale fringe of early bracken, and began the wild keen, or crying for the dead. Each old woman, as she took her turn in the leading recitative, seemed possessed for the moment with a profound ecstasy of grief, swaying to and fro, and bending her forehead to the stone before her, while she called out to the dead with a perpetually recurring chant of sobs.

All round the graveyard other wrinkled women, looking out from under the deep red petticoats that cloaked them, rocked themselves with the same rhythm, and intoned the inarticulate chant that is sustained by all as an accompaniment.

The morning had been beautifully fine, but as they lowered the coffin into the grave, thunder rumbled overhead and hailstones hissed among the bracken.

In Inishmaan one is forced to believe in a sympathy between man and nature, and at this moment when the thunder sounded a death-peal of extraordinary grandeur above the voices of the women, I could see the faces near me stiff and drawn with emotion.

When the coffin was in the grave, and the thunder had rolled away across the hills of Clare, the keen broke out again more passionately than before.

This grief of the keen is no personal complaint for the death of one woman over eighty years, but seems to contain the whole passionate rage that lurks somewhere in every native of the island. In this cry of pain the inner consciousness of the people seems to lay itself bare for an instant, and to reveal the mood of beings who feel their isolation in the face of a universe that wars on them with winds and seas. They are usually silent, but in the presence of death all outward show of indifference or patience is forgotten, and they shriek with pitiable despair before the horror of the fate to which they all are doomed.

Before they covered the coffin an old man kneeled down by the grave and repeated a simple prayer for the dead.

There was an irony in these words of atonement and Catholic belief spoken by voices that were still hoarse with the cries of pagan desperation.

A little beyond the grave I saw a line of old women who had recited in the keen sitting in the shadows of a wall beside the roofless shell of the church. They were still sobbing and shaken with grief, yet they were beginning to talk again of the daily trifles that veil from them the terror of the world.

When we had all come out of the graveyard, and two men had rebuilt the hole in the wall through which the coffin had been carried in, we walked back to the village, talking of anything, and joking of anything, as if merely coming from the boat-slip, or the pier.

One man told me of the poteen drinking that takes place at some funerals.

"A while since," he said, "there were two men fell down in the graveyard while the drink was on them. The sea was rough that day, the way no one could go to bring the doctor, and one of the men never woke again, and found death that night."

The other day the men of this house made a new field.
There was a slight bank of earth under the wall of the yard,
and another in the corner of the cabbage garden. The old man
and his eldest son dug out the clay, with the care of men working in a gold-mine, and Michael packed it in panniers—there
are no wheeled vehicles on this island—for transport to a flat
rock in a sheltered corner of their holding, where it was mixed
with sand and seaweed and spread out in a layer upon the
stone.

Most of the potato-growing of the island is carried on in
fields of this sort—for which the people pay a considerable
rent—and if the season is at all dry, their hope of a fair crop is
nearly always disappointed.

It is now nine days since rain has fallen, and the people are
filled with anxiety, although the sun has not yet been hot
enough to do harm.

The drought is also causing a scarcity of water. There are a
few springs on this side of the island, but they come only from
a little distance, and in hot weather are not to be relied on.
The supply for this house is carried up in a water-barrel by
one of the women. If it is drawn off at once it is not very nauseous, but if it has lain, as it often does, for some hours in the
barrel, the smell, colour, and taste are unendurable. The water
for washing is also coming short, and as I walk round the
edges of the sea, I often come on a girl with her petticoats
tucked up round her, standing in a pool left by the tide and
washing her flannels among the sea-anemones and crabs.
Their red bodices and white tapering legs make them as beautiful as tropical sea-birds, as they stand in a frame of seaweeds
against the brink of the Atlantic. Michael, however, is a little
uneasy when they are in sight, and I cannot pause to watch
them. This habit of using the sea water for washing causes a
good deal of rheumatism on the island, for the salt lies in the
clothes and keeps them continually moist.

The people have taken advantage of this dry moment to
begin the burning of the kelp, and all the islands are lying in a
volume of grey smoke. There will not be a very large quantity
this year, as the people are discouraged by the uncertainty of

the market, and do not care to undertake the task of manufacture without a certainty of profit.

The work needed to form a ton of kelp is considerable. The
seaweed is collected from the rocks after the storms of autumn
and winter, dried on fine days, and then made up into a rick,
where it is left till the beginning of June.

It is then burnt in low kilns on the shore, an affair that takes
from twelve to twenty-four hours of continuous hard work,
though I understand the people here do not manage well and
spoil a portion of what they produce by burning it more than
is required.

The kiln holds about two tons of molten kelp, and when
full is loosely covered with stones, and left to cool. In a few
days the substance is as hard as the limestone, and has to be
broken with crowbars before it can be placed in curaghs for
transport to Kilronan, where it is tested to determine the
amount of iodine it contains, and paid for accordingly. In former years good kelp would bring seven pounds a ton, now
four pounds are not always reached.

In Aran even manufacture is of interest. The low flame-
edged kiln, sending out dense clouds of creamy smoke, with a
band of red and grey clothed workers moving in the haze, and
usually with some petticoated boys and women who come
down with drink, forms a scene with as much variety and
colour as any picture from the East.

The men feel in a certain sense the distinction of their
island, and show me their work with pride. One of them said
to me yesterday, "I'm thinking you never saw the like of this
work before this day?"

"That is true," I answered, "I never did."

"Bedad, then," he said, "isn't it a great wonder that you've
seen France, and Germany, and the Holy Father, and never
seen a man making kelp till you come to Inishmaan."

All the horses from this island are put out on grass among
the hills of Connemara from June to the end of September, as
there is no grazing here during the summer.

Their shipping and transport is even more difficult than that of the horned cattle. Most of them are wild Connemara ponies, and their great strength and timidity make them hard to handle on the narrow pier, while in the hooker itself it is not easy to get them safely on their feet in the small space that is available. They are dealt with in the same way as for the bullocks I have spoken of already, but the excitement becomes much more intense, and the storm of Gaelic that rises the moment a horse is shoved from the pier, till it is safely in its place, is indescribable. Twenty boys and men howl and scream with agitation, cursing and exhorting, without knowing, most of the time, what they are saying.

Apart, however, from this primitive babble, the dexterity and power of the men are displayed to more advantage than in anything I have seen hitherto. I noticed particularly the owner of a hooker from the north island that was loaded this morning. He seemed able to hold up a horse by his single weight when it was swinging from the masthead, and preserved a humorous calm even in moments of the wildest excitement. Sometimes a large mare would come down sideways on the backs of the other horses, and kick there till the hold seemed to be filled with a mass of struggling centaurs, for the men themselves often leap down to try and save the foals from injury. The backs of the horses put in first are often a good deal cut by the shoes of the others that arrive on top of them, but otherwise they do not seem to be much the worse, and as they are not on their way to a fair, it is not of much consequence in what condition they come to land.

There is only one bit and saddle in the island, which are used by the priest, who rides from the chapel to the pier when he has held the service on Sunday.

The islanders themselves ride with a simple halter and a stick, yet sometimes travel, at least in the larger island, at a desperate gallop. As the horses usually have panniers, the rider sits sideways over the withers, and if the panniers are empty they go at full speed in this position without anything to hold on to.

More than once in Aranmor I met a party going out west with empty panniers from Kilronan. Long before they came in sight I could hear a clatter of hoofs, and then a whirl of horses would come round a corner at full gallop with their heads out, utterly indifferent to the slender halter that is their only check. They generally travel in single file with a few yards between them, and as there is no traffic there is little fear of an accident.

Sometimes a woman and a man ride together, but in this case the man sits in the usual position, and the woman sits sideways behind him, and holds him round the waist.

Old Pat Dirane continues to come up every day to talk to me, and at times I turn the conversation to his experiences of the fairies.

He has seen a good many of them, he says, in different parts of the island, especially in the sandy districts north of the slip. They are about a yard high with caps like the "peelers" pulled down over their faces. On one occasion he saw them playing ball in the evening just above the slip, and he says I must avoid that place in the morning or after nightfall for fear they might do me mischief.

He has seen two women who were "away" with them, one a young married woman, the other a girl. The woman was standing by a wall, at a spot he described to me with great care, looking out towards the north.

Another night he heard a voice crying out in Irish, "A mháthair tá mé marbh" ("O mother, I'm killed"), and in the morning there was blood on the wall of his house, and a child in a house not far off was dead.

Yesterday he took me aside, and said he would tell me a secret he had never yet told to any person in the world.

"Take a sharp needle," he said, "and stick it in under the collar of your coat, and not one of them will be able to have power on you."

Iron is a common talisman with barbarians, but in this case the idea of exquisite sharpness was probably present also, and, perhaps, some feeling for the sanctity of the instrument of toil, a folk-belief that is common in Brittany.

The fairies are more numerous in Mayo than in any other

county, though they are fond of certain districts in Galway, where the following story is said to have taken place.

"A farmer was in great distress as his crops had failed, and his cow had died on him. One night he told his wife to make him a fine new sack for flour before the next morning; and when it was finished he started off with it before the dawn.

"At that time there was a gentleman who had been taken by the fairies, and made an officer among them, and it was often people would see him and her riding on a white horse at dawn and in the evening.

"The poor man went down to the place where they used to see the officer, and when he came by on his horse, he asked the loan of two hundred and a half of flour, for he was in great want.

"The officer called the fairies out of a hole in the rocks where they stored their wheat, and told them to give the poor man what he was asking. Then he told him to come back and pay him in a year, and rode away.

"When the poor man got home he wrote down the day on a piece of paper, and that day year he came back and paid the officer."

When he had ended his story the old man told me that the fairies have a tenth of all the produce of the country, and make stores of it in the rocks.

It is a Holy Day, and I have come up to sit on the Dun while the people are at Mass.

A strange tranquillity has come over the island this morning, as happens sometimes on Sunday, filling the two circles of sea and sky with the quiet of a church.

The one landscape that is here lends itself with singular power to this suggestion of grey luminous cloud. There is no wind, and no definite light. Aranmor seems to sleep upon a mirror, and the hills of Connemara look so near that I am troubled by the width of the bay that lies before them, touched this morning with individual expression one sees sometimes in a lake.

On these rocks, where there is no growth of vegetable or

animal life, all the seasons are the same, and this June day is so full of autumn that I listen unconsciously for the rustle of dead leaves.

The first group of men are coming out of the chapel, followed by a crowd of women, who divide at the gate and troop off in different directions, while the men linger on the road to gossip.

The silence is broken; I can hear far off, as if over water, a faint murmur of Gaelic.

In the afternoon the sun came out and I was rowed over for a visit to Kilronan.

As my men were bringing round the curagh to take me off a headland near the pier, they struck a sunken rock, and came ashore shipping a quantity of water. They plugged the hole with a piece of sacking torn from a bag of potatoes they were taking over for the priest, and we set off with nothing but a piece of torn canvas between us and the Atlantic.

Every few hundred yards one of the rowers had to stop and bail, but the hole did not increase.

When we were about half way across the sound we met a curagh coming towards us with its sail set. After some shouting in Gaelic, I learned that they had a packet of letters and tobacco for myself. We sidled up as near as was possible with the roll, and my goods were thrown to me wet with spray.

After my weeks in Inishmaan, Kilronan seemed an imposing centre of activity. The half-civilised fishermen of the larger island are inclined to despise the simplicity of the life here, and some of them who were standing about when I landed asked me how at all I passed my time with no decent fishing to be looking at.

I turned in for a moment to talk to the old couple in the hotel, and then moved on to pay some other visits in the village.

Later in the evening I walked out along the northern road, where I met many of the natives of the outlying villages, who had come down to Kilronan for the Holy Days, and were now wandering home in scattered groups.

The women and girls, when they had no men with them,

usually tried to make fun of me.

"Is it tired you are, stranger?" said one girl. I was walking very slowly, to pass the time before my return to the east.

"Bedad, it is not, little girl," I answered in Gaelic, "it is lonely I am."

"Here is my little sister, stranger, who will give you her arm."

And so it went on. Quiet as these women are on ordinary occasions, when two or three of them are gathered together in their holiday petticoats and shawls, they are as wild and capricious as the women who live in towns.

About seven o'clock I got back to Kilronan, and beat up my crew from the public-houses near the bay. With their usual carelessness they had not seen to the leak in the curagh, nor to an oar that was losing the brace that holds it to the toll-pin, and we moved off across the sound at an absurd pace with a deepening pool at our feet.

A superb evening light was lying over the island, which made me rejoice at our delay. Looking back there was a golden haze behind the sharp edges of the rock, and a long wake from the sun, which was making jewels of the bubbling left by the oars.

The men had had their share of porter and were unusually voluble, pointing out things to me that I had already seen, and stopping now and then to make me notice the oily smell of mackerel that was rising from the waves.

They told me that an evicting party is coming to the island to-morrow morning, and gave me a long account of what they make and spend in the year, and of their trouble with the rent.

"The rent is hard enough for a poor man," said one of them, "but this time we didn't pay, and they're after serving processes on every one of us. A man will have to pay his rent now, and a power of money with it for the process, and I'm thinking the agent will have money enough out of them processes to pay for his servant-girl and his man all the year."

I asked afterwards who the island belonged to.

"Bedad," they said, "we've always heard it belonged to Miss————, and she is dead."

When the sun passed like a lozenge of gold flame into the
sea the cold became intense. Then the men began to talk
among themselves, and losing the thread, I lay half in a dream
looking at the pale oily sea about us, and the low cliffs of the
island sloping up past the village with its wreath of smoke to
the outline of Dun Conor.

Old Pat was in the house when I arrived, and he told a long
story after supper:—

There was once a widow living among the woods, and her
only son living alone with her. He went out every morning
through the trees to get sticks, and one day as he was lying on
the ground he saw a swarm of flies flying over what the cow
leaves behind her. He took up his sickle and hit one blow at
them, and hit that hard he left no single one of them living.

That evening he said to his mother that it was time he was
going out into the world to seek his fortune, for he was able to
destroy a whole swarm of flies at one blow, and he asked her
to make him three cakes the way he might take them with him
in the morning.

He started the next day a while after the dawn, with his
three cakes in his wallet, and he ate one of them near ten
o'clock.

He got hungry again by midday and ate the second, and
when night was coming on him he ate the third. After that he
met a man on the road who asked him where he was going.

"I'm looking for some place where I can work for my living," said the young man.

"Come with me," said the other man, "and sleep to-night in
the barn, and I'll give you work to-morrow to see what you're
able for."

The next morning the farmer brought him out and showed
him his cows and told him to take them out to graze on the
hills, and to keep good watch that no one should come near
them to milk them. The young man drove out the cows into
the fields, and when the heat of the day came on he lay down
on his back and looked up into the sky. A while after he saw a

black spot in the north-west, and it grew larger and nearer till he saw a great giant coming towards him.

He got up on to his feet and he caught the giant round the legs with his two arms, and he drove him down into the hard ground above his ankles, the way he was not able to free himself. Then the giant told him to do him no hurt, and gave him his magic rod, and told him to strike on the rock, and he would find his beautiful black horse, and his sword, and his fine suit.

The young man struck the rock and it opened before him, and he found the beautiful black horse, and the giant's sword and the suit lying before him. He took out the sword alone, and he struck one blow with it and struck off the giant's head. Then he put back the sword into the rock, and went out again to his cattle, till it was time to drive them home to the farmer.

When they came to milk the cows they found a power of milk in them, and the farmer asked the young man if he had seen nothing out on the hills, for the other cow-boys had been bringing home the cows with no drop of milk in them. And the young man said he had seen nothing.

The next day he went out again with the cows. He lay down on his back in the heat of the day, and after a while he saw a black spot in the north-west, and it grew larger and nearer, till he saw it was a great giant coming to attack him.

"You killed my brother," said the giant; "come here, till I make a garter of your body."

The young man went to him and caught him by the legs and drove him down into the hard ground up to his ankles.

Then he hit the rod against the rock, and took out the sword and struck off the giant's head.

That evening the farmer found twice as much milk in the cows as the evening before, and he asked the young man if he had seen anything. The young man said that he had seen nothing.

The third day the third giant came to him and said, "You have killed my two brothers; come here, till I make a garter of your body."

And he did with this giant as he had done with the other

two, and that evening there was so much milk in the cows it was dropping out of their udders on the pathway.

The next day the farmer called him and told him he might leave the cows in the stalls that day, for there was a great curiosity to be seen, namely, a beautiful king's daughter that was to be eaten by a great fish, if there was no one in it that could save her. But the young man said such a sight was all one to him, and he went out with the cows on to the hills. When he came to the rocks he hit them with his rod, and brought out the suit and put it on him, and brought out the sword and strapped it on his side, like an officer, and he got on the black horse and rode faster than the wind till he came to where the beautiful king's daughter was sitting on the shore in a golden chair, waiting for the great fish.

When the great fish came in on the sea, bigger than a whale, with two wings on the back of it, the young man went down into the surf and struck at it with his sword and cut off one of its wings. All the sea turned red with the bleeding out of it, till it swam away and left the young man on the shore.

Then he turned his horse and rode faster than the wind till he came to the rocks, and he took the suit off him and put it back in the rocks, with the giant's sword and the black horse, and drove the cows down to the farm.

The man came out before him and said he had missed the greatest wonder ever was seen, and that a noble person was after coming down with a fine suit on him and cutting off one of the wings from the great fish.

"And there'll be the same necessity on her for two mornings more," said the farmer, "and you'd do right to come and look on it."

But the young man said he would not come.

The next morning he went out with his cows, and he took the sword and the suit and the black horse out of the rock, and he rode faster than the wind till he came where the king's daughter was sitting on the shore. When the people saw him coming there was great wonder on them to know if it was the same man they had seen the day before. The king's daughter called out to him to come and kneel before her, and when he kneeled down she took her scissors and cut off a lock of hair from the back of his head and hid it in her clothes.

Then the great worm came in from the sea, and he went down into the surf and cut the other wing off from it. All the sea turned red with the bleeding out of it, till it swam away and left them.

That evening the farmer came out before him and told him of the great wonder he had missed, and asked him would he go the next day and look on it. The young man said he would not go.

The third day he came again on the black horse to where the king's daughter was sitting on a golden chair waiting for the great worm. When it came in from the sea the young man went down before it, and every time it open its mouth to eat him, he struck into its mouth, till his sword went out through its neck, and it rolled back and died.

Then he rode off faster than the wind, and he put the suit and the sword and the black horse into the rock, and drove home the cows.

The farmer was there before him, and he told him that there was to be a great marriage feast held for three days, and on the third day the king's daughter would be married to the man that killed the great worm, if they were able to find him.

A great feast was held, and men of great strength came and said it was themselves were after killing the great worm.

But on the third day the young man put on the suit, and strapped the sword to his side like an officer, and got on the black horse and rode faster than the wind, till he came to the palace.

The king's daughter saw him, and she brought him in and made him kneel down before her. Then she looked at the back of his head and she saw that place where she had cut off the lock with her own hand. She led him in to the king, and they were married, and the young man was given all the estate.

That is my story.

Two recent attempts to carry out evictions on the island came to nothing, for each time a sudden storm rose, by, it is said, the power of a native witch, when the steamer was approaching, and made it impossible to land.

This morning, however, broke beneath a clear sky of June, and when I came into the open air the sea and rocks were shining with wonderful brilliancy. Groups of men, dressed in their holiday clothes, were standing about, talking with anger and fear, yet showing a lurking satisfaction at the thought of the dramatic pageant that was to break the silence of the seas.

About half-past nine the steamer came in sight, on the narrow line of sea-horizon that is seen in the centre of the bay, and immediately a last effort was made to hide the cows and sheep of the families that were most in debt.

Till this year no one on the island would consent to act as bailiff, so that it was impossible to identify the cattle of the defaulters. Now, however, a man of the name of Patrick has sold his honour, and the effort of concealment is practically futile.

This falling away from the ancient loyalty of the island has caused intense indignation, and early yesterday morning, while I was dreaming on the Dun, this letter was nailed on the doorpost of the chapel:—

"Patrick, the devil, a revolver is waiting for you. If you are missed with the first shot, there will be five more that will hit you.

"Any man that will talk with you, or work with you, or drink a pint of porter in your shop, will be done with the same way as yourself."

As the steamer drew near I moved down with the men to watch the arrival, though no one went further than about a mile from the shore.

Two curaghs from Kilronan with a man who was to give help in identifying the cottages, the doctor, and the relieving officer, were drifting with the tide, unwilling to come to land without the support of the larger party. When the anchor had been thrown it gave me a strange throb of pain to see the boats being lowered, and the sunshine gleaming on the rifles and helmets of the constabulary who crowded into them.

Once on shore the men were formed in close marching

order, a word was given, and the heavy rhythm of their boots came up over the rocks. We were collected in two straggling bands on either side of the roadway, and a few minutes later the body of magnificent armed men passed close to us, followed by a low rabble, who had been brought to act as drivers for the sheriff.

After my weeks spent among primitive men this glimpse of the newer types of humanity was not reassuring. Yet these mechanical police, with the commonplace agents and sheriffs, and the rabble they had hired, represented aptly enough the civilisation for which the homes of the island were to be desecrated.

A stop was made at one of the first cottages in the village, and the day's work began. Here, however, and at the next cottage, a compromise was made, as some relatives came up at the last moment and lent the money that was needed to gain a respite.

In another case a girl was ill in the house, so the doctor interposed, and the people were allowed to remain after a merely formal eviction. About mid-day, however, a house was reached where there was no pretext for mercy, and no money could be procured. At a sign from the sheriff the work of carrying out the beds and utensils was begun in the middle of a crowd of natives who looked on in absolute silence, broken only by the wild imprecations of the woman of the house. She belonged to one of the most primitive families on the island, and she shook with uncontrollable fury as she saw the strange armed men who spoke a language she could not understand driving her from the hearth she had brooded on for thirty years. For these people the outrage to the hearth is the supreme catastrophe. They live here in a world of grey, where there are wild rains and mists every week in the year, and their warm chimney corners, filled with children and young girls, grow into the consciousness of each family in a way it is not easy to understand in more civilised places.

The outrage to a tomb in China probably gives no greater shock to the Chinese than the outrage to a hearth in Inishmaan gives to the people.

When the few trifles had been carried out, and the door blocked with stones, the old woman sat down by the threshold and covered her head with her shawl.

Five or six other women who lived close by sat down in a circle round her, with mute sympathy. Then the crowd moved on with the police to another cottage where the same scene was to take place, and left the group of desolate women sitting by the hovel.

There were still no clouds in the sky, and the heat was intense. The police when not in motion lay sweating and gasping under the walls with their tunics unbuttoned. They were not attractive, and I kept comparing them with the islandmen, who walked up and down as cool and fresh-looking as the sea-gulls.

When the last eviction had been carried out a division was made: half the party went off with the bailiff to search the inner plain of the island for the cattle that had been hidden in the morning, the other half remained on the village road to guard some pigs that had already been taken possession of.

After a while two of these pigs escaped from the drivers and began a wild race up and down the narrow road. The people shrieked and howled to increase their terror, and at last some of them became so excited that the police thought it time to interfere. They drew up in double line opposite the mouth of a blind laneway where the animals had been shut up. A moment later the shrieking began again in the west and the two pigs came in sight, rushing down the middle of the road with the drivers behind them.

They reached the line of the police. There was a slight scuffle, and then the pigs continued their mad rush to the east, leaving three policemen lying in the dust.

The satisfaction of the people was immense. They shrieked and hugged each other with delight, and it is likely that they will hand down these animals for generations in the tradition of the island.

Two hours later the other party returned, driving three lean cows before them, and a start was made for the slip. At the public-house the policemen were given a drink while the dense crowd that was following waited in the lane. The island bull happened to be in a field close by, and he became wildly excited at the sight of the cows and of the strangely-dressed men. Two young islanders sidled up to me in a moment or two as I was resting on a wall, and one of them whispered in my ear—

"Do you think they could take fines of us if we let out the bull on them?"

In the face of the crowd of women and children, I could only say it was probable, and they slunk off.

At the slip there was a good deal of bargaining, which ended in all the cattle being given back to their owners. It was plainly of no use to take them away, as they were worth nothing.

When the last policeman had embarked, an old woman came forward from the crowd and, mounting on a rock near the slip, began a fierce rhapsody in Gaelic, pointing at the bailiff and waving her withered arms with extraordinary rage.

"This man is my own son," she said; "it is I that ought to know him. He is the first ruffian in the whole big world."

Then she gave an account of his life, coloured with a vindictive fury I cannot reproduce. As she went on the excitement became so intense I thought the man would be stoned before he could get back to his cottage.

On these islands the women live only for their children, and it is hard to estimate the power of the impulse that made this old woman stand out and curse her son.

In the fury of her speech I seem to look again into the strangely reticent temperament of the islanders, and to feel the passionate spirit that expresses itself, at odd moments only, with magnificent words and gestures.

Old Pat has told me a story of the goose that lays the golden eggs, which he calls the Phoenix:—

A poor widow had three sons and a daughter. One day when her sons were out looking for sticks in the wood they saw a fine speckled bird flying in the trees. The next day they saw it again, and the eldest son told his brothers to go and get sticks by themselves, for he was going after the bird.

He went after it, and brought it in with him when he came home in the evening. They put it in an old hencoop, and they gave it some of the meal they had for themselves;—I don't know if it ate the meal, but they divided what they had themselves; they could do no more.

That night it laid a fine spotted egg in the basket. The next night it laid another.

At that time its name was on the papers and many had heard of the bird that laid the golden eggs, for the eggs were of gold, and there's no lie in it.

When the boys went down to the shop the next day to buy a stone of meal, the shopman asked if he could buy the bird of them. Well, it was arranged in this way. The shopman would marry the boys' sister—a poor simple girl without a stitch of good clothes—and get the bird with her.

Some time after that one of the boys sold an egg of the bird to a gentleman that was in the country. The gentleman asked him if he had the bird still. He said that the man who had married his sister was after getting it.

"Well," said the gentleman, "the man who eats the heart of that bird will find a purse of gold beneath him every morning, and the man who eats its liver will be the king of Ireland."

The boy went out—he was a simple poor fellow—and told the shopman.

Then the shopman brought in the bird and killed it, and he ate the heart himself and he gave the liver to his wife.

When the boy saw that there was great anger on him, and he went back and told the gentlemen.

"Do what I'm telling you," said the gentleman. "Go down now and tell the shopman and his wife to come up here to play a game of cards with me, for it's lonesome I am this evening."

When the boy was gone he mixed a vomit and poured the lot of it into a few naggins of whiskey, and he put a strong cloth on the table under the cards.

The man came up with his wife and they began to play.

The shopman won the first game and the gentleman made them drink a sup of the whiskey.

They played again and the shopman won the second game. Then the gentleman made him drink a sup more of the whiskey.

As they were playing the third game the shopman and his wife got sick on the cloth, and the boy picked it up and carried it into the yard, for the gentleman had let him know what he was to do. Then he found the heart of the bird and he ate it, and the next morning when he turned in his bed there was a purse of gold under him.

That is my story.

When the steamer is expected I rarely fail to visit the boat-slip, as the men usually collect when she is in the offing, and lie arguing among their curaghs till she has made her visit to the south island, and is seen coming towards us.

This morning I had a long talk with an old man who was rejoicing over the improvement he has seen here during the last ten or fifteen years.

Till recently there was no communication with the mainland except by hookers, which were usually slow, and could only make the voyage in tolerably fine weather, so that if an islander went to a fair it was often three weeks before he could return. Now, however, the steamer comes here twice in the week, and the voyage is made in three or four hours.

The pier on this island is also a novelty, and is much thought of, as it enables the hookers that still carry turf and cattle to discharge and take their cargoes directly from the shore. The water round it, however, is only deep enough for a hooker when the tide is nearly full, and will never float the steamer, so passengers must still come to land in curaghs. The boat-slip at the corner next the south island is extremely useful in calm weather, but it is exposed to a heavy roll from the south, and is so narrow that the curaghs run some danger of missing it in the tumult of the surf.

In bad weather four men will often stand for nearly an hour at the top of the slip with a curagh in their hands, watching a point of rock towards the south where they can see the strength of the waves that are coming in.

The instant a break is seen they swoop down to the surf, launch their curagh, and pull out to sea with incredible speed. Coming to land is attended with the same difficulty, and, if their moment is badly chosen, they are likely to be washed sideways and swamped among the rocks.

This continual danger, which can only be escaped by extra-ordinary personal dexterity, has had considerable influence on the local character, as the waves have made it impossible for clumsy, fool-hardy, or timid men to live on these islands.

When the steamer is within a mile of the slip, the curaghs are put out and range themselves—there are usually from four to a dozen—in two lines at some distance from the shore.

The moment she comes in among them there is a short but desperate struggle for good places at her side. The men are lolling on their oars talking with the dreamy tone which comes with the rocking of the waves. The steamer lies to, and in an instant the oars bend and quiver with the strain. For one minute they seem utterly indifferent to their own safety and that of their friends and brothers. Then the sequence is decid-ed, and they begin to talk again with the dreamy tone that is habitual to them, while they make fast and clamber up into the steamer.

While the curaghs are out I am left with a few women and very old men who cannot row. One of these old men, whom I often talk with, has some fame as a bone-setter, and is said to have done remarkable cures, both here and on the mainland. Stories are told of how he has been taken off by the quality in their carriages through the hills of Connemara, to treat their sons and daughters, and come home with his pockets full of money.

Another old man, the oldest on the island, is fond of telling me anecdotes—not folk-tales—of things that have happened here in his lifetime.

He often tells me about a Connaught man who killed his father with the blow of a spade when he was in passion, and then fled to this island and threw himself on the mercy of some of the natives with whom he was said to be related. They hid him in a hole—which the old man has shown me—and kept him safe for weeks, though the police came and searched for him, and he could hear their boots grinding on the stones over his head. In spite of a reward which was offered, the island was incorruptible, and after much trouble the man was safely shipped to America.

This impulse to protect the criminal is universal in the west. It seems partly due to the association between justice and the hated English jurisdiction, but more directly to the primitive feeling of these people, who are never criminals yet always capable of crime, that a man will not do wrong unless he is under the influence of a passion which is as irresponsible as a storm on the sea. If a man has killed his father, and is already sick and broken with remorse, they can see no reason why he should be dragged away and killed by the law.

Such a man, they say, will be quiet all the rest of his life, and if you suggest that punishment is needed as an example, they ask, "Would any one kill his father if he was able to help it?"

Some time ago, before the introduction of police, all the people of the islands were as innocent as the people here remain to this day. I have heard that at that time the ruling proprietor and magistrate of the north island used to give any man who had done wrong a letter to a jailer in Galway, and send him off by himself to serve a term of imprisonment.

As there was no steamer, the ill-doer was given a passage in some chance hooker to the nearest point on the mainland. Then he walked for many miles along a desolate shore till he reached the town. When his time had been put through, he crawled back along the same route, feeble and emaciated, and had often to wait many weeks before he could regain the island. Such at least is the story.

It seems absurd to apply the same laws to these people and to the criminal classes of a city. The most intelligent man on Inishmaan has often spoken to me of his contempt of the law, and of the increase of crime the police have brought to Aranmor. On this island, he says, if men have a little difference, or a little fight, their friends take care it does not go too far, and in a little time it is forgotten. In Kilronan there is a band of men paid to make out cases for themselves; the moment a blow is struck they come down and arrest the man who gave it. The other man he quarrelled with has to give evidence against him; whole families come down to the court and swear against each other till they become bitter enemies. If there is a conviction the man who is convicted never forgives. He waits his time, and before the year is out there is a cross summons, which the other man in turn never forgives. The feud continues to grow, till a dispute about the colour of a man's hair may end in a murder, after a year's forcing by the law. The mere fact that it is impossible to get reliable evidence in the island—not because the people are dishonest, but because they think the claim on kinship more sacred than the claims of abstract truth—turns the whole system of sworn evidence into a demoralising farce, and it is easy to believe that law dealings on this false basis must lead to every sort of injustice.

While I am discussing these questions with the old men the curaghs begin to come in with cargoes of salt, and flour, and porter.

To-day a stir was made by the return of a native who had spent five years in New York. He came on shore with half a dozen people who had been shopping on the mainland, and walked up and down on the slip in his neat suit, looking strangely foreign to his birthplace, while his old mother of eighty-five ran about on the slippery seaweed, half crazy with delight, telling every one the news.

When the curaghs were in their places the men crowded round him to bid him welcome. He shook hands with them readily enough, but with no smile of recognition.

He is said to be dying.

Yesterday—a Sunday—three young men rowed me over to Inisheer, the south island of the group.

The stern of the curagh was occupied, so I was put in the bow with my head on a level with the gunnel. A considerable sea was running in the sound, and when we came out from the shelter of this island, the curagh rolled and vaulted in a way not easy to describe.

At one moment, as we went down into the furrow, green waves curled and arched themselves above me; then in an instant I was flung up into the air and could look down on the heads of the rowers, as if we were sitting on a ladder, or out across a forest of white crests to the black cliff of Inishmaan.

The men seemed excited and uneasy, and I thought for a moment that we were likely to be swamped. In a little while, however, I realised the capacity of the curagh to raise its head among the waves, and the motion became strangely exhilarating. Even, I thought, if we were dropped into the blue chasm of the waves, this death, with the fresh sea saltness in one's teeth, would be better than most deaths one is likely to meet.

When we reached the other island, it was raining heavily, so that we could not see anything of the antiquities or people.

For the greater part of the afternoon we sat on the tops of empty barrels in the public-house, talking on the destiny of Gaelic. We were admitted as travellers, and the shutters of the shop were closed behind us, letting in only a glimmer of grey light, and the tumult of the storm. Towards evening it cleared a little and we came home in a calmer sea, but with a dead head-wind that gave the rowers all they could do to make the passage.

On calm days I often go out fishing with Michael. When we reach the space above the slip where the curaghs are propped, bottom upwards, on the limestone, he lifts the prow of the one we are going to embark in, and I slip underneath and set the centre of the foremost seat upon my neck. Then he crawls under the stern and stands up with the last seat upon his shoulders. We start for the sea. The long prow bends before me so that I see nothing but a few yards of shingle at my feet. A quivering pain runs from the top of my spine to the sharp stones that seem to pass through my pampooties, and grate upon my ankles. We stagger and groan beneath the weight; but at last our feet reach the slip, and we run down with a half-trot like the pace of barefooted children.

A yard from the sea we stop and lower the curagh to the right. It must be brought down gently—a difficult task for our strained and aching muscles—and sometimes as the gunnel reaches the slip I lose my balance and roll in among the seats.

Yesterday we went out in the curagh that had been damaged on the day of my visit to Kilronan, and as we were putting in the oars the freshly-tarred patch stuck to the slip which was heated with the sunshine. We carried up water in the bailer—the "cupeen," a shallow wooden vessel like a soup-plate—and with infinite pains we got free and rode away. In a few moments, however, I found the water spouting up at my feet.

The patch had been misplaced, and this time we had no sacking. Michael borrowed my pocket scissors, and with admirable rapidity cut a square of flannel from the tail of his shirt and squeezed it into the hole, making it fast with a splint which he hacked from one of the oars.

During our excitement the tide had carried us to the brink of the rocks, and I admired again the dexterity with which he got his oars into the water and turned us out as we were mounting on a wave that would have hurled us to destruction.

With the injury to our curagh we did not go far from the shore. After a while I took a long spell at the oars, and gained a certain dexterity, though they are not easy to manage. The handles overlap by about six inches—and at first it is almost impossible to avoid striking the upper oar against one's knuckles. The oars are rough and square, except at the ends, so one cannot do so with impunity. Again, a curagh with two light people in it floats on the water like a nutshell, and the slightest inequality in the stroke throws the prow round at least a right angle from its course. In the first half-hour I found myself more than once moving towards the point I had come from, greatly to Michael's satisfaction.

This morning we were out again near the pier on the north side of the island. As we paddled slowly with the tide, trolling for pollock, several curaghs, weighed to the gunnel with kelp, passed us on their way to Kilronan.

An old woman, rolled in red petticoats, was sitting on a ledge of rock that runs into the sea at the point where the curaghs were passing from the south, hailing them in quavering Gaelic, and asking for a passage to Kilronan.

The first one that came round without a cargo turned in from some distance and took her away.

The morning had none of the supernatural beauty that comes over the island so often in rainy weather, so we basked in the vague enjoyment of the sunshine, looking down at the wild luxuriance of the vegetation beneath the sea, which contrasts strangely with the nakedness above it.

Some dreams I have had in this cottage seem to give strength to the opinion that there is a psychic memory attached to certain neighbourhoods.

Last night, after walking in a dream among buildings with strangely intense light on them, I head a faint rhythm of music beginning far away on some stringed instrument.

It came closer to me, gradually increasing in quickness and volume with an irresistibly definite progression. When it was quite near the sound began to move in my nerves and blood, and to urge me to dance with them.

I knew that if I yielded I would be carried away to some moment of terrible agony, so I struggled to remain quiet, holding my knees together with my hands.

The music increased continually, sounding like the strings of harps, tuned to a forgotten scale, and having a resonance as searching as the strings of the 'cello.

Then the luring excitement became more powerful than my will, and my limbs moved in spite of me.

In a moment I was swept away in a whirlwind of notes. My breath and my thoughts and every impulse of my body, became a form of the dance, till I could not distinguish between the instruments and the rhythm and my own person or consciousness.

For a while it seemed an excitement that was filled with joy, then it grew into an ecstasy where all existence was lost in a vortex of movement. I could not think there had ever been a life beyond the whirling of the dance.

Then with a shock the ecstasy turned to an agony and rage.

I struggled to free myself, but seemed only to increase the passion of the steps I moved to. When I shrieked I could only echo the notes of the rhythm.

At last with a moment of uncontrollable frenzy I broke back to consciousness and awoke.

I dragged myself trembling to the window of the cottage and looked out. The moon was glittering across the bay, and there was no sound anywhere on the island.

I am leaving in two days, and old Pat Dirane has bidden me good-bye. He met me in the village this morning and took me into "his little tint," a miserable hovel where he spends the night.

I sat for a long time on his threshold, while he leaned on a stool behind me, near his bed, and told me the last story I shall have from him—a rude anecdote not worth recording. Then he told me with careful emphasis how he had wandered when he was a young man, and lived in a fine college, teaching Irish to the young priests!

They say on the island that he can tell as many lies as four men: perhaps the stories he has learned have strengthened his imagination.

When I stood up in the doorway to give him God's blessing, he leaned over on the straw that forms his bed, and shed tears. Then he turned to me again, lifted up one trembling hand, with the mitten worn to a hole on the palm, from the rubbing of his crutch.

"I'll not see you again," he said, with tears trickling on his face, "and you're a kindly man. When you come back next year I won't be in it. I won't live beyond the winter. But listen now to what I'm telling you; let you put insurance on me in the city of Dublin, and it's five hundred pounds you'll get on my burial."

This evening, my last in the island, is also the evening of the "Pattern"—a festival something like "Pardons" of Brittany.

I waited especially to see it, but a piper who was expected did not come, and there was no amusement. A few friends and relations came over from the other island and stood about the public-house in their best clothes, but without music dancing was impossible.

I believe on some occasions when the piper is present there is a fine day of dancing and excitement, but the Galway piper is getting old, and is not easily induced to undertake the voyage.

Last night, St. John's Eve, the fires were lighted and boys ran about with pieces of the burning turf, though I could not find out if the idea of lighting the house fires from the bonfire is still found on the island.

I have come out of an hotel full of tourists and commercial travellers, to stroll along the edge of Galway bay, and look out in the direction of the islands. The sort of yearning I feel towards those lonely rocks is indescribably acute. This town, that is usually so full of wild human interest, seems in my present mood a tawdry medley of all that is crudest in modern life. The nullity of the rich and the squalor of the poor give me the same pang of wondering disgust; yet the islands are fading already and I can hardly realise that the smell of the seaweed and the drone of the Atlantic are still moving round them.

One of my island friends has written to me:—

DEAR JOHN SYNGE,—I am for a long time expecting a letter from you and I think you are forgetting this island altogether.

Mr.——— died a long time ago on the big island and his boat was on anchor in the harbour and the wind blew her to Black Head and broke her up after his death.

Tell me are you learning Irish since you went. We have a branch of the Gaelic league here now and the people is going on well with the Irish and reading.

I will write the next letter in Irish to you. Tell me will you come to see us next year and if you will you'll write a letter before you. All your loving friends is well in health.—*Mise do chara go buan.*

Another boy I sent some baits to has written to me also, beginning his letter in Irish and ending it in English:—

DEAR JOHN,—I got your letter four days ago, and there was pride and joy on me because it was written in Irish, and a fine, good, pleasant letter it was. The baits you sent are very good, but I lost two of them and half of my line. A big fish came and caught the bait, and the line was bad and half of the line and the baits went away. My sister has come back from America, but I'm thinking it won't be long till she goes away again, for it is lonesome and poor she finds the island now.—I am your friend....

Write soon and let you write in Irish, if you don't I won't look on it.

The Deep Waters

by
E. PAULINE JOHNSON
(1861–1913)

The two legends of the Flood given here, from the Squamish and the Iroquois, are from Legends of Vancouver, *a fine collection of tales and legends that were told to Pauline Johnson by Joe Capilano, a Squamish chief, in the early years of this century. Johnson, an intriguing figure, half-Mohawk and half-white, seems to have been cast in the role of the "white man's Indian"—moving with apparent ease between cultures. Her strength as a poet and storyteller giving voice to traditional Native values is clearly evident here.*

Far over your left shoulder as your boat leaves the Narrows to thread the beautiful waterways that lead to Vancouver Island, you will see the summit of Mount Baker robed in its everlasting whiteness and always reflecting some wonderful glory from the rising sun, the golden noontide, or the violet and amber sunset. This is the Mount Ararat of the Pacific Coast peoples; for those readers who are familiar with the ways and beliefs and faiths of primitive races will agree that it is difficult to discover anywhere in the world a race that has not some story of the Deluge, which they have chronicled and localized to fit the understanding and the conditions of the nation that composes their own immediate world.

Amongst the red nations of America I doubt if any two tribes have the same ideas regarding the Flood. Some of the traditions concerning this vast whim of Nature are grotesque in the extreme; some are impressive; some even profound; but of all the stories of the Deluge that I have been able to collect I know of not a single one that can even begin to equal in beauty of conception, let alone rival in possible reality and truth, the Squamish legend of "The Deep Waters."

I here quote the legend of "mine own people," the Iroquois tribes of Ontario, regarding the Deluge. I do this to paint the colour of contrast in richer shades, for I am bound to admit that we who pride ourselves on ancient intellectuality have but a childish tale of the Flood when compared with the jealously preserved annals of the Squamish, which savour more of history than tradition. With "mine own people," animals always play a much more important role and are endowed with a finer intelligence than humans. I do not find amid my notes a single tradition of the Iroquois wherein animals do not figure, and our story of the Deluge rests entirely with the intelligence of sea-going and river-going creatures. With us, animals in olden times were greater than man; but it is not so with the Coast Indians, except in rare instances.

When a Coast Indian consents to tell you a legend he will, without variation, begin it with, "It was before the white people came."

The natural thing for you then to ask is, "But who were here then?"

He will reply, "Indians, and just the trees, and animals, and fishes, and a few birds."

So you are prepared to accept the animal world as intelligent co-habitants of the Pacific slope, but he will not lead you to think he regards them as equals, much less superiors. But to revert to "mine own people": they hold the intelligence of wild animals far above that of man, for perhaps the one reason that when an animal is sick it effects its own cure; it knows what grasses and herbs to eat, what to avoid, while the sick human calls the medicine man, whose wisdom is not only the result of years of study, but also heredity; consequently any great natural event, such as the Deluge, has much to do with the wisdom of the creatures of the forests and the rivers.

Iroquois tradition tells us that once this earth was entirely submerged in water, and during this period for many days a busy little muskrat swam about vainly looking for a foothold of earth wherein to build his house. In his search he encountered a turtle also leisurely swimming, so they had speech together, and the muskrat complained of weariness; he could find no foothold; he was tired of incessant swimming, and longed for land such as his ancestors enjoyed. The turtle suggested that the muskrat should dive and endeavour to find earth at the bottom of the sea. Acting on this advice the muskrat plunged down, then arose with his two little forepaws grasping some earth he had found beneath the waters.

"Place it on my shell and dive again for more," directed the turtle. The muskrat did so, but when he returned with his paws filled with earth he discovered the small quantity he had first deposited on the turtle's shell had doubled in size. The return from the third trip found the turtle's load again doubled. So the building went on at double compound increase, and the world grew its continents and its islands with great rapidity, and now rests on the shell of a turtle.

If you ask an Iroquois, "And did no men survive this flood?" he will reply, "Why should men survive? The animals are wiser than men; let the wisest live."

How, then, was the earth repeopled?

The Iroquois will tell you that the otter was a medicine man; that in swimming and diving about he found corpses of men and women; he sang his medicine songs and they came to life, and the otter brought them fish for food until they were strong enough to provide for themselves. Then the Iroquois will conclude his tale with, "You know well that the otter has greater wisdom than a man."

So much for "mine own people" and our profound respect for the superior intelligence of our little brothers of the animal world.

But the Squamish tribe hold other ideas. It was on a February day that I first listened to this beautiful, humane story of the Deluge. My royal old tillicum had come to see me through the rains and mists of late winter days. The gateways of my wigwam always stood open—very widely open—for his feet to enter, and this especial day he came with the worst downpour of the season.

Womanlike, I protested with a thousand contradictions in my voice that he should venture out to see me on such a day. It was "Oh! Chief, I am so glad to see you," and it was "Oh!

Chief, why didn't you stay at home on such a wet day—your poor throat will suffer." But I soon had quantities of hot tea for him, and the huge cup my own father always used was his— as long as the Sagalie Tyee allowed his dear feet to wander my way. The immense cup stands idle and empty now for the second time.

Helping him off with his great-coat, I chatted on about the deluge of rain, and he remarked it was not so very bad, as one could yet walk.

"Fortunately, yes, for I cannot swim," I told him.

He laughed, replying, "Well, it is not so bad as when the Great Deep Waters covered the world."

Immediately I foresaw the coming legend, so crept into the shell of monosyllables.

"No?" I questioned.

"No," he replied. "For one thing there was no land here at all; everywhere there was just water."

"I can quite believe it," I remarked caustically.

He laughed—that irresistible, though silent, David Warfield laugh of his that always brought a responsive smile from his listeners. Then he plunged directly into the tradition, with no preface save a comprehensive sweep of the wonderful hands towards my wide window, against which the rains were beating.

"It was after a long, long time of this—this rain. The mountain streams were swollen, the rivers choked, the sea began to rise—and yet it rained; for weeks and weeks it rained." He ceased speaking, while the shadows of centuries gone crept into his eyes. Tales of the misty past always inspired him.

"Yes," he continued. "It rained for weeks and weeks, while the mountain torrents roared thunderingly down, and the sea crept silently up. The level lands were first to float in sea water, then to disappear. The slopes were next to slip into the sea. The world was slowly being flooded. Hurriedly the Indian tribes gathered in one spot, a place of safety far above the reach of the on-creeping sea. The spot was the circling shore of Lake Beautiful, up the North Arm. They held a Great Council and decided at once upon a plan of action. A giant canoe should be built, and some means contrived to anchor it in case the waters mounted to the heights. The men undertook the canoe, the women the anchorage.

"A giant tree was felled, and day and night the men toiled over its construction into the most stupendous canoe the world has ever known. Not an hour, not a moment, but many worked, while the toil-wearied ones slept, only to awake to renewed toil. Meanwhile the women also worked at a cable— the largest, the longest, the strongest that Indian hands and teeth had ever made. Scores of them gathered and prepared the cedar fibre; scores of them plaited, rolled and seasoned it; scores of them chewed upon it inch by inch to make it pliable; scores of them oiled and worked, oiled and worked, oiled and worked it into a sea-resisting fabric. And still the sea crept up, and up, and up. It was the last day; hope of life for the tribe, of land for the world, was doomed. Strong hands, self-sacrificing hands fastened the cable the women had made—one end to the giant canoe, the other about an enormous boulder, a vast immovable rock as firm as the foundations of the world— for might not the canoe with its priceless freight drift out, far out, to sea, and when the water subsided might not this ship of safety be leagues and leagues beyond the sight of land on the storm-driven Pacific?

"Then with the bravest hearts that ever beat, noble hands lifted every child of the tribe into this vast canoe, not one single baby was overlooked. The canoe was stocked with food and fresh water, and lastly, the ancient men and women of the race selected as guardians to these children the bravest, most stalwart, handsomest young man of the tribe, and the mother of the youngest baby in the camp—she was but a girl of sixteen, her child but two weeks old; but she, too, was brave and very beautiful. These two were placed, she at the bow of the canoe to watch, and he at the stern to guide, and all the little children crowded between.

"And still the sea crept up, and up, and up. At the crest of the bluffs about Lake Beautiful the doomed tribes crowded. Not a single person attempted to enter the canoe. There was no wailing, no crying out for safety. 'Let the little children, the young mother, and the bravest and best of our young men live,' was all the farewell those in the canoe heard as the waters reached the summit, and—the canoe floated. Last of all to be seen was the top of the tallest trees, then—all was a world of water.

"For days and days there was no land—just the rush of swirling, snarling sea; but the canoe rode safely at anchor, the cable those scores of dead, faithful women had made held true as the hearts that beat behind the toil and labour of it all.

"But one morning at sunrise, far to the south a speck floated on the breast of the waters; at midday it was larger; at evening it was yet larger. The moon arose, and in its magic light the man at the stern saw it was a patch of land. All night he watched it grow, and at daybreak looked with glad eyes upon the summit of Mount Baker. He cut the cable, grasped his paddle in his strong, young hands and steered for the south. When they landed, the waters were sunken half down the mountain side. The children were lifted out; the beautiful young mother, the stalwart young brave, turned to each other, clasped hands, looked into each other's eyes—and smiled.

"And down in the vast country that lies between Mount Baker and the Fraser River they made a new camp, built new lodges, where the little children grew and thrived, and lived and loved, and the earth was repeopled by them.

"The Squamish say that in a gigantic crevice halfway to the crest of Mount Baker may yet be seen the outlines of an enormous canoe, but I have never seen it myself."

He ceased speaking with that far-off cadence in his voice with which he always ended a legend, and for a long time we both sat in silence listening to the rains that were still beating against the window.

The Waves
(dusk)

The sun was sinking. The hard stone of the day was cracked and light poured through its splinters. Red and gold shot through the waves, in rapid running arrows, feathered with darkness. Erratically rays of light flashed and wandered, like signals from sunken islands, or darts shot through laurel groves by shameless, laughing boys. But the waves, as they neared the shore, were robbed of light, and fell in one long concussion, like a wall falling, a wall of grey stone, unpierced by any chink of light.

VW

The Little Mermaid

by

HANS CHRISTIAN ANDERSEN

(1805–1875)

Of the world beneath the waves, and cockleshells and shiny pearls… Hans Christian Andersen is always more interesting than the World of Disney would have us believe, and the underworld of the mer-folk in "The Little Mermaid" is a far more dangerous and threatening place than I, for one, remembered it.

In "The Fisherman and His Soul," the Oscar Wilde story which appears earlier in this collection, the fisherman/prince descended into the waves to join his beloved mermaid. Here, the mermaid sprouts legs to walk the earth…but oh, at what a price…

Far, far out to sea the water is as blue as the petals of the loveliest cornflower, and as clear as the clearest glass; but it is deep, very deep, deeper than any anchor has ever sunk. Countless church towers would have to be placed one on top of another to reach from the sea-bed to the surface. Down in those depths live the mer-people.

Now you must not think for a moment that there is nothing down below but bare white sand. No, indeed—the most wonderful trees and plants grow there, with stems and leaves so lithe and sensitive that they wave and sway with the slightest stir of the water; they might be living creatures. All kinds of fish, both large and small, glide in and out of the branches, just like birds in the air up here. In the very deepest part of all is the Mer-King's palace. Its walls are of coral, and the long pointed windows are of the clearest amber, while the roof is made of cockleshells, which open and close with the waves. That's a splendid sight, for each holds a shining pearl; any single one would be the pride of a queen's crown.

The Mer-King here had been a widower for many years; his dowager mother kept house for him. She was a wise old lady, though rather too proud of her royal rank; that's why she always wore twelve oysters on her tail while other highborn mer-folk were allowed no more than six. But she deserved special praise for the care she took of the little mer-princesses, her granddaughters.

There were six of them, all beautiful, but the youngest was the most beautiful of all. Her skin was like a rose petal, pure and clear; her eyes were as blue as the deepest lake. But, like the others, she had no feet; her body ended in a fish's tail. All day long she and her sisters would play down there in the palace, in and out of the vast rooms where living sea-flowers grew from the walls. When the great amber windows were open the fish would swim inside and let themselves be stroked.

Outside the palace was a large garden with flame-red and sea-blue trees. The fruit all shone like gold, and the flowers looked like glowing fire among the moving stems and leaves. The ground itself was of the finest sand, but blue as a sulphur flame. A strange blue-violet light lay over everything; you might have thought that, instead of being far down under the sea, you were high up in the air, with nothing over and under you but sky. On days of perfect calm you could see the sun; it looked like a crimson flower, with rays of light streaming out of its centre.

Each of the little princesses had her own small plot in the garden, where she could dig and plant whatever she wished. One made her flower-bed in the shape of a whale; another made hers like a mermaid. But the youngest had hers perfectly round, like the sun, and the only flowers she planted there were like smaller suns in their glow and colour.

She was a strange child, quiet and thoughtful. While the other sisters decorated their gardens with wonderful things from the wrecks of ships, the only ornament she would have was a beautiful marble carving, a lovely boy made out of pure white stone. This too had sunk to the sea-bed from a wreck. Beside this marble boy she planted a rose-red tree like a weeping willow; it grew apace, its branches bending over the stone figure until they touched the deep-blue sand below.

Nothing pleased the youngest princess more than to hear about the far-off world of humans. She made the old grandmother tell her all she knew about ships and towns, people and animals. It was a strange and wonderful thought to her that the flowers on earth had a sweet smell, for they had none at all in the sea.

"As soon as you are fifteen," the grandmother told her granddaughters, "you may rise to the surface, and sit on the rocks in the moonlight and watch the great ships sail by. If you have enough courage you may even see woods and towns!" The following year the oldest of the sisters would be fifteen; but as for the others—well, each was a year younger than the next, so the youngest of them all still had five years to wait. But each promised to tell the rest what she had seen, and what she had found most surprising in the human world above. Their grandmother never told them enough, and there was so much they wanted to know.

But none of the six had a greater wish to learn about the mysterious earth above than the youngest (the very one who had the longest time to wait), the one who was so thoughtful and quiet. Many a night she would stand at the open window and gaze up through the dark-blue water where the fishes frisked with waving fins and tails. She could see the moon and stars; their light was rather pale, to be sure, but seen through the water they looked much larger than they do to us. If ever a kind of dark cloud glided along beneath them, she knew that it was either a whale swimming over her, or a ship full of human people. Those humans never imagined that a beautiful little mermaid was below, stretching up her white hands towards the keel.

And now came the time when the eldest princess was fifteen, and was allowed to rise to the surface. As soon as she was home again she had a hundred things to tell the others. But what did she like best of all? Lying on a sandbank in the moonlight when the sea was calm, she told them, gazing at the big city, near to the coast, where the lights were twinkling like a hundred stars, listening to the busy noise and stir of traffic and people, seeing all the towers and spires of the churches, hearing the ringing of the bells. And just because she couldn't go to the city, she longed to do this more than anything.

Oh, how intently the youngest sister listened! And later in the evening, when she stood at the open window and gazed up through the dark-blue water, she thought of the great city, and then she seemed to hear the ring of church bells echoing all the way down to her.

The next year the second sister was allowed to rise up through the water and swim wherever she wished. She reached the surface just as the sun was going down and that was the sight that she thought loveliest of all. The whole sky was a blaze of gold, she said; as for the clouds—well, she couldn't find words to describe how beautiful they were, crimson and violet, sailing high overhead. But moving much more swiftly, a flock of wild swans like a long white ribbon had flown across the waves towards the setting sun. She too had swum towards the sun, but it sank in the water, and the brightness vanished from sea and sky.

The year after that, the third sister had her chance. She was the most adventurous of the lot, and swam up a wide river that flowed into the sea. She saw green hills planted with grape-vines; she had glimpses of farms and castles through the trees of the great forests. She heard the singing of birds; she felt the warmth of the sun—indeed, it was so hot that she often had to dive down to cool her burning face. In the curve of a little bay a group of human children were splashing about in the water, quite naked; she wanted to play with them, but they scampered off in a fright.

The fourth sister was not so bold. She kept to mid-ocean, well away from the shore, and that, she declared, gave the best view of all; you could see for miles around. She had seen ships, but so far away that they looked like seagulls. The friendly dolphins had turned somersaults; great whales had spouted jets of water—it was like being surrounded by a hundred waterfalls.

Then came the turn of the fifth sister. Her birthday happened to fall in winter, and so she saw what the others had not seen on their first view of the world above. The sea looked quite green; great icebergs floated about, each one as beautiful as a pearl, she said—yet vaster than the church towers built by men. They appeared in the strangest shapes, glittering like diamonds. She had seated herself on one of the largest, and the sailors in passing ships were filled with terror, and steered in wide curves as far away as they could get from the iceberg where she sat, her long hair streaming in the wind. Late that evening the sky had become heavy and overcast; lightning flashed; thunder rolled and rumbled, and the darks waves lifted huge blocks of ice high into the air. Sails were lowered on all the ships; humans aboard were struck with fear and dread; but the mermaid still sat peacefully on her floating iceberg, and calmly watched the violent flashes of lightning zigzagging down into the glittering sea.

The first time each of the sisters rose above the surface she was enchanted by all the new and wonderful sights; but now that the five were old enough to journey up whenever they liked, they soon lost interest; after a short time at the surface they longed to be home again. The most beautiful place in the world was deep beneath the sea.

Still, there were many evenings when the five sisters would link arms and rise to the surface together. They had lovely voices—no human voice was ever so hauntingly beautiful— and when a storm blew up, and they thought that a ship might be wrecked, they would swim in front of the vessel and sing about the delights of their world beneath the sea; the sailors should have no fear of coming there. But the sailors never understood the songs; they fancied they were hearing the sound of the storm. Nor could they ever see for themselves the paradise down below, for when the ship sank, they were drowned, and only drowned men ever reached the Mer-King's palace.

On those evenings, the youngest was left behind all alone, gazing after them. She would have cried, but a mermaid has no tears, and that makes her feel more grief than if she had.

And then at last she was fifteen.

"There now! We're getting you off our hands at last!" said her grandmother, the old queen Mother. "Come along, and let me dress you up like your sisters." And she put a wreath of white lilies on her head, and every petal was really half a pearl. "Good-bye," the little mermaid said, and floated up through the water as lightly as a bubble.

The sun had just set when her head touched the surface, but the clouds still had a gleam of gold and rose. Up in the pale pink sky the evening star shone out, clear and radiant; the air was soft and mild, and the sea was calm as glass. A great three-masted ship was lying there; only one sail was set, because there wasn't a breath of wind, and the sailors were idly waiting in the rigging and yard-arms. There were sounds of music and singing, and as the night grew darker hundreds of coloured lanterns lit the scene; it looked as if flags of all the nations were flying in the wind.

The little mermaid swam right up to a porthole. Every time she rose with the lift of the waves she could see through the clear glass a crowd of people in splendid clothes—and the handsomest of all was a young prince with large dark eyes. He could not have been much older than sixteen—in fact, this was his birthday, and the cause of all the excitement. Now sailors began to dance on the decks, and when the young prince stepped out among them, over a hundred rockets shot up in the air. They made the night as bright as day, so that the little mermaid was quite terrified, and dived down under the water. But she soon popped up her head again, and then she thought that all the stars of heaven were falling down towards her. She had never seen fireworks. Catherine-wheels were spinning round like suns; rockets like fiery fishes soared into the sky, and all this was reflected in the sea. On the ship itself there was so much light that you could make out the smallest rope, and the features of every face. Oh, how handsome the young prince was! There he stood, shaking hands with one guest after another, laughing and smiling, while the music rang out into the night.

It was growing late, but the little mermaid could not take her eyes from the ship and the handsome prince. The coloured lamps were put out; no more rockets flew up; no more guns were fired. Yet deep down in the sea there was a murmuring and a rumbling. The waves rose higher; great clouds massed together; lightning flashed in the distance—a terrible storm was on the way. And so the crew took in sail as the great ship tossed about. The waves rose like huge black mountains, higher than the masts themselves; but the ship dived down like a swan between the billows and then rode up again on the towering crests. To the little mermaid all this was delightful—but it was no joke to the sailors. The vessel creaked and cracked; its thick planks bent under the pound-ing blows of the waves, the mast snapped in the middle—and then the ship heeled over on its side, and water came rushing into the hold. Now at last the little mermaid realized that they were in danger; even she herself had to look out for the bro-ken beams and planks that were churning about in the water. At one moment it was so pitch black that she could see noth-ing at all; then, when lightning flashed, it was so bright that she could distinguish every one on board. They all seemed desperately trying to save their own lives; but she looked about only for one, the young prince. And just as the ship broke up she saw him, sinking down, drawn below into the deep heart of the sea.

For a moment she felt nothing but joy, for he would be coming into her own country; but then she remembered that humans could not live in the water, and that only as a drowned man could he ever enter her father's palace. No, he must not die! So she swam out through the drifting, jostling beams; they might have crushed her, but the thought never entered her head. Then, diving deep into the water, and rising up high with the waves, she at last reached the young prince, who could scarcely keep afloat any longer in the raging sea. His arms and legs were almost too weak to move; his beautiful eyes were closed, and he would certainly have drowned if the little mermaid had not come. She held his head above the water and let the waves carry the two of them where they would.

When morning came, the storm was over, but not a trace of the ship was to be seen. The sun rose, flame-red and brilliant, out of the water, and seemed to bring a tinge of life to the pale face of the prince; but his eyes remained shut. The mermaid kissed his forehead and stroked back his wet hair. The thought came to her that he was very much like the marble statue in her own little garden; she kissed him again. Oh, if only he would live!

And now she saw dry land in front of her, and high blue mountains whose tops were white with snow. Not far from the shore were lovely green woods, and before them stood a church, or abbey—she did not know what to call it, but a building of that kind. Orange and lemon trees grew in its garden, and tall palms by the gate. Nearby the sea formed a little bay, very calm and still, but deep, with cliffs all round where fine white sand had piled. She swam to this bay with the handsome prince, and laid him on the sand, in the warmth of the sun, taking care that his head was well away from the sea.

Now the bells rang out in the great white building. So the little mermaid swam further out and hid behind some rocks rising out of the water, covering herself in sea foam so that no one would notice her. From there she watched to see who would come to rescue the poor prince lying in the sand. Quite soon a young girl appeared. The sight of the half-drowned figure seemed to frighten her, but only for a moment. Then she went and fetched other people, and the mermaid saw the prince revive and smile at everybody around him. But he did not turn and smile at her, for of course, he had no idea that she was the one who saved him. She felt terribly sad, and after he had been taken into the building she dived down sorrowfully into the water and returned to her father's palace.

She had always been quiet and thoughtful, but now she became much more so. Her sisters asked what she had seen on her first journey into the human world, but she told them nothing.

On many evenings, and many mornings, she glided up to the place where she had left the prince. She saw the fruit grow ripe in the garden, and she saw it gathered in; she saw the snow melt on the high mountains—but she never saw the prince. Her one comfort was to sit in her little garden clasping her arms round the beautiful marble statue which was so much like the prince. But she no longer tended her flowers; they grew like wild things, trailing over the paths, weaving their long stems and leaves in and out of the boughs of the trees until the whole place was in shadow.

At last she could bear it no longer, and told the story to one of her sisters; very soon the others knew it too—nobody else, of course, except one or two other mermaids who told only their best friends. One of these was able to tell her who the young prince was; and where his kingdom lay.

"Come, little sister," said the other princesses. And then, with their arms over one another's shoulders, they rose to the surface and floated in a long row just in front of the prince's palace. It was built of a shining gold-coloured stone with great marble steps, some leading right down into the sea. Towering above the roof were magnificent golden domes, and between the pillars surrounding the building stood marble statues; they almost seemed alive. Through the glass of the tall windows you could see into splendid halls, hung with priceless silken curtains and tapestries. In the centre of the largest hall a great fountain was playing, the water leaping as high as the glass dome in the roof. The sun's rays shone through the dome, lighting the fountain and the lovely plants that grew in the great pool below.

Now that the little mermaid knew where he lived, she would rise to the surface and watch there, night after night. She would swim much closer to land than any of the others had ever dared; she even went right up the narrow canal under the marble balcony, which cast its long shadow over the water. There she would sit and gaze at the young prince, who believed that he was quite alone in the moonlight.

Often in the evenings she would see him setting out in his splendid boat with its flying flags, while music played. She would peep out from between the green rushes, and people who saw a silvery flash thought only that it was a swan spreading its wings. Many a time, late in the night, when the fishermen waited out at sea with their fiery torches, she heard them saying so much that was good about the young prince; this always made her glad that she had saved his life when he lay almost dead on the waves. But he knew nothing at all about that.

She felt closer and closer to human people, and longed more and more to go up and join them. There was so much that she wished to know, but her sisters could not answer her questions. So she asked her old grandmother; *she* knew quite a few things about the upper world, as she very properly called the lands above the sea.

"If humans are not drowned, can they live for ever?" asked the little mermaid. "Do they never die, as we do here in the sea?"

"Yes, indeed," said the old lady, "they too have to die; and their lives are even shorter than ours. We can live for three hundred years, but when our time comes to an end we are only foam on the water; we are like the green rushes. But humans have a soul which lives on after the body has turned to dust. It flies up through the sky to the shining stars. Just as we rise out of the sea and gaze at the human world, they rise up to unknown places which we shall never reach."

"Why, I would give all my hundreds of years in exchange for being a human, even for just one day, if I then had the chance of a place in the heavenly world," said the little mermaid, very sadly.

"You mustn't think such things!" said the old lady. "We are much happier here, and much better off too than the folk up there."

"But is there nothing I can do to get an immortal soul?" asked the little mermaid.

"No," said the old lady. "Only if a human being loved you so dearly that you were more to him than father or mother; only if he clung to you with all his heart and soul, letting the priest place his right hand in yours, promising to be true to you, here and in all eternity—then you too would share the human destiny. But that can never happen. The very thing that is so beautiful here in the sea—I mean your mermaid's tail—they think quite ugly up there on earth. Their taste is so peculiar that they have to have two clumsy props called legs if they want to look elegant."

That made the little mermaid sigh, and look sadly at her fish's tail.

"Let us be cheerful," said the old lady. "Let us make the best of the three hundred years of our life by leaping and dancing; it's a good long time after all. Then when it's over we can have our fill of sleep; it will be all the more welcome and agreeable. Tonight, we'll have a court ball."

This was something far more splendid than any we see on earth. The walls and ceilings of the great ballroom were of crystal glass, thick, but perfectly clear. Several hundred enormous shells, rose-red and emerald-green, were set in rows on either side, each holding a bluish flame; these lit up the whole room and shone out through the walls, giving a sapphire glow to the sea outside. Countless fishes, large and small, could be seen swimming towards the glass, some with scales of glowing violet, others silver and gold.

Through the middle of the ballroom flowed a broad swift stream, and on it mermen and mermaids danced to a marvellous sound—the sound of their own singing. No humans have such beautiful voices—and the sweetest singer of all was the little mermaid. When she sang, the whole assembly clapped their hands; for a moment she felt a thrill of joy, for she knew that she had the most beautiful voice of all who live on earth or in the sea. But she could not forget the handsome prince; and could not forget that she had no immortal soul. And so she slipped out of her father's palace, and sat in her little garden, thinking her sad thoughts.

Suddenly, echoing down through the water, she heard the sounds of horn-music. "Ah, he must be sailing up there," she mused, "the one whom I love more than father and mother, the one who is never out of my thoughts. To win his love and to gain an immortal soul, I would dare anything! Yes—while my sisters are dancing in our father's palace I will call on the old sea witch. I have always been dreadfully afraid of her, but she may be able to tell me what to do."

And so the little mermaid left her garden and set off for the roaring whirlpools, for the old enchantress lived just beyond. She had never taken that grim path before. No flowers grew there, no sea grass even. All she could see was bare grey sand stretching away from the whirlpool, where the water went swirling round as if huge and crazy millwheels were turning all the time, dragging everything caught in them down, down into unknown depths. To reach the sea witch's domain she had to go right through these raging waters, and after that there was no other way but over a long swampy stretch of bubbling mud; the witch called it her peat-bog. Behind this lay her house, deep in an eerie forest. The trees and bushes were of the polyp kind, half creature and half plant; they looked like hundred-headed snakes growing out of the earth. The branches were really long slimy arms with fingers like writhing worms; from joint to joint they never stopped moving, and everything they could touch they twined around and held in a lasting grip.

The little mermaid was terrified as she stood on the edge of this frightful forest. She almost turned back—but then she thought of the prince and the human soul, and plucked up courage. She tied her long flowing hair tightly round her head to keep it from the clutch of the polyp-fingers; then, folding her hands together, she darted along as a fish darts through the water, in and out of the hideous branches, which reached out their waving arms and fingers after her.

Now she came to a large slimy open space in the dreadful forest, where fat water-snakes were frisking about, showing their ugly yellow-white undersides; the sea witch called these her little pets. In the very middle a house had been built from the bones of shipwrecked humans, and here sat the witch herself.

"I know well enough why you are here," said the witch. "It's a foolish notion! However, you shall have your way, for it will bring you nothing but trouble, my pretty princess! You want to get rid of your fish's tail and have two stumps instead, like human beings; then, you hope, the young prince will fall in love with you, and you'll be able to marry him, and get an immortal soul into the bargain." With that, the witch uttered such a loud and horrible laugh that the creatures coiling over her fell sprawling to the ground.

"You've come just in the nick of time," said the witch. "Tomorrow, after sunrise, I wouldn't be able to help for another year. Now I shall make a special potion for you; before the sun rises you must swim with it to the land, sit down and drink it up. Then your tail will divide in two and shrink into what those humans call a lovely pair of legs. But it'll hurt; it will be like a sharp sword going through you. Everyone will say that you are the loveliest child they have ever seen. You will glide along—ah, more gracefully than any dancer, but every step you take will be like treading on a sharp knife. If you are willing to suffer all this, then I will help you."

"Yes, I am willing," said the little mermaid. Her voice trembled, but she fixed her thoughts on the prince, and the chance to gain an immortal soul.

"But remember," said the witch, "when once you've taken a human shape you can never again be a mermaid. You can never go down through the water to your sisters, or to your father's palace! And if you fail to win the prince's love, so that he forgets both father and mother for your sake, and lets the priest join you together as man and wife, you won't get that immortal soul. On the first morning after he marries another, your heart will break, and you will turn into foam on the water."

"I am willing," said the little mermaid. She was now as pale as death.

"But I want my payment too," said the witch, "and it's not a small one either. You have the most exquisite voice of anyone here in the sea. You think that you'll be able to charm him with it, but you're going to give that voice to me. The price of my precious drink is the finest thing you possess. For I shall have to put some of my own blood into it, to make it as sharp as a two-edged sword."

"But if you take my voice?" said the little mermaid, "what shall I have left?"

"Your beauty," said the witch, "your grace in moving, your lovely, speaking eyes—with these you can easily catch a human heart. Well, have you lost your courage? Put out your little tongue; I'll cut it off as my payment, and you shall have the magic drink."

"Well, if it must be so," said the little mermaid, and the witch put her cauldron on the fire to prepare the potion. "Cleanliness is a good thing," she remarked, and wiped out the cauldron with a knotted bunch of snakes. Then she scratched her breast and let some black blood drip down into the pot. The steam rose up in the weirdest shapes, enough to fill anyone with fear and dread. Every moment the witch cast some different item into the cauldron, and when it was really boiling it sounded like the weeping of a crocodile. At last the brew was ready—and it looked like the clearest water.

"There you are!" said the witch, and she cut off the little mermaid's tongue. Now she had no voice; she could neither sing nor speak.

"If those polyps catch hold of you when you are going back through the wood," said the witch, "just throw a drop of the potion on them. You'll see!" But the little mermaid had no need to do that, for the polyps drew back in fear when they saw the potion glittering in her hand like a star. So she came back without delay through the swamp, the forest, and the roaring whirlpool.

She could see her father's palace; the lights were out in the great ballroom—no doubt they were all asleep by now. Yet she dared not go and look, for she was dumb, and she was about to leave them for ever. She felt as if her heart would break with grief. She crept into the garden, took one flower from the flower-bed of each sister, threw a thousand kisses towards the palace, and rose up through the dark-blue sea.

The sun had not yet risen when she came in sight of the prince's palace and made her way up the splendid marble steps. The moon was shining bright and clear. The little mermaid drank the burning drink. A two-edged sword seemed to thrust itself through her delicate body; she fainted, and lay as though dead.

When the sun rose, shining across the sea, she woke, and the sharp pain returned, but there in front of her stood the young prince. His jet-black eyes were fixed on her so intently that she cast her own eyes down—and then she saw that the fish's tail was gone, and that she had instead the prettiest neat white legs that any girl could wish for. But she had no clothes, and so she wrapped herself in her long flowing hair. The prince asked who she was, and how she had come there, but she could only gaze back at him sweetly and sadly with her deep blue eyes, for of course she could not speak. Then he took her by the hand and led her into the palace. Every step she took made her feel as if she were treading on pointed swords, just as the witch had warned her—yet she endured it gladly. Holding the prince's hand, she trod the ground, light as air, and the prince and all who saw her marvelled at her graceful, gliding walk.

She was given rich dresses of finest silk and muslin. All agreed that she was the loveliest maiden in the palace. But she was dumb; she could neither sing nor speak. Beautiful slave girls in silk and gold came forward to sing for the prince and his royal parents. One of them sang more movingly than the rest, and the prince clapped his hands and smiled at her. This saddened the little mermaid, for she knew that her own lost voice was far more beautiful. She thought: "If only he could know that I gave away my voice for ever, just to be near him."

Next, the slave girls danced in graceful gliding motion to thrilling music, and then the little mermaid rose on to the tips of her toes, and floated across the floor, dancing as no one had ever yet danced. With every movement she seemed lovelier, and her eyes spoke more deeply to the heart than all the slave girls' singing.

The whole court was delighted, and the prince most of all; he called her his little foundling. So she went on dancing, though every time her foot touched the ground she seemed to be treading on sharp knives. The prince declared that she must never leave him, and she was given a place to sleep outside his door on a velvet cushion.

He had a boy's suit made for her so that she could go riding with him on horseback. They rode through the sweet-smelling woods, where the green boughs touched her shoulders, and the little birds twittered away in the fresh green leaves. She joined the prince when he climbed high mountains, and though her delicate feet were cut so that all could see, she only laughed, and kept at his side until they could see the clouds sailing beneath them like a flock of birds on the way to distant lands.

At night in the prince's palace, when the others were all asleep, she would go out to the wide marble steps and cool her burning feet in the cold sea water; and then she would think of those down below in the depths of the waves.

One night, her sisters rose to the surface, arm in arm, singing most mournfully as they swam across the water; she waved to them and they recognized her, and told her how unhappy she had made them all. After that, they used to visit her every night; once, in the far distance, she perceived her old grandmother, who hadn't been to the surface for years, together with the Merman-King himself, wearing his crown. They both stretched out their hands towards her, but they would not venture as near to land as her sisters.

As each day passed, the prince grew fonder and fonder of her. He loved her as one loves a dear good child; but the idea of making her his queen never entered his head. And yet, if she did not become his wife she would never gain an immortal soul, and on his wedding morning to another she would dissolve into foam on the sea.

"Do you not love me more than all the rest?" the little mermaid's eyes seemed to say when he took her in his arms and kissed her delicate forehead. "Yes, of course, you are dearest of all to me," said the prince, "because you have the truest heart of all. Besides, you also remind me of a young girl I once saw, and doubt if I shall ever see again. I was on a ship that was wrecked, and the waves drove me to land near a sacred temple, which was tended by many young maidens. The youngest of them found me on the beach and saved my life. I saw her twice, no more, but she was the only one I could ever love in this world, and you are so like her that you almost take her place in my heart. But she belongs to the holy temple, so it is my good fortune that you have been sent to me. We shall never part."

"Ah, he doesn't know that I was the one who saved his life," thought the little mermaid. "He doesn't know that I carried him through the waves to the temple in the wood, that I waited in the foam to see if anyone would come to rescue him, and that I saw the beautiful maiden whom he loves more than me." The mermaid sighed deeply—weep she could not. "The maiden belongs to the holy temple"—those were his words. She will never come out into the world, so they will not meet again. I am here; I am with him; I see him every day. I will care for him, love him, give up my life for him!"

But now the rumour rose that the prince was to be married, to the lovely daughter of the neighbouring king, and because of this he was fitting out a splendid ship. "The prince is supposed to be travelling forth to visit the next door kingdom," people said. "But it's really to call on the king's daughter." The little mermaid shook her head and laughed; she knew the prince's mind better than anyone. "I am obliged to make this journey," he had said to her. "I have to meet the charming princess—my mother and father insist on that—but they cannot force me to bring her home as my bride. I cannot love this stranger! She will not remind me of the fair maid of the temple, as you do. If I have to find a bride, my choice would be you, my dear dumb foundling with the speaking eyes." And he kissed her rose-red mouth.

"You have no fear of the sea, my silent child!" he said, as they stood on the splendid ship that was to carry him to the lands of the neighbouring king. And he told her of storms and calm, of strange fish in the deep, and the marvels that divers had seen down there; she smiled at his accounts, for of course she knew more about the world beneath the waves than anyone.

In the moonlit night, when everyone but the helmsman at the wheel was asleep, she sat by the ship's rail, gazing into the calm water. She thought that she could make out her father's palace, with her old grandmother standing on the highest tower, in her silver crown, peering up through the racing tides at the vessel overhead. Then her sisters came to the surface and looked at her with eyes full of sorrow, wringing their white hands. She waved to them and smiled, and wanted to tell them that all was going well and happily with her; but then one of the cabin boys drew near, and her sisters sank below.

Next morning the ship sailed into the harbour of the neighbouring king's fine city. All the church bells were ringing; trumpets blared from the tall towers, while soldiers stood on parade with flying flags and glinting bayonets. Every day was like a fête; no sooner was one ball or party over than another began—but the princess was not there. She was being brought up in a holy temple, they said, where she was learning the ways of wisdom that her royal role would need. At last, however, she arrived.

The little mermaid waited by, eager to see her beauty, and she had to admit that it would be hard to find a lovelier human girl. Her skin was so delicate and pure, and behind her long lashes smiled a pair of steadfast dark-blue eyes.

"It is you!" said the prince. "You were the one who saved me when I lay almost dead on the shore!" And he held the blushing princess in his arms. "Oh, I am overjoyed," he said to the little mermaid. "My dearest wish—more than I ever dared hope for—has come true. I know you will share in my happiness, because no one anywhere cares for me more than you." The little mermaid kissed his head, though she felt that her heart would break. His wedding morning would bring her death, and turn her to a wisp of foam on the sea.

All the church bells rang out; heralds rode through the streets to proclaim the news. Sweet-smelling oils burned on every altar in precious silver lamps. The priests swung incense vessels; bride and bridegroom joined their hands and received the bishop's blessing. The little mermaid, in silk and gold, stood holding the bridal train, but her ears never heard the festive music, nor did her eyes see the holy ceremony. This was her last day alive in the world, and she thought of all that she had lost.

That evening the bride and bridegroom went aboard the ship. A royal tent of gold and purple had been set up on the main deck with silken cushions and hangings, and there the bridal pair were to sleep in the calm cool pleasant night.

The sails filled out in the breeze, and the vessel flew swiftly and lightly over the shining sea.

As darkness fell, lanterns of every colour were lit, and on the deck the sailors danced merrily. The little mermaid remembered the first time she had come to the surface, and had gazed on just such a joyful scene. And now she too was joining in the dance, lightly gliding and swerving as a swallow does to avoid a pursuer. She could hear the admiring voices and applause, for never before had she danced so brilliantly. Sharp knives seemed to cut her delicate feet, yet she hardly felt them, so deep was the pain in her heart. She could not forget that this was the last night she would ever see the one for whom she had left her home and family, had given up her beautiful voice, and had day by day endured unending torment, of which he knew nothing at all. An eternal light awaited her.

At last, well after midnight, the merrymaking drew to a close. The prince kissed his lovely bride, and they went to the royal tent.

The ship grew hushed and silent; only the helmsman was still awake at the wheel. The little mermaid leaned her white arms on the rail and looked eastwards for a sign of the dawn; the first ray of the sun, she knew, would mean her end. Suddenly, rising out of the sea, she saw her sisters. They were as ghastly pale as she, and their beautiful hair no longer streamed in the wind—it had been cut off.

"We gave our hair to the witch in return for help, for something that will save you from death when morning breaks. She has given us a knife. Look! See how sharp it is! Before the sun rises you must plunge it into the prince's heart; when his warm blood splashes your feet, they will grow together into a fish's tail and you will become a mermaid once again, just as you used to be. You will be able to join us in the depths below and live out all your three hundred years before you dissolve away into salt sea foam. Hurry! Either he or you must die before the first ray of sunrise! Our old grandmother is so full of grief that her white hair has fallen out just as ours fell before the witch's scissors. Kill the prince and come back to us!

Hurry! Do you see that red streak in the sky? In a few minutes the sun will rise and you will be no more." With a strange deep sigh they sank beneath the waves.

The little mermaid drew back the purple curtain from the tent door where the prince and princess slept; she looked up at the sky where the red of dawn began to glow, looked at the sharp knife, and looked again at the prince. The knife quivered in her hand—then she flung it far out into the waves; they shone red where it fell, as though drops of blood were leaping out of the water. Once more she looked at the prince, through eyes half-glazed in death; then she threw herself from the ship into the sea, where she felt her body dissolving into foam.

And now the sun rose from the ocean, and on the foam its beams lay gentle and warm. The little mermaid had no feeling of death. She saw the bright sun, and also, floating above her, hundreds of lovely transparent creatures. Through them she could see the white sails of the ship and the rose-red clouds in the sky. Their voices were like music, but of so ethereal a kind that no human ear could hear it, just as no earthly eye could perceive them. Without wings they floated through the air, borne by their own lightness. And now the little mermaid saw that she had become like them, and was rising higher and higher above the waves.

"Where am I going?" said she, and her voice, too, sounded like those of the other beings, so ethereal that no earthly music could even echo its tune.

"To join with us, spirits of the air," they answered. "We do not need the love of a human being to become immortal. We fly to hot countries where the stifling breath of plague carries death to humans, and we bring them cool fresh breezes; we fill the air with the scent of flowers that bring relief and healing. When we have tried to do all the good we can for three hundred years, we gain an immortal soul and eternal happiness. You, too, poor little mermaid, have striven with all your heart to do good; you have suffered and endured and have raised yourself into the higher world of the spirits of the air. Now, you too can gain an immortal soul for yourself."

The little mermaid lifted her arms towards the heavenly sun. On the ship the bustle of waking life had started again. She saw the prince with his beautiful bride; they were searching for her, gazing sorrowfully into the moving waves. She smiled at the prince, and then, with the other children of the air, she soared up on to the rose-red cloud which floated in the sky.

"In this way, when three hundred years are passed, I shall rise into the kingdom of heaven."

"Perhaps even sooner," one of them whispered. "Unseen, we glide into human homes where there are children, and whenever we find a good child, one who makes its parents happy and deserves their love, God shortens our time of trial. The child never knows when we fly through the room; if its goodness makes us smile with pleasure, a year is taken from the three hundred. But if we see a naughty, evil child, then we must weep tears of sorrow, and each tear adds one day more to our time of waiting."

The Bottle Imp

by
ROBERT LOUIS STEVENSON
(1850–1894)

Robert Louis Stevenson's south sea tales were the final flowering of his short career, and "The Bottle Imp" yet one more dark flower on the bed of his final days. There are some stories that, though not exactly stories of the sea, are nevertheless a part of a larger maritime folklore. "The Bottle Imp" seems to me very much one of these—a sort of genie in the bottle story—though the imp itself is pure Stevenson.

T here was a man of the Island of Hawaii, whom I shall call Keawe; for the truth is, he still lives, and his name must be kept secret; but the place of his birth was not far from Honaunau, where the bones of Keawe the Great lie hidden in a cave. This man was poor, brave, and active; he could read and write like a schoolmaster; he was a first-rate mariner besides, sailed for some time in the island steamers, and steered a whale-boat on the Hamakua coast. At length it came in Keawe's mind to have a sight of the great world and foreign cities, and he shipped on a vessel bound to San Francisco.

This is a fine town, with a fine harbour, and rich people uncountable; and, in particular, there is one hill which is covered with palaces. Upon this hill Keawe was one day taking a walk with his pocket full of money, viewing the great houses upon either hand with pleasure. "What fine houses these are!" he was thinking, "and how happy must those people be who dwell in them, and take no care for the morrow!" The thought was in his mind when he came abreast of a house that was smaller than some others, but all finished and beautified like a toy; the steps of that house shone like silver, and the borders of the garden bloomed like garlands, and the windows were bright like diamonds; and Keawe stopped and wondered at the excellence of all he saw. So stopping, he was aware of a man that looked forth upon him through a window so clear that Keawe could see him as you see a fish in a pool upon the reef. The man was elderly, with a bald head and a black beard, and his face was heavy with sorrow, and he bitterly sighed. And the truth of it is, that as Keawe looked in upon the man, and the man looked out upon Keawe, each envied the other.

All of a sudden, the man smiled and nodded, and beckoned Keawe to enter, and met him at the door of the house.

"This is a fine house of mine," said the man, and bitterly sighed. "Would you not care to view the chambers?"

So he led Keawe all over it, from the cellar to the roof, and there was nothing there that was not perfect of its kind, and Keawe was astonished.

"Truly," said Keawe, "this is a beautiful house; if I lived in the like of it, I should be laughing all day long. How come it, then, that you should be sighing?"

"There is no reason," said the man, "why you should not have a house in all points similar to this, and finer, if you wish. You have some money, I suppose?"

"I have fifty dollars," said Keawe; "but a house like this will cost more than fifty dollars."

The man made a computation. "I am sorry you have no more," said he, "for it may raise you trouble in the future; but it shall be yours at fifty dollars."

"The house?" asked Keawe.

"No, not the house," replied the man; "but the bottle. For, I must tell you, although I appear to you so rich and fortunate, all my fortune, and this house itself and its garden, came out of a bottle not much bigger than a pint. This is it."

And he opened a lockfast place, and took out a round-bellied bottle with a long neck; the glass of it was white like milk, with changing rainbow colours in the grain. Withinsides something obscurely moved, like a shadow and a fire.

"This is the bottle," said the man; and, when Keawe laughed, "You do not believe me?" he added. "Try, then, for yourself. See if you can break it."

So Keawe took the bottle up and dashed it on the floor till he was weary; but it jumped on the floor like a child's ball, and was not injured.

"This is a strange thing," said Keawe. "For by the touch of it, as well as by the look, the bottle should be of glass."

"Of glass it is," replied the man, sighing more heavily than ever; "but the glass of it was tempered in the flames of hell. An imp lives in it, and that is the shadow we behold there moving: or so I suppose. If any man buy this bottle the imp is at his command; all that he desires—love, fame, money, houses like this house, ay, or a city like this city—all are his at the word uttered. Napoleon had this bottle, and by it he grew to be the king of the world; but he sold it at the last, and fell. Captain Cook had this bottle, and by it he found his way to so many islands; but he, too, sold it, and was slain upon Hawaii. For, once it is sold, the power goes and the protection; and unless a man remain content with what he has, ill will befall him."

"And yet you talk of selling it yourself?" Keawe said.

"I have all I wish, and I am growing elderly," replied the man. "There is one thing the imp cannot do—he cannot prolong life; and, it would not be fair to conceal from you, there is a drawback to the bottle; for if a man die before he sells it, he must burn in hell for ever."

"To be sure, that is a drawback and no mistake," cried Keawe. "I would not meddle with the thing. I can do without a house, thank God; but there is one thing I could not be doing with one particle, and that is to be damned."

"Dear me, you must not run away with things," returned the man. "All you have to do is to use the power of the imp in moderation, and then sell it to someone else, as I do to you, and finish your life in comfort."

"Well, I observe two things," said Keawe. "All the time you keep sighing like a maid in love, that is one; and, for the other, you sell this bottle very cheap."

"I have told you why I sigh," said the man. "It is because I fear my health is breaking up; and, as you said yourself, to die and go to the devil is a pity for anyone. As for why I sell so cheap, I must explain to you there is a peculiarity about the bottle. Long ago, when the devil brought it first upon earth, it was extremely expensive, and was sold first of all to Prester John for many millions of dollars; but it cannot be sold at all, unless sold at a loss. If you sell it for as much as you paid for it, back it comes to you again like a homing pigeon. It follows that the price has kept falling in these centuries, and the bottle is now remarkably cheap. I bought it myself from one of my great neighbours on this hill, and the price I paid was only ninety dollars. I could sell it for as high as eighty-nine dollars and ninety-nine cents, but not a penny dearer, or back the thing must come to me. Now, about this there are two bothers. First, when you offer a bottle so singular for eighty odd dollars, people suppose you to be jesting. And second—but there is no hurry about that—and I need not go into it. Only remember it must be coined money that you sell it for."

"How am I to know that this is all true?" asked Keawe.

"Some of it you can try at once," replied the man. "Give me your fifty dollars, take the bottle, and wish your fifty dollars back into your pocket. If that does not happen, I pledge you my honour I will cry off the bargain and restore your money."

"You are not deceiving me?" said Keawe.

The man bound himself with a great oath.

"Well, I will risk that much," said Keawe, "for that can do no harm." And he paid over his money to the man, and the man handed him the bottle.

"Imp of the bottle," said Keawe, "I want my fifty dollars back." And sure enough he had scarce said the word before his pocket was as heavy as ever.

"To be sure this is a wonderful bottle," said Keawe.

"And now good-morning to you, my fine fellow, and the devil go with you for me!" said the man.

"Hold on," said Keawe, "I don't want any more of this fun. Here, take your bottle back."

"You have bought it for less than I paid for it," replied the man, rubbing his hands. "It is yours now; and, for my part, I am only concerned to see the back of you." And with that he rang for his Chinese servant, and had Keawe shown out of the house.

Now, when Keawe was in the street with the bottle under his arm, he began to think. "If all is true about this bottle, I may have made a losing bargain," thinks he. "But perhaps the man was only fooling me." The first thing he did was to count his money; the sum was exact—forty-nine dollars American money, and one Chili piece. "That looks like the truth," said Keawe. "Now I will try another part."

The streets in that part of the city were as clean as a ship's decks, and though it was noon, there were no passengers. Keawe set the bottle in the gutter and walked away. Twice he looked back, and there was the milky, round-bellied bottle where he left it. A third time he looked back, and turned a corner; but he had scarce done so, when something knocked upon his elbow, and behold! it was the long neck sticking up; and as for the round belly, it was jammed into the pocket of his pilot coat.

"And that looks like the truth," said Keawe.

The next thing he did was to buy a corkscrew in a shop, and go apart into a secret place in the fields. And there he tried to draw the cork, but as often as he put the screw in, out it came again, and the cork as whole as ever.

"This is some new sort of cork," said Keawe, and all at once he began to shake and sweat, for he was afraid of that bottle.

On his way back to the port-side, he saw a shop where a man sold shells and clubs from the wild islands, old heathen deities, old coined money, pictures from China and Japan, and all manner of things that sailors bring in their sea-chests. And here he had an idea. So he went in and offered the bottle for a hundred dollars. The man of the shop laughed at him at the first, and offered him five; but, indeed, it was a curious bottle—such glass was never blown in any human glassworks, so prettily the colours shone under the milky white, and so strangely the shadows hovered in the midst; so, after he had disputed awhile after the manner of his kind, the shopman gave Keawe sixty silver dollars for the thing, and set it on a shelf in the midst of his window.

"Now," said Keawe, "I have sold that for sixty which I bought for fifty—or, to say truth, a little less, because one of my dollars was from Chili. Now I shall know the truth upon another point."

So he went back on board his ship, and, when he opened his chest, there was the bottle, and had come more quickly than himself. Now Keawe had a mate on board whose name was Lopaka.

"What ails you?" said Lopaka, "that you stare in your chest?"

They were alone in the ship's forecastle, and Keawe bound him to secrecy, and told all.

"This is a very strange affair," said Lopaka; "and I fear you will be in trouble about this bottle. But there is one point very clear—that you are sure of the trouble, and you had better have the profit in the bargain. Make up your mind what you want with it; give the order, and if it is done as you desire, I will buy the bottle myself; for I have an idea of my own to get a schooner, and go trading through the islands."

"That is not my idea," said Keawe; "but to have a beautiful house and garden on the Kona Coast, where I was born, the sun shining in at the door, flowers in the garden, glass in the windows, pictures on the walls, and toys and fine carpets on the tables, for all the world like the house I was in this day— only a storey higher, and with balconies all about like the King's palace; and to live there without care and make merry with my friends and relatives."

"Well," said Lopaka, "let us carry it back with us to Hawaii; and if all comes true, as you suppose, I will buy the bottle, as I said, and ask a schooner."

Upon that they agreed, and it was not long before the ship returned to Honolulu, carrying Keawe and Lopaka and the bottle. They were scarce come ashore when they met a friend upon the beach, who began at once to condole with Keawe.

"I do not know what I am to be condoled about," said Keawe.

"Is it possible you have not heard," said the friend, "your uncle—that good old man—is dead, and your cousin—that beautiful boy—was drowned at sea?"

Keawe was filled with sorrow, and, beginning to weep and to lament, he forgot about the bottle. But Lopaka was thinking to himself, and presently when Keawe's grief was a little abated, "I have been thinking," said Lopaka. "Had not your uncle lands in Hawaii, in the district of Kau?"

"No," said Keawe, "not in Kau; they are on the mountain-side—a little way south of Hookena."

"These lands will now be yours?" asked Lopaka.

"And so they will," say Keawe, and began again to lament for his relatives.

"No," said Lopaka, "do not lament at present. I have a thought in my mind. How if this should be the doing of the bottle? For here is the place ready for your house."

"If this be so," cried Keawe, "it is a very ill way to serve me by killing my relatives. But it may be, indeed; for it was in just such a station that I saw the house with my mind's eye."

"The house, however, is not yet built," said Lopaka.

"No, nor like to be!" said Keawe; "for though my uncle has some coffee and ava and bananas, it will not be more than will keep me in comfort; and the rest of that land is the black lava."

"Let us go to the lawyer," said Lopaka; "I have still this idea in my mind."

Now, when they came to the lawyer's, it appeared Keawe's uncle had grown monstrous rich in the last days, and there was a fund of money.

"And here is the money for the house!" cried Lopaka.

"If you are thinking of a new house," said the lawyer, "here is the card of a new architect, of whom they tell me great things."

"Better and better!" cried Lopaka. "here is all made plain for us. Let us continue to obey orders."

So they went to the architect, and he had drawings of houses on his table.

"You want something out of the way," said the architect. "How do you like this?" and he handed a drawing to Keawe.

Now, when Keawe set eyes on the drawing, he cried out loud, for it was the picture of his thought exactly drawn.

"I am in for this house," thought he. "Little as I like the way it comes to me, I am in for it now, and I may as well take the good along with the evil."

So he told the architect all that he wished, and how he would have that house furnished, and about the pictures on the wall and knick-knacks on the tables; and he asked the man plainly for how much he would undertake the whole affair.

The architect put many questions, and took his pen and made a computation; and when he had done he named the very sum that Keawe had inherited.

Lopaka and Keawe looked at one another and nodded.

"It is quite clear," thought Keawe, "that I am to have this house, whether or no. It comes from the devil, and I fear I will get little good by that; and of one thing I am sure, I will make no more wishes as long as I have this bottle. But with the house I am saddled, and I may as well take the good along with the evil."

So he made his terms with the architect, and they signed a paper; and Keawe and Lopaka took ship again and sailed to Australia; for it was concluded between them they should not interfere at all, but leave the architect and the bottle imp to build and to adorn that house at their own pleasure.

The voyage was a good voyage, only all the time Keawe was holding in his breath, for he had sworn he would utter no more wishes, and take no more favours from the devil. The time was up when they got back. The architect told them that the house was ready, and Keawe and Lopaka took a passage in the *Hall*, and went down Kona way to view the house, and see if all had been done fitly according to the thought that was in Keawe's mind.

Now, the house stood on the mountain side, visible to ships. Above, the forest ran up into the clouds of rain; below, the black lava fell in cliffs, where the kings of old lay buried. A garden bloomed about that house with every hue of flowers; and there was an orchard of papaia on the one hand and an orchard of bread-fruit on the other, and right in front, toward the sea, a ship's mast had been rigged up and bore a flag. As

for the house, it was three storeys high, with great chambers
and broad balconies on each. The windows were of glass, so
excellent that it was as clear as water and as bright as day. All
manner of furniture adorned the chambers. Pictures hung
upon the wall in golden frames: pictures of ships, and men
fighting, and of the most beautiful women, and of singular
places; nowhere in the world are there pictures of so bright a
colour as those Keawe found hanging in his house. As for the
knick-knacks, they were extraordinary fine; chiming clocks
and musical boxes, little men with nodding heads, books filled
with pictures, weapons of price from all quarters of the world,
and the most elegant puzzles to entertain the leisure of a soli-
tary man. And as no one would care to live in such chambers,
only to walk through and view them, the balconies were made
so broad that a whole town might have lived upon them in
delight; and Keawe knew not which to prefer, whether the
back porch, where you got the land breeze, and looked upon
the orchards and the flowers, or the front balcony, where you
could drink the wind of the sea, and look down the steep wall
of the mountain and see the *Hall* going by once a week or so
between Hookena and the hills of Pele, or the schooners ply-
ing up the coast for wood and ava and bananas.

When they had viewed all, Keawe and Lopaka sat on the
porch.

"Well," asked Lopaka, "is it all as you designed?"

"Words cannot utter it," said Keawe. "It is better than I
dreamed, and I am sick with satisfaction."

"There is but one thing to consider," said Lopaka; "all this
may be quite natural, and the bottle imp have nothing whatever to say to it. If I were to buy the bottle, and got no schooner
after all, I should have put my hand in the fire for nothing. I
gave you my word, I know; but yet I think you would not
grudge me one more proof."

"I have sworn I would take no more favours," said Keawe. "I
have gone already deep enough."

"This is no favour I am thinking of," replied Lopaka. "It is
only to see the imp himself. There is nothing to be gained by
that, and so nothing to be ashamed of; and yet, if I once saw

him, I should be sure of the whole matter. So indulge me so far, and let me see the imp; and, after that, here is the money in my hand, and I will buy it."

"There is only one thing I am afraid of," said Keawe. "The imp may be very ugly to view; and if you once set eyes upon him you might be very undesirous of the bottle."

"I am a man of my word," said Lopaka. "And here is the money betwixt us."

"Very well," replied Keawe. "I have a curiosity myself. So come, let us have one look at you, Mr. Imp."

Now as soon as that was said, the imp looked out of the bottle, and in again, swift as a lizard; and there sat Keawe and Lopaka turned to stone. The night had quite come, before either found a thought to say or voice to say it with; and then Lopaka pushed the money over and took the bottle.

"I am a man of my word," said he, "and had need to be so, or I would not touch this bottle with my foot. Well, I shall get my schooner and a dollar or two for my pocket; and then I will be rid of this devil as fast as I can. For, to tell you the plain truth, the look of him has cast me down."

"Lopaka," said Keawe, "do not you think any worse of me than you can help; I know it is night, and the roads bad, and the pass by the tombs an ill place to go by so late, but I declare since I have seen that little face, I cannot eat or sleep or pray till it is gone from me. I will give you a lantern, and a basket to put the bottle in, and any picture or fine thing in all my house that takes your fancy;—and be gone at once, and go sleep at Hookena with Nahinu."

"Keawe," said Lopaka, "many a man would take this ill; above all, when I am doing you a turn so friendly, as to keep my word and buy the bottle; and for that matter, the night and the dark, and the way by the tombs, must be all tenfold more dangerous to a man with such a sin upon his conscience, and such a bottle under his arm. But for my part, I am so extreme-ly terrified myself, I have not the heart to blame you. Here I go then; and I pray God you may be happy in your house, and I fortunate with my schooner, and both get to heaven in the end in spite of the devil and his bottle."

So Lopaka went down the mountain; and Keawe stood in his front balcony, and listened to the clink of the horse's shoes, and watched the lantern go shining down the path, and along the cliff of caves where the old dead are buried; and all the time he trembled and clasped his hands, and prayed for his friend, and gave glory to God that he himself was escaped out of that trouble.

But the next day came very brightly, and that new house of his was so delightful to behold that he forgot his terrors. One day followed another, and Keawe dwelt there in perpetual joy. He had his place on the back porch; it was there he ate and lived, and read the stories in the Honolulu newspapers; but when anyone came by they would go in and view the chambers and the pictures. And the fame of the house went far and wide; it was called *Ka-Hale Nui*—the Great House—in all Kona; and sometimes the Bright House, for Keawe kept a Chinaman, who was all day dusting and furbishing; and the glass, and the gilt, and the fine stuffs, and the pictures, shone as bright as the morning. As for Keawe himself, he could not walk in the chambers without singing, his heart was so enlarged; and when ships sailed by upon the sea, he would fly his colours on the mast.

So time went by, until one day Keawe went upon a visit as far as Kailua to certain of his friends. There he was well feasted; and left as soon as he could the next morning, and rode hard, for he was impatient to behold his beautiful house; and, besides, the night then coming on was the night in which the dead of old days go abroad in the sides of Kona; and having already meddled with the devil, he was the more chary of meeting with the dead. A little beyond Honaunau, looking far ahead, he was aware of a woman bathing in the edge of the sea; and she seemed a well-grown girl, but he thought no more of it. Then he saw her white shift flutter as she put it on, and then her red holoku; and by the time he came abreast of her she was done with her toilet, and had come up from the sea, and stood by the track-side in her red holoku, and she was all freshened with the bath, and her eyes shone and were kind. Now Keawe no sooner beheld her than he drew rein.

"I thought I knew everyone in this country," said he. "How comes it that I do not know you?"

"I am Kokua, daughter of Kiano," said the girl, "and I have just returned from Oahu. Who are you?"

"I will tell you who I am in a little," said Keawe, dismounting from his horse, "but not now. For I have a thought in my mind, and if you knew who I was, you might have heard of me, and would not give me a true answer. But tell me, first of all, one thing: Are you married?"

At this Kokua laughed out aloud. "It is you who ask questions," she said. "Are you married yourself?"

"Indeed, Kokua, I am not," replied Keawe, "and never thought to be until this hour. But here is the plain truth. I have met you here at the roadside, and I saw your eyes, which are like the stars, and my heart went to you as swift as a bird. And so now, if you want none of me, say so, and I will go to my own place; but if you think me no worse than any other young man, say so, too, and I will turn aside to your father's for the night, and tomorrow I will talk with the good man."

Kokua said never a word, but she looked at the sea and laughed.

"Kokua," said Keawe, "if you say nothing, I will take that for the good answer; so let us be stepping to your father's door."

She went on ahead of him, still without speech; only sometimes she glanced back and glanced away again, and she kept the strings of her hat in her mouth.

Now, when they had come to the door, Kiano came out on his verandah, and cried out and welcomed Keawe by name. At that the girl looked over, for the fame of the great house had come to her ears; and, to be sure, it was a great temptation. All that evening they were very merry together; and the girl was as bold as brass under the eyes of her parents, and made a mock of Keawe, for she had a quick wit. The next day he had a word with Kiano, and found the girl alone.

"Kokua," said he, "you made a mock of me all the evening; and it is still time to bid me go. I would not tell you who I was, because I have so fine a house, and I feared you would think too much of that house and too little of the man who loves you. Now you know all, and if you wish to have seen the last of me, say so at once."

"No," said Kokua; but this time she did not laugh, nor did Keawe ask for more.

This was the wooing of Keawe; things had gone quickly; but so an arrow goes, and the ball of a rifle swifter still, and yet both may strike the target. Things had gone fast, but they had gone far also, and the thought of Keawe rang in the maiden's head; she heard his voice in the breach of the surf upon the lava, and for this young man that she had seen but twice she would have left father and mother and her native islands. As for Keawe himself, his horse flew up the path of the mountain under the cliff of tombs, and the sound of the hoofs, and the sound of Keawe singing to himself for pleasure, echoed in the caverns of the dead. He came to the Bright House, and still he was singing. He sat and ate in the broad balcony, and the Chinaman wondered at his master, to hear how he sang between the mouthfuls. The sun went down into the sea, and the night came; and Keawe walked the balconies by lamplight, high on the mountains, and the voice of his singing startled men on ships.

"Here am I now upon my high place," he said to himself. "Life may be no better; this is the mountain top; and all shelves about me toward the worse. For the first time I will light up the chambers, and bathe in my fine bath with hot water and the cold, and sleep alone in the bed of my bridal chamber."

So the Chinaman had word, and he must rise from sleep and light the furnaces; and as he wrought below, beside the boilers, he heard his master singing and rejoicing above him in the lighted chambers. When the water began to be hot the Chinaman cried to his master; and Keawe went into the bathroom; and the Chinaman heard him sing as he filled the marble basin; and heard him sing, and the singing broken, as he undressed; until of a sudden, the song ceased. The Chinaman listened, and listened; he called up the house to Keawe to ask if all were well, and Keawe answered him "Yes," and bade him go to bed; but there was no more singing in the Bright House;

and all night long, the Chinaman heard his master's feet go round and round the balconies without repose.

Now the truth of it was this: as Keawe undressed for his bath, he spied upon his flesh a patch like a patch of lichen on a rock, and it was then that he stopped singing. For he knew the likeness of that patch, and knew that he was fallen in the Chinese Evil.*

Now, it is a sad thing for any man to fall into this sickness. And it would be a sad thing for anyone to leave a house so beautiful and so commodious, and depart from all his friends to the north coast of Molokai between the mighty cliff and the sea-breakers. But what was that to the case of the man Keawe, he who had met his love but yesterday, and won her but that morning, and now saw all his hopes break in a moment, like a piece of glass?

Awhile he sat upon the edge of the bath; then sprang, with a cry, and ran outside; and to and fro, to and fro, along the balcony, like one despairing.

"Very willingly could I leave Hawaii, the home of my fathers," Keawe was thinking. "Very lightly could I leave my house, the high-placed, the many-windowed, here upon the mountains. Very bravely could I go to Molokai, to Kalaupapa by the cliffs, to live with the smitten and to sleep there, far from my fathers. But what wrong have I done, what sin lies upon my soul, that I should have encountered Kokua coming cool from the sea-water in the evening? Kokua, the soul ensnarer! Kokua, the light of my life! Her may I never wed, may I look upon no longer, her may I no more handle with my loving hand; and it is for this, it is for you, O Kokua! that I pour my lamentations!"

Now you are to observe what sort of a man Keawe was, for he might have dwelt there in the Bright House for years, and no one been the wiser of his sickness; but he reckoned nothing of that, if he must lose Kokua. And again, he might have wed Kokua even as he was; and so many would have done, because they have the souls of pigs; but Keawe loved the maid

---

* Leprosy

manfully, and he would do her no hurt and bring her in no danger.

A little beyond the midst of the night, there came in his mind the recollection of that bottle. He went round to the back porch, and called to memory the day when the devil had looked forth; and at the thought ice ran in his veins.

"A dreadful thing is the bottle," thought Keawe, "and dreadful is the imp, and it is a dreadful thing to risk the flames of hell. But what other hope have I to cure my sickness or to wed Kokua? What!" he thought, "would I beard the devil once, only to get me a house, and not face him again to win Kokua?"

Thereupon he called to mind it was the next day the *Hall* went by on her return to Honolulu. "There must I go first," he thought, "and see Lopaka. For the best hope that I have now is to find that same bottle I was so pleased to be rid of."

Never a wink could he sleep; the food stuck in his throat; but he sent a letter to Kiano, and about the time when the steamer would be coming, rode down beside the cliff of the tombs. It rained; his horse went heavily; he looked up at the black mouths of the caves, and he envied the dead that slept there and were done with trouble; and called to mind how he had galloped by the day before, and was astonished. So he came down to Hookena, and there was all the country gathered for the steamer as usual. In the shed before the store they sat and jested and passed the news; but there was no matter of speech in Keawe's bosom, and he sat in their midst and looked without on the rain falling on the houses, and the surf beating among the rocks, and the sighs arose in his throat.

"Keawe of the Bright House is out of spirits," said one to another. Indeed, and so he was, and little wonder.

Then the *Hall* came, and the whale-boat carried him on board. The afterpart of the ship was full of Haoles* who had been to visit the volcano, as their custom is; and the midst was crowded with Kanakas, and the forepart with wild bulls from Hilo and horses from Kaü; but Keawe sat apart from all in his sorrow, and watched for the house of Kiano. There it sat, low

---

* Whites

upon the shore in the black rocks, and shaded by the cocoa palms, and there by the door was a red holoku, no greater than a fly, and going to and fro with a fly's business. "Ah, queen of my heart," he cried, "I'll venture my dear soul to win you!"

Soon after, darkness fell, and the cabins were lit up, and the Haoles sat and played at the cards and drank whiskey as their custom is; but Keawe walked the deck all night; and all the next day, as they steamed under the lee of Maui or of Molokai, he was still pacing to and fro like a wild animal in a menagerie.

Towards evening they passed Diamond Head, and came to the pier of Honolulu. Keawe stepped out among the crowd and began to ask for Lopaka. It seemed he had become the owner of a schooner—none better in the islands—and was gone upon an adventure as far as Pola-Pola or Kahiki; so there was no help to be looked for from Lopaka. Keawe called to mind a friend of his, a lawyer in the town (I must not tell his name) and inquired of him. They said he had grown suddenly rich, and had a fine new house upon Waikiki shore; and this put a thought in Keawe's head, and he called a hack and drove to the lawyer's house.

The house was all brand new, and the trees in the garden no greater than walking-sticks, and the lawyer, when he came, had the air of a man well pleased.

"What can I do to serve you?" said the lawyer.

"You are a friend of Lopaka's," replied Keawe, "and Lopaka purchased from me a certain piece of goods that I thought you might enable me to trace."

The lawyer's face became very dark. "I do not profess to misunderstand you, Mr. Keawe," said he, "though this is an ugly business to be stirring in. You may be sure I know nothing, but yet I have a guess, and if you would apply in a certain quarter you might have news."

And he named the name of a man, which, again, I had better not repeat. So it was for days, and Keawe went from one to another, finding everywhere new clothes and carriages, and fine new houses and men everywhere in great contentment, although, to be sure, when he hinted at his business their faces would cloud over.

"No doubt I am upon the track," thought Keawe. "These new clothes and carriages are all the gifts of the little imp, and these glad faces are the faces of men who have taken their profit and got rid of the accursed thing in safety. When I see pale cheeks and hear sighing, I shall know that I am near the bottle."

So it befell at last that he was recommended to a Haole in Beritania Street. When he came to the door, about the hour of the evening meal, there were the usual marks of the new house, and the young garden, and the electric light shining in the windows; but when the owner came, a shock of hope and fear ran through Keawe; for here was a young man, white as a corpse, and black about the eyes, the hair shedding from his head, and such a look in his countenance as a man may have when he is waiting for the gallows.

"Here it is, to be sure," thought Keawe, and so with this man he noways veiled his errand. "I am come to buy the bottle," said he.

At the word, the young Haole of Beritania Street reeled against the wall.

"The bottle!" he gasped. "To buy the bottle!" Then he seemed to choke, and seizing Keawe by the arm carried him into a room and poured out wine in two glasses.

"Here is my respects," said Keawe, who had been much about with Haoles in his time. "Yes," he added, "I am come to buy the bottle. What is the price by now?"

At that word the young man let his glass slip through his fingers, and looked upon Keawe like a ghost.

"The price," says he; "the price! You do not know the price?"

"It is for that I am asking you," returned Keawe. "But why are you so much concerned? Is there anything wrong about the price?"

"It has dropped a great deal in value since your time, Mr. Keawe," said the young man, stammering.

"Well, well, I shall have the less to pay for it," says Keawe.

"How much did it cost you?"

The young man was as white as a sheet. "Two cents," said he.

"What?" cried Keawe, "two cents? Why, then, you can only sell it for one. And he who buys it—" The words died upon Keawe's tongue; he who bought it could never sell it again, the bottle and the bottle imp must abide with him until he died, and when he died must carry him to the red end of hell.

The young man of Beritania Street fell upon his knees. "For God's sake buy it!" he cried. "You can have all my fortune in the bargain. I was mad when I bought it at that price. I had embezzled money at my store; I was lost else: I must have gone to jail."

"Poor creature," said Keawe, "you would risk your soul upon so desperate an adventure, and to avoid the proper punishment of your own disgrace; and you think I could hesitate with love in front of me. Give me the bottle, and the change which I make sure you have all ready. Here is a five-cent piece."

It was as Keawe supposed; the young man had the change ready in a drawer; the bottle changed hands, and Keawe's fingers were no sooner clasped upon the stalk than he had breathed his wish to be a clean man. And, sure enough, when he got home to his room, and stripped himself before a glass, his flesh was whole like an infant's. And here was the strange thing: he had no sooner seen this miracle, than his mind was changed within him, and he cared naught for the Chinese Evil, and little enough for Kokua; and had but the one thought, that here he was bound to the bottle imp for time and for eternity, and had no better hope but to be a cinder for ever in the flames of hell. Away ahead of him he saw them blaze with his mind's eye, and his soul shrank, and darkness fell upon the light.

When Keawe came to himself a little, he was aware it was the night when the band played at the hotel. Thither he went, because he feared to be alone; and there, among happy faces, walked to and fro, and heard the tunes go up and down, and saw Berger beat the measure, and all the while he heard the flames crackle, and saw the red fire burning in the bottomless pit. Of a sudden the bank played *Hiki-ao-ao*, that was a song that he had sung with Kokua, and at the strain courage returned to him.

"It is done now," he thought, "and once more let me take the good along with the evil."

So it befell that he returned to Hawaii by the first steamer, and as soon as it could be managed he was wedded to Kokua, and carried her up the mountain side to the Bright House.

Now it was so with these two, that when they were together, Keawe's heart was stilled; but so soon as he was alone he fell into a brooding horror, and heard the flames crackle, and saw the red fire burn in the bottomless pit. The girl, indeed, had come to him wholly; her heart leapt in her side at sight of him, her hand clung to his; and she was so fashioned from the hair upon her head to the nails upon her toes that none could see her without joy. She was pleasant in her nature. She had the good word always. Full of song she was, and went to and fro in the Bright House, the brightest thing in its three storeys, carolling like the birds. And Keawe beheld and heard her with delight, and then must shrink upon one side, and weep and groan to think upon the price that he had paid for her; and then he must dry his eyes, and wash his face, and go and sit with her on the broad balconies, joining in her songs, and, with a sick spirit, answering her smiles.

There came a day when her feet began to be heavy and her songs more rare; and now it was not Keawe only that would weep apart, but each would sunder from the other and sit in opposite balconies with the whole width of the Bright House betwixt. Keawe was so sunk in his despair, he scarce observed the change, and was only glad he had more hours to sit alone and brood upon his destiny, and was not so frequently condemned to pull a smiling face on a sick heart. But one day, coming softly through the house, he heard the sound of a child sobbing, and there was Kokua rolling her face upon the balcony floor, and weeping like the lost.

"You do well to weep in this house, Kokua," he said. "And yet I would give the head off my body that you (at least) might have been happy."

"Happy!" she cried. "Keawe, when you lived alone in your Bright House, you were the word of the island for a happy man; laughter and song were in your mouth, and your face was as bright as the sunrise. Then you wedded poor Kokua; and the good God knows what is amiss in her—but from that day you have not smiled. Oh!" she cried, "what ails me? I thought I was pretty, and I knew I loved him. What ails me that I throw this cloud upon my husband?"

"Poor Kokua," said Keawe. He sat down by her side, and sought to take her hand; but that she plucked away. "Poor Kokua," he said, again. "My poor child—my pretty. And I had thought all this while to spare you! Well, you shall know all. Then, at least, you will pity poor Keawe; then you will understand how much he loved you in the past—that he dared hell for your possession—and how much he loves you still (the poor condemned one), that he can yet call up a smile when he beholds you."

With that, he told her all, even from the beginning.

"You have done this for me?" she cried. "Ah, well, then what do I care!"—and she clasped and wept upon him.

"Ah, child!" said Keawe, "and yet, when I consider of the fire of hell, I care a good deal!"

"Never tell me," said she; "no man can be lost because he loved Kokua, and no other fault. I tell you, Keawe, I shall save you with these hands, or perish in your company. What! you loved me, and gave your soul, and you think I will not die to save you in return?"

"Ah, my dear! you might die a hundred times, and what difference would that make?" he cried "except to leave me lonely till the time comes of my damnation?"

"You know nothing," said she. "I was educated in a school in Honolulu; I am no common girl. And I tell you, I shall save my lover. What is this you say about a cent? But all the world is not American. In England they have a piece they call a farthing, which is about half a cent. Ah! sorrow!" she cried, "that makes it scarcely better, for the buyer must be lost, and we shall find none so brave as my Keawe! But, then, there is France; they have a small coin there which they call a centime, and these go five to the cent or thereabout. We could not do better. Come, Keawe, let us go to the French islands; let us go to Tahiti, as fast as ships can bear us. There we have four centimes, three centimes, two centimes, one centime; four possible sales to come and go on; and two of us to push the bargain. Come, my Keawe! kiss me, and banish care. Kokua will defend you."

"Gift of God!" he cried. "I cannot think that God will punish me for desiring aught so good! Be it as you will, then; take me where you please: I put my life and my salvation in your hands."

Early the next day Kokua was about her preparations. She took Keawe's chest that he went with sailoring; and first she put the bottle in a corner; and then packed it with the richest of their clothes and the bravest of the knick-knacks in the house. "For," said she, "we must seem to be rich folks, or who will believe in the bottle?" All the time of her preparation she was as gay as a bird; only when she looked upon Keawe, the tears would spring in her eye, and she must run and kiss him. As for Keawe, a weight was off his soul; now that he had his secret shared, and some hope in front of him, he seemed like a new man, his feet went lightly on the earth, and his breath was good to him again. Yet was terror still at his elbow; and ever and again, as the wind blows out a taper, hope died in him, and he saw the flames toss and the red fire burn in hell.

It was given out in the country they were gone pleasuring to the States, which was thought a strange thing, and yet not so strange as the truth, if any could have guessed it. So they went to Honolulu in the *Hall*, and thence in the *Umatilla* to San Francisco with a crowd of Haoles, and at San Francisco took their passage by the mail brigantine, the *Tropic Bird*, for Papeete, the chief place of the French in the south islands. Thither they came, after a pleasant voyage, on a fair day of the Trade Wind, and saw the reef with the surf breaking, and Motuiti with its palms, and the schooner riding withinside, and the white houses of the town low down along the shore among green trees, and overhead the mountains and the clouds of Tahiti, the wise island.

It was judged the most wise to hire a house, which they did accordingly, opposite the British Consul's, to make a great parade of money, and themselves conspicuous with carriages and horses. This it was very easy to do, so long as they had the bottle in their possession; for Kokua was more bold than Keawe, and, whenever she had a mind, called on the imp for twenty or a hundred dollars. At this rate they soon grew to be remarked in the town; and the strangers from Hawaii, their riding and their driving, the fine holokus and the rich lace of Kokua, became the matter of much talk.

They got on well after the first with the Tahitian language, which is indeed like to the Hawaiian, with a change of certain letters; and as soon as they had any freedom of speech, began to push the bottle. You are to consider it was not an easy subject to introduce; it was not easy to persuade people you were in earnest, when you offered to sell them for four centimes the spring of health and riches inexhaustible. It was necessary besides to explain the dangers of the bottle; and either people disbelieved the whole thing and laughed, or they thought the more of the darker part, became overcast with gravity, and drew away from Keawe and Kokua, as from persons who had dealings with the devil. So far from gaining ground, these two began to find they were avoided in the town; the children ran away from them screaming, a thing intolerable to Kokua; Catholics crossed themselves as they went by, and all persons began with one accord to disengage themselves from their advances.

Depression fell upon their spirits. They would sit at night in their new house, after a day's weariness, and not exchange one word, or the silence would be broken by Kokua bursting suddenly into sobs. Sometimes they would pray together; sometimes they would have the bottle out upon the floor, and sit all the evening watching how the shadow hovered in the midst. At such times they would be afraid to go to rest. It was long ere slumber came to them, and, if either dozed off, it would be to wake and find the other silently weeping in the dark, or, perhaps, to wake alone, the other having fled from the house and the neighbourhood of that bottle, to pace under the bananas in the little garden, or to wander on the beach by moonlight.

One night it was so when Kokua awoke. Keawe was gone. She felt in the bed and his place was cold. Then fear fell upon her, and she sat up in bed. A little moonshine filtered through the shutters. The room was bright, and she could spy the bottle on the floor. Outside it blew high, the great trees of the avenue cried aloud, and the fallen leaves rattled in the verandah. In the mist of this Kokua was aware of another sound; whether of a beast or of a man she could scarce tell, but it was as sad as death, and cut her to the soul. Softly she arose, set the door ajar, and looked forth into the moonlit yard. There, under the bananas, lay Keawe, his mouth in the dust, and as he lay he moaned.

It was Kokua's first thought to run forward and console him; her second potently withheld her. Keawe had borne himself before his wife like a brave man; it became her little in the hour of weakness to intrude upon his shame. With the thought she drew back into the house.

"Heaven!" she thought, "how careless have I been—how weak! It is he, not I, that stands in this eternal peril; it was he, not I, that took the curse upon his soul. It is for my sake, and for the love of a creature of so little worth and such poor help, that he now beholds so close to him the flames of hell—ay, and smells the smoke of it, lying without there in the wind and moonlight. Am I so dull of spirit that never till now I have surmised my duty, or have I seen it before and turned aside? But now, at least, I take up my soul in both the hands of my affection; now I say farewell to the white steps of heaven and the waiting faces of my friends. A love for a love, and let mine be equalled with Keawe's! A soul for a soul, and be it mine to perish!"

She was a deft woman with her hands, and was soon apparelled. She took in her hands the change—the precious centimes they kept ever at their side; for this coin is little used, and they had made provision at a Government office. When she was forth in the avenue clouds came on the wind, and the moon was blackened. The town slept, and she knew not whither to turn till she heard one coughing in the shadow of the trees.

"Old man," said Kokua, "what do you here abroad in the cold night?"

The old man could scarce express himself for coughing, but she made out that he was old and poor, and a stranger in the island.

"Will you do me a service?" said Kokua. "As one stranger to another, and as an old man to a young woman, will you help a daughter of Hawaii?"

"Ah," said the old man. "So you are the witch from the eight islands, and even my old soul you seek to entangle. But I have heard of you, and defy your wickedness."

"Sit down here," said Kokua, "and let me tell you a tale." And she told him the story of Keawe from the beginning to the end.

"And now," said she, "I am his wife, whom he bought with his soul's welfare. And what should I do? If I went to him myself and offered to buy it, he would refuse. But if you go, he will sell it eagerly; I will await you here: you will buy it for four centimes, and I will buy it again for three. And the Lord strengthen a poor girl!"

"If you meant falsely," said the old man, "I think God would strike you dead."

"He would!" cried Kokua. "Be sure he would. I could not be so treacherous—God would not suffer it."

"Give me the four centimes and await me here," said the old man.

Now, when Kokua stood alone in the street, her spirit died. The wind roared in the trees, and it seemed to her the rushing of the flames of hell; the shadows tossed in the light of the street lamp, and they seemed to her the snatching hands of evil ones. If she had had the strength, she must have run away, and if she had had the breath she must have screamed aloud; but, in truth, she could do neither, and stood and trembled in the avenue, like an affrighted child.

Then she saw the old man returning, and he had the bottle in his hand.

"I have done your bidding," said he. "I left your husband weeping like a child; to-night he will sleep easy." And he held the bottle forth.

"Before you give it me," Kokua panted, "take the good with the evil—ask to be delivered from your cough."

"I am an old man," replied the other, "and too near the gate of the grave to take a favour from the devil. But what is this? Why do you not take the bottle? Do you hesitate?"

"Not hesitate!" cried Kokua. "I am only weak. Give me a moment. It is my hand resists, my flesh shrinks back from the accursed thing. One moment only!"

The old man looked upon Kokua kindly. "Poor child!" said he, "you fear; your soul misgives you. Well, let me keep it. I am old, and can never more be happy in this world, and as for the next—"

"Give it me!" gasped Kokua. "There is your money. Do you think I am so base as that? Give me the bottle."

"God bless you, child," said the old man.

Kokua concealed the bottle under her holoku, said farewell to the old man, and walked off along the avenue, she cared not whither. For all roads were now the same to her, and led equally to hell. Sometimes she walked, and sometimes ran; sometimes she screamed out loud in the night, and sometimes lay by the wayside in the dust and wept. All that she had heard of hell came back to her; she saw the flames blaze, and she smelt the smoke, and her flesh withered on the coals.

Near day she came to her mind again, and returned to the house. It was even as the old man said—Keawe slumbered like a child. Kokua stood and gazed upon his face.

"Now, my husband," said she, "it is your turn to sleep. When you wake it will be your turn to sing and laugh. But for poor Kokua, alas! that meant no evil—for poor Kokua no more sleep, no more singing, no more delight, whether in earth or heaven."

With that she lay down in the bed by his side, and her misery was so extreme that she fell in a deep slumber instantly.

Late in the morning her husband woke her and gave her the good news. It seemed he was silly with delight, for he paid no heed to her distress, ill though she dissembled it. The words stuck in her mouth, it mattered not; Keawe did the speaking. She ate not a bite, but who was to observe it? for Keawe cleared the dish. Kokua saw and heard him, like some strange thing in a dream; there were times when she forgot or doubted, and put her hands to her brow; to know herself doomed and hear her husband babble, seemed so monstrous.

All this while Keawe was eating and talking, and planning the time of their return, and thanking her for saving him, and fondling her, and calling her the true helper after all. He laughed at the old man that was fool enough to buy that bottle.

"A worthy old man he seemed," Keawe said. "But no one can judge by appearances. For why did the old reprobate require the bottle?"

"My husband," said Kokua, humbly, "his purpose may have been good."

Keawe laughed like an angry man.

"Fiddle-de-dee!" cried Keawe. "An old rogue, I tell you; and an old ass to boot. For the bottle was hard enough to sell at four centimes; and at three it will be quite impossible. The margin is not broad enough, the thing begins to smell of scorching—-brrr!" said he, and shuddered. "It is true I bought it myself at a cent, when I knew not there were smaller coins. I was a fool for my pains; there will never be found another: and whoever has that bottle now will carry it to the pit."

"O my husband!" said Kokua. "Is it not a terrible thing to save oneself by the eternal ruin of another? It seems to me I could not laugh. I would be humbled. I would be filled with melancholy. I would pray for the poor holder."

Then Keawe, because he felt the truth of what she said, grew the more angry. "Heighty-teighty!" cried he. "You may be filled with melancholy if you please. It is not the mind of a good wife. If you thought at all of me, you would sit ashamed."

Thereupon he went out, and Kokua was alone.

What chance had she to sell that bottle at two centimes? None, she perceived. And if she had any, here was her husband hurrying her away to a country where there was nothing lower than a cent. And here—on the morrow of her sacri-fice—was her husband leaving her and blaming her.

She would not even try to profit by what time she had, but sat in the house, and now had the bottle out and viewed it with unutterable fear, and now, with loathing, hid it out of sight.

By-and-by, Keawe came back, and would have her take a drive.

"My husband, I am ill," she said. "I am out of heart. Excuse me, I can take no pleasure."

Then was Keawe more wroth than ever. With her, because he thought she was brooding over the case of the old man; and with himself, because he thought she was right, and was ashamed to be so happy.

"This is your truth," cried he, "and this your affection! Your husband is just saved from eternal ruin, which he encountered for the love of you—and you can take no pleasure! Kokua, you have a disloyal heart."

He went forth again furious, and wandered in the town all day. He met friends, and drank with them; they hired a car-riage and drove into the country, and there drank again. All the time Keawe was ill at ease, because he was taking his pas-time while his wife was sad, and because he knew in his heart that she was more right than he; and the knowledge made him drink the deeper.

Now there was an old brutal Haole drinking with him, one that had been a boatswain of a whaler, a runaway, a digger in gold mines, a convict in prisons. He had a low mind and a foul mouth; he loved to drink and to see others drunken; and he pressed the glass upon Keawe. Soon there was no more money in the company.

"Here you!" says the boatswain, "you are rich, you have been always saying. You have a bottle or some foolishness."

"Yes," says Keawe, "I am rich; I will go back and get some money from my wife, who keeps it."

"That's a bad idea, mate," says the boatswain. "Never you trust a petticoat with dollars. They're all as false as water; you keep an eye on her."

Now, this word stuck in Keawe's mind; for he was muddled with what he had been drinking.

"I should not wonder but she was false, indeed," thought he. "Why else should she be so cast down at my release? But I will show her I am not the man to be fooled. I will catch her in the act."

Accordingly, when they were back in town, Keawe bade the boatswain wait for him at the corner, by the old calaboose, and went forward up the avenue alone to the door of his house. The night had come again; there was a light within, but never a sound, and Keawe crept about the corner, opened the back door softly, and looked in.

There was Kokua on the floor, the lamp at her side; before her was a milk-white bottle, with a round belly and a long neck; and as she viewed it, Kokua wrung her hands.

A long time Keawe stood and looked in the doorway. At first he was struck stupid; and then fear fell upon him that the bargain had been made amiss, and the bottle had come back to him as it came at San Francisco; and at that his knees were loosened, and the fumes of the wine departed from his head like mists off a river in the morning. And then he had another thought; and it was a strange one, that made his cheeks to burn.

"I must make sure of this," thought he.

So he closed the door, and went softly round the corner again, and then came noisily in, as though he were but now returned. And, lo! by the time he opened the front door no bottle was to be seen; and Kokua sat in a chair and started up like one awakened out of sleep.

"I have been drinking all day and making merry," said Keawe. "I have been with good companions, and now I only come back for money, and return to drink and carouse with them again."

Both his face and voice were as stern as judgement, but Kokua was too troubled to observe.

"You do well to use your own, my husband," said she, and her words trembled.

"O, I do well in all things," said Keawe, and he went straight to the chest and took out money. But he looked besides in the corner where they kept the bottle, and there was no bottle there.

At that the chest heaved upon the floor like a sea-billow, and the house span about him like a wreath of smoke, for he saw he was lost now, and there was no escape. "It is what I feared," he thought; "it is she who has bought it."

And then he came to himself a little and rose up; but the sweat streamed on his face as thick as the rain and as cold as the well-water.

"Kokua," said he, "I said to you to-day what ill became me. Now I return to carouse with my jolly companions," and at that he laughed a little quietly. "I will take more pleasure in the cup if you forgive me."

She clasped his knees in a moment; she kissed his knees with flowing tears.

"O," she cried, "I asked but a kind word!"

"Let us never one think hardly of the other," said Keawe, and was gone out of the house.

Now, the money that Keawe had taken was only some of that store of centime pieces they had laid in at their arrival. It was very sure he had no mind to be drinking. His wife had given her soul for him, now he must give his for hers; no other thought was in the world with him.

At the corner, by the old calaboose, there was the boatswain waiting.

"My wife has the bottle," said Keawe, "and, unless you help me to recover it, there can be no more money and no more liquor to-night."

"You do not mean to say you are serious about that bottle?" cried the boatswain.

"There is the lamp," said Keawe. "Do I look as if I was jesting."

"That is so," said the boatswain. "You look as serious as a ghost."

"Well, then," said Keawe, "here are two centimes; you must go to my wife in the house, and offer her these for the bottle, which (if I am not much mistaken) she will give you instantly.

Bring it to me here, and I will buy it back from you for one; for that is the law with this bottle, that it still must be sold for a less sum. But whatever you do, never breathe a word to her that you have come from me."

"Mate, I wonder are you making a fool of me?" asked the boatswain.

"It will do you no harm if I am," returned Keawe.

"That is so, mate," said the boatswain.

"And if you doubt me," added Keawe, "you can try. As soon as you are clear of the house, wish to have your pocket full of money, or a bottle of the best rum, or what you please, and you will see the virtue of the thing."

"Very well, Kanaka," says the boatswain. "I will try; but if you are having your fun out of me, I will take my fun out of you with a belaying pin."

So the whaler-man went off up the avenue; and Keawe stood and waited. It was near the same spot where Kokua had waited the night before; but Keawe was more resolved, and never faltered in his purpose; only his soul was bitter with despair.

It seemed a long time he had to wait before he heard a voice singing in the darkness of the avenue. He knew the voice to be the boatswain's; but it was strange how drunken it appeared upon a sudden.

Next, the man himself came stumbling into the light of the lamp. He had the devil's bottle buttoned in his coat; another bottle was in his hand; and even as he came in view he raised it to his mouth and drank.

"You have it," said Keawe. "I see that."

"Hands off!" cried the boatswain, jumping back. "Take a step near me, and I'll smash your mouth. You thought you could make a cat's-paw of me, did you?"

"What do you mean?" cried Keawe.

"Mean?" cried the boatswain. "This is a pretty good bottle, this is; that's what I mean. How I got it for two centimes I can't make out; but I'm sure you shan't have it for one."

"You mean you won't sell?" gasped Keawe.

"No, *sir!*" cried the boatswain. "But I'll give you a drink of the rum, if you like."

"I tell you," said Keawe, "the man who has that bottle goes to hell."

"I reckon I'm going anyway," returned the sailor; "and this bottle's the best thing to go with I've struck yet. No, sir!" he cried again, "this is my bottle now, and you can go and fish for another."

"Can this be true?" Keawe cried. "For your own sake, I beseech you, sell it me!"

"I don't value any of your talk," replied the boatswain. "You thought I was a flat; now you see I'm not; and there's an end. If you won't have a swallow of rum, I'll have one myself. Here's your health, and good-night to you!"

So off he went down the avenue towards town, and there goes the bottle out of the story.

But Keawe ran to Kokua light as the wind; and great was their joy that night; and great, since then, has been the peace of all their days in the Bright House.

by
STEPHEN LEACOCK
(1869–1944)

Aargh, Billy Leacock, full sail, full sail! Them's pirates be a-starboard, and Spaniards to the port! This story, one of Leacock's best, is a sort of Treasure Island *with a Leacockian twist, and the whole thing soaked in seaweed...*

It was in August in 1867 that I stepped on board the deck of the *Saucy Sally*, lying in dock at Gravesend, to fill the berth of second mate.

Let me first say a word about myself.

I was a tall, handsome young fellow, squarely and powerfully built, bronzed by the sun and the moon (and even copper-coloured in spots from the effect of the stars), and with a face in which honesty, intelligence, and exceptional brain power were combined with Christianity, simplicity, and modesty.

As I stepped on deck I could not help a slight feeling of triumph, as I caught sight of my sailor-like features reflected in a tar-barrel that stood beside the mast, while a little later I could scarcely repress a sense of gratification as I noticed them reflected again in a bucket of bilge water.

"Welcome on board, Mr. Blowhard," called out Captain Bilge, stepping out of the binnacle and shaking hands across the taffrail.

I saw before me a fine sailor-like man of from thirty to sixty, clean-shaven, except for an enormous pair of whiskers, a heavy beard, and a thick moustache, powerful in build, and carrying his beam well aft, in a pair of broad duck trousers across the back of which there would have been room to write a history of the British Navy.

Beside him were the first and third mates, both of them being quiet men of poor stature, who looked at Captain Bilge with what seemed to me an apprehensive expression in their eyes.

The vessel was on the eve of departure. Her deck presented that scene of bustle and alacrity dear to the sailor's heart. Men were busy nailing up the masts, hanging the bowsprit over the side, varnishing the lee-scuppers and pouring hot tar down the companion-way.

Captain Bilge, with a megaphone to his lips, kept calling out to the men in his rough sailor fashion:

"Now, then, don't over-exert yourselves, gentlemen. Remember, please, that we have plenty of time. Keep out of the sun as much as you can. Step carefully in the rigging there, Jones; I fear it's just a little high for you. Tut, tut, Williams, don't get yourself so dirty with that tar, you won't look fit to be seen."

I stood leaning over the gaff of the mainsail and thinking— yes, thinking, dear reader, of my mother. I hope that you will think none the less of me for that. Whenever things look dark, I lean up against something and think of mother. If they get positively black, I stand on one leg and think of father. After that I can face anything.

Did I think, too, of another, younger than mother and fairer than father? Yes, I did. "Bear up, darling," I had whispered as she nestled her head beneath my oilskins and kicked out backward with one heel in the agony of her girlish grief, "in five years the voyage will be over, and after three more like it, I shall come back with money enough to buy a second-hand fishing-net and settle down on shore."

Meantime the ship's preparations were complete. The masts were all in position, the sails nailed up, and men with axes were busily chopping away the gangway.

"All ready?" called the Captain.

"Aye, aye, sir."

"Then hoist the anchor in board and send a man down with

the key to open the bar."

Opening the bar! the last sad rite of departure. How often in my voyages have I seen it; the little group of men soon to be exiled from their home, standing about with saddened faces, waiting to see the man with the key open the bar—held there by some strange fascination.

Next morning with a fair wind astern we had buzzed around the corner of England and were running down the Channel.

I know no finer sight, for those who have never seen it, than the English Channel. It is the highway of the world. Ships of all nations are passing up and down, Dutch, Scotch, Venezuelan, and even American.

Chinese junks rush to and fro. Warships, motor yachts, icebergs, and lumber rafts are everywhere. If I add to this fact that so thick a fog hangs over it that it is entirely hidden from sight, my readers can form some idea of the majesty of the scene.

We had now been three days at sea. My first sea-sickness was wearing off, and I thought less of father.

On the third morning Captain Bilge descended to my cabin.

"Mr. Blowhard," he said, "I must ask you to stand double watches."

"What is the matter?" I inquired.

"The two other mates have fallen overboard," he said uneasily, and avoiding my eye.

I contented myself with saying, "Very good, sir," but I could not help thinking it a trifle odd that both mates should have fallen overboard in the same night.

Surely there was some mystery in this.

Two mornings later the Captain appeared at the breakfast-table with the same shifting and uneasy look in the eye.

"Anything wrong, sir?" I asked.

"Yes," he answered, trying to appear at ease and twisting a fried egg to and fro between his fingers with such nervous force as almost to break it in two—"I regret to say that we have lost the bosun."

"The bosun!" I cried.

"Yes," said Captain Bilge more quietly, "he is overboard. I blame myself for it, partly. It was early this morning. I was holding him up in my arms to look at an iceberg, and, quite accidentally I assure you—I dropped him overboard."

"Captain Bilge," I asked, "have you taken any steps to recover him?"

"Not as yet," he replied uneasily.

I looked at him fixedly, but said nothing.

Ten days passed.

The mystery thickened. On Thursday two men of the starboard watch were reported missing. On Friday the carpenter's assistant disappeared. On the night of Saturday a circumstance occurred which, slight as it was, gave me some clue as to what was happening.

As I stood at the wheel about midnight, I saw the Captain approach in the darkness carrying the cabin-boy by the hind leg. The lad was a bright little fellow, whose merry disposition had already endeared him to me, and I watched with some interest to see what the Captain would do to him. Arrived at the stern of the vessel, Captain Bilge looked cautiously around a moment and then dropped the boy into the sea. For a brief instant the lad's head appeared in the phosphorus of the waves. The Captain threw a boot at him, sighed deeply, and went below.

Here then was the key to the mystery! The Captain was throwing the crew overboard. Next morning we met at breakfast as usual.

"Poor little Williams has fallen overboard," said the Captain, seizing a strip of ship's bacon and tearing at it with his teeth as if he almost meant to eat it.

"Captain," I said, greatly excited, stabbing at a ship's loaf in my agitation with such ferocity as almost to drive my knife into it—"You threw the boy overboard!"

"I did," said Captain Bilge, grown suddenly quiet, "I threw them all over and intend to throw the rest. Listen, Blowhard, you are young, ambitious, and trustworthy. I will confide in you."

Perfectly calm now, he stepped to a locker, rummaged in it a moment, and drew out a faded piece of yellow parchment, which he spread on the table. It was a map or chart. In the centre of it was a circle. In the middle of the circle was a small dot and a letter T, while at one side of the map was a letter N, and against it on the other side a letter S.

"What is this?" I asked.

"Can you not guess?" queried Captain Bilge. "It is a desert island."

"Ah!" I rejoined with a sudden flash of intuition, "and N is for North and S is for South."

"Blowhard," said the Captain, striking the table with such force as to cause a loaf of ship's bread to bounce up and down three or four times, "you've struck it. That part of it had not yet occurred to me."

"And the letter T?" I asked.

"The treasure, the buried treasure," said the Captain, and turning the map over he read from the back of it—"The point T indicates the spot where the treasure is buried under the sand; it consists of half a million Spanish dollars, and is buried in a brown leather dress-suit case."

"And where is the island?" I inquired, mad with excitement.

"That I do not know," said the Captain. "I intend to sail up and down the parallels of latitude until I find it."

"And meantime?"

"Meantime, the first thing to do is to reduce the number of the crew so as to have fewer hands to divide among. Come, come," he added in a burst of frankness which made me love the man in spite of his shortcomings, "will you join me in this? We'll throw them all over, keeping the cook to the last, dig up the treasure, and be rich for the rest of our lives."

Reader, do you blame me if I said yes? I was young, ardent, ambitious, full of bright hopes and boyish enthusiasm.

"Captain Bilge," I said, putting my hand in his, "I am yours."

"Good," he said, "now go forward to the forecastle and get an idea what the men are thinking."

I went forward to the men's quarters—a plain room in the front of the ship, with only a rough carpet on the floor, a few simple armchairs, writing-desks, spittoons of a plain pattern, and small brass beds with blue-and-green screens. It was Sunday morning, and the men were mostly sitting about in their dressing-gowns.

They rose as I entered and curtseyed.

"Sir," said Tompkins, the bosun's mate, "I think it my duty to tell you that there is a great deal of dissatisfaction among the men."

Several of the men nodded.

"They don't like the way the men keep going overboard," he continued, his voice rising to a tone of uncontrolled passion. "It is positively absurd, sir, and if you will allow me to say so, the men are far from pleased."

"Tompkins," I said sternly, "you must understand that my position will not allow me to listen to mutinous language of this sort."

I returned to the Captain. "I think the men mean mutiny," I said.

"Good," said Captain Bilge, rubbing his hands, "that will get rid of a lot of them, and of course," he added musingly, looking out of the broad old-fashioned port-hole at the stern of the cabin, at the heaving waves of the South Atlantic, "I am expecting pirates at any time, and that will take out quite a few of them. However"—and here he pressed the bell for a cabin-boy—"kindly ask Mr. Tompkins to step this way."

"Tompkins," said the Captain as the bosun's mate entered, "be good enough to stand on the locker and stick your head through the stern port-hole, and tell me what you think of the weather."

"Aye, aye, sir," replied the tar with a simplicity which caused us to exchange a quiet smile.

Tompkins stood on the locker and put his head and shoulders out of the port.

Taking a leg each we pushed him through. We heard him plump into the sea.

"Tompkins was easy," said Captain Bilge. "Excuse me as I enter his death in the log."

"Yes," he continued presently, "it will be a great help if they mutiny. I suppose they will, sooner or later. It's customary to do so. But I shall take no step to precipitate it until we have first fallen in with pirates. I am expecting them in these latitudes at any time. Meantime, Mr. Blowhard," he said, rising, "if you can continue to drop overboard one or two more each week, I shall feel extremely grateful."

Three days later we rounded the Cape of Good Hope and entered upon the inky waters of the Indian Ocean. Our course lay now in zigzags and, the weather being favourable, we sailed up and down at a furious rate over a sea as calm as glass.

On the fourth day a pirate ship appeared. Reader, I do not know if you have ever seen a pirate ship. The sight was one to appal the stoutest heart. The entire ship was painted black, a black flag hung at the masthead, the sails were black, and on the deck people dressed all in black walked up and down arm-in-arm. The words "Pirate Ship" were painted in white letters on the bow. At the sight of it our crew were visibly cowed. It was a spectacle that would have cowed a dog.

The two ships were brought side by side. They were then lashed tightly together with bag string and binder twine, and a gang plank laid between them. In a moment the pirates swarmed upon our deck, rolling their eyes, gnashing their teeth and filing their nails.

Then the fight began. It lasted two hours—with fifteen minutes off for lunch. It was awful. The men grappled with one another, kicking one another from behind, slapping one another across the face, and in many cases completely lost their temper and tried to bite one another. I noticed one gigantic fellow brandishing a knotted towel, and striking right and left among our men, until Captain Bilge rushed at him and struck him flat across the mouth with a banana skin.

At the end of two hours, by mutual consent, the fight was

declared a draw. The points standing at sixty-one and a half against sixty-two.

The ships were unlashed, and with three cheers from each crew, were headed on their way.

"Now, then," said the Captain to me aside, "let us see how many of the crew are sufficiently exhausted to be thrown overboard."

He went below. In a few minutes he reappeared, his face deadly pale. "Blowhard," he said, "the ship is sinking. One of the pirates (sheer accident, of course, I blame no one) has kicked a hole in the side. Let us sound the well."

We put our ear to the ship's well. It sounded like water.

The men were put to the pumps and worked with the frenzied effort which only those who have been drowned in a sinking ship can understand.

At six p.m. the well marked one half an inch of water, at nightfall three-quarters of an inch, and at daybreak, after a night of unremitting toil, seven-eighths of an inch.

By noon of the next day the water had risen to fifteen-sixteenths of an inch, and on the next night the sounding showed thirty-one thirty-seconds of an inch of water in the hold. The situation was desperate. At this rate of increase few, if any, could tell where it would rise to in a few days.

That night the Captain called me to his cabin. He had a book of mathematical tables in front of him, and great sheets of vulgar fractions littered the floor on all sides.

"The ship is bound to sink," he said, "in fact, Blowhard, she is sinking. I can prove it. It may be six months or it may take years, but if she goes on like this, sink she must. There is nothing for it but to abandon her."

That night, in the dead of darkness, while the crew were busy at the pumps, the Captain and I built a raft.

Unobserved we cut down the masts, chopped them into suitable lengths, laid them crosswise in a pile and lashed them tightly together with bootlaces.

Hastily we threw on board a couple of boxes of food and bottles of drinking fluid, a sextant, a cronometer, a gas-meter, a bicycle pump and a few other scientific instruments. Then taking advantage of a roll in the motion of the ship, we launched the raft, lowered ourselves upon a line, and under cover of the heavy dark of a tropical night, we paddled away from the doomed vessel.

The break of day found us a tiny speck on the Indian Ocean. We looked about as big as this (.).

In the morning, after dressing, and shaving as best we could, we opened our box of food and drink.

Then came the awful horror of our situation.

One by one the Captain took from the box the square blue tins of canned beef which it contained. We counted fifty-two in all. Anxiously and with drawn faces we watched until the last can was lifted from the box. A single thought was in our minds. When the end came the Captain stood up on the raft with wild eyes staring at the sky.

"The can-opener!" he shrieked, "just Heaven, the can-opener." He fell prostrate.

Meantime, with trembling hands, I opened the box of bottles. It contained lager beer bottles, each with a patent tin top. One by one I took them out. There were fifty-two in all. As I withdrew the last one and saw the empty box before me, I shroke out—"The thing! the thing! oh, merciful Heaven! The thing you open them with!"

I fell prostrate upon the Captain.

We awoke to find ourselves still a mere speck upon the ocean. We felt even smaller than before.

Over us was the burnished copper sky of the tropics. The heavy, leaden sky lapped the sides of the raft. All about us was a litter of corn beef cans and lager beer bottles. Our sufferings in the ensuing days were indescribable. We beat and thumped at the cans with our fists. Even at the risk of spoiling the tins for ever we hammered them fiercely against the raft. We stamped on them, bit at them and swore at them. We pulled and clawed at the bottles with our hands, and chipped and knocked them against the cans, regardless even of breaking the glass and ruining the bottles.

It was futile.

Then day after day we sat in moody silence, gnawed with

hunger, with nothing to read, nothing to smoke, and practically nothing to talk about.

On the tenth day the Captain broke silence.

"Get ready the lots, Blowhard," he said. "It's got to come to that."

"Yes," I answered drearily, "we're getting thinner every day."

Then, with the awful prospect of cannibalism before us, we drew lots.

I prepared the lots and held them to the Captain. He drew the longer one.

"Which does that mean?" he asked, trembling between hope and despair. "Do I win?"

"No, Bilge," I said sadly, "you lose."

But I mustn't dwell on the days that followed—the long quiet days of lazy dreaming on the raft, during which I slowly built up my strength, which had been shattered by privation. They were days, dear reader, of deep and quiet peace, and yet I cannot recall them without shedding a tear for the brave man who made them what they were.

It was on the fifth day after that I was awakened from a sound sleep by the bumping of the raft against the shore. I had eaten perhaps overheartily, and had not observed the vicinity of land.

Before me was an island, the circular shape of which, with its low, sandy shore, recalled at once its identity.

"The treasure island," I cried, "at last I am rewarded for all my heroism."

In a fever of haste I rushed to the centre of the island. What was the sight that confronted me? A great hollow scooped in the sand, an empty dress-suit case lying beside it, and on a ship's plank driven deep into the sand, the legend, "*Saucy Sally*, October, 1867." So! the miscreants had made good the vessel, headed for the island of whose existence they must have learned from the chart we so carelessly left upon the cabin table, and had plundered poor Bilge and me of our well-earned treasure!

Sick with the sense of human ingratitude I sank upon the sand.

The island became my home.

There I eked out a miserable existence, feeding on sand and gravel and dressing myself in cactus plants. Years passed. Eating sand and mud slowly undermined my robust constitution. I fell ill. I died. I buried myself.

Would that writers who write sea stories would do as much.

Sleep

by
EMILY CARR
(1871–1945)

Emily Carr recognized early in life that our native peoples were very much worth listening to. This small episode would have taken place sometime in the early 1880s I suppose. On the one hand, this is a small sketch from a long time ago; on the other, it still speaks volumes...

When I was a child I was staying at one of Victoria's beaches.

I was down on the point watching a school of porpoises at play off Trial Island when a canoe came round the headland. She was steering straight for our beach.

The Government allowed the Indians to use the beaches when they were travelling, so they made camp and slept wherever the night happened to fall.

In the canoe were a man and woman, half a dozen children, a dog, a cat and a coop of fowls, besides all the Indians' things. She was a West Coast canoe—dug out of a great red cedar tree. She was long and slim, with a high prow shaped like a wolf's head. She was painted black with a line of blue running round the top of the inside. Her stern went straight down into the water. The Indian mother sat in the stern and steered the canoe with a paddle.

When the canoe was near the shore, the man and the woman drove their paddles strong and hard, and the canoe shot high up on the pebbles with a growling sound. The barefoot children swarmed over her side and waded ashore.

The man and the woman got out and dragged the canoe

high on to the beach. There was a baby tucked into the woman's shawl; the shawl bound the child close to her body. She waddled slowly across the beach, her bare feet settling in the sand with every step, her fleshy body squared down on to her feet. All the movements of the man and the woman were slow and steady; their springless feet padded flatly; their backs and shoulders were straight. The few words they said to each other were guttural and low-pitched.

The Indian children did not race up and down the beach, astonished at strange new things, as we always were. These children belonged to the beach, and were as much a part of it as the drift-logs and the stones.

The man gathered a handful of sticks and lit a fire. They took a big iron pot and their food out of the canoe, and set them by the fire. The woman sat among the things with her baby—she managed the shawl and the baby so that she had her arms free, and her hands moved among the kettles and food.

The man and a boy, about as big as I was, came up the path on the bank with tin pails. When they saw me, the boy hung back and stared. The man grinned and pointed to our well. He had coarse hair hanging to his shoulders; it was unbrushed and his head was bound with a red band. He had wrinkles everywhere, face, hands and clothing. His coat and pants were in tatters. He was brown and dirty all over, but his face was gentle and kind.

Soon I heard the pad-pad of their naked feet on the clay of the path. The water from the boy's pail slopped in the dust while he stared back at me.

They made tea and ate stuff out of the iron pot; it was fish, I could smell it. The man and the woman sat beside the pot, but the children took pieces and ran up and down eating them.

They had hung a tent from the limb of the old willow tree that lolled over the sand from the bank. The bundles and blankets had been tossed into the tent; the flaps were open and I could see everything lying higgledy-piggledy inside.

Each child ate what he wanted; then he went into the tent and tumbled, dead with sleep, among the bundles. The man, too, stopped eating and went into the tent and lay down. The dog and the cat were curled up among the blankets.

The woman on the beach drew the smouldering logs apart; when she poured a little water on them they hissed. Last of all she too went into the tent with her baby.

The tent full of sleep greyed itself into the shadow under the willow tree. The wolf's head of the canoe stuck up black on the beach a little longer; then it faded back and back into the night. The sea kept on going slap-slap-slap over the beach.